THE PENGUIN CONTEMPORARY
AMERICAN FICTION SERIES

SOLOMON'S DAUGHTER

C. E. Poverman was born in New Haven,
Connecticut, and graduated from Yale University. He spent two years in India on a Ful-
bright and traveled extensively in Southeast
Asia before returning to the United States to
take his M.F.A. at the University of Iowa. His
collection of short stories, *The Black Velvet
Girl,* received the Iowa School of Letters
Award for Short Fiction in 1976 and was published the same year as his first novel, *Susan.*
He has taught at the University of Hawaii
and at Yale University. He currently teaches
English at the University of Arizona in Tuc-
son, where he lives with his wife.

Solomon's Daughter

C. E. Poverman

PENGUIN BOOKS

Penguin Books Ltd, Harmondsworth,
Middlesex, England
Penguin Books, 625 Madison Avenue,
New York, New York 10022, U.S.A.
Penguin Books Australia Ltd, Ringwood,
Victoria, Australia
Penguin Books Canada Limited, 2801 John Street,
Markham, Ontario, Canada L3R 1B4
Penguin Books (N.Z.) Ltd, 182–190 Wairau Road,
Auckland 10, New Zealand

First published in the United States of America by
The Viking Press 1981
Published in Penguin Books 1983

LIBRARY OF CONGRESS CATALOGING IN PUBLICATION DATA
Poverman, C. E., 1944–
Solomon's daughter.
I. Title.
PS3566.O82S6   1983   813'.54   82-16512
ISBN 0 14 00.6280 7

Printed in the United States of America by
R. R. Donnelley & Sons Company, Harrisonburg, Virginia
Set in Primer

Grateful acknowledgment is made to Addison-Wesley
Publishing Company, Inc., for permission to reprint
a selection from *The World Is Round* by Gertrude
Stein, A Young Scott Book. Copyright © Gertrude
Stein, 1939, 1967.

SOLOMON awake now, but breath still coming rapidly, that dream again, familiar, the glittery underwater light, something awful coming toward him, what is it? Solomon can't remember. He becomes aware of Bea's breathing, heavy, regular, warm against his shoulder.

In another moment, it starts coming to him in bright pieces how things will be in the morning: the vague smell of carbon tetrachloride in the operating room, checking the instrument table; the inflatable tourniquet in place, then, sliding the X rays on the viewing box, the glow of the bones like pale-blue candles, studying the foot a moment more. . . .

Solomon looks at the clock. After two. He listens. The house quiet. Low electric hum of the clock. He closes his eyes. Drifts. The glittery underwater light, that dream. He turns over, watches the second hand circling. In the morning . . .

. . . the clean nurse will hold the gown and he will extend his arms for the sleeves. She will tie the gown behind him, then hold the gloves, the cuffs bent down over her fingers, and he will place his hands in the gloves and peel them up over his wrists.

He can hear himself talking to the resident. The Achilles tendon has already been lengthened, they are moving on to the second part of the operation. "Now, before sewing up, make sure the foot comes to a right angle . . ."

Solomon turns onto his back. The next part of the operation, his voice still calm, steady, the resident at his side.

"Carry the incision down to the bone." He watches his incision curve from the back of the heel to the dorsum of the foot, the knife exposing the yellow fat under the skin, then the yellow-white of the deep fascia.

1

His voice calm. ". . . now in this case, because the peroneal muscles have been paralyzed, you don't have to worry about damaging them when you retract. But ordinarily, be careful."

Solomon stares across the bedroom. The soft glow of the windows.

"Now here, pry the soft tissues away from the bone. On top of the foot, you want to stick close to the bone. Otherwise, you might damage the dorsalis pedis artery. The problem here is that you can't see the artery. Just stick close to the bone and you'll be all right."

Voice calm. That's what will be odd about it, his voice no different, the resident will be wondering about him, won't he? They are all wondering about Solomon. Even Nick. Nick's saying, "Look, Dad, everybody knows doctors don't operate on members of their families . . ."

". . . by this method, you expose the astragalus, os calcis, the cuboid, the scaphoid . . ." Picking up the osteotome and mallet. ". . . removing the surfaces of these three joints, you have to get your angles right, and this can be tricky."

. . . the cuboid, the scaphoid, fusion of the bones of the foot . . .

Solomon listens to Bea's breathing. Heavy, exhausted. For some reason, the last few days Solomon has been remembering a summer night they'd gone fishing, God, it was back just before the start of the Korean War, Rose had found some new fishing spot she wanted to show him. . . .

Rose hopped up on the trunk first, a huge tree fallen across a pool, her feet glowing in the flashlight loom, a dark shadow beneath each high arch, the lower halves of her feet a pale glow where her tan stopped; the flashlight bobbed, shined down into the water, came back up onto the trunk, "Okay, Daddy." Her fly rod glittered in the light, disappeared back into the dark.

Solomon felt for a handhold, tried several branches, hoisted himself heavily, caught his breath a moment, felt his way out onto the trunk, wondering if this were such a good idea after all. The space quickly opened between them until Rose was alone far out over the pool, the woods circled dark around them. Once she waved the light down the trunk, held it for him at his feet, whispered, "Come on, Daddy!"

Across the pool, a low fall raised a cool rush of air, a sweetness of water; the echo rushed into the woods. Smell of pine and 6-12. Again the light bounced, a festoon of bright flies on Rose's vest, a sleeve, red-and-black checkerboard of a flannel shirt. Solomon saw her feet flicker in and out of the light. Surefooted.

She whispered back to him, "I scouted this yesterday afternoon. You put your line out that way. I'll put mine on this side. There's plenty of room. Rose waved the light. "Come on, come on."

"You're right, it's a wonderful spot, but not for me. I'm going to fish from shore."

Silence. Rose's disapproval. Loudly whispered, "But, Daddy, I want you to be with me."

"I do, too, but then don't go places I can't go anymore."

"Dad, you're only forty-one. And you're rich. Great doctors are rich. We're rich, aren't we?"

"Why do you think I'm a great doctor?"

"By the way those people come to the house and bring you presents and kiss you and that old woman who always remembers your birthday and bakes you a cake. And when you have dinner parties and the other doctors come, the way they talk to you. They get a special voice for you."

"How would you know the way other doctors talk to me?"

"I just know."

"It wouldn't be because someone is up on the landing in the dark when she's supposed to be sleeping and eavesdrops? Some little mouse . . ."

"Just tell me how rich?"

"At eight, never mind money. Money doesn't concern you. You've got what you need. Little bottom isn't bare, is it? Don't go to bed hungry? And, I'm not forty-one, I'm forty-two, which is too old to be standing out on this damned tree trunk in the dark waiting for the sun to come up if I hope to see forty-three in one piece. Now shine the light down here."

"*Damn*. Daddy swore." She laughed. The light on her face a moment. Golden-brown eyes, several freckles across the bridge of her nose, hair parted in the middle. Braids. And always that willful look around her mouth.

"Yes, Daddy swore and it's nothing to what Daddy's going to do if he falls in the water. Now keep the light on the tree for me, I'm not a monkey."

"Daddy, stop talking so loud, you'll scare the fish away." Solomon laughed as he made it back to shore.

As Solomon lies in the dark he remembers finding her white figure skates the other day, one of the bells missing off the toes, he suddenly feels like getting up and going down to the basement; he wants to touch them.

"You make another incision up the front of the leg. Pull the tendon up through the fourth incision and make a fifth incision on the top of the foot."

Solomon pushes the covers back. The bathroom. The light falling across the bed, Solomon glances back. Bea goes on sleeping. Books on her night table. *Psychic Discoveries Behind the Iron Curtain, Born to Heal.*

Solomon closes the bathroom door. If only he could have slept through the night. He would have gotten up in the morning, next thing be operating, it would be over; that would be that. He squints against the lights in the mirror; wisps of gray hair, gray mustache, circles under his eyes, cheeks sunken. He doesn't look like himself. He looks old.

Nick's voice: "But do you think she'll be able to walk again afterward?"

"No."

But Nick had been insistent. What chance of success? What odds? One in ten? One in fifty? He had finally given up against Solomon's refusal to speculate—to say. And in exasperation, finally, "If there's no chance, then what's the point of it all. Why not just leave her alone."

"It will make her more comfortable. She's going to have to live this way a long time. And she, herself, wants it done. Wants me to do it."

He pours himself a swallow of brandy, recalls Rose lying in the intensive-care unit—four years already . . . Rose, her body sweet with lotions, acid with drainages, and the hospital bed, luminous with the abeyance of coma, body bowed against the mattress with paralysis. And the eyes, sometimes partially

4

open, a mysterious glaze of light between the lids. Or closed, lids rippling, eyes fluttering. Sometimes, as Solomon sat by the bed, he would look up, startled to see her teeth bared. She seemed to be grimacing at him, snarling or laughing. Though he knew it was the paralysis, could name the affected areas of her brain, still that didn't make it better, the grimace, the bared teeth, the hoarse intake of breath.

"She knows everything," Bea's voice, quiet. Bea had started that business in the intensive-care unit right after the accident.

"She is aware. She knows we are with her, don't you, sweetie? We love you. We have always loved you. Wake up, now, Rose. Rose, wake . . ." Bea staring down at Rose. Solomon would sometimes abruptly walk out of the room.

Later, he might return and Bea would still be there by Rose's bed, holding her clenched hand, tugging on her clenched fingers. Bea would be talking softly, trying to move her rigid arms and legs, and Solomon would say, "That's enough for now, Bea." He would take Bea's hand. "Bea, that's all for now."

"But what if she comes to and we're not here? I don't want her to come to when we're not here. Alone. Tubes in her arms and nose and throat. She'll be terrified."

"You can't stay by this bed twenty-four hours a day, you've been at this now for weeks."

Bea's clothes hanging on her, lines deepened at the corners of her mouth, her eyes. Cords in her neck. Bea who had always looked so young.

Solomon would say, "Come on now."

Bea would stand by the bed a moment longer, squeeze Rose's clenched fist. "We are with you, Rose, with you all the time. I am with you."

Solomon would lead Bea to the door. Gently cradling her elbow, feeling her thinness through her clothes, Solomon would guide Bea out.

Now Solomon wipes his face with a warm washcloth, glances around the bathroom, pushes open the door. The light across the bed, Bea frowning in her sleep, her night table, *Psychic Discoveries* . . . Solomon finds his bathrobe, switches

5

off the light, darkness, feeling for the doorknob.

He hesitates on the landing. Listens. Breathing. Murmurs. He stands beside the door to Nick's old room. Trophies on the bookshelves and dresser, gleaming in the light from the hall. High school. College. Nick standing on the wrestling mat, hair cropped, dark with sweat, raising the trophy, 1961.

Rose's children in the rooms now. Toys on the floor. Nick's bed still where it had been since high school. Now Tim sleeps soundly, murmuring, holding the spotted neck of a giraffe. Six years old. The crib, no longer needed, folded against the wall. One of Nick's trophies on the floor, arm broken off. Solomon picks the trophy out of the toys, carefully places it back among the others.

At the other end of the hall, Solomon glances into the den. Richard, older, eight now, lank blond hair spread across the pillow, covers kicked back, one foot hanging off the bed. Richard, so compulsive, so neat. Toys arranged on the shelf just so. Bed tucked in, sheet folded back and smoothed. The Sleep-Sound whirring softly in the silence. It helps him get to sleep. Stay asleep. Everything tucked in. Yet as he sleeps, he kicks back the covers, tears the bed apart. Like Nicky. Light from the hall. Clay dinosaurs, pencils, and burned spark plugs stabbed into their backs. Solomon lifts Richard's foot, gently places it back onto the mattress, covers him.

Solomon hesitates at Rose's now-empty room.

Downstairs, red glow of the burglar alarm. On. Solomon reaches for the living-room lights. The white rug, the high mantel. Bookshelves, floor to ceiling. Medical books, encyclopedias, novels, Solomon's fly-fishing library.

In the kitchen, he looks around the counters. Cigarettes. The nurses usually leave them lying around everywhere. He looks, but nothing. In the back hall, he turns the trash over lightly. A crumpled pack covered with coffee grounds. Solomon untwists the pack. Tears it open. One cigarette, bent. Solomon smooths it through his fingers, looks it over a moment, finds a match. Solomon smokes, remembering back to the intensive-care unit, the sense he had that his feelings would come later—that he had put them somewhere and later he would have to find them wherever, however, but then in the bright lights, the glare of white tile and stainless steel, he had wanted to find out everything, everything he could, maybe they had overlooked something. The massive cuts and contusions, bad, yes, but they heal. The eye, he caught his breath, eyes can be repaired, removed if need be, the way it lay out on her cheek . . . But no, he saw it immediately, the body rigid, toes pointed down and inward, head turned to the right. He had held Bea's hand tightly. A broken neck. It must be a broken neck. Outside the intensive-care unit, he removed the mask and went over it again with the neurosurgeons. Yes, massive transfusions, massive cortisone injections to shrink the brain, tracheotomy two hours ago to help the breathing. Solomon requested the X rays once more and again they showed him the X rays and again he held them up to the lights and hunted, looking for hemorrhage. If only there were a hemorrhage, it might be drained, release pressure on the brain. There were no signs of hemorrhage. If only it had been that.

He overheard a nurse talking about her. "She was . . ." They had not expected her to last the night; she was not expected to live the morning. "She was . . ."

Solomon sits in the living room and smokes. An ophthalmologist had looked at the eye several days after the accident and told Solomon that if she lived, it would probably draw back in the socket, the vision greatly diminished or gone but the eye would not have to be removed. For some reason, Solomon felt relieved. She was not even supposed to be alive at that point. She seemed to be living from breath to breath. Each breath a hoarse gasp rising, stretching tauter, thinner, almost breaking, momentary silence; then the next gasp, sudden, hoarse a rush, like someone held too long underwater suddenly breaking the surface.

Bea said, "Oh, I'm not amazed that she lived the night or anything else, the moment I saw her, I knew she was going to be all right, I started telling her, sending messages to her. . . ."

Solomon had never argued with Bea on this.

"Do you think I've come fourteen hundred miles to let her die? So she chose to live her life away from us and fine, so she lived it her way, but now we are here again. I didn't raise a daughter to have her die like this. And I don't go in for all this nay-saying. They don't know her like I know her. I raised her. I *know* her. She will start a new life, this will be the beginning of a new life for her."

Bea squeezing his hand. Squeezed his hand harder.

Solomon had nodded. If it helped Bea now, so much the better. She would have to adjust later, but that would be better, too. She would do so at her own pace. He certainly wasn't going to sit here in the motel room and argue the clinical aspects with her. That was the last thing he wanted to start doing.

IT is late and he doesn't want to feel sluggish in the morning. He has to be alert. Even the most routine operation could be complicated. Paul Holland, a fine surgeon, one of the best. He'd lost a son in Vietnam. Seemed all right. Went in to operate on a deformity of the elbow. Scar tissue, the patient couldn't straighten his arm. He'd been trying to loosen the anterior ligaments of the elbow—tried stripping them with a periosteal elevator. Scar tissue too dense. He tried a scalpel, the scalpel slipped, cut the brachial artery without his noticing. The tourniquet released, no pulse; the arm turned white, later had to be amputated. This out of what started out as a simple, routine operation. What a way to end a practice.

Solomon sighs. Feels the silence in the house. Tonight more than ever. All the nights the phone had rung for him in the silence. The night of Rose's accident, the phone ringing in the silence. Four years ago. This call for him.

A woman's tired voice, "Is this Dr. Solomon—with a daughter Rose? Is this Boston?"

He hesitated. "Yes. Yes." Is this Dr. Solomon? . . . Is this Boston?

Bea stirring in the dark beside him. The bathroom light.

He listened. She didn't have many details. "When did it happen?"

"Yesterday afternoon."

Solomon looked at his watch. Twelve hours ago. After a moment, "Where's Price?"

"Away on a hunting trip."

"So he doesn't know yet?"

"No, he doesn't know yet."

After Solomon set the phone down, he looked up. Bea was dressed and packing a suitcase.

"What are you doing?"

"It was about Rose, wasn't it?"

Solomon nodded.

"She's been in an accident. We have to get there immediately."

Solomon sat blankly a moment. "How did you know?"

"I've felt uneasy all night. Some kind of disturbance."

During the flight to Wisconsin, Solomon had watched the clouds coming out of the dark, the stars fading, the sky getting bluer. He looked at the orange light on the tops of the clouds, felt the confinement of the plane. An odd feeling of distraction continued—he kept going over the conversation. He could feel the plane starting to descend. He held Bea's hand tightly and said, "It's probably not that bad. Price is away and this Lynn somebody has panicked. So we're being on the safe side, aren't we?" But there was something he was trying to remember.

THEY—Solomon and Lynn Welsh—had been sitting alone in an empty waiting room. He looked at the circles under her eyes, the curly blond hair coming out in all directions beneath a floppy wide-brimmed hat, long silver earrings. She glanced at Solomon, tried to smile. Her lips quivered. She put her hand to her mouth, pressed her lips, looked away. Voice muffled from behind her hands. "Please don't say anything for a minute."

Solomon was silent. After a moment, Lynn turned back. She forced a smile. "I'm okay." She fumbled for a cigarette in her purse.

"This is just so typical. Just when we really need Price, he's off on one of his hunting or fishing trips." She looked at her hands.

"You know, Doctor, I was crazy about Rose." Lynn stopped uneasily. "I mean I *am* crazy about Rose. I will be crazy about her. She'll live. Rose was inventive, exciting. I'm kind of boring." She began talking quickly. "Rose loved operas. Crazy about them. Operas all over the house. Drove Price crazy. Price hates operas. And her spending twenty dollars a crack on these things, those big albums weren't cheap. I'd come over at ten in the morning and she'd be standing there in the middle of the kitchen, dishes piled in the sink, Price gone off to work, the dog up on his hind legs licking cereal out of the bowl on the table—another thing that drove Price crazy, a dog that wasn't disciplined—and she'd be wearing sunglasses, a long dress, white gloves buttoned up to her elbows, a cigarette holder yea long, and she'd have Beverly Sills or Joan Sutherland powered up there, eighty watts on the stereo, and she'd be going at it. The postman would be standing there dumbstruck, she'd waltz out to him on the icy walk in that outfit, slide one arm under his mailbag, take his hand with the other, take a turn with him out there on the ice while singing some aria, take the mail, and sing back into the house. The neighbors were probably ready to call the cops. She'd be singing away, Richard would be crawling around on the floor in his diapers, probably figuring all mothers started their day like this. It made you feel terrific. . . ."

Lynn went on speaking rapidly, urgently. There was something about all of this which made Solomon uneasy. Almost as though by the rapidity of her speech, Lynn was trying to keep Rose alive. Wasn't that it?

"She had a terrific memory. Knew all of those operas cold. Italian, German, French. And she could sing them beautifully. Even with the cigarettes. She was taking voice lessons. The thing is, I think she really could have done it. Been an opera singer. Hell, I don't think Joan Sutherland or Beverly Sills really got going until their thirties and she was—is—only twenty-seven." Lynn's voice trailed off. She shook her head. Then smiled again.

"She had half the kids in the neighborhood following her around singing operas. Even my kid—my husband and I separated last year. My kid's nine. Rose was just great with her. So kind. You know, she had a feeling for how bad Karen was feeling about it all and she made her feel important and like

10

she cared a lot. Which she did. Karen followed her around singing *Tosca*—my little midwestern kid singing *Tosca*—she taught Karen to fly-fish—she taught the other kids in the neighborhood, too. That was another thing, she was always discovering little things, places to fish. She took us out once to a place somewhere out in the woods. We were going to practice our casting. She had Karen and three or four of these kids with baseball hats on standing there on shore singing all these jumbled words to *The Magic Flute* and Rose was up there wearing her vest with all of these beautiful flies she tied, making beautiful casts and . . ."

As Lynn went on, Solomon realized that Lynn, in some unconscious way, was eulogizing Rose.

". . . the kids were lined up on the banks of this pool. At first they'd been singing, then they'd just laughed, it was great to hear them all laughing, and finally they stopped and were standing there watching her. There she was casting and singing and her voice was floating off into the woods—the sun was going down. . . ."

Lynn drifted off before continuing. Her eyes were bloodshot. "I'm going on, aren't I? You're a doctor and you probably think my going on is a sign of hysteria. Do you think so?"

Yes, Solomon thought so, but then why not? Except for the faint ringing in his ears, he was so calm he wondered if he were hysterical himself.

"Why did it take you so long to call—to reach me?" Solomon's voice was gentle. "Twelve hours is a long time."

Lynn placed the back of her hand to her lips. Keeping her eyes on him, almost as though to keep him at bay, she groped for another cigarette out of her bag. She stared at him as she lit the cigarette. Took a deep drag. Said quietly, "Maybe that's why I've been talking so much . . . that question. . . . Well, first off, there wouldn't have been any problem if Price weren't away. He just would have called you himself and that would have been that. But he was away. Still is. Doesn't even know yet . . . Isn't that unbelievable?" Lynn nodded toward the intensive-care unit. "After what you've seen in there I doubt that what I'm going to tell you could bother you much, but I'm— Look, Rose Summer Turner, Doctor. I only knew her as

11

Rose *Summer* Turner. I didn't find out her maiden name was Solomon until two a.m. And even then it was just because I got lucky that I found out at all."

"So she's in there unconscious and you're calling all over the place trying to find her father—me—a nonexistent Dr. Summer. How finally, did you find out her name—my name?"

"Well, I'm lying there, Price gone, I'm exhausted, it comes to me slowly, maybe I've got her name wrong—I've tried different spellings and so on, but now it starts occurring to me, maybe I've just got her name *entirely* wrong. So I get up and start wandering around the house like a sleepwalker, I'm taking books out of shelves, emptying drawers, I really don't know what I'm looking for, maybe some writing in a margin, an old letter, something with a spelling of her name on it. I'm getting to the point where I'm wondering if for all I know, maybe she'd been married once before, and Summer was from her first marriage and she'd never ever mentioned it."

"And what did you find?"

"A book with her name in it. Rose Solomon. Euclid Ave., Boston, Mass. I went right over to the phone, called and got you. I don't know what it was all about, her different name. And right now, I don't want to know."

"I'll tell you—"

"Another time. Please. I want to think of her singing *Tosca* and dancing around. I don't want to know anything more. Not now."

Solomon's head felt muffled. "I'd like that better right now, myself."

"Well, I shouldn't ask this, Doctor, but I want to know. What are her chances?"

Solomon said, "I'm not a neurologist. I'm an orthopedist. But from what I've seen, at this point, I'm amazed she's still alive."

"And if she does live?"

"I can't even begin to think of that now." Solomon stood up.

"Doctor . . ." As Lynn stood, her purse opened, fell on the floor. "No, no, I've got them . . . Please."

They both got down, picked things up. Lipstick, tampons, car keys, birth-control pills, comb, cigarettes. . . . "God, I'm so embarrassed, this is embarrassing."

"Terrible, just terrible." Solomon smiled. He handed back some of her things.

"Doctor, can I tell you one last thing?" She brushed some hair out of her eyes. "About Rose. Why I know Rose is going to live. Can I tell you?" She barely waited for Solomon's nod.

"We were in this little bar. Rose and I, just a couple of days ago. Rose was playing the pinball machine and she'd been playing for about half an hour on one quarter—terrific, drinking her drink, playing her last ball, picking up points and games, she'd cleaned up. She was wearing tight jeans and twitching around and paying no attention to anything at all but that ball and her drink and some guy comes up behind her and puts his hand on her rear end—oh hell, he goosed her.

"She turned right around and just let him have it, whap, right across the face. And hard. Never hesitated.

"This guy reels back and grabs his cheek. There were several tables full of rowdy guys and some people at the bar and everyone in the bar just shut up. All of a sudden I'm scared to hell. We stand there for a second and it's one of those long—I mean long, like Gary Cooper in *High Noon*—silences. Then one of the guys pushes back his chair and it scrapes on the floor and my heart is pounding, I want to run. He stands up and starts clapping all by himself. He's a little drunk, but nonetheless—then a couple of more stand up and clap. Then the whole place was clapping and cheering and the guy she slapped just slunk out. They loved her, Doctor. They clapped like hell."

Lynn smiled. "I never would have had the nerve to do that. It might have been smart, it might have been dumb, but she had nerve. Or at least her own way of doing things."

Lynn's voice softened: "When we got back in the car, I guess I was gawking at her because she looked over at me, started the car, and said, 'Well, beside grabbing my ass, he made me lose my quarter.'"

They were walking toward the door and when she reached the corridor, she said, "I've got to go see about the kids. I've got them—mine. Hers. The kids. They're safe." She shook Solomon's hand once, hard, turned, walked quickly down the hall, blond curls bounding out from beneath the black hat.

Slapping some guy in a bar. Nerve. Or her own way of doing things. Solomon recalls a pair of bright-red shoes lying in the middle of the kitchen floor, one heel snapped off. Rose hadn't walked so much as teetered in them.

Bea saying, "Go ahead, then, they're your feet. But, beside the fact that people don't generally wear jeans and three-inch high heels to country-club dances, you're going to be awfully uncomfortable."

And a couple of days later, they—Solomon and Bea—heard about it from a friend. Rose had been marvelous, simply marvelous. Who else would have been clever enough to wear jeans to one of those stuffy dances. And those red high heels were really a touch of genius. Brilliant. She'd danced with everyone; they'd all been intrigued.

Bea had smiled vaguely.

BUT whether it was shoes or anything else, Rose did have her own way of doing things. The summer she was fourteen she'd taken riding lessons at a stable near the cabin. After each lesson, Rose walked the horse, then she watered him by the lake while she sat on the horse's back, read *Gone With the Wind* and dangled her bare feet in the water. Everything was *Gone With the Wind* and she read it day and night until she finished, stumbled upon a water-stained copy of Gertrude Stein's *The World Is Round* and started reading and talking like Gertrude Stein.

She was still talking like Gertrude Stein when they returned from the lake in late August. She would sit on the terrace in a halter and shorts and read under the tree and was doing so the afternoon Dominic Ferrara delivered the groceries. Dom's entry into the driveway was not so much an entry as an advent, first a heraldry of music, which came to one like an auditory hallucination; then the sound of the mufflers, the music suddenly louder, confirming to the listener an earthly or corporeal existence; all followed by the flash of light, a blaze of fire, as Dom would pull in, flames painted at the skirts, chrome shining; and finally Dom himself, tight T-shirt, Luckies rolled into his sleeve, tight muscles.

Nick peered into the car, stared at the pink dice still swaying. Gaped at the plastic suicide knob. A plastic breast with a large red nipple on the end.

Solomon looked up from his sandwich and novel.

"How's your father, Dom?"

Dom patted his hair into place, smoothed one of the wings of his D.A. Hoisted a box of groceries.

"He got the back brace on this morning, Doc. He lifted too much yesterday."

"I told him not to overdo it."

"I told 'em what you told 'em. He don't listen, Doc. Ya gotta sit on that guy."

"Well, have him call me."

"Okay. All this stuff—the corn, the tomatoes, the zucchini, he picked it out for ya himself. The best."

"Wonderful. Now you tell him the other thing that would make me happy would be for him to get in bed and stay in bed until his back quiets down."

Dom made several quick trips, gold cross, chain and medallion jangling, on each leg into the house his hair fell out of place, on each leg back to the car he would pat and comb the hair back into place, looking once in the sideview mirror before picking up the next box, each time glancing quickly at Rose's legs as she sat reading Gertrude Stein. Rose ignored him. The record player: "Shake, Rattle and Roll."

Nick stared through the open door at the black leather seats. Dom giving him a gentle hand on the shoulder as he went for a last box.

"Get out of his way, Nick."

"Nah, nah, that's okay, Doc. Come on, you wanna go for a ride. Hey, ya like that, Nicky. I just got that last week. A record player. In a car! What they don't think of!"

Dom pulled out a stack of forty-fives. Rose glanced quickly out of the corner of her eye.

"Go on, pick one."

Nick went through the stack, handed one to Dom.

Solomon playfully covered his ears. "What is that noise?"

"Doc, that's the Penguins—'Earth Angel.'"

15

Dominic glanced over at Rose. His voice tense. He looked away from Nick. "Uh, you wanna ask your sister?"

"No."

"But that would be nice."

"Nick, leave Dominic alone, he's working."

"No, no, Doc, I'm finished." Dom patted his hair, walked over to Rose. "Rose, ya wanna go for a ride with Nick."

Rose looked up from *The World Is Round*, colored. Then closed the book.

" 'And I am here and here is There Oh where oh where is there Oh where.' "

Dominic looked around at the ground.

"Yes?"

" 'I am Rose My eyes are blue. I am Rose and who are you? I am Rose. . . .' "

Solomon said, "Rose, give him a straight answer, for God's sake!"

" 'And when I sing, I am Rose like anything!' "

Dom looked from one to the other.

"Earth Angel" came to an end.

Dom changed the record, turned, looked momentarily inspired, "I am Dom, my car is blue. I am Dom. . . ."

Rose smiled at him.

"Yes."

She got up and walked toward the car and Dom ran to open the door.

For several weeks after there were secret comings and goings—the hallucinatory music, the sudden rumble of the mufflers. Solomon ran into a friend who told him he'd had some uninvited guests in his pool one night. Two or three couples, the girls swimming in bras and underpants, he'd been about to come down and throw them out when he'd heard a familiar laugh and recognized it as Rose's. He'd noticed a car at the end of the driveway. Flames at the skirts. Chrome.

Solomon nodded. "White walls and pink furry dice?"

"Dice, anyway. I couldn't see if they were pink or furry."

"They were. Thanks for not throwing them out. Rose is basically sensible. I think this will take care of itself in its own good time."

Which it had done. Mr. Ferrara started delivering the groceries in his back brace. Rose eventually stopped talking like Gertrude Stein and went on to reading other things with equal fascination. *Peyton Place, To the Lighthouse.* The only remnant being Nick, who wore his pants too low on his hips.

But Rose had been basically sensible. Hot-tempered, yes. Her own way of doing things, yes. But sensible. Then something had changed in her and Solomon hadn't understood it.

That next summer she had gone West on a tour—trail-riding through the Grand Tetons. When she'd returned in late August, she was different. Cool. Distant. She had bleached her hair blond, taken up smoking, though she denied it; let her fingernails grow long, started using a lot of makeup. She seemed uncomfortable. Solomon would catch her staring vacantly. He'd seen something of that look before, at the Emmanuel Home for the Aged. She'd been staring at a bronze plaque. Next to each name, there had been a light. Some lit. She'd been wearing brown-and-white saddle shoes. Bea's mother approaching Rose, hugging her, Rose closing her eyes and stiffening, keeping her arms at her sides, letting herself be hugged.

In the car, Rose complained bitterly, "I hate her kissing me. And Sunday, wasted. The same thing. Always gray, always raining, too. And it's like death in there. And that horrible plaque with those names, the lights are on because they're dead, aren't they? And all those old people waiting to die, too."

"Rose . . ."

"I get a chill when I walk in there. A chill. And that is what they're doing, isn't it?"

"People get old and sick."

"She's so gloomy."

"It's not been an easy life for her."

"Well, if you really cared about her, you wouldn't stick her in that horrible place. I get the chills in there." Rose looked at Bea. "She wants to live with us. But Mother doesn't want her. That's why I get dragged here every Sunday, because Mother can't stand her mother."

Solomon and Bea looked at each other. In the rearview mirror, Solomon saw Rose nodding.

"I know I'm right. When I'm right, you give each other that stupid look. I know."

Solomon glanced in the mirror. His eyes met Rose's. She nodded, her eyes fixed on him in the mirror. He could hear her voice behind him, "I know, I know . . ."

And that same look, but now masked after that summer out West. Rose with her beautiful rust-gold hair now bleached blond. Long red fingernails and a sense of secrecy. She was then fifteen.

SOLOMON stands. He is tired. Beyond tired. He stretches, knocking over an ashtray. He listens for Rose, habit, before he remembers that of course she isn't in her room, in the house. He bends to pick up the ashtray, breathing into the silence with relief. When Rose came home after the accident, Solomon sensed she never slept; she lay in her room, tv screen gray at the foot of her bed, stations off the air for the night. No one ever really knew what Rose could or couldn't hear; Bea claimed she had excellent hearing—and that she felt things, knew things, knew everything, really. Even the slightest sound could set off a tantrum. She would scream, and then in the middle of the night the children would wake and cry. Nick—when Nick had been home, before his leaving—Nick would come down from the attic room, blinking, jaw clenched, glare, get that look on his face, and then Nick wouldn't go back to sleep. He might go out and walk half the night—or pace around the house, or go down to the basement.

Solomon breathes easily, enjoying the deep silence of the house. Odd that he hasn't become aware until just this moment that she had been lying there, listening, always listening. Tense. How tense he's been. He eyes the mail table. What a clutter. Piles of mail, magazines, newspapers. Who can keep up with it all? Catalogues. Saks Fifth Avenue. Bea isn't really interested in this stuff, not like some women. Solomon gathers up a stack of catalogues, throws them in the hall basket, then retrieves the Saks catalogue. Bea might still enjoy looking; he smooths a crease out of the cover, places it back on the table.

The mail. That's when they had first really become aware of

18

it, actually seen the name, Summer. It must have been during college. She hadn't finished. 1961? 62? Bea had been sorting the mail. She'd stopped, glanced at an envelope. "Another one. Same thing. The address right. And the first name—Rose. But Rose Summer. This is the third or fourth one. I see what she must have done. She changed apartments last summer, left a forwarding address with the post office, but she must have written in our home address unthinkingly."

Solomon shrugged. "It's junk mail. Somebody got her name wrong. Leave it for the mailman."

Bea started to say something more. She studied the envelope. Set it aside. "I have the oddest feeling about this."

"Go on, what odd feeling?"

"Just a feeling. And I'm going to ask Rose about it next time she's home."

1959. The beat of the sprinkler through the screens. Solomon leafed the *Globe*. Khrushchev visiting Ike at Camp David, and here, more on Castro in the Sierra Madre. Bea called once more.

In the kitchen, Bea read Solomon a letter from "Dear Abby." Then read Solomon his horoscope.

He made a sound of impatience and walked into the dining room. Bea laughed. They went through this ritual every night.

Rose came to the table, glanced at her plate, wrinkled her nose. . . .

"Broccoli! Liver! Mother, you know I don't like broccoli! And liver! You know it! You do this on purpose! Every night, she does this to me. Last night it was lamb. The night before, one of her icky casseroles."

"All right, Sarah Bernhardt. What would you like to eat?"

Solomon looked at Rose. Blue eyeshadow. Bright lipstick. She looked pretty enough, yes, but he liked her better without makeup. Her nails were long and filed to points. Lately, Bea and Rose had argued about the nails, along with everything else.

"They don't suit you, Rose."

"Yes, Mother Dear."

"Joe, can you talk to her? I can't."

"Oh, can't you, now? She used to tell me not to bite my nails. *Now* my nails are too long to suit her majesty. Nothing I do is right."

"Oh, come on, you poor thing."

Along with Rose's love of makeup, she delighted in bizarre clothes. Dresses from the twenties, wide-brimmed floppy hats, gold high heels, feather boas.

In the last few months, Bea had gotten notes home from the headmistress of Rose's school saying she had been out of school uniform several times in her classes. Obviously, she had changed between leaving the house and getting to school. Bea had talked to her while Rose looked at a place on the ceiling. Finally she put her hands to her ears, said, "Blue skirts and white blouses. Every day, every day! Nothing but girls. I'm sick of it! I can't take it another minute!"

"Oh, cut it out."

"You cut it out."

Solomon put down his paper. "There's no argument here. You'll follow the rules like everyone else."

"Dad . . ."

"That's it. No argument."

" 'No argument,' " she mimicked. "What if I don't?"

Solomon glared at her. "There are a few things you like to do which you won't get to do. That's it, Rose. No argument."

That, too, almost a nightly discussion.

Now Bea read Rose's horoscope. Rose pretended not to listen, frowned, and blurted, "I thought you asked us not to read at the table, Mother."

"We haven't sat down yet, Rose."

"You don't even keep your own rules."

Bea and Solomon looked at each other. Bea smiled. "Oh, have a little sense of humor, Rose. What's bothering you anyway?"

Solomon nodded slightly to Bea.

Bea said, "Sit down, Nicky." Bea glanced at his shirt; a loud-pink Hawaiian shirt which he wore with great self-conscious pleasure.

She started to say something, looked at Solomon . . . he

shook his head, no. Bea smiled slightly, "Never mind, Nicky, just sit down now."

Rose looked at her plate, pushed it away.

"May I leave the table?"

"Eat your dinner, Rose."

"I'm not going to eat this junk so why do I have to sit here and waste time?"

"What do you have to do that's so important?"

Rose stared at Bea. Bulged her eyes at her. Mimicked her, " 'What do you have to do . . .' I hate to listen to the sound of you chewing, if you must know, Mother Dear."

Solomon looked at Rose. "You won't talk to your mother like that and you'll sit and eat your dinner."

"She cooks food she knows I hate, then I have to sit here and listen to her chewing."

She looked at Solomon. "And why is my horoscope always bad when that woman reads it?"

"*That woman* is your mother. And I just said I don't want to hear you talking to her like that. And where do you get this business anyway? *That woman?*"

"Have you noticed that, Dad? Whenever she reads my horoscope, it's bad?"

"Of course, she prints a special edition of the paper with a special horoscope—terrible!—just for you."

"I'm serious."

"Well, so am I! I wouldn't kid about a thing like your horoscope."

Rose pushed abruptly back from the table. She looked at Nick.

"Nicky's so good, sitting over there eating all of the little greens Mother Dear made for him so he'll grow big and strong, right, Nicky?"

Nick looked uncertainly at Rose, bounced in his chair once, looked at Bea, at Solomon, laughed uneasily.

"That's it, Nicky, do just whatever they want you to do. You're so spoiled, you get just what you want, don't you? Where did you get that ugly pink shirt? From one of your little friends?" Rose stared at him a moment. Her voice softened. "He is so cute. Nicky, you really are. That's the only word for you. Cute. Cute enough to be a girl. Much too cute for this family." He started to smile, shrugged. "But look at those big paws of his—that's just what they look like, too. Paws."

Nick stopped chewing a moment, looked at his hands.

"Bowwow, Nicky-pooh, bowwow. Where did he ever get hands like that? Look at Dad's hands, so delicate."

Bea said, "Go ahead and eat, Nicky. You have lovely hands."

Solomon smiled at Nick. "Hold up your hand, Nicky."

Nick held up his hand.

Solomon pressed his palm against Nick's. "Look at that." The fingers of Nick's hand were almost as long as Solomon's. Solomon smiled with pleasure, suddenly interlocked fingers with Nick to bend his hand back, but Nick saw it coming. Their hands trembled and slowly Nick bent Solomon's hand back.

"Nicky, that's enough, you'll hurt your father! Why you two play these games—"

Solomon turned red pushing against Nick's hand.

"And at the table, dear."

"All right, Nick, let go. Hey . . ." Solomon pulled his hand free, flexed the fingers. "That's the hand that feeds us, boy. Go easy on your old dad."

Bea shook her head. "Exerting yourself like that while you're eating. You're red in the face."

"Go on."

"Bowwow, Nicky. Paws."

"They're going to be fine for him. Just fine." Solomon smiled at Nick. "He's going to be a lot bigger than his dad. And you know something? For every inch he is taller than me, I'm as happy as can be."

"He's going to be big and dumb."

"Since when have you started thinking of your brother that way, Rose? No one in this family's dumb."

"You are, Mother Dear."

"Of course I am."

"That's enough of that to your mother, Rose!"

Rose pushed back from the table again."

"Where are you going, Rose?"

"Don't worry, Mother Dear, I'll be right back, go on chew-chew-chewing."

"You could ask to be excused."

Rose went into the kitchen, returned with a large bowl of ice cream covered with chocolate sauce, sat down, and started to eat with exaggerated relish.

Bea and Solomon exchanged looks.

"So who are you kidding? Am I supposed to be upset by this?"

Rose went on eating the ice cream and chocolate sauce.

Bea said quietly, "Did something happen at school today?"

Rose went on eating the ice cream.

"Rose, I'm talking to you. What happened? What was it?"

"Nothing, Mother Dear, I can't hear you."

The phone began to ring in the kitchen.

Bea stood, shook her head. "Why does it always ring at dinner? If it's that Mrs. Reynolds with the back pain again, I'm just going to tell her once and for all she's starting to give me a back pain!"

Bea went to the phone. "The doctor is at dinner now. Who is this? I see. May I take a message?"

Everyone stopped eating and listened. Rose stared at her ice cream, then glanced at Solomon. She looked both annoyed and pleased. She said to no one in particular, "Always Dad. They all want him."

Bea held her hand over the mouthpiece as she started writing something on a pad. "The emergency room . . . an accident . . . Sounds bad . . . is bad. . . ."

Rose watched Bea writing on the pad. "Mother Dear, Dad's great protector from the world."

Solomon took the phone out of Bea's hand. "This is Dr. Solomon . . . No, it's all right, go ahead. . . ."

He spoke to the resident for several minutes. When he sat back down, Rose and Bea were still at it.

"Oh, this is so ridiculous. Do you think eating a bowl of ice cream with chocolate sauce is good for you? Good for your complexion?"

Rose suddenly turned on Bea, banged the spoon hard into the bowl, "What difference does it make about my complexion?! I'm not pretty!"

"Whatever gave you that idea?

" 'Whatever gave you that idea?' " Rose mimicked.

23

"You're being hateful."

"Am I, Mother Dear?"

"Yes, you are. If you want to believe you're not pretty, that's too bad for you."

"If you come from an ugly family, you'll be ugly."

"Your grandmother was known for being a real beauty—you look just like her. Enormous light-brown eyes—you even have the gold fleck in the right eye. Reddish-blond hair. Just the same. And many people have told me so. What more do you want? I'll show you some pictures after dinner."

"Oh, keep your pictures! And what's the difference, I'm not one of your little beauties."

"Who's been telling you you're not pretty?"

"No one!"

"Rose, look at me."

Rose stared down at the table. She began eating ice cream. Then she glared at Nick. "What are you looking at?"

Nick shrugged.

Rose pointed at him. "You're so smug with your pretty little baby face and green eyes. What a waste. And that little baby nose." Rose turned and looked at Solomon. "What a waste! He's just going to get his little nose broken playing football or something asinine like that. Boys don't need looks anyway."

"I thought you said everyone in this family is ugly."

"You certainly are, Mother."

Bea looked at Solomon. "She's beautiful, she doesn't know she's beautiful. What can I do?"

Solomon took a deep breath. "I've had about enough of this."

Nick glanced away from the table, pulled something out of his lap and up onto his head; he faced the table and went on eating, looking down at his plate.

He was wearing a pair of one-way, silver sunglasses which hid his eyes, and what was that he had pulled over his ears? Like earmuffs, tied in a bow under his chin.

"Dad! Mother! Look, stop him!" Rose half stood out of her chair.

"Sit down, Rose, we'll take care of this. Nick, Nick, I agree with your sister, this isn't the least bit clever. Take that off! Immediately."

24

"He's been in my bureau drawers."

Nick went on eating quietly.

"Dad! Do something!"

The padded cups stood out over each ear. Solomon glanced at Bea, looked down at his plate, tried to keep from laughing.

"No, dear, you're just encouraging him now."

"He's been in my things!"

Solomon tried to keep from laughing.

"Take it off, Nicky."

"I want him punished! Punish him, DAD!"

"We'll take care of it, Rose."

"No, you'll let him get away with it."

Solomon said, "All right, Nick, take it off. Now!"

Nick untied the bra.

"And the sunglasses, Nick."

Nick placed the sunglasses on the table.

Solomon looked down at his plate, caught his laugh. Looked up to see Rose staring at him. "That's right, Dad, laugh at him. He has everything and he does this to me and you laugh."

"We'll take care of this," Bea said. "And look, Rose, what do you mean, he has everything? There's nothing wrong with you. He's nice-looking, you're nice-looking, too. You have lovely eyes. . . ."

"Brown eyes!"

"Half the world has brown eyes."

"Precisely! Brown eyes! How common."

"Somehow people manage to live with brown eyes. Think of that. How amazing."

"Even you, Mother Dear, have green eyes. And of course pretty little Nicky with Mother's green eyes."

"You want to be exceptional? Do something exceptional. It's not the color of your eyes. And anyway, you have extraordinary eyes! They're not brown. They're gold. People tell me all the time how pretty you are. I don't ask them. They just tell me."

"Your stupid insincere friends!"

"My friends couldn't be anything but stupid and insincere."

"You said it yourself."

"You have nice features."

"Look at my nose!"

"Yes, let's. What's wrong with your nose. Show me."

Rose turned in profile. Ran her fingertip up and down her nose.

"Here. See."

"No, I don't see."

"I'm just not right. Here." Rose pressed the bridge of her nose. "Look."

"I can't see anything."

"No, you wouldn't, stupid. Look across the table at your little brat. Look at Nicky."

"You're being ridiculous, just ridiculous. Childish. Just how would you like to look, Rose?"

"Like Elizabeth Taylor."

Bea laughed. "Shoot me for not making you Elizabeth Taylor."

"I'd like to. And go ahead, laugh your fake laugh."

Rose went on eating the ice cream.

"I don't know what's happened, but someone, somewhere, has been feeding you a line and you haven't been strong enough to stand up for yourself. You've swallowed it all—hook, line, and sinker."

"Yes, Mother Dear."

Bea shrugged. "Can I say any more to make you see? I guess not. So be miserable. My grandmother used to have an expression: *gornish helfin.* Do you know what that means?"

"I don't care about your grandmother and don't talk that stupid language to me!"

"I'll tell you what it means and hope you can come to appreciate it someday."

Rose plugged her ears. "Dad, will you talk to this woman?"

"In about one minute, Rose—"

"Mother and her ba-sooms."

"Oh Rose, really, how childish, at seventeen I expect more from you than this."

Nick giggled.

Bea looked over at Nick, "All right, Nicky, you know the word, *bosom.* You've never had to go outside this house to learn that word or any other word. You could always ask. And you got honest answers. So what's so amusing?"

Nick giggled, looked at his plate, and tried not to laugh.

"Look at me."

Rose said, "Don't look at her, Nicky."

"Look at me. Nicky, look at me."

Nick looked up at Bea. She said his name softly, "Nicky."

He looked embarrassed. "I'm sorry, Mom."

She said softly, "It's unnecessary, dear."

"I know, Mom."

Rose stared at Nick. "How sickening you are, Nicky. Letting her fool you like that!"

Nick looked down at his plate.

"Nicky! *Ba-zooms. Ba-zooms. Ba-zooms!*"

Nick looked down, looked quickly at Bea.

"*Bazoooooooms,* Nicky."

Nick burst out laughing.

"Rose, you want to leave the table, go ahead," Bea said.

Rose spooned over the melted ice cream and chocolate sauce in her dish, looked toward the kitchen. "Billy!"

The dog came to the open door, hesitated, pranced. "Come here! Billy!"

Billy bounded into the room, under the table.

"Billy! Billy!"

Billy snorted, pranced, ran quickly in and out under the table.

"Billy, in the kitchen! Rose, why you're doing this, I don't know. Congratulations, you've disrupted another dinnertime. Your father has a right after working all day to come home to a little peace and quiet."

Rose set the bowl on the floor, Billy suddenly stopped by the chair, lapped quickly, chocolate syrup and ice cream speckling the rug.

"Rose!" Bea stood up, grabbed Billy by the collar.

"Billy! Billy!"

Billy licked the chocolate sauce out of his whiskers as Bea dragged the labrador toward the kitchen, returned with a damp cloth.

"Mother and her precious rug." Rose reached out and touched Bea's breast. "*Ba-zoom, Nicky!*"

Solomon dropped his fork. "Goddammit, Rose, you've been

27

trying to provoke me and now you've succeeded. Now leave this table!"

"Dad—"

"Leave this table immediately!"

"I get blamed!" Rose turned red, looked over at Nicky. "You little bastard."

"NOW!"

Bea looked at Solomon. "You're red, this isn't good for you."

Solomon rose quickly from his chair, and Rose pushed back her chair, a frightened look on her face, looked at Bea, "I hate you."

Solomon threw his napkin on the chair and followed her into the hall. She ran up the stairs, and Solomon heard her door slam; he started up the stairs as Bea caught his arm. He took several steps, then yielded to her pulling him back.

"That's just what she's been trying to do—cool off. She is unhappy with everybody and everything. Just let her go now. Come back and finish your dinner. I'm sorry. Deep in her heart, she's sorry, too. That's the pity of it."

Solomon took a deep breath and let Bea lead him back to the table.

"Oh, of course, I know what girls go through at this age, and it's not easy—but sometimes, for reasons I don't begin to understand, I think this is the only way she knows how to show love."

Solomon made a sound of disgust.

"Have your dinner, dear. This too will pass."

THE one thing which seemed to make Rose happy was singing. She had a strong, natural voice; she loved musicals and had dozens of albums from Broadway shows. *Damn Yankees, Oklahoma!, South Pacific.* She knew them all by heart. She would stand in the living room looking out the window and sing for hours. She would put round spots of rouge on each cheek, get into a long dress, and become Eliza Doolittle in *My Fair Lady.* She would dress in black leotard and black fishnet stockings and become Lola from *Damn Yankees* with shadowed eyes, red lips, high-heel shoes, and a slinky walk.

She came home from school one day happier than Solomon had seen her in a long time. She had been made soprano soloist of her singing group at school. Her teacher told her that she had a genuine voice, a rare, big voice—Solomon interrupted her by putting his hands over his ears and saying, "I can attest to that."

Rose laughed. "Stop, listen." She went on. The teacher had said she might really do something with her voice. Perhaps even be an opera singer if she worked hard enough, but that she would have to start doing just that, working hard, and training her voice. Could she?

Solomon had thought it was a fine idea, maybe now she would calm down, settle down, become involved with something, stop carrying on. So Rose started voice lessons.

But except for the singing, she went on complaining about school. She hated the school uniform, fought with Bea almost every morning about wearing it, complained that there were no boys.

Once Solomon got fed up and said, "Look, if you want to go to the public high school, go, I can save the two thousand-plus dollars, and I'm sure if I think hard enough, I'll find something I can use it for. So don't do me any favors."

Rose looked at Solomon a moment.

"Is that what it costs? Two thousand dollars?"

"Yes, that's what it costs—what did you think it cost? Maybe it's time you learned a little about money."

She looked pleased. "Well, if it costs that much, at least they could have decent lunches."

"Go to the high school and eat their lunches instead. See if they're to your liking." But Rose didn't say more. She had a slight smile on her face and seemed to be thinking.

Bea shrugged. "It would probably be the same for her wherever she went now. She makes things so hard for herself. You know how she is the night before an exam. She gets so worked up, she defeats herself—she gets A's, but the misery . . . Where she's gotten this idea she must be perfect, I don't know. All of her teachers tell me how bright she is. Moody, yes. Volatile, yes. But rewarding to have in a class." Bea shook her head. "She's pretty, she doesn't believe she is pretty; she's smart, she doesn't believe she's smart. Whatever I say, she gets angry at me. She doesn't *get* angry. She *is* angry at me. She's angry at me all the time. What have I done?"

"You've done nothing, Bea. She is just angry."

"I can do nothing right for her."

"Leave her alone, you yourself have said, she'll get through this, whatever it is, she'll go on, she'll be fine, like everyone else in the world."

"I sometimes wonder."

"Go on."

Bea sat down on the sofa. Solomon sat down beside her, took her hand.

"Bea . . ." She looked at him. "She'll be all right. . . . She's difficult now . . . sure, what kids aren't. . . . So she's excitable—maybe more than most. But she's bright as hell, and a lot of that is your doing. You've interested her in books without forcing anything on her, just by your own genuine interest. That's your doing, too. Sure, we read, but there was a time when she would talk to you about books—and you were great with her, with Nick too. You've always treated them like people—real people."

"Maybe that's part of her problem."

"What her problem is . . . Look, no matter what she says now she's always known you've been there for her."

"Maybe I've been there too much. . . ."

"Bea . . . listen to me. She knows that you love her—and even though she's upset now, she knows you still love her."

Bea sighed. "I'm really starting to wonder . . . she's so angry. . . ."

Solomon hugged her. "You've been fine—it's not your fault. Really, the less fuss now, the better. It will sort itself out."

ONE afternoon Rose's voice teacher gave Rose a ride home and came into the house to tell Solomon and Bea what a remarkable voice Rose had. Beautiful tone quality, fine sense of pitch, and added to her own natural gifts was what every voice teacher hopes for—Rose's "insurmountable desire to sing."

After she left, Bea couldn't resist saying, "Well, your horrible ugly family couldn't have been so bad, you seem to have your gifts."

Rose turned. "If I do, they didn't come from you, Mother Dear."

"Of course not."

"Oh, you're so sarcastic, so clever, you always have something clever to say. *That,* incidentally, is just so Jewish."

"*What* is so Jewish?"

"That kind of cheap word cleverness."

Bea flushed. Struggling to control herself, she turned and walked out of the room.

"Just who do you think you are and where the hell do you get that kind of thing?"

"Don't swear at me, Father. We aren't supposed to swear. Your rule, it isn't nice. And it's true what I said. Isn't that why they're such good lawyers? Everyone knows Jews are clever with words. They twist meanings."

Solomon shook with anger.

"Don't you ever talk like that to your mother again! And don't ever say things like that about Jews—or any other group of people—again. You never got *that* in this house. And God-dammit, I won't have it!"

"Yes, Father. Shout. Just what you tell me not to do."

Solomon walked out of the room.

Rose shouted after him. "And it's true! You know it is! You can't stand the truth!" She slammed the door hard.

LATER, Bea said to Solomon, "I do not know where she is getting this about Jews. It's a private school, but there are girls from all kinds of families."

"I'm afraid she's just going to have to have her ears pinned back by someone who really won't stand for it. She'll learn the hard way."

Bea was quiet. After a time, she said, "It *is* disturbing. A little adolescent rebellion is one thing. Does she have even the slightest idea what happened to Jews during the war?"

"She will learn, she will learn the hard way. The way she seems to do everything else, lately."

ROSE was given the lead solo in the Fall Concert. There had been, according to her teacher, virtually no competition. A friend of hers from the Juilliard School was planning to attend; Rose might even find herself with a scholarship.

Rose came home with the music and spent the evening playing various passages on the piano. She got up, paced, leafed through the music, sat back down, played. She did this for three nights in a row, testing her voice, trying passages, consulting with her voice teacher. She would stop and start. Then one evening, suddenly, the whole piece, "Entrata di Butterfly," seemed to be flowing out of her, filling up the house. Solomon put down his paper, looked up. Bea glanced over. They listened.

Bea said, "My God, it's really a beautiful voice."

They walked quietly into the front hall. The singing louder. The deep glow of the mahogany piano. The rust-gold of Rose's hair in the light. Rose went on singing, her voice clear, strong, her eyes half closed. She looked and sounded radiant. Then she caught sight of Bea. Her face went rigid. She banged the piano keys. "What are you doing, Mother?"

"It's beautiful, simply beautiful."

"No, it's not."

"It's wonderful. The tone. It's . . . like your hair, if you could see the gold in your hair in the light."

"You don't know anything about voices. Or hair."

Solomon took a deep breath. Bea shrugged, "I'm your mother, I know nothing," and walked slowly up the stairs.

At the landing Solomon took her hand. Then put his arms around her. After a moment, Rose slapped the keys—once— the dissonance, a single sharp clatter jumping up the stairs. Solomon felt Bea stiffen, and held her tight against him.

AT about this time, Solomon noticed several packs of cigarettes and tins of Schimmelpennincks—small cigars—missing from his top drawer. He counted the packs, watched until he was certain they were disappearing.

One evening he knocked on Rose's door, which was always closed after dinner. He knocked, then pushed the door open.

Rose at her desk. Biology book open. Clothes, sheet music, record albums scattered on her bed and the floor. Taped to her dresser mirror, a magazine photo of Gertrude Stein. Beneath, a full-page color photo of Ezio Pinza and Mary Martin in *South Pacific*. Another of Robert Wagner. Rose sat furiously writing something at her desk. When she wrote, she wrote with her head almost touching the paper, her whole body bent over. She had her face completely made up.

"Am I interrupting?"

"No."

"What are you writing so intently?"

"A letter."

"To whom?"

"Sam Shepherd."

"Who?"

"Sam Shepherd, Dad."

She handed him a pile of clippings. Solomon went through them quickly. Trial. Testimony. F. Lee Bailey. Shepherd found guilty. Appeals. People who had known him—patients—all saying it was impossible, he couldn't have killed his wife. Prison.

Solomon nodded. "How long have you been following this?"

"Since the beginning."

"And what are you writing to him?"

"That I believe he's innocent. I know they'll let him go."

Solomon looked down at the clippings. "Why do you care so much about him?"

"What's wrong with it, Dad?"

"No one said there was anything wrong with it. You believe he's innocent?"

"I wouldn't be writing to him if I didn't. A lot of other people do, not just me."

"A lot of people think he's guilty, too."

"They're wrong."

"I see. How can you tell?"

"I just know. What did you knock for?"

Solomon decided not to say anything about the cigars.

"Nothing. I just came in to say hello. Can't anyone come in to say hello anymore?"

"*You* can."

Solomon looked around the room. Rose followed his eyes. "I'll pick it up, Dad, don't worry."

"I'm not worried. How's your music coming?"

Rose shrugged. "Oh, I don't care about it."

"You don't care? I thought you cared more about music and singing than anything. Your teachers say you have the talent to be a serious singer."

"They just say that."

"What I hear sounds good to me."

"Oh, Dad . . . it would to you."

"No, really. And why would your teachers say that you had a talent if you didn't?"

"Dad, you don't understand anything."

"I don't understand much, but I understand one thing."

Rose looked at the letter she'd been writing. Picked up her pen.

"Do you want to hear?"

"No, but you want to tell me."

"That's right, I do. A real talent like yours—a gift—is also a responsibility. You're going to have to work like hell."

"Have you been talking to Mother again?"

"What's your mother have to do with it?"

"That endless Jewish moralizing of hers."

"Listen, Rose. I've told you not to talk like that in this house. If you want to talk like an ignorant bigot, do it somewhere else."

Solomon turned and walked toward the door. Rose watched him.

"Do you want the door open or shut?"

"Dad . . ."

"What is it?"

"Stay here with me a minute."

"Suppose you think things over for a while." Solomon pulled the door shut.

Rose shouted, "They're true!"

SEVERAL nights later, Solomon again noticed the small cigars missing from his top drawer; bad enough that she was sneaking cigarettes, but cigars . . . . He debated. He could imagine the scene, the anger, the screams, the looking away, stopping her ears with her hands, the childish denial. He sighed. The hell with it. He'd had a long day. He picked up the paper. Threw down the paper.

At her closed door, he paused, knocked hard, and walked in. She looked up at him. "To what do I owe the honor?"

"I have a question for you. I want you to tell me the truth."

"Do you realize you're interrupting my studying?"

"This won't take long."

She closed her eyes, opened them, and looked at her nails. "Yes, Father Dear."

"Rose, I want to know if you are helping yourself to the cigars and cigarettes in my top drawer."

Rose colored, stared hard at Solomon, and then said in a loud voice, *"No! Did she* put you up to this?"

"If this *she* is your mother, no."

"I'm not listening." Rose put her fingers in her ears, looked at the ceiling.

"Do you think cigarettes are good for your voice? Cigarettes and cigars?"

"I don't care about my voice and I don't hear you."

"What do you care about?"

"And they can't hurt. I wasn't smoking."

"They can't hurt? You think they'll help?"

Rose closed her eyes, *"I was not* smoking your precious little cigarettes!"

Rose took her fingers out of her ears, pointed a long red fingernail at Solomon. *"That's* why you came in here the other night. 'I just came in to say hello,'" she mimicked. "Pretending to be interested in me."

"Rose, I am interested in you, I don't have to pretend—"

"You wouldn't even stay when I asked you to."

"To tell you the truth, when you are behaving that way, I don't find you very pleasant to be around."

"You really wanted to ask me about the cigarettes, didn't you?"

"No."

"Yes, you did! I thought I could trust you. She's turned you against me. Get out of *my* room."

"Cigarettes and cigars won't help your voice."

"Get out!"

Solomon pulled the window closed.

"What are you doing to *my* window?"

"The Kellys don't have to hear this!"

"The Kellys! The Kellys! *Get out!*"

"That screaming won't help your voice either."

"Out!"

"Look at yourself in the mirror when you do that. Is that the way you want to be? To look?"

"Out!"

"Yes, be alone." Solomon turned and walked out.

"BEA, she denies taking the cigarettes. Of course. And now she says she doesn't care about her singing."

"She cares."

"Has she stopped practicing?"

"Of course not, she practices, but she practices secretly. She does some at school, some at the Kellys. I pretend not to know. Of course she cares. She doesn't want us to know how much she cares."

SOLOMON woke in the middle of the night. Rose was kneeling by the bed.

"Dad. Dad." Her voice was hoarse. "I can't sleep. I'm having trouble breathing."

Solomon got up, examined her nose and throat, felt her glands, took her temperature and pulse.

"Rose, I can find nothing."

"Dad, there is something."

"Sweethert, there may well be, but I can find nothing."

"I can't lie there all night gasping for breath. I can't."

"What would you like me to do?"

"I don't know."

"I can make an appointment for you to see someone tomorrow. But I myself can find nothing now. And I can't start calling someone in the middle of the night."

"Why not?"

"Because, Rose, I think you'll be all right until morning. If I didn't, don't you think I'd do something immediately?"

"No." But she smiled.

"I'll tell you what. I'll get you a glass of brandy. Would you like that?"

She nodded. "And sit with me—just a little."

"All right."

He returned with the brandy. "Get back in bed."

Solomon pulled a chair close to the bed as Rose sipped the brandy.

He watched her. "Were you having a bad dream?"

"No."

"Can you describe the trouble you had breathing?"

She closed her eyes and touched the area beneath her eyes and around her nose. "It feels closed. And when I open my mouth and take a deep breath, I can still hardly breathe." Rose sipped the brandy. "Maybe I injured myself the other night."

"Injured yourself? How?"

"I woke up in the middle of the night and I was lying on the floor. I had fallen out of bed."

Rose sipped the brandy. "My nose and cheeks were sore and I had a headache. . . . In the morning, I noticed my nose was swollen and I was black and blue. Here." Rose touched the area beneath her eye.

"When was this?"

"Monday."

"Why didn't you say something to me then?"

"I didn't want to worry you."

"I didn't notice anything. . . . Monday?"

"You didn't look."

He studied Rose. Was she making this up?

Rose took another sip of brandy.

Maybe she believed something had happened, maybe something in fact had. Feeling helpless, he hesitated. Then he said in a professional voice, "All right, Rose, come here." He led her to the desk, turned up the light, and aimed it into her eyes.

"Dad, it's blinding me."

"Please, bear with this. How do you expect me to see?"

"Maybe it can't be seen. Maybe it's in my sinuses."

"Oh, if there's anything to find, I'll find it. Now sit down here and close your eyes."

She did so. He took her face tenderly in his hands, held her face. Looked for traces of hemorrhage. Felt the bridge of her nose—the septum—for swelling. Finally said, "Okay, Rose," and switched off the light.

She looked at him expectantly. "Did you find it?"

"No, Rose, I think you're fine."

He smiled. He wanted her to smile. He pinched her cheek.

"Dad! Don't." She pushed his hand away.

"Well, Rose, first thing in the morning, I'll call and make an appointment with an ear, nose, and throat specialist and he'll check you out completely."

She got back in bed and pushed down under the covers. Stared up at the ceiling.

"Here, finish your brandy."

Rose took a last sip. "Stay another minute, Dad."

Rose closed her eyes. Her breath deepened slightly, her lips parted. Solomon listened, but could hear no obstruction in her breathing. Relaxed in sleep, her face was beautiful. Solomon put the glass down on the night table. Her lips moved once. She said something he couldn't understand.

In the morning, Solomon told Bea. "Whatever is or isn't wrong, I am going to take her seriously. I'll make an appointment with John Castle—he's one of the best in the country— she'll get completely checked out, and that will be that."

SOLOMON took her for the examination. Afterward, the doctor told her he could find nothing wrong.

Rose flushed. "There *is* something."

Dr. Castle said quietly, "There *may* be something. I only said I could not find it."

Rose stood, glared at him, glared at Solomon, and walked out, slamming the door.

"John, I apologize for her behavior. She's going through some kind of stage—it'll pass—and I'm not always sure how to deal with it."

"It's all right, you don't have to apologize."

"I myself feel this is a psychosomatic episode. I thought a negative finding on an examination would put an end to it. Apparently it hasn't. I'm sorry she was so rude."

In the car, Rose stared straight ahead. "A stupid little man!"

"He's the best there is, Rose. You're lucky he took the time to see you. I'd like you to go back in there and apologize to him. Not for me, the apology. For you. It would be good for you. Rose. Look at me when I talk to you!"

"I'll find another doctor!"

"And slam *his* door?" Solomon started the car. "Do you think you can go through life slamming doors?"

"On stupid little men, I can!"

Rose went on complaining. Night after night she woke Solomon, insisting she could not breathe, could not sleep.

Bea would say, "Really, Joe, you have to get some sleep. I wish I could do something. I would sit with her if she would let me."

"Well, there's not much point in going into that. She's hardly talking to you."

And Solomon would throw on his bathrobe, get up, and sit beside Rose's bed. Sometimes they played checkers or cards. . . . But mostly she wanted him to tell stories.

"Tell me about the patient you had in a cast—the one who decided to die. . . ."

Solomon would look blank. Then joke, "All my patients live."

"No, Dad, you remember, the old Italian man . . . you went to his house and he was sitting up in bed under a picture of Jesus with a bleeding heart and cutting himself out of his body cast with a kitchen knife."

"But you already know the story. . . ."

"I've almost forgotten and anyway, I love the way you tell it—tell it from the beginning."

Rose would lie there with a pleased smile on her face and

listen. "Tell me about your old chief, Gutman, how he would drive up to the hospital every day in a Rolls-Royce and you were the chief resident and you stood at the steps and opened the door and took his coat . . . and how he would sit on a raised platform during grand rounds. . . ."

"Oh, Rose, I've told you this a thousand times."

"But I like to hear it. I like the way you tell it. Tell me how tough he was again. And how great he was. . . . I like to hear it . . . the things you did were so hard."

"If you want something, you work for it."

She would ask him to tell her about the time he'd delivered the baby in a farmhouse near the cabin and the baby had been born with a full head of red hair.

"Tell me how beautiful the red hair was . . . and how you went for a walk in the new snow afterward, and the moon was rising."

Or about the time Solomon's uncle had swum to Hoboken from the Battery on a bet, was that really true?

She would ask him to tell her how he used to get up at three in the morning with his father. They'd go to the farmer's market and buy produce for the store.

"Tell me about the horses and the lanterns."

She would lie there and ask him to tell her about riding the ambulance when he'd been an intern. . . .

Once she said, "Things were more real then, weren't they?"

"What do you mean? Things were more real? This is real, every day's real to me."

"No, Dad, people were more wonderful then. Dr. Gutman. And your uncle's swimming from the Battery to Hoboken. People don't do things like that anymore."

"Of course they do."

"It's not the same . . . horses, lanterns, you working in a factory when you were fourteen. . . ."

"Everyone I knew worked, we worked all the time . . . nothing wonderful about working in a factory."

"I wish I had."

"I'm damned glad you don't."

"And the fights you got into."

"Rose, I only fought when I had to. . . ."

Rose smiled up at the ceiling. "No, Dad, you're wrong, things were more real then."

They would talk into the night. Night after night, Solomon would get up with her, sit with her, talk to her, quietly, tenderly.

BEA took Rose to look for a simple white dress for the concert.

She returned harried and exhausted. "Rose is impossible. We get into a store and she shouts at me. People turn around, the salesgirls are shocked. It's so awful. I'm not going to try again. She says she'll wear what she wants and buy what she wants." Bea shrugged. "She can do whatever she feels like as far as I'm concerned. I'm fed up."

Liz Kelly saved the day. Bea mentioned she was having a hard time getting Rose a dress for the concert, and Liz said, "Don't worry, let me take her shopping, I have a tough time with my own, too."

Afterward, Rose returned with something she would not show anyone. She walked smugly past Bea and Solomon, kissed Liz Kelly on the cheek, and with a large dress box under her arm, mussing Nick's hair, she'd disappeared up the stairs.

"How did you do it?" Bea asked Liz.

"She was great. Relaxed. Charming. So much fun to be with. Really."

Later, Bea sat at the kitchen table. Solomon lowered the paper. "Bea. Bea. What are you thinking about?"

"Nothing . . . really. . . ."

"Whatever it is, I can see from the look on your face that it's not good."

"I'm just a little tired, Joe."

"Try to be a little philosophical. . . ."

She smiled faintly. "Yes, what else."

ROSE kept after Solomon, wouldn't he *please* take her to another specialist, didn't he know she was in pain? Didn't he care about her? And Solomon tried to joke with her, of course he knew she was in pain, no, of course he didn't care about her, she was only his daughter. . . . He played for time, hoping she would drop her obsession with seeing a specialist. He hoped that after her concert, she would relax and the whole business would come to an end.

She continued to wander around the house in the middle of the night, and Solomon, several times rousted out of an exhausted sleep, had almost lost his temper, but realizing she couldn't control whatever she was doing, had gotten hold of himself and patiently sat up with her.

Rose came down to breakfast one morning and said, "All right, if you won't take me to see someone, I'll just have to go by myself."

"Good morning, Rose. You could say good morning."

"Look at those paws." Rose mussed Nick's hair as she passed him.

"I'm going to have my sinuses cleared—I have an obstruction."

"But Dr. Castle could find nothing."

"I have an obstruction—and I am going to have it cleared so I can breathe. And while I'm having that done, I'm going to have this," she touched the bridge of her nose, "removed so I can be pretty."

"On whose money?"

"Doctors don't charge each other."

"You're not a doctor."

"Then I'll charge it to you."

"No, you won't. You will spend not a cent of my money, ever, without my consent."

"Then I'll get the money."

"Where, Rose?"

"I'll get it. I'm not going to go on suffering because you're too cheap—"

"Look, Rose, money really has nothing to do with it. I'm keeping my eye on you. Good doctors observe patients before deciding to operate. I *don't* do something just for the sake of doing it. I'm certainly not going to let you suffer or be uncomfortable. Do you think I would?"

"Yes."

Solomon looked at the circles under her eyes and suddenly felt annoyed, not because he didn't believe she was suffering but because he really didn't know what the hell was wrong. Why couldn't she just go to school, do her work, have fun. . . .

"You don't believe that for a second."

She didn't answer.

"Do you?"

AFTER she'd left for school, Solomon said to Bea, "I can just imagine the scene if we suggested she see a psychiatrist."

Bea shook her head. "Here. Did you see the program? Rose brought one home yesterday. Of course, she didn't offer it to us, but made sure to leave it where we'd find it. Look what she's singing. She's really half the concert. The 'Entrata di Butterfly,' two songs from *West Side Story*, more from *Showboat* . . ."

"Bea? You don't think we could get her to a psychiatrist, do you?"

Bea put the program down. "I have the feeling she's waiting for us to suggest that." Bea didn't say anything more.

"Bea . . . well?"

"Well, what?"

"Why do you say that? Do you think she would go?"

"No, of course not."

Solomon waited in exasperation.

"Well, what is your point? Why would you say she's waiting for us to suggest she see a psychiatrist when she wouldn't go?"

"Because then she can say we're suggesting she's crazy."

"Now that you mention it, Bea, do you think she is?"

They looked at each other in silence. Solomon sighed, stood, picked up his briefcase and several brown envelopes of X rays.

"What is it, Bea?"

"Look at you. Circles under your eyes. And I can see from the way you're moving, you're exhausted. She hugged him. "I don't really understand what she's doing. I don't think she knows what she's doing herself."

Solomon started to say something, but found he had nothing to say.

Bea kissed him. "Never mind. Enough for now. Go to work, forget it for a while. We'll think of something."

ON the day of the concert, Rose spent the day agonizing over her hair. It was too curly.

"My God, it's not too curly, it's hanging in beautiful ringlets."

"No, Mother, it is too . . ." Then she spent a long time showering and a longer time dressing.

It was getting late and Bea knocked lightly on her door, "Rose, can I give you a hand?"

"No."

Rose came out of her room. Her eyes were heavily mascaraed. She wore bright lipstick and matching nail polish. She was wearing a cobalt-blue dress—it looked satiny—Oriental, slit to midthigh.

Solomon and Bea looked at each other.

Bea said tentatively, "Dear, did you tell Mrs. Kelly what the dress was for?"

"Yes, Mother Dear, what's the matter, don't you like it?"

"I didn't say that. I only asked."

Rose turned, walked back into her room, and slammed the door.

Solomon said, "I'd better handle this. Why don't you see if Nick's ready. He was having trouble with his tie. Help him, you'd think a fourteen-year-old would know how to tie a tie."

"Well, dear, I don't know how to tie a tie either."

"Then just make sure he brings it. I'll do it for him in the car."

Bea shrugged and shook her head. "She couldn't have told Liz what the dress was for. I can't believe Liz would have let her get something like that. I know she wouldn't have."

Solomon whispered, "That's enough, Bea. Just take Nick and go downstairs."

Solomon stood in the hall. Smell of autumn coming in the

open windows, fragrance in the house. He took a deep breath, walked to Rose's door, knocked.

"Go away."

Solomon turned the knob slowly. "Rose. . . ."

"Go away."

"It's time to go now."

Solomon opened the door. Fragrance, Chanel No. 5.

Rose sat in her desk chair, arms crossed in front of her; she stared out the window.

Solomon spoke softly. "Come on now. You look fine—smell wonderful, too."

Rose didn't answer.

"Rose, what's the matter?"

"I saw the way you looked at each other when I came out, you and Mother."

"What do you mean?"

"You know!"

Solomon sighed. He looked at his watch. "It's getting late, Rose. Let's go."

"I'm not going."

Solomon sat down on the bed. "Rose, look at me."

Rose stared out the window.

"You know, sometimes before I operate, I'm afraid, too."

"I'm not afraid."

"I'm afraid because the patient is weak or badly hurt. Or the operation's dangerous. It's natural to fear."

"I'm not going."

"Whatever I feel, I do the operation. If I don't, the patient will be worse off and I'll be worse off, too."

"Is this going to be another one of your lectures?"

"Look, Rose, people are depending on you. Your classmates. People have hopes for you. Your voice teacher. What about her? All the time she's spent with you."

"For the money!"

"No, not for the money. Not for the money. People do things for reasons other than money. And she has brought people to hear you. Can you think of other people for a change?"

Rose stared out the window.

"You'll regret this, Rose."

"Don't threaten me!"

Solomon laughed sadly. "I'm not threatening you. Not at all. That's the last thing I'm doing. What are you going to do—sit there in that chair all night?"

Rose didn't answer.

Solomon stood. He felt exhausted.

"Well, Rose, what do you want me to do?"

"Call them and tell them I'm not going to sing."

"And what reason should I give?"

"That I'm sick."

"I won't lie for you. If you want to lie, then do it yourself."

Solomon looked at his watch. "You still have time to change your mind and make it. I'll be downstairs."

He walked to the door. Rose did not move.

He said quietly, "Rose, if you don't sing tonight, I'm afraid you will regret it for the rest of your life. That's all I can say."

Solomon stepped out of the room, closed the door quietly. He checked his watch again.

Downstairs, Bea and Nick sat at opposite ends of the kitchen table, Nick uncomfortable in jacket and shirt, the shirt buttoned to the top button, ready for a tie. Hair neatly parted, the water drying and tufts of hair popping up.

"Let me talk to your mother alone for a minute, Nicky."

Nick started for the door.

Solomon placed his hand on Nick's shoulder. "Nick, don't go upstairs—why don't you wait for us in the sunroom?"

Nick looked uncertain, looked at Bea.

Bea said softly, "Go ahead, dear."

"And close the door, Nick, please."

"I don't think she's going to sing, Bea," he said when Nick had left.

"And no doubt it was the way we—I—reacted to the dress. All I did was ask her if she had told Liz about—"

"I know, Bea."

"The fact that we didn't want to see her make a fool of herself. It's a beautiful dress, but ridiculous for a seventeen-year-old girl."

"Never mind that. The question is what do we do now? Call the school?"

"Oh, I don't know what to tell them, Joe. I don't even know if she has an understudy. I think I recall her saying she did. But whether we should call now, or wait . . ."

"We'll wait a few minutes, she might change her mind. But I don't think so."

Bea looked at her tightly folded hands. "I've been trying to convey to her silently that I—that we—believe in her. I don't know if she ever had any real intention of singing. She was looking for an out. She probably didn't do it consciously, but she bought a dress she knew was unsuitable. And she knew we would think so. Even a single glance from us was enough excuse—so now it's the old pattern, it's our fault." Bea corrected herself. "My fault."

Solomon looked at the kitchen clock. "A few more minutes and it won't matter either way. Except for her. She'll have to live with this."

"And we'll have to live with her. If only I could go in there and talk to her."

"Well you can't, so forget it."

Solomon lit a cigarette.

"I hate to see you smoke, Joe."

Solomon waved his hand at her. "Bea, please."

Bea stood up.

"Don't go up there, Bea."

Bea crossed the kitchen, hesitated, listened. "Do you think Nicky is all right? He's been very distant lately."

"Ah, he's all right."

"No, lately he looks troubled. He never used to keep things so much to himself and this isn't good for him."

"It's not good for any of us. She is tyrannizing the whole house."

Bea started as the phone rang.

"What do we say?"

"I told her I would not lie for her and I'm not going to. I'm for letting it ring until she answers it."

"Oh, Joe, don't be ridiculous, she won't answer it."

"Well, if someone doesn't pick it up and say something . . ."

The phone rang again.

"Dear . . ."

"Bea! Answer it!"

"Oh, dear . . ."

Bea answered the phone. Solomon took a deep drag on his cigarette, threw it toward the sink, a shower of ashes and a hiss. Bea followed the flight of the cigarette into the kitchen sink, covered the mouthpiece momentarily, "Joe!"

Solomon fished out another. "Just tell them she is not coming. That's all. That's it."

Bea turned her back.

He couldn't make out the conversation. He paced. Once he said out loud, "Tell them exactly why she won't sing . . . the real reason." Solomon hesitated. "The real reason, that she's too goddamned afraid!"

He caught several phrases. Migraine headaches. Pains in her sinuses. That, at least, was part true.

He caught sight of the program with her name on it.

Solomon crumpled it and threw it away.

He thought of her voice teacher, the program disrupted completely. Did she at least have an understudy?

Did she think she was getting even with him—with all of them—for some terrible thing they had done to her? If so, what, just exactly what, in her mind?

Bea hung up the phone. She looked exhausted.

"What'd you tell them?"

Bea walked to the sink, picked the wet cigarette butt out of the water, and threw it in the trash. She returned, ran the water in the sink, dried her hands. Said softly, "I hate lies. And I end up lying for her."

"*What did* you say?"

"Because, that's what it really is, isn't it? A lie?"

"Bea! Never mind that! What did you say?"

"I said she had a migraine headache. I tried to explain. She *has* been up the last few weeks? with pains in her head."

"How did they react?"

"They were polite but very upset. She does have an understudy, but they say she's poorly prepared . . . it ruins the program. What a real shame. Her beautiful voice, all the work she's done, and now no one will hear it."

48

"I've heard enough of it for one day."

"Getting angry isn't going to help. We have to fight giving in to that . . . Joe? Did you hear me?"

"I heard you."

Nick appeared at the door, a questioning look on his face.

"Are we going, Dad?"

"No, Nicky, we are not."

Nick looked confused. He hesitated. "Then can I unbutton this button?"

"Is it so terrible for you to button your shirt like a gentleman?"

Solomon leveled his index finger at Nick. Nick winced.

Solomon felt Bea squeeze his arm.

"Dear, that's fine, you can undo the top button now."

A hurt and confused look on Nick's face.

"Your father's sorry, Nick."

"Why aren't we going?"

Bea opened her mouth. Solomon checked her with a cautioning look.

Bea said, "Because, Nicky, your sister is too upset to sing. She's not feeling well."

"What's she upset about?"

"Many things, Nicky."

"Like what?"

"Look, Nicky, that's enough! She is! So that's that!"

Bea said quietly, "Your father doesn't mean to raise his voice. Rose is upset about many things, some we understand, some we don't."

Nick looked curious. "Like what?" he repeated.

"That's enough, now, Nicky, we'll talk about it later, your father and I have some things to discuss."

Bea put her arms around him, kissed him, leaving lipstick on his cheek. "Wait." Bea smiled. She rubbed at the smudge with a tissue. She held Nick at arm's length, a hand on each shoulder. "Remember that movie you wanted to see?"

"*The Creature from the Black Lagoon*?"

"Yes, how'd you like to go later—you and a couple of your friends?"

Nick nodded, smiled.

A door slammed upstairs, Bea felt Nick stiffen. She touched his face. "It will be all right, Nicky."

Rose coming down the stairs, clattering into the kitchen, unsteady in her high heels. She had a glass in one hand.

"Father Dear, I would like the car keys."

"You must be out of your mind."

"I would like the car keys," Rose repeated, emphasizing each word.

"Where do you think you're going?"

"May I have the car keys or not?"

"No, you may not have the car keys!"

"Joe, keep your voice down."

"That's right, Mother Dear, always the hypocrite. Afraid the neighbors might hear?"

"I've had enough histrionics for one day."

Nick held up his hands. Tried to smile. "Paws, Rose."

"Shut up!"

"Your brother was just trying to joke, Rose."

"What are you drinking?"

"None of your business!"

Solomon took the glass out of her hand. "You're drunk. Where did you get this?"

"It's your own precious Scotch, Father Dear, how else did you think I got to sleep every night after you ignored me?"

"Ignored you? I didn't take you to the best doctor in Boston? . . ."

"A stupid little man."

"I didn't sit up with you night after night . . ."

"You wouldn't really help me in the way that mattered! Now may I, or may I not, have the car keys?" Rose put her hands on her hips.

"And just where is it you have to go so urgently now, Rose?"

"I am going to sing."

"Sing? Sing where?"

"Sing at school!"

Solomon pointed at the clock. "You should have made up your mind a while ago, it's too late for that now, tootsie."

"Don't tootsie me! I am going to sing whether you like my dress or not."

"Yes, that's what I wanted you to do an hour ago. That is

just what I wanted you to do. Sing. But now it's too late and there's nothing I or anyone else can do about it, Rose."

"I am still going to sing!"

"It's too late, Rose. And you're drunk."

"Are you going to give me those car keys or not? No?"

Rose walked unsteadily to the phone. Dialed information. "The number of the Yellow Cab Company, please. Thank you." Rose hung up, started to dial.

Solomon took the phone. "You had your chance, you are going nowhere, now!"

Rose snatched the phone back. "You can't keep me here. I'll call the police."

She pushed Solomon. Solomon staggered backward, recovered his balance, snatched the phone from her.

She shoved past Solomon. Started for the door. "I am getting out of this house. *Out! Now!*"

Solomon stepped in front of her. "You are going nowhere!"

She flailed at him. Solomon caught her wrists, her nails dug into his skin. Blind look in her eyes, close boozy smell, perfume. Rose kicked at him, staggered, tried to kick him again.

"Let me go!" She intoned it in a rhythm as she tried to kick him. *LET-ME-GO!*"

Her foot wobbled, her heel broke, she slipped, hit her head against the stove. On both knees, silent; she put her fingers to the side of her head. Slowly, carefully, she felt the side of her head. Her voice soft, "There's a bump there."

"Rose. . . ."

She said quietly, "You pushed me. . . ."

Rose let out a sound somewhere between a wail and a scream. "You pushed me!"

Nick in the doorway. Rigid. Hand on his top button, motionless, staring.

"Bea, take care of him . . . get him out of here, will you?"

Rose pulled herself up, came at Solomon again, kicking, scratching, flailing. He pulled her arms down to her sides, pushed her to the floor, and held her down until her wails and screams subsided into an exhausted, semiconscious monologue. Once or twice she tried to sing, raising her head, panting out several shrill notes.

51

Finally she became still, passed out, and Solomon carried her upstairs in his arms and put her to bed.

SOLOMON glances down at his bathrobe, half-expecting to find what he'd discovered as he'd come out of her room that evening. His shirt buttons ripped off, the sleeves and shirt front streaked with lipstick and rouge; as though pieces of her had come off on him as they'd fought. His hands and wrists and neck were scratched but he had not felt anger; instead, a strange calm, which soon gave way to exhausted depression.

AFTER the Fall Concert, Rose stayed home from school for several days, remaining in her room, not talking to anyone, occasionally coming out to make herself a cup of tea. All day her door was closed and neither Bea nor Solomon went in. Then one morning Rose came down to breakfast—dressed, quiet—and went back to school.

An uneasy calm followed, and then Rose again started complaining, she had pains in her head, she had pains in her sinuses, she could not breathe, and once again she was up during the night . . . if Solomon didn't do something then Rose would do it herself.

Solomon finally made up his mind to take Rose to a plastic surgeon.

Bea said, "I don't believe in what these girls do. Every girl who doesn't like something about herself or her face runs to a doctor and has her face changed. And their parents let them. Is this right? Is this the way to do things? She claims she has an obstruction. Dr. Castle found nothing. We know there's nothing. I think this is all just an excuse for her . . ."

"That's too simple."

". . . to have her nose done. What a tragedy that would be, she's beautiful right now. I feel helpless. I really do."

"I don't like it any better than you do, and no one's saying anything about right or wrong, but let's face it, Rose isn't just another unhappy teenager. . . ."

"Don't you see, it's not going to help. And after this, she'll just find something else, don't you see? She is determined to be unhappy. . . ."

"No, I don't see that."

"Look, I really can't see anything wrong with her nose or her looks. What I do see is that she hates herself. She doesn't feel good enough. Why, I really don't know. We've both always been supportive. She hates her looks, she hates Jews, which is shocking, she hates me, and that is marvelously convenient for her—in her mind I represent everything terrible. So what's the big psychological mystery, Joe? Some things are straightforward. I don't believe in mystifying. I think she can learn to live with—"

"I've told you, this is not just another unhappy teenager we are dealing with and you are being a little slow to grasp—or accept—that fact."

"You're reinforcing her, saying yes, fine, go ahead, yell, scream, you will get what you want. She has browbeat everyone. You give in."

"No."

"She's blackmailed you. Now she thinks this is the way—a way—to get what she wants. Whoever forced anything on her? Did you? Did I? If we were narrow-minded people—"

Bea mused a moment.

"You know, in many ways, I was closer to my grandmother than my mother."

Her voice softened. "She had no real education, but she was so wise. At the end of first semester my freshman year, my first time back home, my grandmother made me lunch, meat and oh, something, I forget what—cheese—I think it was, on the same plate. I looked up at her surprised and she said—and there wasn't a trace of martyrdom— 'Yes, I will keep kosher, but I know you don't so why should you keep up something you don't believe?' And that was all there was to it.

"What a wonderful, remarkable woman." Bea drifted off, her face young and open, for a moment. "Oh, don't look so impatient, Joe. My point is that I don't come from rigid people, you've always thought for yourself, we've encouraged them to do so."

"And this is what she's done with it."

"No, not at all. What she's done with it has made us out to be rigid." Bea flushed. "We're bending over backward. She thinks by shouting she will get what she wants. *She's* the one who's rigid. And you advocate giving in to her. . . ."

"No, I don't."

"I say, let her learn to live with herself."

"But that's my point, Bea. She's not learning. What do you suggest? Bea? Just exactly what do you suggest? We've talked about sending her to a psychiatrist and you yourself said she wouldn't go, that our suggesting it would only be playing into her hands."

"Dear . . . I don't have any answers right now, but—"

"You don't have any answers."

"Not yet, but I know this isn't the way. And I wish you wouldn't take that tone of voice—I'm starting to feel browbeaten by all of you!"

"Look, Bea, if I refuse, what do you think she'll do. The first chance she gets, she'll get the money somehow, she'll find a good friend who knows so-and-so, who is just a wonderful doctor, and very cheap, and off she'll go to this very wonderful, very cheap doctor. And this wonderful cheap doctor will make a mess of her because he's such a big bargain."

"Oh, she won't go running off to any doctor, Joe. . . ."

"The hell she won't. This is a very willful girl."

"Like her father."

"Hear me out. This way I take her, at least I can get her the best doctor; she has this done, and whatever is supposed to happen in her mind, it happens. And we've helped her. We who are not supposed to be on her side. We—who she thinks don't love her— Now we love her in her mind, don't you see?"

"No, I don't see at all."

"Listen to me. When I was a resident, we had a young woman—twenty—twenty-two. She came in and she was bent over like this." Solomon showed her. "She was bent over and she could hardly shuffle along. Have I ever told you about this woman?"

"Not that I remember."

54

"We examined her, went over her with a fine-tooth comb. Nothing. Perfectly healthy. But there she was, bent over. So Gutman—Gutman was not fooled—Gutman found out from social workers that she had some kind of bad family situation. . . ."

"Rose doesn't have a bad family situation. She is making—"

"Will you listen to me?"

"I'm listening. You can lower your voice." Bea quietly closed the bedroom door. "And stop glaring at me."

"Well, sometimes, Bea."

"Go on."

"Gutman called the woman in and made a great show of examining her. He sat her down in front of his desk and once again studied her records and X rays. Then he stood up and said grandly, 'My dear, you shall have the operation. It will be a difficult, risky operation, but if it is successful, you will be fine. Are you sure you want to take the risk?

" 'Oh, yes, sure, let's get on with it.' This woman can't have the operation soon enough.

"So we set the date and everyone scrubbed. I remember this very well. We went through the procedure just as though we were going to operate. Caps. Gowns. The works. The patient was wheeled in and Gutman made sure that she got a good look at all of us. Dramatic effect. Then Gutman said, 'Now we are going to give you an anesthetic'; he took some harmless, foul substance on a rag to simulate ether and he put it over her nose."

Bea looked at him questioningly.

"He wanted her to be awake, Bea, through this procedure so that she would feel what he was going to do! He wanted her to *feel* it! That was the point!"

"You don't have to be so impatient with me, Joe."

"I'm not! *Feel it!*"

"Yes, dear."

"So then he touched her in several places along her spine, 'Can you feel that? That?'

"Oh, no, she could not feel a thing. Each place he touched her she volunteered that she could not feel his touch. She was in a state of autohypnosis.

"Gutman then said in a theatrical voice, 'The patient is ready! Proceed!' Gutman produced a huge needle. Oh, Christ, it must have been this long." Solomon holding his hands so far apart. "And the needle was hitched up to a galvanic shock machine. Gutman took the needle and stuck it in her back and then he administered a series of shocks—he must have done this ten times. Each time the woman's body jolted. It would have knocked over a horse, but this woman never let out a whimper of pain. Not one. Then Gutman said once again in a theatrical voice, 'Bring the patient out of it.'

"At which point, we stepped forward, turned the woman over, and sat her up. Gutman took the woman's hand and said, 'My dear, the operation is a great success, better than any of us could have ever hoped for, get up, stand straight, and walk.'

"And you know something, Bea? She did. I saw it with my own eyes. She got up off that table, stood straight, and walked. We never heard from her again."

Bea didn't say anything for a long time.

"Bea, I cannot let Rose go on tyrannizing this household."

"We've indulged her."

"Oh, hell, Bea, we've indulged her . . . the hell we have. Give me a decent alternative."

"She has gotten her way and this is wrong, Joe. It will just be something else after this."

Neither of them said anything.

Finally Solomon said, "Look, you have some blocks about this, Bea. I'm not exactly sure what this represents to Rose—I'm no psychiatrist, don't pretend to be. I'm not certain she knows herself, but we both know we're not getting her to a psychiatrist. We have to do what we can."

Bea shook her head. "It's just so unnecessary. So unnecessary."

"That may be. But this is the way it is."

"I don't agree."

"And this is the way it's going to have to be."

And that's the way it had been. During Christmas vacation of her senior year, Solomon took Rose to a plastic surgeon, and she had her nose done. He found nothing wrong with her sinuses.

Rose came home with two black eyes, which slowly faded. There was an uneasy peace around the house, in which for the most part, Rose seemed pleased with herself. She spent hours experimenting with makeup, and, with a mirror held to one side, studying her profile. She would gently stroke the bridge of her nose with the tip of her index finger, sometimes as though in disbelief, at other times as though to renew or rediscover the pleasure—whatever it was—of her new nose, still other times, perhaps nervously, as though she suddenly felt exposed and vulnerable. Solomon noticed her doing this secretly, privately, a nervous gesture, an unconscious habit— reaching up, stroking her nose.

LONG after Rose had been married, Solomon recalled a tortured, long call—another crisis.

When he'd hung up, Nick had given him an angry look. "You'll never win with her."

"Why look angry at me?"

They'd gotten into a heated exchange over Rose. Nick suddenly, with a look of contempt, "You encouraged her, I remember her black eyes, grotesque. . . . I couldn't even recognize her for two weeks. . . ."

"Encouraged?! Look, you don't know a goddamned thing about it. Encouraged! You have no idea what we were going through with her at that time in her life. Her misery was far deeper than you or I can understand. And don't look at me like that. And, as a matter of fact, almost nothing was done to your sister. We went through this with her because we thought it would make her like herself better. What would you have done?"

"I don't know, but—"

"Uh huh, you and your mother, you don't know, *but. But* is easy. Just what would you have done?"

"I don't know, I—"

"You don't know!"

"Let me finish!"

"Go ahead, Mr. *But.*"

"I would have sent her to a shrink, I guess."

Solomon made a sound of disgust. "Oh, look, Nick, you have no idea about this. None at all."

"Well, why not?"

"That's what I'm trying to tell you. We never would have gotten your sister to a shrink. Never."

"But why?"

"It was beyond that. At times, when I try to figure her out, I sometimes think she might have actually been brain-injured at birth."

Nick's incredulous look. "You're kidding."

"Why kidding?"

"Because it's so convenient to put it off on something like"— Nick laughed uneasily—"an injury. . . ."

"Put it off? When have you ever known your father to duck responsibility?"

"It's like one of those bad jokes, I act funny, someone dropped me on my head."

"So it's a big joke. The facts are your mother had a bad re-action to the anesthesia. Your sister got held up. The obstetrician had to make a quick decision and it was a high forceps delivery. I damned well remember because I looked at those two red marks on her temples for ten days afterward and thought some long thoughts.

"It was after that experience your mother decided to practice what they now call natural childbirth with you. Where do you think she gets some of these notions of hers about holistic healing and ESP or whatever it is. I can hardly get her to take two aspirins when she has a headache. Why not? Oh, she's concentrating, oh, concentrating. She's dealing with the inner disturbance or whatever the hell else. I tell her fine, take the two aspirins and deal with the inner disturbance better. I can tell her nothing."

"I think that's ridiculous, putting it off on something like that—what? A forceps delivery."

"A *high* forceps delivery."

"Yeah, whatever it is."

"How can it be ridiculous if you don't know what it is?"

"Your attitude toward it. And what is it?"

Solomon took hold of Nick's head. "It's when the doctor

takes hold of the baby like this and yanks it out with forceps."

Solomon and Nick looked at each other. Solomon said, "They don't do them anymore, it's so ridiculous."

Nick with a blank look. Rubbing his head.

"No, go ahead and think I encouraged your sister, what-ever."

"I only said—"

"I know what you said!"

Rose seemed nervous and for a period moved self-con-sciously, as though afraid she might hurt herself. Once, Nicky, horsing around, bumped into her. Her hand went to her face. She screamed at him. Without thinking, he said, "That's still not even you yet."

Rose took a new singing teacher. Nothing was ever said about the Fall Concert. Things did in some ways seem bet-ter. The house calmer, Rose more pleased with herself. She didn't scream or slam doors as much—she now reacted to Bea with a restrained sarcasm, an occasional outburst: "Oh, say what you want, Mother Dear, soon I'll be out of this house and away from you and the sound of your voice."

Several times she looked at Bea with a gloating expression and said, "I'm glad at least someone around here wanted to see me happy, aren't you, Mother?"

To which Bea would say nothing.

Solomon found himself looking at Rose's face, and feeling blank, almost as though he were waking up and not knowing where he was. And he had the growing sense that Rose was disappearing—there was a secretiveness, a distance. Out of that distance, that new insulation, there would be an incon-gruous word or gesture, oddly accented, elaborate, or con-trived, which Solomon had never seen before, and which gave him the uneasy sense she was inventing herself—a new self, a pastiche of gestures, words, scenes, arrivals, departures, crises—from novels, movies, and her beloved musicals.

And an odd incident occurred. Dozens of old family photo-graphs disappeared, mostly ones with Rose in them. Bea fi-nally gave up looking for them. "Maybe she's hidden them, but most likely she's destroyed them. And I am not going to have another scene with her over it. I know what she's done and why she's done it and it's too bad. They weren't her pictures. They were ours. You took them. And I wanted them."

Solomon didn't say anything. He still felt he had done the only possible thing in taking her to the doctor. He couldn't have let her go on the way she was. But he was beginning to have the sense that it hadn't changed anything—just as Bea had said. Whatever Rose was doing had taken on a different, secret form.

SOLOMON stands. Stretches. Back stiff. Knees. Looks at his watch. Again debates the sleeping pill. Glances over at the mail table. Gets up, walks over and throws the remainder of the unopened *Wall Street Journal*s into the basket. Remembers Bea's turning from the mail table, "Here"—holding a letter out to him, "Here, there's more of it, Rose Summer, this address, it can't be a mistake."

Solomon looking at the letters. "Miss Rose Summer."

"I don't know, Bea. We'll just wait until the next time she comes home. Look, it's junk mail, what's the difference?"

"No, this mail coming to the house represents an unconscious mistake. A plea for our help. Some part of her wants help."

"I would call that wishful thinking of the highest magnitude. Pure projection. I don't think she wants a damned thing to do with us. We see her three times a year now—if we're lucky. Occasionally—more than occasionally—she asks for money. That's the kind of help she likes."

THE letters, Rose Summer, this had been after college. She'd been living in New York at that time. She'd gone to Oberlin, studied voice, majored in drama, almost flunked out she spent so much time doing plays and musicals, had suddenly become disenchanted with music, stopped it cold, had made vague references to studying medicine. After two years and a difficult summer-school session, she had dropped out, moved to New York, and started working. Secretive. Vague. A theatrical style, a sweeping walk, histrionics in her gestures. Closing her eyes. Opening them slowly. Staring. Deep inhalations of cigarettes. She often smoked little cigars. Said, "What of it? I'll do as I please." And did. The bizarre contrast of her brightly painted long fingernails, the dark Schimmelpennincks, the deep smell of raw leaf tobacco, her perfume, the downward glance of her eyes, the lids heavily shadowed, blues, almost black. Her curly reddish-blond hair. And several times wearing a dark wig with silky, shoulder-length hair, Solomon momentarily not recognizing her. The same man's voice answering the phone at her apartment over a period of time, but her never saying a thing about him, Solomon wondering, but never asking.

. . . Picking her up at the station. "Father"—her kissing his cheek. Something theatrical about that. And her new way of walking. Important. Long strides. The city walk, New York. She didn't arrive. She swept in.

They'd talked about politics—the 1964 election. "Who are you voting for?"

"Let me put it this way, I'm not going to vote for our friend Johnson, the giveaway artist."

"No, of course not, you'd vote for Goldwater."

"At least he tells the truth."

"And in the last election, you probably voted for Nixon."

"That's my business."

"Of course, you voted for Nixon. If I'd been able to vote in sixty, I'd have voted for Kennedy and canceled your vote. Kennedy. He was gorgeous. What blue eyes."

"That's a good reason."

"He was too good to last."

"He wasn't so hot."

"Johnson and Goldwater and Nixon, a bunch of uglies. And now, of course, you'll vote Republican—all the mean old men with bank accounts—"

"Old man Kennedy has a dollar or two, and don't you forget it."

"The Kennedy's money is different from other people's money."

61

"Is that right? How so?"

"It just is."

"That's right, it is. Joe Kennedy made his bootlegging. I—and by referring to myself I assume I'm one of the mean old men, though I'm not so old, yet—made mine fixing broken arms and legs."

"I don't include you, Dad."

In the house, Rose walked quickly from room to room, then took off her coat. Looked at the living room.

"I always thought this was a beautiful room. The light. The piano. I think about this room."

Looking almost wistful. "Promise me you'll never sell this house," she said suddenly.

"We're not about to."

"I mean *never* sell it."

Solomon looked at her questioningly. "I couldn't bear the thought of other people in this room. It always has to belong to you." Rose sat at the piano. Played the beginnings of several songs. Slammed the cover. Then going into the dining room to the liquor cabinet she poured herself a Scotch.

"You're pretty handy with that stuff, aren't you, Rose?"

"Oh, Dad, you've done it for years."

"A drink or two before dinner. It's barely noon, now. How often have you seen me take a drink at noon?"

"Dad—"

"Just how much do you drink?"

"Nothing, Dad. Nothing at all."

"I can only ask. I can't be with you and watch twenty-four hours a day."

"Don't worry, Dad."

Rose went up to the attic. Searching for something.

Solomon and Bea looked at each other, and Bea said, "I am going to ask her, just ask her. No one is going to raise his or her voice. But it has to be done . . . doesn't it?"

Rose came down from the attic with a box smelling of moth balls. A sweater. "I thought I remembered putting it away sometime in college. And there it was. I'm going skiing. . . ."

"When did you learn to ski?"

"Oh, I learned—" Rose stopped. She looked from one to the other. Rolled her eyes.

"Uh, oh, I see something's wrong. I've only been home five minutes, but I've done something wrong already. Mother has that calm, carefully composed look. What has she put you up to now, Father? Mm? What is it, Mother Dear? What have I done? Just one minute. I think I'll fortify myself."

Rose returned from the dining room with a full glass of Scotch.

"So? What is it now?"

"Oh, really, Rose."

"Oh, really yourself, Mother."

"Your attitude hasn't changed toward us one iota since you were sixteen."

"Yours hasn't changed, either."

"Childish."

"Whatever you say."

"Why don't we sit down, have a talk where no one raises his or her voice."

"Just tell me what's wrong! It's always something! What have I done now?"

"Why do you think it's always something? What do *you* think you've done?"

"Always the little psychological ploys, Mother. So thin, so transparent. 'What do *you* think you've done?' " Rose mimicked.

"This is a grown woman? You can't act like this toward other people—you just can't. You wouldn't have any friends."

"I have friends, but they don't treat me the way you do."

"How do I treat you?"

"That's right, Mother, play the innocent?"

"It's a fair question, what has your mother done?"

"Are you going to take her side, Father?"

"I'm not taking anyone's side. I'm only asking a question. What's your mother done to you that's so terrible?"

"Oh, never mind."

"Why don't you answer?"

Rose took a deep drink of her Scotch.

"You don't answer because you don't know, you aren't interested in change, you're only interested in hurting and accusations, aren't you?"

"Who are you going to vote for, Mother Dear?"

"What's that got to do with anything?"

"Republican."

"What makes you think I'll vote Republican, Rose?"

"You do whatever Dad does, don't you, Mother Dear!"

"A minute ago you were asking me what your mother put me up to. Which is it? Which of us is the terrible manipulator?"

Rose didn't answer.

Bea said, "As a matter of fact, in 1956 I voted for Adlai Stevenson. And your father voted for Eisenhower." Bea shrugged. "But I want to know, you say I've done something to you. . . . Something so terrible. So tell me. What is this terrible thing?"

Rose glared at Bea.

"Okay, Rose, no need for that. I get the message. Foolish of me to have asked. I live, I breathe, I am your mother. That in itself is enough. That's what I have done. I got the message a long time ago. Foolish of me to hope you'd grow up. You must be very happy inside."

"I am. When I'm away from here."

"So who's keeping you here? Did I ask you to come home?"

"No, you wouldn't."

"You don't want to be here. But you're angry I haven't asked you. You've got me coming and going. I give up."

Bea picked up the stack of mail. "Here. These belong to you."

Solomon shook his head, lipped silently, "No, not now."

"They do, don't they?"

Rose looked at the stack of letters without taking them.

Bea replied to the shake of Solomon's head. "And no, now is as good a time as any! Because, don't you see, there is never a right time for anything between us. . . . And there's never going to be. Here, Rose, take your mail."

Rose took the stack of mail. Flushed.

"Where did you get these?"

"They came to the house—or is that my fault, too?"

Rose sorted through the letters a moment.

"Are they for you?"

Rose didn't answer.

64

"What I've done to you, I can understand, the list of injuries must be so long and complex, you can hardly begin to answer—"

"Yes, Mother, your Jewish sarcasm. Say one thing, mean another."

"Well, I don't see what could be more direct than asking you if these letters are for you. It requires a simple yes or no. You're the one who is indirect. And you can keep your anti-Semitic diatribes out of my house!"

"Dad's house. He's the one who's done all the work. Made the money!"

"Our house," Solomon said quietly. "Yours, too. . . ."

"I'm asking you a simple yes-or-no question. Are these letters for you?"

"They are my own business!"

"We don't open your mail. And we didn't ask that they come to the house."

"They shouldn't have!"

"No, Rose?"

"No."

"Why don't you answer the question. If they're not for you, there's no problem, we'll just give them back to the postman, tell him there is no such person at this address, that will end it."

"Oh, Mother, really, you are so clever and smart." Rose put the letters in her purse.

"I guess that answers us."

"Yes, they're mine! Does that satisfy you? Goddamn you!"

"Thank you for an honest answer at last. And no, it does not satisfy me. If they're for you, then you are Rose Summer. So you have become Rose Summer. When did you change your name?"

Rose looked away.

"Do you feel better with your new name? Happier?"

"Goddamn you, Mother!"

"Why be angry? If you're proud of your new name, why hide it? We're interested in knowing. Tell us. We'll be the first to call you by your new name. Rose Summer."

"You're *so* smart, aren't you, Mother? Safe in your little

house, Father taking care of you—you don't know anything."

"If I'm such an ignoramus, why don't you enlighten me?"

"Just forget it. I'm sorry I came home. I came home in a good mood. I'll go."

"Can I ask you one more question, Rose?"

"Oh, sure, Dad, anything. Why not? Anything."

"Well, I'll only ask you the obvious question. Why did you change your name?"

"Is it a crime?"

"That's not what I asked."

"If I were married, I would have a different last name."

"But you're not."

"Actresses do it all the time."

"You're not an actress. Maybe I should take that back. Maybe you are an actress. Pretending to be anyone and everyone but yourself."

"Okay, Dad, anything you say. I thought *you* at least understood me."

"I'm trying."

"Rose, we're wrong for being upset that you've changed your name?"

"Yes, Mother, you are."

"Do you think Mrs. Kelly next door would be upset if Kitty came home and announced she'd changed her name?"

"I didn't announce it."

"No, you didn't. That's true. You at least had enough shame left not to do that."

"And Kitty wouldn't have to change her name."

"You change your name and expect to find us dancing? You are utterly insensitive. I'd think you'd be proud of your father's name. What do you have to hang your head about? Is your father a bank robber?"

"I'm not listening to you, Mother."

"No, I suppose not. And you never have. Your father's worked hard for his name, it means something to people, a lot of people. Everyone but you. You don't have the brains to know what you've done. It's the only name he, this man right here—no matter what you may think of me, your terrible mother—this man standing here is the only father you'll ever have."

66

"I knew you'd say something like this."

"It takes your father thirty-five years to make his name mean something and you throw it in the garbage in two minutes and pick a name out of the phone book."

Bea crossed the room, looked out the window, her arms folded, her shoulders hunched, hugging herself.

Solomon glanced at Rose, drink in one hand, Schimmelpenninck in her other. Rings, large stones. New rings.

He shook his head slightly.

"What are you shaking your head at, Father?"

"Nothing."

"Me, aren't you? I'm just so awful, aren't I?"

"You're afraid someone will think you're a Jew. To be a Jew is so terrible, you should change your name, run, hide, be ashamed?"

"Dad . . . Please. . . ."

"No, tell me. I really don't understand what it is like to feel that way. Freud, Marx, Einstein . . . Jesus . . . Chagall, the painter you've always loved so much, he painted villages exactly like the one your grandmother came from in Russia. . . . Chagall is a Jew, Mahler—"

The look suddenly changed on Rose's face. Her eyes hard. "I'm not even Jewish anyway."

"Oh, you're not. How is that?"

"You had an Irish step-uncle, you told me that yourself."

"What does this mean to you, why is it so important? We never made anything out of it. Maybe we should have. But neither your mother nor I are religious. No one ever forced anything on you. Why is it so important?"

"It's not."

"People don't change their names for nothing."

"Dad, please. I don't want to argue with you. I've never wanted to argue with *you*."

"I don't even go to temple."

"You don't have to."

Solomon looking at Rose questioningly. "Don't have to?"

"You're a great doctor."

"I'm a good doctor. And what's one have to do with the other?"

Rose said, "I'm *not* Jewish, so it doesn't concern me."

"What's one got to do with the other? Rose?"

Rose glanced over at Bea's back. Bea was still hugging herself and looking out the window.

"That's so stagey. Mother's looking out the window. Are you supposed to be rejecting me, Mother? Are you? Well, I reject you, too. Isn't that a psychological word you'd understand? Reject?"

Bea didn't answer. Rose looked at Solomon.

Solomon said, "You may not be Jewish, but I am. And your mother is. And if anyone ever asks me, you can bet I'll tell them."

"I'm not."

"I don't know how you arrive at that with an Irish step-uncle, great-uncle for you, and a Jewish mother and father, but good for you."

Rose glanced over at Bea again. "What do you see out there, Mother Dear?"

Bea turned. Solomon surprised by the look on her face, which was no longer hurt and angry, but thoughtful.

"Uh oh, Mother's got a thoughtful look on her face."

"How could I, I'm an ignoramus, remember?"

"How could I forget?"

"In my stupidity, I think I see a few things—your stupid Jewish mother. This changing your name wouldn't have anything to do with the man who answers your phone? Would it, Rose?"

" 'Would it?' " Rose mimicked.

"Uh huh, I thought so."

"What *do you* think?"

"I know you, Rose, I know you a lot better than you think I do."

"Yes, Mother."

"I wonder if you know what you've done to yourself."

"Oh yes, Mother."

"And I wonder what he would think of you if he could see you now. You and the way you're behaving now?"

"Is Mother using her precious psychology on me again?" Rose took a deep drag of the Schimmelpenninck.

Solomon jarred by the deep red of her lipstick, the cigar. Bea shook her head.

68

"Shake your head, Mother. Go ahead."

"Yes, I shake my head at what I see. This man—or his parents—are anti-Semitic, that means in simple language, since you accuse me of indirectness—Jewish indirectness, since I *am* Jewish—that they don't like Jews. You are a Jew, so your feelings are hurt—deeply hurt."

"Oh yes, Mother Dear. As a matter of fact, his parents like me. For myself."

"Do they know your real name?"

Rose didn't answer.

"Do they? Uh huh, I see. They like you for yourself. Tell me about it. Since you've never accepted yourself."

"Yes, Mother Dear."

"Then what would make more sense, you would fall in love with a man who wouldn't accept you for who—"

"Always correct English, Mother—"

"Yes, for who you really are."

"Yes, Mother Dear, you know nothing about it, nothing at all."

"Tell me if I'm wrong, Rose. I want to be the first to know. Tell me I'm wrong. I *want* to be wrong."

"Mother the great psychologist."

"It doesn't take much psychology to see the obvious. He—or his parents, or both—don't like Jews. Wonderful."

"I'm not Jewish."

Bea laughed.

"You think you've fooled them. And he's encouraged you. Because he loves *you* so much. You're not like all the other terrible Jews. So they'll make an exception for you."

"He hasn't encouraged me!"

"Don't you think that if he really loved you, he'd stand up for you. Even though you don't have the brains to stand up for yourself. He wouldn't try to pass you off as something other than yourself."

"I *am not* Jewish."

Bea laughed again.

Rose stamped her foot. "Go ahead and laugh. And it is *not* for him."

"Who's it for?"

"I was going to do it anyway. As a matter of fact, I had

started before I met him. I picked the name—"

"Wonderful. Not for him. You were going to do it anyway. You'd picked the name. Wonderful. For his parents. And so now you're suffering. Of course you're suffering. I feel sorry for you."

"I'm not. And don't."

"I do. Be Rose Summer now. Be happy. Live with it. I see the rest of this pattern now. Since you've gone to all this trouble, you'll marry your wonderful man. We're as good as dead now anyway. Call us when you need money. I'll try to help you by dropping dead quickly."

"I wish you would, Mother!"

"That's enough!"

"And have a good life, Rose Summer."

"I will!"

Snatching up her coat, Rose threw the sweater on the floor and stormed out, slamming the front door.

NICK's face close. Again, Nick's persistence. His questioning really did irritate the hell out of Solomon.

Solomon studied Nick another moment—his square jaw, reddish curly hair. Bea's green eyes. Solomon fought to control his annoyance. "You seem to have it in your head that *we,* your mother and I, did something to cause her unhappiness— that something we did made her change her name. Nothing could be further from the truth."

"I don't have any such thing in my head. Where do you get that?"

"Something in the tone of your voice, the belligerent look on your face."

"You're always telling me I have a belligerent look on my face. According to you, I was born with a belligerent look on my face."

"No, you weren't and you haven't always had it, either. But you've had it now for a good while."

"I don't have a belligerent look on my face."

"You can't see yourself."

"I don't feel belligerent. I'm only asking what happened."

70

Solomon sighed. "Nicky, I'm telling you, I don't know what happened to her. You know, you can only do so much for your kids. You'll find that out yourself someday. After that, they've got to live their own lives."

"Okay, Dad, okay."

"So okay-Dad me. You see them hurt themselves and you can do nothing. Plenty of times I've asked you not to do something I thought was unwise—and you've ignored me, told me in no uncertain terms to mind my own business. So what was I supposed to do? Your sister wanted to change her name, she did. Your sister always did what she wanted. Once she had made up her mind, that was it. The rest of the world could go to hell."

"Dad, I ask you something—you look up from your book, like it was a big favor to me. Why anyone would always be reading about World War Two like some kid, anyway, is beyond me."

"Samuel Eliot Morison is no kid."

"I don't mean Samuel Eliot Morison. Not him. You. You're the kid."

"He's a hell of a writer."

"Great, he's a hell of a writer."

"Read him, see for yourself."

"That's not my point."

"But that's my point since you raise it!"

"Okay, hand over the book! I'll read it as fast as I can. My point is you won't talk to me—except in three-word phrases."

"I tell you the facts."

"The facts! What a mind you have. Black and white."

"What more is it you want!"

"You act like there's some big dark secret here."

"There's no big dark secret. If there's a big dark secret, it's in your mind, not mine. I tell you. I've told you. But you look at me as if you expect something more."

"You're annoyed that I ask. As though I'm supposed to know—or remember everything."

"Well, you are a member of this family, aren't you? You might have taken an interest."

"And when you answer, you answer with this tone. Disdain. Defensive."

"Oh, the hell I'm defensive. Defensive about what? What do I have to be defensive about? Did I do something?"

"I don't know, Dad. Everything's cut and dried. Like a case history. And your attitude, everything so obvious, how could I even ask. And will you take your finger out of that book so I can talk to you?"

"We can talk with my finger in the book. And let's lower our voices. Someone else in this family used to conduct all human transactions at a rather high-decibel level, remember? Look, I told you, your sister's mail came to the house—your mother felt something was wrong. Your mother confronted your sister—and that, let me tell you, was never an easy thing. Your mother never ducked what she thought was her responsibility. She confronted your sister and after hemming, hawing, and dodging around, your sister came out and admitted, yes, she had changed her name. Professed not to understand what the big deal was, why we should be upset. She was ashamed the world would know she was Jewish. Solomon. Jewish. Big deal to her. Why, I honestly don't know. A terrible thing to be Jewish in her mind. Why, I just don't know. She doesn't get it from me. Or your mother. We never pushed anything on her. Who knows. Maybe we should have. I don't know. But have I ever been one of those guys up there in the first three seats in the temple mumbling his prayers ten times a day? Have I ever been? Have I ever made you? No. I do my work, I live, that's it. So one morning Rose gets up and being Jewish is a terrible thing, she can't live, she changes her name. And, of course, Price played a part in it. How much, I don't know. At that time, your mother and I had no idea who or what Price was— knew nothing whatsoever about him. You talk about secrets. It was your sister who was the big one for secrets. Melodrama. Everything a big deal. But again, here, your mother guessed. And she guessed right. I might add. She guessed right."

"Family myth: Mother intuitive."

"I'm not saying she's perfect. She can be wrong on a few things, too. I'm sure the Turners had—and still have—no use for Jews. Fine with me. I have no illusions. I tell you, when people come running to me in the middle of the night with a compound fracture, I don't start asking them about Mary and

72

Joseph. And you know something else? They have a funny way of not asking me if Solomon is a Jewish name at that moment, either."

"Why be so bitter, Dad?"

"Bitter? I'm not bitter. I'm telling you how it is. Old man Turner isn't a bad guy, but Mama runs that outfit and she's got some ideas, she's a little—" Solomon tapping his temple.

Nick still looking.

"So your sister—who knows what she was thinking—and Price, they thought they would fool Mama. Very clever. But of course Mama figured it all out. You have got to get up very early in the morning to fool Mama Turner. She is shrewd and she is willful." Solomon paused. "Like someone else we know."

Nick looked questioningly at Solomon.

"Oh, look, Nick. Shrewd and willful. Like Rose, Nick!"

"*That* tone of voice. Why should it be so obvious to me?"

"You ask. I tell you. Pay attention. Follow."

"Is this a classroom?"

"Not for me, it isn't."

Nick gazed at Solomon with an amazed look. "I don't understand you. What's *that* mean?"

Solomon returned to his book. Looked up. "Never mind. That's all, Nick. Your sister and Price didn't fool anyone, least of all Mama. Maybe Price thought he was getting back at Mama. For what I don't know. Price has a problem or two himself. He never finished college, his father spoiled the hell out of him—gave him whatever he wanted, then cut him off. Old Man Turner would think nothing of getting up one morning, buying five motorcycles, using them two days, and then letting them sit in the garage. Not exactly the best way to give your children a sense of perspective, is it? Price probably manages money by going out, charging whatever the hell he feels like, and not paying the bills—I think that's one of the things your sister and Price fight about. If I taught her nothing else, I taught her to pay her bills—though why that rubbed off, I don't know. Not much else did. I don't have any idea what Price's mother taught him. I don't think she ever said two consistent things to him in her life. And I wouldn't be a bit surprised if he has some rather antiquated right-wing John Birch Society ideas—about Jews, Negroes, and Communists. Which your sister probably shares with him. So your sister storms out of here, yes, she'd changed her name, we can all go to hell, and next thing we know, she calls up and says, 'We're married, come meet your new son-in-law.' Wonderful. They'd gone to a justice of the peace. Very quaint. Some old man with a cat sleeping on the piano. That's what your sister said. A cat sleeping on the piano, for Christ's sake. Isn't that wonderful? And the man's old wife was a witness. A Norman Rockwell cover for the *Saturday Evening Post*."

Nick silent a moment. "Well, Dad . . . look on the bright side; at least she saved you the expense of a wedding."

"Gee, Nick, I never thought of it that way. Terrific. I should have gone out and bought three new cars. Wonderful."

"I'm kidding. Take it easy. What *did* you say to her?"

"When?"

"When she called you up—the cat on the piano, the justice of the peace."

"Me? What did I say? I'm just a mean old guy with a bank account."

"Why do you always say that?"

"It's true, isn't it? A mean old guy with a bank account. Who fixes broken arms and legs. And like to read about trout fishing. And I count myself as fortunate. Because if I forget who or what I am, you and your sister remind me. What one doesn't remind me of, the other one does. I'm lucky. So what would an ordinary guy like me say when his daughter who changes her name calls up and says, 'I'm married'?"

"I don't know, Dad. What does he say?"

"He says, *mazel tov!* Congratulations. What's your name now?"

Nick looking sad.

"Don't look sad. Nothing to be sad about."

"I thought I only looked belligerent."

"This is the way things are. So? More? You want more? Your mother was delighted, too. But Rose was very reassuring. She informed us that they didn't invite his parents, either. You see, they played no favorites, here, that was the idea. And I

74

guess they made whatever point they wanted to make. Your mother said, 'He must have a wonderful relationship and high regard for his family, too. Now it will be both of you against the awful world, is that it?'

"Then, your sister wanted to know, would we come meet him?

"Your mother said, 'Now's a nice time to be asking us. Sure we'll rush right down, just give me time to change my dress and powder my nose.'

"Your sister says, 'I'm serious. Price wants to meet you.'

"And your mother: 'He had plenty of chances, didn't he? Who stopped him before?'

"This went back and forth, 'Oh, you don't understand, Mother,' and the rest of it, and finally your mother said she'd think about it.

"And Rose, tactful as a meat cleaver, kept insisting. 'But he wants to meet you *now*.'

"You can imagine how pleased your mother was by this— that Price wanted to meet her *now*."

"What did she say? Mother?"

"As a matter of fact, I remember it clearly: she said, 'He wants to meet me now. How nice. You've always accused me of Jewish sarcasm—isn't that how you put it? Jewish indirectness? So now, just so there won't be an confusion, let me give you some directness—some Jewish directness—so you'll never be in doubt again. You and your new husband— whoever he is—can go straight to hell. Is that hard to understand? Is it indirect? Can I say it any clearer?' "

"Mother said that?"

"Oh, you're surprised? There's a lot you don't know about your mother."

"I'm not surprised."

"That's what she said. There was a long silence on Rose's end of the phone. I think she was actually surprised and hurt that we didn't want to come running that instant. Let me say that your sister's sense of reality can be slightly wanting at times. I think she was actually surprised.

"But surprised or not, it didn't take her long to answer your mother in her customary way. How exactly did she say it?

Something like, 'Oh, you're so small.' No. It was, 'Oh, you're such a small person.' That was it. 'A small person.'

"Your mother said, 'Yes, if this makes me a small person, you can bet I'm small.'

"Then Rose asked to talk to me.

"Your mother said, 'If you didn't want his name, why do you want him to come now?'

"Rose said something to the effect, 'Always so clever, Mother.' You know how Rose can talk to your mother.

"Your mother didn't even reply. She just went right on. 'And when—and if—I get around to meeting this man, your husband, it will be when I'm damned good and ready! And don't forget it!'

"You see what small people we are, your mother and I?"

"Hey, remember who you're talking to—"

"*Whom* you're talking to."

"Sure, Dad, *whom*. Just remember, it wasn't me."

"So I took the phone and your sister started her whole song and dance, 'Talk sense to that woman'; 'At least *you* come'; 'Oh, I know you'll come'—and all the rest of it."

"And what did you say?"

"I said there was no *you* come. It's either *we* come or forget it. And I said I'd think about it."

"You just accepted it."

"I didn't say that! I said I'd think about it."

"You went."

"Why say it like that? Eventually I did go, yes. What the hell was I to do? Why take that tone with me? Just what was I supposed to do? You know, Nick, you have a way of acting superior at times—like your sister, as a matter of fact. Superior and completely out of touch with reality. This was the situation. Rose is my daughter, she will always be my daughter, no matter what, misguided, whatever you want to say about her. Would it help her or me or anyone else to pull this—you know, I've seen a few guys pull this routine, with their kids, yank their hair out, I never want to see or hear you again, you're dead to me. What's it get them? Who are they kidding?"

"I would have told her to get stuffed!"

"Sure you would. You seem to have one characteristic approach to things. You tell me I'm a guy who sees things black

76

or white. You would have told Rose to get stuffed—as you put it. Your way of dealing with the world is to tell everyone to get stuffed, pow, punch everyone in the nose. You're a big guy, you wrestle, lift weights, and you think this is a way to do things. You weren't always this way. But now, this gets you somewhere: pow. Your mother told her to go to hell—at that moment. Understandable. Me, I'm just an ordinary guy, I live in an imperfect world. A guy breaks a hip. I don't promise him the moon. I fix it as best I can.

"I eventually prevailed upon your mother to go in with me and meet them for a drink. And *that*, let me tell you, was no easy thing, either. Your mother's damned willful when she wants to be. Tavern on the Green, I think it was. Sure, Tavern on the Green. You know something, Nick, I think, more than anything else—hurt, anger—I felt sorry for your sister."

"That's just a defense."

"Fine, a defense, know-it-all. Do you want to listen? Or are you so busy judging?"

"Dad . . ."

After a moment, Solomon continued. "Here is a girl who feels so bad about herself that first she tries to change her looks, changes her name, is so afraid of her parents' opinion of her—"

"And ashamed of her parents, don't forget that."

"I tell you, I'm sorry for her, a girl's wedding day is one of the happiest moments of her life—she shares it with everyone she loves, her mother and father, her relatives, her friends. Your sister runs off to get married by some old justice of the peace she looks up in a phone book, his wife whom she's met a minute before is a witness, a cat is sleeping on a piano. Bronxville, I think it was. Get married by a stranger. Then hop on a train back to New York five minutes later. This is your sister's wedding. Am I wrong to feel sorry for her?"

Nick didn't answer.

"Am I? Uh huh, not so wrong, am I? And then she doesn't understand how her parents can be less than excited. Sure, I felt sorry for her."

"Oh, you should have taught her a lesson and told her to go to hell, once and for all."

"You just don't discard people. Rose will always be my

daughter. And for that reason, after I cooled off, we went to meet her and her husband. Price. This was wrong? This makes me a bad guy in your eyes?"

Nick stared at the cover of the book.

"Nick?"

"Did I say that? Did I say one word about your being a bad guy?"

"Not in so many words." Solomon shrugged. "If this makes me a bad guy, then I'm a bad guy."

"Oh, stop."

"Yes, I went to meet your sister and her husband. Another father would have said—as you put it—get stuffed. I cooled off and went to meet them for a drink. I believe in working with the situation at hand. I went."

Solomon looked at his watch, carefully marked the place in his book, got up with a grunt. "You want a cup of coffee?"

"No thanks."

"Tea?"

"No, nothing."

"Well, I'm going in the kitchen. You sure? Your mother put some Cranapple juice in the refrigerator this morning."

"No, nothing! Why the hell can't she buy either apple juice or cranberry juice! Cranapple! That's Mother. Cranapple. Jesus."

Solomon returned with a cup of coffee, spilling it into the saucer with each step, spilling more as he sat down; he felt for the pedal on the recliner—let himself down slightly. Nick shifted in his chair, Solomon sipped the coffee, Solomon took up the Samuel Eliot Morison, setting it on his lap, but not opening the book.

Nick shifted again, the chair creaked under his weight. Solomon glared at him.

"What?"

"Can't you sit still in a chair?"

"No. So what?" Nick glared back.

Solomon gazed up at the ceiling. He said absently, "Well, you're old enough, you should be able to sit still."

"So you went."

Solomon looked at Nick. "So I went?"

"So you went to meet them at Tavern on the Green. With Mother? Was she with you?"

"When have you ever known your mother and me to go anywhere without each other? We went together. We met them. And do you want to know my honest reaction the moment I saw her? The truth?"

"No, lie to me."

"I caught sight of them as they were following the waiter across the room. Your sister looked beautiful. She looked self-assured, she wasn't wearing piles of makeup. Sure, she still had the long nails. Except now she's also wearing a rock about this big." Solomon showing Nick. "Now where Price got this, I'll never know. I don't think Price has had that much money at one time in a year. I suddenly thought, as I saw her coming toward us, this might not be such a bad thing for her. That's the truth. That's what I felt."

"And what did you think of Price?"

"I thought he was a nice-looking guy. He was wearing a blue suit, he had a nice haircut, I thought he looked a little like William Holden. Just a regular-looking guy. You're nicer-looking."

Nick laughed again.

"Why are you laughing?"

"You."

"I'm so funny? Your father's a funny guy. A lot of laughs."

"Was it awkward?"

"Sure it was awkward. Could it have been much else? Your sister gave me a big kiss. She looked at Mother and said, 'Hello, Mother Dear.' That's all. No kiss, nothing. Then she introduced us to Price. She didn't let go of his arm once. I don't think your mother said three words the whole time. She ordered a drink, folded her hands so tightly I thought she was going to cut off the circulation in her ring finger, and looked at some point about three inches past the salt shaker."

"Uh, oh. I know that look of Mother's."

"If you think you've seen looks, you know nothing. The worst was yet to come. But for the time, we sat—Price looked me in the eye and started in, oh he loved Rose and not to worry, he would take care of her. To my mind, this was right out of Dickens. Have you ever read Dickens?"

"I read *David Copperfield*. Had to—school."

"Good, at least they did that much for you. That's all?"

"That's all."

"Well, read him. He's a great writer."

"As soon as I finish Samuel Eliot Morison, okay?"

"Don't read him. It's your loss. When I was a boy, I would go to the library every Saturday just after work. . . ."

"Where were you working then?"

"At that time I worked in the shop with my father. He was still a locksmith. I've told you this many times. I wonder if you ever listen. You're so busy wiggling around in that chair. . . ."

Nick looked thoughtful.

"I loved Kipling, Ryder Haggard, Conan Doyle, H. P. Love-craft. And Charles Dickens. And Tolstoy. Dickens and Tolstoy wrote things exactly the way they were. Especially Tolstoy. I read them all. There used to be a sign in front of the librar-ian's desk: *A book is like a leaky ship, a little knowledge must seep in.*

Nick creaked in his chair, looked at the floor.

Solomon stared out the window at the lawn. "What re-minded me of this was Price. A scene right out of Dickens, the suitor petitioning for the daughter's hand; except, this was a slightly different version. 1964. Postwedding." Solomon sighed.

"And Mother wasn't having any of it?"

"Not one damned bit. She barely raised her eyes from the table. Price, I don't have to tell you, can be very smooth, and he was smooth that day. . . ."

"You were having it, weren't you? I'll bet he talked about fishing. His ocean racing, that bit."

"Yes, as a matter of fact, you know, he'd been in the *Finis-terre* when she won the Bermuda Race in 1960. I was inter-ested."

"He conned you."

"He was smooth all right. Your sister was twenty-two and had a few crazy ideas, this guy was thirty, thirty-two, he'd been around the block, I don't blame your sister for being sucked in. He'd traveled a lot, been a ski instructor, a hunter, he'd been on the *Finisterre*, very glamorous to your sister, who thinks life is going to be a picnic. He'd been an extra in a couple of Westerns and war movies. He'd been a stunt man."

"And Mother stared at the tablecloth."

"Yes, and I'm not so sure that was the best way to behave, either. I understand it, but I'm not sure it was the best thing. I know, you would have had me punch him in the nose and drag your sister out of there by the hair. Wonderful. Later I said to your mother, 'I know what you're thinking, but this might not be such a bad thing for her.' Your mother glared at me.

"As I recall, you weren't exactly clairvoyant about him—you went skiing and fishing with him a couple of times when they lived in California. Seemed to like it well enough. Am I wrong?"

Nick got up and stretched. He looked out the window.

"Nick? Am I wrong?"

Nick didn't say anything.

"Uh, huh, so don't be superior with me, Nick. Don't *Finisterre* me. . . . I can remember telling you about this—or trying to tell you—on the phone. I think you were a big Dartmouth freshman then. And you know what your reaction was?"

"No, I don't remember."

"Oh, now someone doesn't remember. I'll tell you what your reaction was. You couldn't have given less of a damn."

"Come off it."

"Why would I be making this up? You just couldn't have given less of a damn. I remember it very well. You were on your way to a party with one of your girls—very important at the time—two months later you don't know one from the other, it's so important. You couldn't have cared less."

"That's not true."

"Not true? I turned to your mother and said, 'He's not interested. I don't get it.' I remember what she said. Do you want to hear?"

"No."

"She said, 'Why be surprised? Nothing they do surprises me anymore. Nothing.'"

"And she had *that* look on her face, didn't she?"

"I don't remember."

"You remember everything else." Nick puffed his cheeks, sighed. Nervous a moment. "When you were in Tavern on the Green, you said, the worst of her looks was yet to come."

"Sure, you've never seen a look like this on your mother's face. Your sister had planned another one of her little surprises. Your sister nudged Price and said, 'Here they come.' We look over and there's a couple following our waiter across the floor. They're coming right toward us, the guy looks a little like Price—an older version, about my vintage."

"You're kidding."

"What's to kid about? So we hike up out of our seats and start shaking hands again all around, your mother is just the color of ash. I mean it. Ash. That's no exaggeration. Just two red flush marks across her cheekbones."

Solomon touching his cheekbones. "Here. And here. But the rest of her, ash. She looks at your sister once, just stares at her. If looks could kill . . .

"Well, you've met Mama Turner. You know what she's like. Oh, she had just been in to see her designer. *Her* designer, if you please. They're on their way to their apartment in Paris—and she's off, a mile a minute yapping like one of these little goddamned, what do you call them—Pekinese dogs. Jesus, and looking like a Great Dane, she must be a good six feet tall. I took one look at this dame and said to myself, Hysterical personality. She's wearing some dress that looks to me like a potato sack, your mother wouldn't be caught dead in it; she's got a serape flung over her shoulder, your sister must have thought this was very exotic. I'm thinking, If this is what your designer is doing for you lady, why bother. It's cheaper to shop the basement at Gimbels after Mother's Day—"

"Okay, Dad—"

"I'm not kidding. She's waving her hands around, she's got more rocks on each finger, bracelets, necklaces, Christ, she looked to me like a walking advertisement for Tiffany's. The old man, Price Senior, you know, I never really minded him—and that's the truth. He was kind of a sweet-tempered guy. He doesn't say much, he just shakes hands, gives your sister a peck on the cheek, sits down, orders a drink. He gets that

82

quiet smile on his face, for all I know he's thinking about his island in the Caribbean. Did you know he owned an island in the Caribbean? No? Because it's just when I'm sitting down again, it starts to dawn on me, from the looks of Mama and Papa, that they are the Turners who own—actually *own*, and Papa is chairman of the board—Turner and Beebe Lumber Corp."

There was a long silence. Nick played with his fingers. Shifted in the chair.

"But what happened when you introduced yourself?"

"What do you mean, 'What happened'?"

"Well, Rose had been passing herself off as Rose Summer, Queen of the Rose Bowl or something . . ."

"Nothing happened. You can goddamned well bet every nickel you've got and will ever make that I introduced myself as Dr. Solomon. And in case they hadn't heard me right, I said, 'And this is Mrs. Solomon.' "

"That's what I'm talking about. Solomon with this daughter Rose Summer. She'd been telling them she was Rose Summer. What did they do? What did Rose do?"

"It was the goddamnest thing I ever saw. No one bats an eyelash. No one. Not your sister. Not Mama Turner. Not Papa Turner. No one.

"Mama Turner doesn't miss a beat, she just launched into her song and dance, the famous Dr. Solomon, she takes my hand, she's heard such marvelous things about me, she'd always hoped to meet me, but not in a professional capacity, of course. Big joke. And she starts pumping my hand again, I thought she was going to break my arm, Oh, did I know so-and-so? I did this, that and the other thing for him. He was miserable, spent half his life going from doctor to doctor until he found me. I was his salvation. Did I remember him?

"No, I didn't remember him. Before I can say anything more, she's off again. And Mrs. so-and-so? She'd had this, that, and the other thing wrong with her. Miserable. And so on and so forth. Did I remember her? No? Well, she remembers me. She talked about me all the time. Said a prayer for me, lit three candles morning, noon, and night for me in the church, whatnot. And before I can get in two words, she's off again. Did I know such-and-such?

"Finally I told her, 'Mrs. Turner, I've had a few patients in the last twenty-five years.'

"No one batted a goddamned eyelash—neither your sister, Price, or his parents, these great blue-blooded WASPs who probably thought they were doing me a big favor to have a drink with me.

"While Mama Turner is going on with the great-doctor routine, your sister, Rose Summer, was looking proud as hell about her father, the Jewish Dr. Solomon. Then Mama Turner starts about how lucky she is to have such a father and me, to have such a daughter, such a smart daughter, it's good to get some brains in the family, if you get my meaning: *smart*."

"No, I don't get your meaning, *smart*."

"Oh, *smart*. I took it she's saying, all you Jews are so smart, that business."

"I don't think that is what she was saying. Not at all."

"No? You weren't even there. I'm telling you."

"You're defensive, you really—"

"Go on, defensive! I'm telling you, *smart*. And your sister, so smart she can't get out of her way for being dumb, is sitting there so proud of her daddy, I swear, I look at your sister, and I think, Am I nuts? Is she nuts? Are we all nuts here at this table?

"What can I do but hope this will turn out for the best from this great, auspicious beginning. I feel utterly helpless. I look at your sister across the table and she might as well be a million miles away sandwiched in between Price Junior, her new husband, Price Senior, with that vague amused smile on his face, and Mama Turner yapping away like an enormous Pekinese."

"And no one ever said a word about Rose's name? Or your name? The obvious: that they didn't match?"

"Not a word. It was crazy, but then what exactly would you have said if you were there? Your mother didn't say two words. She sat at the table looking like she wanted to kill everyone. I don't believe I have ever seen your mother's face like that before or since. She might have been the only sane one at the table. I don't know.

"So there we were all sitting. And Mama Turner takes over.

No one can get a word in edgewise. The old man, Price Senior, probably gave up a long time ago. He sits there with his drink. Your mother, as I've said, is not exactly thrilled. But Mama Turner is patting this cheek and giving Rose little pecks on that cheek, saying how wonderful Rose was, the new addition to the family. She was such a lady, such a little lamb."

"She had them fooled."

"I don't believe she had anyone fooled. Not for one minute. Except maybe herself. She had Price fooled. But certainly not Mama Turner. You have to get up very early in the morning to fool her. I think that Mama Turner had figured out this was the best way to deal with Price. Maybe Mama Turner was a little smarter than your mother on this score. But oh, what a load of crap. Mama Turner really carried on. Rose was the best thing for Price since cod-liver oil. Now he'd settle down. Price had finally met a woman—a real woman—who would make him toe the line.

"I'm looking at Rose and Price and thinking, This poor bastard has no idea at all what he's in for. None." Solomon paused.

"Anyway, Mama Turner goes on with her palaver and next thing, she has reached into a pocketbook—she's got a pocketbook the size of a creel and pulls out a box, pops it open, and she holds up a necklace that must have had three million diamonds, rubies, this, that . . . Well, Mama Turner is not a lady you can easily miss. Since she has come in, six tables on this side, five tables on that, if you get me, have been looking over to see what all the fuss is about. Now Mama Turner raises this necklace. She has that same look you had when you landed that big rainbow—"

"Which one?"

"Oh, which one! Which one! A couple of years ago. Don't you remember anything?"

"I—"

"Anyway, she holds this necklace up over her head like this . . ."

Solomon showing Nick. "You need sunglasses to look at this thing. And everyone's looking, I'm telling you. Half the place falls silent. Three waiters here, four waiters there, the maître d'. Everyone just stops and gapes. This necklace would have been the cause of more than a few slipped discs.

"I'm no different. I gape. I admit it. I don't see people waving necklaces around like this in restaurants every day.

"Mama Turner half rises out of her seat—which for her is no easy thing, she's about thirty pounds overweight—and she says in this sugary voice, 'Rose, sweetheart.' Rose bows her head meek and sweet as a little lamb. Mama Turner slips the necklace on over her head. Rose just bows her head slightly like this." Solomon bowed his head. "Like this is a coronation of the Queen of England. Mama Turner kisses her on both cheeks, she kisses Price on both cheeks, toasts all around."

"But not Mother."

"No, not your mother. She didn't toast anyone."

"But you did!"

"I did. I made a toast. Yes, I did. I really felt the thing to do here was make the best of the situation. So I toasted her. Then your sister's wearing this necklace and sipping her Manhattan. She's on top of the world. Dream come true, I guess. She's brought your mother and me in for this little performance, she thought she now had the goods—she had Price, she had the name Turner, she has this necklace. Christ, you would need a hell of a trapezius to hold your head up with this thing on." Solomon fell silent a moment.

"How a person could wear such a necklace, I honestly don't know. I wouldn't want to have anything that valuable and conspicuous on my person—I'd feel like one hell of a walking target. I don't think a person could take three steps without getting conked on the head. Maybe you could wear it in a locked bathroom. I wouldn't sleep soundly with this thing lying around my house." Solomon shook his head. "We've never gone in for this kind of stuff. What's the point?"

"And Rose just wore the necklace out of there?"

"Sure."

"What's she done with it?"

"I don't know that, either. But what a performance Mama Turner put on that day. She walked out of there, and as far as I can see, except for making a show when Richard and Tim were born, I'll bet she's washed her hands of them. I don't think she gives them the time of day."

"But it doesn't make sense. If Price had been around so much and knew something about women, he would have seen Rose was impossible. I don't see what could have been the point of attraction."

"First, let me say that Rose can make herself quite beautiful when she wants. She's always attracted attention. You're her brother, you might not see that. And she's always had a way about her. And then Price has always been the black sheep of the family, that kind of thing. He never finished college, he went in the Army, bounced here, bounced there. As a matter of fact, even before he tried college, they were having problems with him. They sent him to some military academy in Virginia, you know, one of these places where the boys wear uniforms and they have Civil War cannons all over rolling lawns. Price once told me he showed up for parade with a button missing. Anyway, for this great crime, a couple of upperclassmen dressed him in full winter gear—long johns, winter uniform, coat, hat, gloves, the works—sat him on a radiator turned up all the way and started him doing the manual of arms. He told me he lasted about half an hour before he passed out cold." Solomon shook his head, said more to himself than Nick, "Imagine sending your kid to a place like that . . . Anyway, Mama Turner, I'm telling you, Nick, she's crazy, she was always telling Price he was a nothing and a nobody. At the table that day, she had a few deprecating remarks to make to him: if you'd finished college, you wouldn't always be in a bind for money. And these are people with millions, Nick. Millions.

"I don't think there was a lot of love lost between them. Your sister comes along, she's more than slightly confused herself. She's impressionable. She falls for him. He's been around. To his mother he's a bum. To your sister, this makes him a very exciting guy. At that time, he was working as a two-bit associate editor for some magazine like *Cycle World* or some such. New York. A two-room apartment. I was there a couple of times before they moved. Move *número uno*. You know, it had zebra hides on the floor, some hide shields on the walls. Three spears in each corner. Price brought them back from Ethiopia. Very exciting. Maybe your sister thought she had walked into one of those musicals she loved so much when she was growing up."

"I wonder if she still loves them. Musicals and operas."

"Your sister thought all of this was marvelous. Much more exciting than living in the same house in the suburbs all your life. That refers to this house. And so much more exciting than plodding along doing the same thing. That also referred to me, the doctor. You know, your sister, she let me know how she felt about each and every thing in no uncertain terms. I apologized for being such a boring guy. You know what her reply was? 'Well, he's only done a lot of the things you'd always hoped to do yourself. Traveled. Lived in different countries. He just decided not to wait around forever. He wanted to do things when he was still young.' As you see, I have no guts, either.

"Now, of course, two kids and three moves later—or what is it now, four moves later?—she sees things differently. Living in one place doesn't look so boring to her now. She was complaining recently on the phone. She's just gotten the house the way she likes it, now it looks like Price is going to get fired. Again. Which means yet another move. The big difference being that she's fed up with it."

"What's he getting fired for this time?"

"The same thing he's always gotten fired for. He and his bosses have little disagreements. It's always the same. Your sister used to tell me it was because Price was such an innovator, such a genius, so talented that his higher-ups felt threatened. The simple truth of the matter is that he doesn't know how to get along with people on the most simple level. Well, now your sister's just plain fed up. Only now she's got two kids."

Solomon sighed. "Can you blame her? You set up a house, make friends, boom, you're moving. You were asking about that necklace. I wouldn't be surprised if it had been sold a long time ago."

"No."

"I really wouldn't. I can remember another long speech your sister made to me about how grubby it was to sell real estate and insurance. You know. All the people who keep the world going and don't say much. Well, now she's trying to sell real estate to help make ends meet."

"So what is your point, Dad? Are you happy to be right?"

"I would rather have been wrong. I get no satisfaction from this. I'm telling you something. People do change. Do you know part of the reason she is selling real estate?"

"How would I know. She doesn't communicate with me. To make ends meet, like you said."

"Yes, how would you know, as a matter of fact, since you don't take an interest. She wants the money to help pay for voice lessons."

"Singing?"

"Singing."

"Did she tell you?"

"Of course she didn't tell me."

"Then how do you know?"

"Your father knows a thing or two. Do you know something else?"

"I guess not."

"Don't glare at me. It's true. You don't take an interest in your sister anymore."

"That's not true. But she's made it hard. She's never been home. She was always shouting."

"She has loved you dearly."

"Come on."

"When you were in elementary school, she walked with you, took care of you, protected you. Never let anyone lay a hand on you. She would wait until she saw you coming out of school. I remember once you were getting bullied and she went up and blackened some kid's eye. A boy."

"Come on, Dad."

"You don't remember anything. I remember, because the boy's father called me up. He was damned mad. I think the thing that annoyed him the most was that his son got his black eye from a girl."

"But—"

"Look, if you'd really wanted to be close to her, you could have found a way."

Nick sighed. "Okay, Dad."

"So, okay. All of these years, she has taken voice lessons and practiced her singing in secret. She has never told anyone. And she never thought anyone knew, but she won't give up smoking. She wouldn't give it up when she was pregnant with the boys, either. I can remember her six months' pregnant and Price pleading with her not to smoke. She'd do anything for her children, but she won't give up smoking. Two packs a day. Pall Malls. And she's there taking singing lessons. Still. And smoking."

"On her way to the Met."

"That's not beyond your sister to think. In one way, she has never changed. She has never stopped blaming your mother for everything that's ever gone wrong in her life. But I will say this for her. She's a good mother, herself. She really loves her children."

Nick walked to the window, looked out. "Big deal," he said. "Anyone can be a mother."

"Big deal? So she could be a bad mother. There are plenty of those, too. Nothing's a big deal to you."

"No, I guess I don't think being a mother's a big deal."

"I'll tell you why it's a big deal for your sister. At least, she has learned to care about someone other than herself. That, for your sister, is a big deal. Maybe the biggest deal of all. Because that's what it's all about. Someone else around here could stand to learn a little of that."

Nick looked back at Solomon, a closed hurt look, and Solomon picked up his book and began to read.

SOLOMON stares at a plastic dinosaur on the piano. Richard's. He listens. Tim crying. Someone crying. The pulse of blood in his ears. Maybe Richard, another nightmare. Solomon listens, but nothing. He glances at the clock. It isn't too late to cancel. He could call first thing in the morning, go to the hospital, explain to Rose that he really isn't the right person. Or someone else could do it, she'd never know.

Solomon looks at the empty chair by the window. After Saint Mary's, when they'd finally brought Rose back to the house, Nick had slumped in that chair day after day, there in the morning, still there in the evening. First his pacing. All day. All night. Then finally, his sitting. Circles under his eyes. Unshaven. Hardly talking or looking at anyone. And walking right past Bea that last morning without even glancing at her. He had not spoken to her for weeks. And now? Weeks since they'd heard one word from him.

And Nick, that closed angry look on his face, one of the last conversations they'd had, Nick's dogged questioning, "But do you think she'll be able to walk again afterward?"

"No, she won't walk. Why keep asking?"

"Then what's the point? You must believe there's some chance."

"Little chance."

"Then why do it?"

"Look, Nick."

"One in ten?"

"No."

"One in fifty?"

"Look, Nick, this isn't a guessing game."

"One in a hundred?"

"Nick, when have you ever known me to guess? I don't guess. Now that's enough."

"You don't guess because that way you're never wrong."

"She wants it done."

"If she doesn't walk?"

"I've said there's little chance of that, but I'll have tried."

"And if she does?"

"I've told everyone, don't expect the moon."

The conversation had gone on. Somehow that business about the other doctors had come up.

"Hey, this isn't just my opinion. Remember Tad Wilson, that guy I used to wrestle with—177—yeah, well, he's a resident now. He's the one who told me—it's what he's hearing. You know where he's getting it? From doctors, your peers. It's what they're saying."

SOLOMON suddenly feels, what? Angry, almost vengeful. A bunch of residents and doctors gossiping about him. That was easy for them. They were completely out of the situation. Probably their point. And Nick, is that why he was so angry, he chose to believe *them* rather than his own father, what the hell was so wrong with it, anyway, Gutman had done what he could, hadn't Harry Albright delivered both of his daughters?

Solomon thinks back. When he asked Tom Baldwin to do the anesthesia, Baldwin had not hesitated for a moment. He could have. If he'd had any doubts, wouldn't he have said something to Solomon? But no, not a word, a glance. He'd squeezed Solomon's shoulder, said he'd be glad to. Wouldn't Solomon have seen it in his face if there'd been anything?

. . . if you make a mistake. That's not likely. But Paul Holland, a routine procedure, deformity of the elbow, loosening the anterior ligament. Lost his son in Vietnam. The tourniquet released, no pulse, the arm white, later had to be amputated.

And Gutman operating until he was seventy-five. Maybe toward the end, he had been doing more harm than good, maybe there was simply a time to step down and leave things to other men, younger men.

Solomon recalled Gutman. Short. Powerful. Impatient with the least sign of hesitation or uncertainty. He asked a question once and expected an immediate answer. That gesture, cutting residents off in the middle of a sentence with a sweep of his hand. If you didn't know it cold, you didn't know it. Gutman had studied orthopedics in Germany before and then again after WWI. Great pathologists. And then the veterans to operate on. Gutman had it all. All the great ones. Swift. Decisive. Never hesitant. Gutman reached for an instrument, used it quickly, discarded it. Never put back an instrument once he'd picked it up. Speed. Dexterity.

After his residency in orthopedics under Gutman, he would spend Saturdays and Sundays dissecting corpses, come home, eyes stinging, neck and shoulders stiff, and after a shower, Bea would kid him, "I can still smell it." She would rub the stiffness out of his shoulders and Solomon would think of the fluid certainty he'd seen in Gutman's fingers.

Speed counted. Back then, there'd been no endotracheal anesthesia and the operations and their lengths had been severely limited by the kinds of anesthesia and the possible positioning of the patient on the table. Speed. Less trauma. But back then, there'd been no blood storage, no hip nailing, no sulfas, no penicillin—pneumonia had been called the Old Man's Friend, and Solomon remembers the wards full of people dying, his feeling helpless, and nothing to be done, but hold down the fever; there'd been no artificial joints. . . . Speed, too, lessened the incidence of aerobic-borne infection, though for some reason, then, they'd had the notion that operating rooms should be hot and Solomon, just the thought of heat. . . .

Solomon prides himself on being quick. Back then, a doctor referred a patient and scrubbed with you. His operations had been a showcase for speed and technique and in a short time doctors had spread the word.

Occasionally, even now, in the middle of an operation, he could feel that sense of awe and beauty he had first felt, something he really couldn't put into words. He would feel it during bloodless surgery when all of the anatomy would suddenly manifest itself—tendons, muscles, arteries, veins, ligaments, the glow of the bones—and in some way he could sense the intelligence of it, the clarity and beauty of design.

Solomon suddenly thinks ahead to the morning: the electrocardiogram on the monitor, the electric blurp.

Rubber tube on the arm, the pentathol, sudden sleep. Then the mask: nitrous oxide, oxygen.

Solomon will sit waiting on the stool and watch Tom Baldwin as he has hundreds of times before.

The insertion of the airway into the mouth. Now Tom watching the patient closely. More nitrous oxide.

His bending over, pulling back the eyelid, examining the pupil.

Now taking blood pressure. Watching the gauge.

Now turning from the table, Tom's voice slightly muffled behind the mask. "Okay, Joe."

He will rise from the stool.

People want younger doctors now. When he looks at himself in the mirror, he is surprised to see an old man. Gray hair, mustache gray, cheeks sunken, eyes hollow. He doesn't feel old. Tired, yes, but not old. As good as he's always been. But he looks old to his patients. Too old? He has an urge to look at himself again in the hall mirror. He starts to get up, feels light-headed, sinks back into the sofa.

He dreams again the sound of her breathing, each breath harsh, drawn gasp, the beginning of the next breath. The intensive-care unit. Slipping forward in his chair, dozed, head against the restraining bar.

Another hoarse gasp.

Solomon had jerked awake, his head still against the restraining bar, seen Rose's hands clenched, wrists and ankles bound to the bed, body straining in paralysis against the mattress, the nail polish on the thumbnail half grown out, half red, half white—the pale moon. . . .

A chain of bubbles rose slowly through the iv bottle.

His hand had brushed something hanging on the restraining bar. The weight as he took it in his palm. Familiar. A charm bracelet. Jingling softly. For her ninth, tenth birthday? A megaphone for cheers, a record, a heart. He was sweating. Another hoarse breath. Sudden pause. He had glanced uneasily at the charm bracelet. From where? . . . He dropped it into his pocket.

Solomon remembers Price across from him in mask and gown. When? Sometime, before? After? Solomon couldn't see his face, just his eyes, circles beneath, bloodshot, pale-blue eyes. The sound of her breathing.

Price said something, muffled through the green mask. "Rose . . ." Price's voice trailed away. Solomon couldn't make out the rest.

Outside, Price dropped the mask and gown into the bin; unshaven, some white in his whiskers. His shoulders sagged. He was still wearing a hunter's vest with empty cartridge pockets, the game bag on the back was a flat purple in places. Blue jeans, hunting boots.

Hair long, the part breaking in several directions. Solomon gathered an odor in his nostrils. Deep smell of woods, pungency of wood? Smoke? Or was that his imagination?

Price half turning. Eyes out of focus. Chin almost on his

chest, flannel shirt. Something jowly, the lines running from the corners of his mouth to the midpoint of his nose—a fold, a crease. Solomon realizing it had been some time—several years—since he'd seen Price. That last time—ice fishing. Freezing. Sound of ice suddenly cracking in the silence. Silence between them. Two years, three?

Solomon noticed a well-chewed pipe in a cartridge holder, a lighter in another.

"It rained the last night and the roads were mud, pure mud . . . just couldn't get out. We got stuck. It was five miles to a phone. I started, but the woods were full of black flies. . . . I had to turn back." Price's finger groped toward the pipe. Worked the curve of the bowl. Drew the pipe part way out. Pushed it back.

The electronic beat of heart monitors; around the intensive-care unit, doors, closed.

Price glanced obliquely toward Solomon. "What will . . ." His voice trailed away.

After a time, Solomon said, "We don't know. No one knows. I don't know. They don't know. Have you talked to them yet?"

Price shook his head. "No. Not yet. I came here first. I didn't think it would be anything like this."

Price looked back at the closed doors of the intensive-care unit. Solomon started to say something. Stopped. Let the neurosurgeons tell him.

They walked toward the doors. In the corridor, Bea still in mask and gown. Solomon couldn't see her face. Just her eyes. She looked at Price. Walked past him. Price watched her open the door. Disappear.

Price again touched the pipe. Mumbling. His eyes damp. Solomon noticed he was white.

"Maybe you better sit down."

Price shook his head. "No . . . no . . . can't sit. I'm going to find the doctors. Get cleaned up. Take care of the boys." Price walking slowly toward the elevator.

After a moment, Solomon said, "Where were you?"

"When?"

"The last few days."

"On a story. Hunting."

The elevator came.

Solomon said, "Did you get it?"

"What?"

They looked at each other confused.

"The story."

Price stepped into the elevator.

"Yeah, we got it." He looked at Solomon another moment as if to ask if there were some significance he'd missed in what Solomon had said. Quick suspicious glance.

Price repeated, "We got it."

Solomon nodded, waved his hand for him to go, "I'll see you in a while."

LATER, Solomon would think about that last look he'd seen on Price's face. That glance. If Price hadn't already made up his mind right there at the hospital, then it didn't take long. Maybe after the doctors told him. The sagging shoulders, the tears, the halting manner. All an act. A damned good act. But that's what Price always . . .

Next thing Solomon knew was from Lynn. Price had gotten some girl to move in, with the children, take care of them, and that was the last anyone had heard of him.

BEA said, "I'm not in the least surprised. I never expected anything of him. So fine, when she recovers, she will start her life over completely—and it will be without him. She'll have her children." Bea fell silent. She gazed off.

Solomon looked at her. "What?"

"Oh dear . . . sometimes . . . I keep thinking about Patricia Neal. Patricia Neal had a series of strokes which left her paralyzed and speechless."

"This isn't a stroke!"

"And I remember reading about her husband, how he never gave up. He stayed with her, loved her, talked to her, fed her, carried her to the bathroom. And she recovered. But she didn't just recover, she *acted*. She was determined. But the basic thing was that she had her husband's love. She made a complete recovery." Bea became quiet. "I have no doubts, love makes the difference. Love is the—" She met Solomon's gaze. "Well, it will be us . . . dear . . . And I do have this overpowering feeling she will respond to Nick."

"I see no point in having Nick see her as she is now. It can do no good. And it will scare the hell out of him. Look, I called him, he knows there's been an accident, he offered to come, and I told him to stay where he is. He has no idea how bad this is and that's all I think he should know for now."

Bea had been noncommittal. But as Rose had gone on day after day Bea said, "I think he should be here. His presence will help."

And after a few more days:

"Rose always did have a special feeling for Nick."

Bea glanced over at him sharply. Her voice was softer than her glance.

"No, I mean it. In some way, he could always kid her when no one else could. He could get a laugh out of her."

"I don't know, Bea, it's been a damned long time. . ."

"If he could be here—sit with her—talk to her—the sound of his voice alone, dear, you know that *she* knows that we're here with her—then she would hear his voice and be comforted by it. She would respond."

Solomon put her off. He evaded. He changed the subject. The way Rose looked, her eye alone . . .

"I don't want him to see her like this. If there were something to be gained. But there's nothing to be gained. And nothing he can do. He'll be helpless like the rest of us."

"But he might be the right one. I know. I feel it. And she has old resistances to us."

"Bea . . . Bea, please."

"All right." She sighed. "But I do not see what he is doing that is so much more important that he doesn't have time for this. I really don't. What is so important? Remodeling houses. Whatever. And why is he doing that, anyway, with a degree from Dartmouth? He could go back and finish up his master's. . . ."

"Hold on! No one said a word about anything being more

important than this. Or his not having the time. Or any other thing. I am saying there's little he can do now. Nothing. Those are the plain facts. And it is very disturbing to see her."

"There is something he can do, that is my point."

But Solomon did not call Nick.

After yet another few days, Bea suddenly said, "Is he or is he not a member of this family, that is what I'd like to know! I do not see that there is anything in the world he might be doing that is more important than this! Nothing."

"Bea! I've said before. I'm saying now. No one has ever said one word about his having anything more important to do. Why are you going on about that? I haven't asked him to come because— Oh, look, we've been all through this."

"And about his being disturbed, he is, at twenty-four, supposedly an adult. Let him be disturbed! It is disturbing, yes! This, too, is part of living in the world."

NIGHTS, when Bea could no longer stay in the hospital with Rose, she was restless; she would sit on the bed, write in her journal. She would close her eyes.

Often she sat motionless for such long periods of time, Solomon would think she was asleep.

Once Solomon said her name softly, "Bea? Bea? Are you awake?"

She nodded.

"What are you doing there with your eyes closed?"

"Concentrating."

"On what?"

"Rose. On reaching Rose."

Finally Solomon called Nick. Without going into detail, he suggested Nick might come now—his presence might have a beneficial effect on Rose. Did Solomon mind if Nick came in a week, he was just finishing up a room addition?

Solomon glanced at Bea, who was watching him. "Well, it's nothing to be alarmed about, but I think you should come now and leave the room addition for your partner—if you can."

Nick hesitated. Yes, he could. He'd be there in a couple of days. Which he was.

NICK stopped uncertainly in front of his parents' open door, leaned in to check the number.

Bea suddenly up, hugging Nick. Pushing him back to look at him, hugging him hard again.

"Mom . . ." He kissed her cheek. Patted her shoulders uneasily. "Okay, Mom." She hugged him harder. Nick made a tentative gesture to push her away. Laughed uneasily. "Hey, you're going to break my neck."

Finally he pushed her away. Looked uncertain.

"You look wonderful, Nicky. A little tired. And that hair . . ." Bea reached up and grabbed a handful.

"Okay, Mom."

"Oh, 'Okay, Mom,'" Bea mimicked, "wonderful." She touched his whiskers. "Can't afford a razor, times must be tough."

"What's up here? One of Mom's alarmist reactions?" He looked from one to the other, smiled uneasily.

"That's right, Nick. Just one of your Mom's alarmist reactions."

"Everything is going to be all right, Nicky. All right. Even your gloomy father knows that, deep in his heart, don't you, dear?"

Bea kissed Solomon on his cheek. She patted his cheek. "Don't you, dear?"

Her eyes. Their appeal. Nick's uneasiness.

"Your father tends to lose sight of a few things at times," she said in a slightly mocking, playful voice. "Oh, the world. So black. I can remember times, your father, up until two, three in the morning worried about a patient—and they were always fine. You see, I have a feeling about things. Deep in his heart, he knows, too. That's what I'm here for—to remind him, aren't I, dear?"

"Oh, that's for sure."

Nick glanced uneasily from one to the other.

After he'd gone to his room, Bea was excited. "Tomorrow, you take him to the hospital in the morning, just you boys go together. Then you might leave him alone with her for a while.

I know hearing his voice will be good for her. In a way, I think she loved Nick more than anyone else— Oh, of course they had their little squabbles. But he had a feeling for her. It might be good for Nick to be alone with her. Just be with her. Hold her hand. Say her name. Communicate with her. I think she'll have some response."

Solomon said in a quiet way, "I wouldn't expect too much, Bea."

"You might be surprised."

"I might be," he said quietly. "I think I'll walk over to Nicky's room and help him get settled. I've been giving him a rough idea of what to expect on the phone. Now that he's here, I'm going to give him a little more. And tomorrow, at the hospital, he'll get the rest, won't he? And Bea, when he sees her, he might not be in any shape to communicate anything to anyone. So don't get your hopes up."

SOLOMON sat in a chair beside the bed. Nicky lay on his back, hands under his head, and stared at the ceiling. As Solomon spoke, Nick showed little reaction. Once Nick closed his eyes for so long Solomon stopped abruptly.

"Are you listening? Maybe your mother's right about you."

Nick opened his eyes, turned his head slowly, looked at Solomon a long time. "What do you mean right about me?"

"You could have been here sooner!"

"I would have. But you told me not to come."

"Well, I had my reasons for waiting. But now you could show some concern!"

"I'm listening to every word; I drove twelve hours today and my eyes are burning."

"Well, that's no damned good either. If you'd broken up the trip, you wouldn't be so exhausted."

"I'm not exhaused. My eyes are tired. Go on. I *am* listening."

Nick turned and looked back up at the ceiling, eyes wide, hands under his head.

"And you can take your boots off the bed."

Nick didn't move his feet. "Go on, Dad. I *am* listening."

Solomon looked at Nick's boots. Continued. When he got to

100

the part about the car, Nicky again closed his eyes until he finished.

Then Nick opened his eyes, turned to Solomon, said in a quiet voice, "Can you go over that, again?"

"I thought you were listening."

"Dad . . ."

"Nick . . ."

"It's a lot to absorb."

So again Solomon told Nick what he himself had been told. The facts seemed no different in character than those from any one of ten thousand other accidents and patient case histories. No matter how much Solomon went over them, what the doctors had said, revealed nothing. Still, Solomon went through it again.

"She was driving Price's Triumph. From what was left of it, they knew she'd been speeding. Anything different about that day? She always drove fast. Had anyone ever been able to tell Rose anything? Or anyone else in this family, for that matter?" Nick not taking his eyes from the ceiling. "And of course, no seat belt. Never wore seat belts. They were for other people. No telling her anything on that score, either. I don't know if you remember in high school she piled up your mother's car—didn't faze her in the least. She shrugged it off, 'It's only a car, you can afford it.' " Solomon stopped. "So I've told you the rest. What more is it you want to hear?"

Nick didn't react.

Solomon sighed, went on: "It happened in the country. She hit a curve too fast—broke through the guard rail, hit a tree. From where they found her . . . Look Nick, I'm telling you, she must have traveled a long way in the air and lay there God knows how long before someone happened along and found her. If you had seen her the first morning. Your mother never flinched. I don't know how Rose lived, how anyone could have lived. I still don't know."

Nick sat up slowly, let his legs over the side of the bed. Let out a breath.

"And the last part?"

"I told you."

Solomon didn't say anything for several moments. Finally he

said, "The police reported no brake marks."

"At three in the afternoon?"

"Three. Three-thirty. People fall asleep at the wheel at three in the afternoon. And what business you have driving twelve straight hours—"

"Or get drunk . . . at three in the afternoon."

"Or get drunk. I've thought of that. I don't have any illusions about your sister. But the doctors' report showed very little alcohol in her blood."

"And the car was totaled?"

"Pulverized."

"So she fell asleep." Nick seemed preoccupied, spoke softly, "Or was a little drunk."

"But I told you, the doctors' report—"

"Or did not choose to apply the brakes."

Solomon was silent.

"You've thought of that, Dad, haven't you?"

Solomon let out a breath. "Yes, I have thought of that, Nick. And it is not entirely out of character. I have thought of that. But I don't accept that."

"No?"

Neither of them said anything for some time.

"No. Because, Nick—no matter what else might have been wrong, and I know there was a lot wrong, always had been— still, I don't think she would do such a thing."

Nick didn't say anything.

"Her children, Nick. No matter what else she might have felt about any of us, she loved her children."

Nick said quietly, "Other people have loved their children and—"

"I just don't think she did it, Nick." They both looked at the floor. "I don't, Nick. I really do not."

Nick stood and started unbuttoning his shirt. "And no one's seen or heard from Price in two weeks?"

Solomon shook his head. "I'm telling you, he came, he looked for two minutes, turned white—I'm telling you, white— mumbled 'I can't bear to see her this way,' and that's the last we've seen or heard of him. He gave some farm girl a few bucks and told her to stay with the boys—surprised he even did that much. What in the world Rose was ever doing with this guy in the first place . . ."

"At one time I remember your telling me it might not be such a bad thing."

"I never said any such thing. Or if I did you misunderstood me."

"Okay, have it your way."

Nick started unbuttoning his shirt again.

"What are you going to do now?"

"Take a shower."

"Have you eaten?"

"I'm not hungry."

"You're not hungry. When have I ever known you not to be hungry? Christ, there's a place across the street. Go eat." Solomon hesitated. "Come on, I'm not hungry, but I'll go with you."

"No thanks, Dad. Really. I just want to be by myself. Don't get that look on your face."

"I've got no look on my face; you want to be by yourself. I understand, be by yourself." Solomon pulled out a twenty. "But go eat."

"My father the Jewish mother."

Solomon looked Nick over. He pulled out three more twenties. "And here. Do me a favor. Do it for your mother before she says anything."

"What?"

"There's a barbershop . . ."

"Dad . . ."

"You're not a bad-looking guy. Cut some of that hair. Buy some regular slacks. Don't you get tired of jeans? And a shirt, a real shirt, Christ, anyone who saw you would think you had no education, knew nothing, were some ignorant slob. . . ."

"Dad . . ."

"Okay, Nick, I'm asking." Solomon placed the money on the dresser.

Nick took off his shirt, started for the bathroom.

"And Nick . . ."

Nick turned.

"Don't tell your mother we've talked about this."

Nick glanced questioningly at him.

"No brake marks. Because it's all speculation. It could have been anything, true; but you know something? Your sister always drove too fast and in the final analysis I think it's nothing more than it appears to be. An accident."

Nick gave him an odd look.

"No, I really think so. I'd thought of other possibilities, too."

"And now Price is gone."

"That's something else, his being gone. He's a coward and he has no stomach for this. Oh, you should have seen the act he put on in the hospital. . . . Do you know, his parents have not even called us to say one word. Not *one* word. I mean, they may have thought what they thought about us but they should have called. I'm telling you, Nick, the world we're living in . . ."

Nick didn't say anything.

Solomon studied him. "I must say you're taking this rather coolly, yourself."

Nick looked at Solomon, looked away. "What do you want? I've been listening to you."

"Never mind, I don't want you to say anything about our conversation to anyone. And especially your mother."

"I—"

"Get me?"

"Yes, don't raise your voice."

"I want that clear in no uncertain terms!"

"It's clear."

"Good. She's suffering enough. She has certain unreal notions at this point. They're keeping her going. There'll be time enough later for reality. . . . Look, you'll see for yourself, you'll get a bellyful of it. Just remember what I said. Not a word."

"No, not a word, Dad." Nick stepped into the bathroom. Solomon started for the door.

"Dad?" Solomon turned at the door. "One last thing. When was the last time anyone spoke to Rose? You? Or Mother? Which one was it anyway?"

Solomon saw himself in the mirror. Nick walking slowly into the mirror. Nick. Powerful. Reddish-blond hair on his forearms. Thick neck, thick-veined hands. Nick moved toward the mirror.

Nick stopped in front of him. "Do you remember?"

"Oh, I'm not sure, Nick. I spoke to her. Maybe a few days before."

"And what'd you talk about?"

"Oh, this and that. Not a damned thing, really. It wasn't one hell of a lot different than ninety-four other conversations we'd had. Kids wonderful, not enough money. . . . Price going to lose his job again. Price no help, the two of them miserable. No money . . . remember how she was going to find a man who would support her in the manner to which she was accustomed?"

"I remember. I remember from your telling me. And what'd you say?"

"Oh, Christ, Nick, I've had a few other things on my mind in the last few weeks." Solomon spotted the four twenties on the dresser. "And don't leave money lying around like this."

"There's no one here."

"I don't care. It's still a bad habit to get into. Where's your wallet?" Nick reached into his pocket, flipped Solomon the wallet, shook his head. "So shake your head at me."

Nick closed the bathroom door, turned on the shower.

OUTSIDE, Solomon walked slowly across the motel court. Thought of Nick's studying him. "What'd you say to her?"

Solomon could remember one part. Rose, complaining something typical, ending by saying, "Oh, you wouldn't understand, Dad."

". . . Of course not, how could I understand, I'm just a mean old man with a bank account. Remember?"

There'd been a long pause.

Then Rose's voice, tired, sad. "Are you always going to bring that up, Dad?"

Her voice, tired and lonely, and he'd wanted to say something, but what, and he'd said nothing.

Finally, "Well? It's true, isn't it? Just a mean old . . ."

She hadn't replied.

Solomon couldn't remember the rest. He couldn't even remember if that had been the last time he spoke to her. Or some other time.

He walked slowly across the motel court back to their room, where Bea was sitting upright in a chair, hands folded in her lap, tight lines around her mouth; her eyes were closed in concentration.

NICK touched her hands tentatively. Her arm. He took hold of a finger and pulled at it.

He looked up at Solomon. Eyes above the mask. Touched her finger again.

"It's rigid. It feels as though something hard has been poured under her skin."

"She's paralyzed. What do you think paralysis means?" He softened his voice, "What did you think I was trying to tell you last night?"

"I don't know. I just got a different idea from Mother. She didn't really say anything specific, but I somehow half expected to come in here and find Rose sitting up and complaining."

"Your mother's got a few ideas. I was trying to tell you about that, too."

"Is this for good?" Nick tugged at her finger.

"I don't know. Your mother thinks—"

"You just said she's got some weird ideas. You're the doctor."

"I'm way out of my field here. And even the neurologists can't always be sure. It doesn't look . . ." Solomon suddenly lowered his voice to a whisper, ". . . good."

"What?"

"We'll discuss it outside."

"Can she hear us?"

"Your mother thinks so."

Nick looked down a moment at Rose, let go of her finger, walked toward the door.

IN the hallway, Nick walked toward the waiting room, pushed open the door, stopped, looking at the people, turned abruptly, walked to the other end of the hallway, looked out the window.

106

Solomon caught up with him. "Are you all right, Nick?"

Nick looked vaguely at Solomon. "Where *is* Price?"

"I don't know."

"Why don't you know?"

"Why don't I know?"

Nick glanced over his shoulder at people approaching the elevator. "What happens now?"

"We wait."

"For what?"

"For her to come to."

"She will definitely come to?"

"There is no 'definitely' in this. Get rid of the notion right now. There is no 'definitely.' And if she comes to, we have no idea who or what she'll be if anything. I don't know. The neurosurgeons don't know—for sure. Though they've told me, not your mother, she won't be more than—" Solomon halted. "No one knows. One person thinks she knows. Your mother. Everything will be wonderful, Rose will be fine."

"And if she doesn't come to?"

"Never mind if she doesn't come to. For now we wait."

"But for how long?"

"Nick, we just wait! For as long as we have to. Two months can be nothing in a thing like this."

Nick stared out the window. After a time, he mumbled something, stopped abruptly.

"What?"

"Nothing."

"No, tell me. What?"

"If you really want to know, I started to say this was inevitable. It's like everything else she ever did. I always knew it would be something like this. And suddenly, now, we're her family again."

"Yes, we're her family. But not again. We've always been her family—"

"No."

"Yes. And we're her family now. And why do you say 'inevitable'?"

"Why? How could it have been any other way? Why!" Nick stared out the window, arms crossed in front of him. He

107

pressed his lips together and rocked suddenly. Looked at Solomon.

"All right, Nick, relax. You're having a reaction. Calm down."

"I'm not having a reaction."

"The hell you're not. You wouldn't be normal if you weren't having a reaction."

"Okay, I'm having a reaction and I'm normal, okay. Whenever I say something you don't like or agree with, you can tell me I'm having a reaction from now on." He rocked again. Shirt stretched across his shoulders. Arms crossed. His eyes moved everywhere quickly. Sudden smell of sweat. His upper lip and hair line glistened, his pupils looked large and dark.

"Take a deep breath, Nick."

Nick started to say something. Solomon put his hand on Nick's shoulder.

Nick took a deep breath. He looked exhausted. His cheeks sagged. He mumbled something. "You know . . ."

"Okay, Nick, it's not easy. I've seen plenty of intensive-care units at all hours of the day and night and I still find this hard to look at. So just take it slow."

"I'm calm. I'm fine. You don't see it, do you?" Nick shook his head. "No, you don't. You wouldn't. You'd be the last to see it." Nick glanced around him. "Doesn't all of this seem familiar to you?"

"If you mean hospitals, yes, I work in hospitals. I'm not intimidated by hospitals."

"This feels familiar to me. All of it. We've lived through this before. You, me, Mother, Rose. All of us. Like this."

"Calm down, Nick."

"She's finally gotten even with you."

"Gotten even with me?" Nick drifted off. "Even with me?"

"No, more than that." Nick glanced at Solomon, distracted; he pronounced each word precisely. "No, she has not gotten even with you. She has finally defeated you."

"Defeated me?"

"You're helpless now."

"I don't know what you're talking about."

"All her life she's been trying to kill you with her life."

Nick started walking toward the elevator. Solomon watching him, then followed. He caught up. Nick kept his eyes on the flashing numbers.

Solomon held up his hands. "Kill me with her life—all her life? What did I ever do, Nick, except love her and want to see her happy? Nick?"

Nick kept his eyes on the numbers. They stopped, the bell rang, the doors opened.

"Nick? Defeated me?"

Solomon followed Nick into the elevator. A nun moved into the corner. They rode down in silence.

"How did he react, Joe? Did he try to talk to her?"

"He had one hell of a strange reaction."

"Her appearance . . ."

"There *is* her appearance."

"If I could help him learn to look beyond—"

"There *is* her appearance! And that wasn't what was strange about his reaction, Bea." Bea waited. "Look, let's not go into it. He was upset and just talked a lot of nonsense. Let's just let him alone for now. I don't even think he knew what he was saying."

FOR the next few days, Solomon heard Bea talking to Nick about remaining open and undisturbed, about looking beyond Rose's appearance, which would change, and concentrating on sending Rose positive messages. Bea told Nick about Patricia Neal and how at one point Patricia Neal had been as badly off as Rose. She hadn't been able to utter a word. Not one word. And Patricia Neal's husband . . .

Nick listened and stared uneasily at the floor or glanced up at the news.

Bea told Nick about the boy who had been in a motorcycle accident. He had been unconscious for several months and then one morning, he raised his head and asked if he might please have a glass of cold orange juice, ". . . he asked just as clearly as you and I are talking now, Nicky." The intensive-

109

care nurses had seen it themselves. And they also told Bea that the entire neurological staff had given up hope, but they, too, were astounded. And they had no explanations. None. They still had no idea what had caused the change. But they were genuinely astounded.

Bea talked softly."But I am not astounded, Nick. Not at all. I have told your father for years that there are many things about healing and the mind that we know nothing about. Your father believes more than he lets on. He likes to play to your expectations of him, but he believes. So many times he's seen patients do things he couldn't explain, that old man—called his family around him and died—you said he was in good health . . . Primitive civilizations . . ." Bea drifted off for a moment. "Have you heard of Uri Geller?"

Nick shook his head, no.

"Or some of the Soviet experiments in telepathy?"

Nick shook his head no again.

"And this Arigo in Brazil . . . Surgeon with a Rusty Knife . . . Well, you wouldn't believe them. They are doing astounding things. Doctors don't know everything, Nick. You are disturbed because you see this whole situation in a conventional way. But the brain is a mystery and there are forms of healing and communication we know nothing about. You can't let yourself be upset by the way she looks. That is yielding to the negative energy."

Bea offered Nick a book from her bedside table. *The Crack in the Cosmic Egg.* Nick stared at several Holiday Inn postcards on the dresser. "I know you will be fascinated by these books. You, especially, have always been very intuitive about things. When you were a little boy, you used to say the most insightful things about people. Things that would just astound me. I would think, How does he know these things? I remember once, the first time you met Blanche North, remember her?"

"Sure."

"You took one look at her, looked at me, and the first moment we were alone you said, 'Something bad has happened to her.' You couldn't have been more than seven. And something had happened. Her husband had died."

110

"Oh, Mom, come on . . . Please . . ."

"Perhaps children have insight and communicative capacities and greater feeling for one another and through some quirk in evolution we have lost them. Like whales with their ventral fins. But I don't think we have lost these capacities. I think they are simply dormant in us." Bea looked out the window. She reached over and touched Nick's cheek. "You especially, Nick." Her voice soft. "You've always had some special feeling."

Nick stared at the postcards. The Holiday Inn. He glanced over at Solomon. Solomon ignored his glance and watched Walter Cronkite.

Bea handed Nick the books and he took them, pressed his lips together, looked at the covers. Solomon glanced over.

The Crack in the—pale blue cover, enormous white egg, jagged crack. He glanced back at Cronkite.

"Sit with Rose, Nick. Concentrate on making your mind close to hers. We're her parents. Her mother and father. That complicates things. I have no illusions. I'm not unaware. I realize she has mixed and troubled feelings about your father and I. But maybe you can get through to her."

LATER, when they were alone, Nick looked at Solomon and shrugged. "I really don't understand what I'm supposed to do. These books. I've heard of John Lilly. But this *Crack* in whatever. Look at the cover. It's hard to believe Mother could go for this stuff—even in this situation. And that Jeane Dixon and Edgar Cayce—"

"She's always had an interest in this aspect of things."

"She's cum laude from Radcliffe. . . ."

"Magna cum laude . . ."

"All right, magna cum laude, so much the worse."

"So she's not the first and won't be the last to go in for this stuff in a situation like this. I don't need to tell you I find this way of thinking alien. I'm scientifically trained. Before I draw a conclusion, I want evidence. But for now, don't say anything to your mother. Don't try to have a rational conversation with her about any of this. There is absolutely no point. I have tried, your mother has twenty irrational answers. So leave her alone on this score. When she starts in, just nod, uh huh, you agree, or you're sympathetic, or whatever, and she usually gets off onto something else in a short time. It saves wear and tear on everyone. Eventually she'll come around . . . I hope."

"Horoscopes from the paper are one thing, but I really wouldn't have believed this of her."

Solomon looked at Nick. He thought of what Nick had said in the hospital. Started to say something. Changed his mind.

"There are a lot of things I wouldn't have believed," Solomon said.

"I'm still asking, what am I supposed to do now?"

"As I say, don't debate this with your mother. Go to the hospital. Sit with your sister. Repeat her name. Repeat your name. Maybe she hears, maybe it registers in some way, I really don't know. I doubt it, but who knows. It can't hurt. And it will help your mother, that much I do know."

"But how long can this go on?"

"You asked me that before and I still say, I don't know. For now we'll do this and see. We'll take it one step at a time."

"I've got a partner—we've got a lot of work lined up. Some projects I'm committed to do. I'm going to have to get back to work sometime."

"I know. I know all about it. I have patients. We all have things to do, places to be. But for now, they are going to have to wait."

EACH day, Nick would go to the hospital, and later Bea would ask Nick or Solomon, "How did it feel to you—being with her?"

Nick would look confused.

Bea would say, "I mean, just the general feeling you got from her."

"I don't know, Mom. She's just lying there . . . and that hoarse breathing . . ."

"Well you must have felt something. Just reach into yourself."

Nick would look a little exasperated, but control himself,

and try to give Bea some kind of answer that would please her, but which didn't seem to be a lie to himself.

After a few more days, Bea said, "You know, Nicky, you could get a haircut. I'm not saying short, your mother's not exactly a square, I realize you boys like your hair longer these days. And some of it can be very nice, but a trim, some shaping . . ." She grabbed a handful of Nick's curls in the back. "This mop. Look, why don't you let me trim these in back? And don't you have any other clothes besides jeans and these shirts?"

Nick glanced at Solomon, and Solomon nodded at him and said in a quiet voice, "Uh huh, Nick . . ."

Bea said, "It all contributes, everything, in subtle ways, to how you feel about yourself. These jeans and T-shirts, unconsciously, what do you think you're saying to the world?"

"Oh, Mom, I'm not saying anything unconsciously or any other way. I feel fine about myself."

"Well, feel finer," Bea tried to joke. She patted Nick's cheek. "So let me make like a mother, already."

"You're doing that, all right."

And again when they were alone in Nick's room, Solomon said, "Nick, now will you please do what I asked you to do in the first place?"

"I'm a little old for this, Dad."

"That's right. You are. Too bad, when at your age your father has to start following you around and telling you when to get a haircut."

"He doesn't. That's the problem."

"All right, Nick. Give me an argument. In this situation you can do it for your mother, whether you agree or not."

Nick started to say something, turned away, suddenly turned back to Solomon. "You stand here like an idiot telling me to cut my hair, as if that's suddenly the most important thing when you don't have any idea where Price is. Her husband. He comes, he looks two minutes, he leaves, you say Price's run out, shrug, and take it."

"Good, I should have him tied up."

"He's run and left us the mess and you stand here nagging me about getting a haircut. Give me a break!"

"I, for one, do not know what Price has or has not done, but you stay away from him. As a matter of fact, if you see him coming down the street, cross the street and go the other way."

"I'll do that, Dad."

"Yes, you will. He is unpredictable, and he is a lot of trouble. Christ, his own goddamned mother would be the first to acknowledge that. You may be big, but this is different. Don't think for one minute Price looks at the world like you and I do. He doesn't."

"Just my point!"

"Listen! As far as I can tell, he's lost every job he's ever had. I'm sure he's got some paranoid and unsavory notions about blacks—I myself think he was a member of the John Birch Society."

Nick raising an eyebrow . . .

"Look, Nick, I've had a few conversations with Price which don't quite add up. Price went on some hunt up in Alaska, came back telling me that *they* were building concentration camps up there big enough to hold twenty million people. Oh, who is *they*, I ask him. *They* is *they*. Price can't tell anyone. Not me, not anyone. But he has documents and photographs to prove it. At the right moment, he'll put them into the hands of the right people. The right moment, I tell you, it sounds to me like a touch of messiah mixed with more than a touch of paranoia—"

"Dad—"

"I'm not finished. I've never personally liked guns or hunting, but I can understand a few guns for sport—rifles, shotguns, whatever. But one day Price starts talking about getting an M-16 and a submachine gun. What the hell would he do with these things? I ask him, 'You'd use them on a person?' Price says if the civil peace breaks down, they would be the best friends he ever had. Anyone coming through his front door is dead. Your sister, she's sitting there nodding her head and going right along with all this. Your sister. I tell you, what a world these two are living in.

"Now you stay the hell away from him! This just isn't a guy you punch in the nose, college wrestling rules and whatnot."

Neither said anything.

"You know, if I recall rightly, a week ago, you came steaming out of the intensive-care unit and went off half-cocked and said a few things."

Nick stared straight ahead.

"Shall I repeat them?"

"Say what you want."

"Fine, I will. Thanks for permission. About your sister's accident being her way of getting even with me. For what, you didn't say. Next thing, that wasn't good enough, she hadn't just gotten even with me. So, she had defeated me. Have I quoted you correctly?"

"Yes."

"Good, because I don't want to be accused of quoting you incorrectly. What these high-handed remarks meant, again you chose not to say. I'd still like some explanation of these remarks, though I think I won't get any. Do you know why I think I won't get any explanation?"

"Nope."

"Because you don't have any explanation. You don't know what the hell you're talking about, do you?"

"Why ask me if I don't know what the hell I'm talking about?"

Solomon had the feeling Nick wanted to stand up and hit him. Nick smiled slightly.

"Well, if you have an explanation, you'll give it to me straight from the shoulder like a man—why are you shaking your head at me like that?—all right, shake your head, and, if not, I'll assume you don't have any reason for these remarks and go on."

Solomon paused.

"Fine, I thought so. So one day you say to me, Rose has gotten even, no, defeated me, that's it. Defeated me. What you're talking about, I have no idea. That's what you say the first day you're here. You know something? You don't know what the hell to think. You're a little confused, buster. So you know something else?"

"No, Dad. Tell me."

Solomon turned abruptly and walked toward the door.

"Yes, I'll tell you. Why don't you just sit here and think for a while and get unconfused."

Solomon fumbled with the knob a moment, stepped out, and slammed the door.

Nick became more withdrawn and sullen; Bea, quizzical.

Several times she said to Solomon, "There is something so destructive in the way he's going about this."

"Oh, go on." Solomon looked away. "As a matter of fact, I saw him sitting by her bed last night. He'd been there for hours; he had fallen asleep, but he was still holding her hand."

"That's not what I'm talking about. It's something intangible, his attitude, an air he has."

"I woke him up and told him to go back to his room, take a shower, maybe see a movie. He's upset, but he'll be fine."

"That's not what I mean. He has such a negative attitude. How can Rose respond to such negative feelings toward her? And I sense his frustration. This isn't making him happy. It's not the way he wants to be. He does have strong, positive feelings toward her, but he doesn't know how to free them."

Bea. Haggard. Tight lines around her mouth. Her eyes as always, beautiful, green, intense, slightly distracted, and a little out of focus, partially from thought, partially from not bothering to wear her glasses.

Solomon watching her as she went on speaking.

". . . very strong, positive feelings in him . . . but these positive feelings have been blocked and overwhelmed by his negative energies."

Solomon studied her. The circles under her eyes, her gaunt cheeks, the way her clothes hung on her; he thought of Nick's closed sullen face, felt the heaviness in his own arms and legs, thought, He'd have to get them away, soon. How he—they— could leave Rose, he didn't know.

That night, Solomon had the dream for the first time, a dream he would have many times. In the dream, Rose's eye had been removed, Rose didn't know yet, Solomon tried to cover the mirror, but he couldn't move, he watched her drifting into the mirror, see her empty eye socket, she began to scream. . . .

Solomon kicked awake.

Her eye had never been removed, but had drawn back into the socket as the ophthalmologist had predicted. Still, he kept having the dream.

Bea had been talking to Nick for some time. They were at dinner. Across the street, the motel. Solomon gazed out the window. Lifted his eyes and stared through the gray-tinted glass into the fading light.

". . . this look on your face . . . so resentful . . . it's so obvious you have no respect for yourself or us. Your clothes, your hair, everything about the way you carry yourself. The message is, we can go to hell, isn't that it? . . . Nick? Isn't that it?"

Nick gave Solomon a look of appeal, but Solomon stared out the window a moment longer, "You can listen to your mother . . . with respect."

Nick looked around him, lowered his head.

Bea went on softly. "You used to have so much feeling for others as a little boy. What's happened to you, Nick? I know you. I can see you're not happy. Not just because of all this. I can just see you're not happy . . ."

Solomon gazing up into the fading light. Swallows. Diving. Fluttering. Feeding on insects, invisible in the air.

". . . Living for yourself and yourself alone, your own pleasures, your own whims. This won't lead to happiness."

Nick swore softly.

"Maybe the trouble is, we've indulged you and your sister. . . ." She looked back at Nick. "You're secretive with us. Evasive. Why? What's the big secret? What are you hiding?"

"Nothing."

"You can't hide your attitude, Nick. Not from me. Not from yourself. And not from Rose."

"From Rose? She's unconscious. And what attitude?"

"This one. This angry, negative attitude."

"I didn't have any attitude, I just came to have dinner."

"You know what I'm talking about."

"I don't. What have I done?"

"If this is the way you feel, why take the trouble to hide it?

117

Why bother? It really would be better if you just stayed away from her altogether. Don't go to the hospital and stay away. Like someone else has done."

"Dad—"

"You cannot hide your negative attitude. That's what you don't seem to understand. Rose knows everything you're feeling."

Nick, a stricken look on his face. Bea suddenly reached for Nick's hand. "Nicky."

Nick pulled back. He reached into his back pocket, dropped a copy of Jeane Dixon's *A Gift of Prophecy* on the table.

"This is where you get this stuff about my attitude. Second-rate."

Bea looked at him. Drew herself up. "What do you take me for? A complete fool?"

Nick looked down at the picture of Jeane Dixon staring into a crystal ball and shook his head.

"Much of this I don't take literally. I use these different ideas eclectically. To create a field . . ." Bea faltered. ". . . of positive thought. Of . . . association . . ."

"Sure, Mom. Sure you do."

"There's much we don't know."

"Sure, Mom, sure there is."

Bea quivered slightly, drew back her hand, said in a soft voice, "You are the one who has always accused your father of seeing black and white. But it is really you who are intolerant!"

Nick pushed his way out of the booth.

"Sit back down, Nick. Can't we discuss this like rational beings without—"

Nick hesitated. Suddenly said, "I see what you did to Rose."

"Yes, Nick, of course. What changes? And you, just like her, will blame me for what you don't like in your life. That's it, Nick, run when you don't like hearing something. Run. Like her, too."

Solomon watched Nick go out of the restaurant. He dropped his napkin.

"Christ almighty, Bea, this is one time—"

"Sit down, Joe. I don't want your dinner ruined."

"You should have thought of that before you started."

"Where are you going?"

"To talk to him."

Nick stood on the curb, napkin still in his hand.

"Nick!" Solomon caught up with him. "Step back from the curb." Nick stepped back. "Over here."

Nick followed him onto the circle of grass in front of the restaurant.

"Why couldn't you just have done a few of the simple things I'd asked you when you first arrived? Were they so much, considering the circumstances?"

"Why can't you let me be?"

"Your actions concern others, that's why."

"What have I done? Why are you both so angry at me?"

"It's what you haven't done. I made a few simple requests. I asked you to do them for your mother. You have chosen not to carry them out. And I asked you—emphasized this, Nick, went out of my way to make a special point here—I asked you not to clash with your mother on this goddamned psychic business of hers."

"I haven't. Did I start? Was it me?"

"I don't care who started. What were you doing back in there when you yanked out the book and threw it on the table like that?"

"Beside the fact that it's insulting to anyone's intelligence, I wouldn't really care what she wanted to believe, but she says all these things to me, all this stuff she sees in me. Dad, look what she was saying to me, crazy."

"Well, goddammit, Nick. She's been heroic on this. I've seen plenty of people go to pieces completely in the face of this. Just at the sight of what we saw the first day. Plenty! You know, throw their hands in the air, 'I can't bear it,' a big show, weeping and wailing, and they're gone. 'You take care of it, pal.' Off they go. Your mother's not that way. She has not flinched. And right now, if it is helping her hold on to believe she communicates with your sister—"

"I don't care what she believes. She can believe whatever she wants. But all this about my attitude—"

"I don't need any goddamned mental telepathy to see she's right! what she's saying about you!"

119

Nick looked down at the ground. "Okay, Dad, sure it's true. You called me, I came, I'm here, but it's wrong."

"I asked you on this, Nick. I asked you. A few things."

"Okay, Dad, my fault . . ."

"You've brought this on yourself between you and your mother."

"No, I haven't."

"It could have been avoided."

"I can't say anything here. I have ideas about the accident, but they're—"

"If you mean our conversation, that's right. You do have ideas. Distorted ideas."

"I can't have any opinions on this psychic mania, even when—"

"That's right. Not now. Any opinions you have, keep to yourself."

Nick walked in a circle.

"Look, Nick, I don't like this extrasensory-perception business, either. Just don't confront her on it now. Lean over backward if you have to."

"I'm backward."

"You weren't a few minutes ago. And let me put something to you. Who's to say, finally, she's so wrong?"

"You're kidding me. Not you, too?"

"The first day we arrived, the neurosurgeons told us she wasn't going to live and if she did she'd be a vegetable. That's right. Why should I mince words? A vegetable. They said, forget it, forget her, stick her in a nursing home and try to forget."

"What did Mother say?"

"She never hesitated. Half of the university neurological staff didn't know anything. Your mother's always had intuitions about this, that, and the other thing."

"What did they say—the doctors?"

"They thought she was crazy—or in shock."

"That means you were ready to do what they said—forget her."

"Why does it mean I was ready? I just saw the facts. Nick?"

"What?"

"I just saw the facts based on years of experience as a doctor. And tell me, what about her children? You see how concerned Price is? Should we just abandon her, abandon her children? They deserve a chance. Tell me."

"Dad."

"Tell me. They say forget it. If she lives, she'll be nothing."

"Is that what they do—just put them in nursing homes?"

"Of course."

"Like that place Grandmom's—"

"That was different!"

"How?"

"It was!"

"Okay, it was. Then what happens to them?"

"What's to happen? You think they have champagne and chorus girls? They get fed, they get taken to the bathroom—if it's a good nursing home. In a few years, if no one visits them, they develop secondary complications—kidney infections, pneumonia—they die. Everyone is relieved. No one has to pay the bill, no one has to feel guilty, no one has to be reminded of anything. They can go on about their business."

It was dark. Solomon could hardly see Nick's face. Overhead, he heard the swallows in the summer air. "It may come to that. But not if I can help it. Now I'm going back inside to your mother. . . ."

After a moment, Nick said, "Then what's the point of it all—the nursing home. If they just die?"

"What are we supposed to do? Take them out and shoot them? Abandon them? Is that what you want us to do, Nick?"

After a long time, Nick's voice, hushed, "No."

Nick's silhouette in the dark.

"You want to do something. Go out to the house. Take Richard. Spend some time with him. The kid's scared as hell. He's three years old. His mother's gone. His father's gone. There's a dumb farm girl there with him. Your mother and I have been out there a couple of times, but we're spending almost all of our time here. You'd be better for this anyway. You're a young man. I don't need to tell you how attached he was to his father. How Price could just disappear I don't know—whatever was wrong. Never mind. Will you do that?"

Solomon took a step back toward the restaurant. Turned back to Nick. Overhead, the sound of the swallows swooping, feeding in the dark.

"Nick?"

"What?"

"I honestly don't understand what's going on between you and your mother. I know you used to be so close to her. Whatever's going on, please stop it. Don't clash with her. . . . Nick?"

Solomon could see Nick's silhouette moving toward the road.

AT Rose's house, Solomon had almost expected to meet Price, but of course he hadn't been there. The house looked a mess. Dishes in the sink, clothes scattered about. Rose never kept the place this way. Solomon sat down to wait, but couldn't sit still. He paced. Glanced at his watch. He could wait a little longer. He wanted to see the children, but he also wanted to get back to the hospital. What the hell was wrong with this girl, Doris? He'd said two-thirty, maybe she'd heard it as three-thirty. Who knows what she'd heard? She certainly didn't sound as though she understood one hell of a lot.

Solomon stood at the sliding glass door. Turned. Glanced at a number of pictures on the piano. Skiing. With a couple he didn't recognize. And this one of them looking down out of a hansom cab in Central Park—that must have been Rose's idea—bright-eyed, life going to be a picnic. And more recent pictures. Richard. Then here, the baby. Tim. And this one, hadn't that been used in an article Rose sent them? Another of the baby. And something here in Rose's face. Solomon leaned closer, her eyes wider, dark, no longer looking at the camera, but at some point beyond.

Solomon glanced around the bedroom. Looked in the closet. One side empty. Price's clothes gone. On Rose's bedside table, a photograph. He didn't recognize the girl. Fat, thin mouth, thick glasses. Her arm around a tall thin boy, also in glasses. They stood in front of a hot rod—Solomon made out the name. The Green Machine. Beside the picture, a marble angel the

122

size of a fist, wings spread; it held a cross, its eyes raised toward heaven. Solomon touched the angel. Cold. What a thing. Solomon glanced toward the bed. Supposed the girl was sleeping in Rose's bed, too. What the hell was the difference now, really. The guy in the picture, with her . . . the two of them in Rose's bed? He glanced at his watch. Goddammit, two-thirty meant two-thirty. . . .

He looked out the sliding glass door. Lawn gently sloping down to the shore of the lake. He noticed a Sailfish pulled up on the grass. . . .

Last time he'd been here, he'd been on his way back from an American College of Surgeons meeting, San Francisco. Though she'd been expecting him, she'd answered the door suspiciously. Looked relieved when she'd seen it was him. Shifted the cookbook, which she held so tightly with both hands her fingertips were white. An old cookbook. Thick. Hearts. *The Way to a Man's Heart* . . .

She tucked it under her arm and hugged him hard, awkwardly.

Later, drinks in hand, they'd stood by the window, Rose, himself—dark outside, snow tailing off, they'd looked out into the dark, the more complete darkness of the lake.

He'd noticed lights, they were lights, drifting, floating in the dark.

Rose glanced at him. "They're headlights, Dad. They're driving across the lake." She looked at the expression on his face, laughed. "It's thick enough."

Solomon turned from the door. Noticed a new upright piano.

"So. A new piano."

Rose moved toward the piano, with a quick gesture, hid something, put the cover down. Solomon decided to go along with not noticing whatever it was she didn't want him to notice. Piles of sheet music. Albums. Operas. Musicals.

"Play me something."

"Oh, later, Dad. Richard's in his high chair. I want to feed him something, get dinner. And there are some clothes in the dryer, I want to get them folded while they're still warm."

"Here." She patted an easy chair. "Sit. Make yourself comfortable." She turned on the tv. "Walter Cronkite. All the comforts of home. Price should be home any minute."

"What's he doing these days?"

"Oh, some story on cross-country skiing or snowshoeing, I'm not sure."

"Snowshoeing? He can have it."

Rose looked out the window a moment. She turned and walked heavily toward the kitchen. The pregnancy had started to show.

Solomon hesitated at the piano, opened the cover. A coupon book. Buying the piano on installment. The last two not met. He replaced the book, closed the cover.

The back door slammed. Price. Price and Rose talking. Their voices loud. The kitchen door swung shut. Voices muted, but still loud.

Then Price came out, smiled, shook Solomon's hand.

"Freshen that drink for you, Doctor?" Snow in Price's hair. Price took his glass, returned with two drinks. They talked, Price dropped a cushion off the sofa, lay down on the floor, propped himself up on one elbow. The cushion under him. They watched the news.

After a few minutes, Rose out of the kitchen. "Price, I know you've been working all day, but you really could help me with the laundry. Just fold it while it's still warm, that makes things so much easier. I'm feeding Richard, and trying to get dinner. And I have asked you please not to put *that* cushion on the floor. Look, there are six—one, two, three, four, five, six others."

Price put down his drink. Rose and Price stared at each other. Then Price hoisted himself up, carefully placed the cushion back on the sofa. "Excuse me, Doctor."

He walked toward the kitchen staring at Rose. She glared at him as he passed, said, "Well, really, Price, I've only got two hands—it's not so much, it'll take you ten minutes."

Rose and Solomon talked during dinner, Price said little, and, toward the end, no one said anything. When they finished, Rose lit a cigarette. Price shook his head, pressed his lips together. Rose said, "It won't hurt. And a pipe isn't any better. Probably worse."

"It won't hurt. I'm not the one who's pregnant. Even if you

don't care about yourself . . . ask your father about pregnancy and smoking. He's a doctor, maybe you'll believe him." Price stood up, dropped his napkin on his chair, "Excuse me, Doctor."

"You can at least carry out your own plate to the kitchen."

Price walked into the kitchen without looking back. After a few minutes, the back door slammed.

Rose sighed. "Is it asking too much for him to fold the clothes? I'm five months' pregnant—they're his clothes too. And not to put a cushion, which I spent a long time embroidering, on the floor."

Solomon was about to say "I can remember a few times you were asked precisely the same thing and what a fuss . . ." He didn't.

Rose went on: "It's not as though I want him to be uncomfortable." Rose sighed. "Sometimes I feel like I've got two kids here, not just one."

"Relax, maybe he had a bad day. Come on, I'll help you with the clothes."

"You're a guest here. And he did not have a bad day. It's the same every day."

"He is right about the cigarettes, you know. You could at least smoke a filter. Let me see, Pall Malls? At least a filter."

Rose sighed. "You too, huh? Let's not talk about it. Stay put, I'll get the baby to bed. Stay put, Dad. I'm starting coffee. Don't you dare touch a dish."

Solomon sat at the empty table. Rose came through with Richard. He yawned. His eyes were closing.

"Isn't he a sweetie? Say hello to your grandfather. Want to hold him a minute, Dad?"

Solomon held him.

"He is so good, he makes all the rest of it worthwhile. How does he look?"

"Wonderful."

"No, I mean to your doctor's eye. Healthy?"

"Oh, just wonderful, Rose. He looks fine."

"Watch, Dad."

Rose fit her pinky into Richard's palm. He closed his fingers around Rose's palm. Rose gently pulled. Richard held on. Rose smiled at Solomon. Tugged a little harder. Richard still hung on. Rose gently pulled her finger away. "You do it, Dad."

Solomon did, feeling the baby's hold. "Wonderful, Rose."

Rose gathered him up. "Wait until you see him in a few years—he is going to be so handsome."

"A few years, you mean you think your old father's going to last a few more years, Rose?"

"That's not even funny, Dad. And don't call yourself old, don't even joke. You'll never get old. You're not the kind." She rocked Richard, leaned over and kissed Solomon on the cheek. Touched his hair. "You look so distinguished. Did you give a paper at the conference?"

"Me? No, I went to listen."

"Oh, I don't believe you."

"I'm serious. Some of the doctors are doing artificial knees, they actually are using a kind of glue to hold the artificial joints, right where the condyles would be . . . if anyone had ever told me I'd live to see the day when they used glue." He laughed. "Nope, someone else gave the paper, I listened. Fine with me, I'm getting on."

"No, you're not."

"I've done damned near everything I've wanted to do in surgery. I'm ready to step aside for the younger men—the patients want younger doctors anyway."

"Oh, Dad! Of course not—"

"And I can't say I blame them. You go on too long, maybe you lose a little ground, better to leave while you've still got it. And you know, I'm at a point where who the hell needs it, the stress, the problems with the hospital bureaucracy. I'm telling you, it was nothing like this mess now when I started, nothing—but beating your brains out . . . financially, I'm fine. We've lived modestly. You know what I'd like to do . . . sell the house."

"No, Dad."

"Sell the place in Maine . . ."

"Dad!"

". . . buy a condominium in Florida . . . go to the Caribbean, the Bahamas—your mother and I . . ."

"Mother!"

"All right, Rose."

"And how can you retire, Dad? Just stop? You can't."

"I'm tired, Rose. I want to relax, too. A lot of the doctors my age are starting to hang it up . . . if they haven't already."

"You'd never be happy sitting around."

"Five years ago—even two years ago—I'd have agreed. But now . . . And you're wrong, the patients do want the younger men. And you know something—that, too, is the way of the world, that's just the way it should be."

Rose rocked Richard a moment, "You'll never get old," she said quietly, kissed him again on the cheek. "I'll be right back, just sit."

Solomon gazed across the living room. The piano. The zebra-hide shields. From a darkened bedroom, Solomon heard a soft laugh, Rose. Then Richard, a baby's chuckle. Rose talking to Richard, nothing Solomon could understand, just a soft stream of words, several laughs . . . Richard's chuckle. Then Rose singing softly, nothing Solomon knew, but her voice was clear and as Solomon listened to her singing softly in the dark, he felt a sense of calm, the calm spreading through him, and in another moment, it started turning to a gentle sadness—the sense of snow around the house, so much of Rose's life lived so far away, something inside of her always having pushed her away. She went on singing softly, the sadness deepening for Solomon as he sensed her loneliness.

Solomon recalled Bea's return home after his birth. "I didn't feel welcome. She's just become a mother herself and she won't let me love her—share it—being mothers.

"Mama Turner came the next day—Rose couldn't have been more delighted to see her—she had baby clothes, blankets, a crib. You should have seen the two of them carrying on. One on each side of the crib. Rose starts in, 'He gets his blue eyes and blond hair from your side of the family.' "

"That again."

"That still. And Mama Turner took it up, 'Any brains this boy has will come from your side of the family, not from that dumb son of mine.'

"Well, Rose didn't want me around, so I left. I'm not sure she even noticed."

Bea said, "Rose was too young to remember my father, but he had the bluest eyes and his hair was so blond it was almost white. He was a towhead." Bea shook her head. "Of course, Rose never wanted to hear anything about her family. There was never any telling her. There still isn't. Oh, what's the point. My father, the sweetest, most gentle man, with his lovely blond hair, a towhead, and the bluest eyes." She burst into tears. Solomon put his arms around her.

Solomon listened to Rose singing, stood, gathered up the plates. He was absorbed in the dishes when Rose gently pushed him aside.

"I told you, sit. How do you like your coffee? Cream still, right?"

Her face was clear, her eyes soft, gentle. She brought him coffee.

"Where's Price? I thought he was in here."

Rose pointed at the wall. "Out there."

"There?"

"Fishing."

"Fishing?"

"Ice fishing."

"Oh, Jesus. It's freezing out."

"He's got a shack. He's gone all day and then comes home and spends half the night out there. He says I can come if I want, but he doesn't really want me with him."

Rose lit a Schimmelpenninck, left two wet marks on the paper.

"Oh, Rose."

"Just one." Rose shrugged. "If he wants to spend his evenings in an ice shack . . ." her voice trailed away.

She picked up the damp cigar, inhaled.

". . . then let him. How's Mother?"

"Just how much are you smoking, Rose?"

"Oh, not so much."

"Is she still just the same?"

"How much?"

"A pack, a little more."

"Maybe two is more like it."

"Once in a while. A great while."

128

"Well, you definitely should cut down and smoke filters—if you must smoke. And your mother's fine."

Solomon sat in the breakfast nook, watched her from the side. The look of contempt on her face.

"And, Rose, can I ask you something, perhaps long overdue? Maybe now we can talk, just the two of us, while we have this opportunity. What is it you have against your mother?"

"There's no use talking to you about it, Dad. She's always had you completely brainwashed to do what she's wanted."

"Brainwashed? Rose, this contempt, what exactly, in your mind, has she done to you? I'd really like to know."

"In my mind. It's not in my mind. Look, Dad, let's not talk about this."

"Rose."

"*Dad!*"

"Why don't you see a doctor, get some help on this."

"*Dad!*"

"All right, Rose."

Rose went on washing the dishes. After a time she said quietly, "I'm sorry I yelled at you, Dad."

She reached in, let the water out of the sink, dried her hands on her apron. "I didn't mean to yell at you. I do love you."

Solomon sighed. "I know you do. Give me one of those cigars."

"Dad, you quit."

"One won't kill me, either."

"Dad . . ."

"Cut it out. Give me one. Come on."

She sat down, gave him a cigar. They sat in the breakfast nook and smoked.

"Do you get out—out of this house—at all?"

"Oh, the market, here and there. You know, when they're Richard's age it's constant attention."

"Yes, I seem to recall a thing or two about it. And now a second one on the way. Look, you can't stay cooped up forever. Don't you want to get out?"

"If Price would take the baby once in a while, of course I'd like to get out. He's actually very good when he makes up his

129

mind. I could commute to Madison. Or even the campus up here at Oshkosh. I'd like to take some courses in music. Maybe I can transfer credits, get the degree . . ." Rose looked quickly at Solomon, looked away. He didn't say anything.

"Do you have any friends here?"

"Of course I have friends, what do you take me for?"

"I'm only asking."

"I have a really good friend a few blocks from here. Lynn."

"Maybe I can meet her."

Rose suddenly seemed uncomfortable, vague.

"I'd like to meet a few of your friends, that's all."

"Well, with this heavy snowfall . . . What's tonight, Wednesday . . ." Rose suddenly looked relieved. "Lynn takes a course tonight. Real estate."

They smoked. Solomon said, "Maybe I'll see what this ice fishing is all about. Do you think Price would mind?"

"No. Go ahead. He's out there somewhere." She laughed bitterly.

Solomon noticed a clumsy blond streak in her hair. It looked as though she'd backed up into paint. He reached across the table, patted her hand.

Her long bright-red fingernails.

"And maybe when you come back, I'll play the piano for you."

"Good."

"I'll turn the backyard flood on—just walk down to the shore." In the living room, she pointed out into the dark, "See that light? The lantern?"

After a moment, Solomon saw a point of light.

"That's it. It's about a quarter of a mile. Are you sure you want to go, Dad, it's cold."

"I'll be fine."

Rose threw on the backyard flood. Snow. Light catching the flakes.

On the way out, Rose tugged Solomon's sleeve, pulled him toward a doorway, pointed at Richard sleeping. She smiled. Solomon nodded, smiled. The gun rack, line of guns upright, shadowed behind the reflection on the glass.

Solomon pointed. "Keep this locked at all times." Solomon

pointed emphatically toward the baby's room.

"Oh, we do, Dad. They're locked and unloaded. Price's a stickler for gun safety. He keeps the bolts separately."

Solomon stared at the guns. "Rose, I have to tell you, I don't even like to see guns. Guns are for one thing and one thing only."

"Now you sound like Mother."

"That is just what I am talking about, Rose. How does this in any way sound like your mother?"

"Oh, her whole hypocritical thing. I remember, she didn't even want Nicky to own a cap pistol, for Christ's sake. Any tv program with shooting—"

"Well, what's wrong with that? And Nicky did have cap guns. All over the house. Seems like I was always breaking my neck stepping on one."

"Dad, let's not talk about Mother!"

"You brought it up. I'll say one last thing on this. I would like to see you get some professional help and I would be will- ing to pay—"

"Dad!"

"Do you really feel comfortable having these things around you?"

"Price and I used to hunt together. Where do you want us to keep them, Dad?"

"And the hunting. I don't understand, Rose, when you were a little girl, I remember how you used to hate to see any- thing—anything—hurt. I remember one summer up at the cabin you found a baby raccoon, nursed it with a bottle . . . he used to follow you around like a puppy, don't you remem- ber?"

Rose sighed. "Oh, Dad, it's different, it's a sport—it's not meant to be cruel, and we do keep the gun cabinet locked, please don't worry."

They walked toward the kitchen.

"Guns are like anything else, Dad. They have a place. In their place, they're fine. You're just not used to them."

"And I don't intend to get used to them, either."

"Never mind, when you come back, I'll play the piano for you."

131

Solomon walked through the deep snow around the house, through the floodlit yard at the back. At the edge of the lake, he hesitated, then stepped down into the dark. Felt uncertainly with his foot. The unevenness of the ice. Packed snow. And bare places. The wind rose in the pines along shore. He stepped out on the crusted old snow and ice, took several uneasy flat-footed steps in the dark, suddenly felt the immensity of the lake opening around him. He walked a few feet, stopped, started walking again. A sudden boom. He stopped. Looked back. The floodlight behind the house, distant, pale. Ahead, the point of light. Again, a sudden booming sound in the freezing air. A jagged cracking. Solomon felt the frozen black water beneath him. He started walking. After some time, the lantern brighter, and he could make out an ice shack. He knocked, hesitated, felt for the door, a latch . . . He pulled the door open.

Price standing. Snow-mobile suit, ash-white in the glow of the Coleman.

Price looked blindly into the dark, Solomon stepped in. Price nodded, then pulled up a camp chair. Several northern pike on the ice. Beautiful, silver, perfect.

Price's eyes, ash-blue, almost colorless in the Coleman.

A radio played softly beside his chair.

"Like a drink?"

Price pulled out a flask, carefully unscrewed the cap, handed Solomon the shot. Bourbon. Solomon hated bourbon. He sat. Sipped the bourbon.

They sat unspeaking, the radio playing softly, and after a time, Solomon thought of something to ask Price, something about ice fishing, and Price started to explain slowly and precisely ice fishing and the winter habits of the northern pike. As he spoke, he stared at the hole in the ice. His voice warmed for a few moments. When he finished, he got up, squatted by the Coleman, pumped and adjusted it, examined the mantle, and sat back down.

Once Price stood and stepped toward the hole. He seemed to listen with his whole body. Then he sat back down.

They sat in silence a long time and then Solomon stood. He walked to the door, hesitated. Price staring at the hole in the ice. Rush of the Coleman. The radio.

"Coming?"

Price glanced up, almost as though startled. He didn't look at Solomon. "No, Doctor, not just yet."

"Rose would like us both back at the house, don't you think?"

"I'll be there shortly," Price said.

The fish on the ice. Perfect. Silver. Eyes round and dark. Solomon stepped outside into the wind and darkness. Waited for his eyes to adjust. Found the floodlight on shore, pale, nebulous, like a face on a distant screen. The booming and sudden splitting of ice in the cold. He walked toward shore.

In the living room, Rose had fallen asleep in a chair, mounds of folded laundry stacked around her. A cigarette burned down in an ashtray. As Solomon stepped lightly toward her, she sighed in her sleep. Stirred. Solomon could see the soft swelling of her stomach against her dress. The nicotine stains on her index and third fingers. Her fingers suddenly twitched in her sleep, she murmured something Solomon couldn't make out. Solomon crushed out the cigarette. Glanced at the piano a moment, walked to the sliding glass door, looked out into the dark.

In the morning, the crying of the baby, smell of coffee; Solomon in bed, quiet.

Then in the living room, the clothes still surrounding the chair, some having toppled over. Beyond, the lake, the ice shack tiny in the distance, the sky bright blue and the sun blinding on the snow. Price already gone to work.

"Do you want to change your flight, Dad? I'd like you to stay another day."

But Solomon couldn't. He had a full day of surgery booked already, and a patient he didn't want to leave any longer.

Breakfast, refrigerator door opening, a fishtail protruding from waxed paper.

Rose was a long time bundling up the baby. She sang to him, made him laugh, talked softly to him as she lifted his legs into his snowsuit, carefully pulled them through, pulled his

133

arms through. "Ready, Dad? I don't want him to get over-heated in the house."

She zipped him up, careful not to catch his chin. "There we are."

The baby let out a delighted laugh.

Outside, the squeak of snow underfoot; once Rose took Solomon's arm and leaned heavily against him—the snow, her pregnancy, the weight of Richard. The dog hopping in the backseat.

"What's that?" Solomon pointing at the red sports car in the garage."

"A Triumph. TR-3. Price got a good buy on it."

Solomon didn't say anything.

"Oh, Dad. Dammit!"

"Did I say one word?"

"Sometimes you don't have to."

"Well, you know how I feel and why I feel the way I do about them."

"Please."

"I didn't say anything, did I?"

Rose opened her mouth, started to say something, shook her head. "Dad, Dad," she said softly.

In the terminal, they faced each other.

"We didn't get much chance to talk. And I was going to play the piano and sing for you."

"We'll make it another time. You were tired. Rose, I know you don't like my saying this, but I truly feel I would be remiss as your father . . ."

"Uh oh, remiss as my father . . ."

"No need for 'uh oh.' Remiss as your father if I didn't say what I believe. I feel strongly that you might consider a few of the things I mentioned last night."

"Dad."

"I'd be willing to foot the bill. No one need know, not a soul. No one. Not Price, not your mother, no one. Just you and me. You can pick whomever you like, just as long as he—or she—is qualified, not one of these fly-by-night radical-therapy guys. You don't have to tell me anything at all."

"I don't need it, Dad."

"Will you at least consider the possibility? Sometimes there are more pressures—greater—than we are aware of."

"Dad—"

"You're pregnant. One at this age is tough, but two will be very tough. Price, from the looks of it, is gone a good part of the time, you have some tensions and attitudes—"

"Dad!"

"Rose. Please. Just think about it."

She sighed. Unzipped Richard's jacket halfway. Took off his cap, smoothed his hair, kissed his cheek. "All right, I'll think about it, but I'm telling you—"

"That's all. That's all I'm asking. Thank you." Solomon glanced away. Nudged Rose. "Give me another one of your cigarettes."

"Dad, really . . ."

"Come on."

Rose reached awkwardly into her pocket. Pulled out a cigarette. Solomon smoked.

His flight was called, passengers started standing, picking up handbags, moving.

Solomon turned. Kissed Rose on the cheek. Patted her. The baby.

"Have a safe trip, Dad."

"I will."

He turned, took several steps. "Dad. Dad!"

He turned again.

She walked quickly toward him, hugged him hard, "Dad, Dad." He felt her pregnant weight; she was trembling. He hugged her.

"All right now, Rosie, stay in touch, you can call me collect at the office if need be. If anything's wrong, don't hesitate, call. Or if you have to, get on a plane."

She tried to say something, swallowed. He turned, walked toward the departure gate. Turned to wave. She tried to smile, waved Richard's hand at him.

That had been a couple of years ago. . . .

Now a red Sailfish moved across the lake in a good breeze. Solomon glanced at his watch. Where the hell was Doris? He paced. In the hall, noticed the gun rack. Empty. He touched the glass tentatively. Reflection. Himself. He tugged the handle. The door swung silently open. It had always been locked. The faint smell of lemon oil and silicone. He stared a moment longer, pushed the door closed, felt something go through him; he remembered the other gun.

In the kitchen, the sticker on the dryer. *The West Wasn't Won with Registered Guns.* He glanced around, she'd had the goddamned thing since L.A. A birthday present from Price. Who exactly in his right mind would give a birthday present like that? Solomon pulled out several cookbooks on the counter, opened them, no, no, he opened several in succession, no, maybe she had gotten rid of the damned thing. He opened several kitchen cabinets. No, nothing there. A carton of Pall Malls. He hesitated, opened a pack, lit one, felt a dizzy rush.

He looked thoughtfully around the kitchen. Riffled the pages of several cookbooks. Nothing.

The odd way she held it in both hands, one hand above, one below. And the cover. An old book. The outline of a heart, a procession of smiling chef-hatted bakers marching through the heart and disappearing into the distance. Below: *The Way to a Man's Heart Is Through His Stomach.*

Yes, she nodded, Price had given it to her. And she was always to carry it to the door with her when she was home alone. Her fingertips white from the pressure.

He sat in the breakfast nook and looked around. The washer, dryer. Cabinets, refrigerator, he glanced out at a cluttered bookshelf in the hall, walked toward the bookshelf, stopped suddenly, reached up to the top of the refrigerator. He felt around.

Cautiously lifted the book down.

The procession of bakers. Smiling. Cherubic round cheeks with squares to represent highlights, scrubbed faces. High chef's hats, they proceeded through the heart, diminished into the distance: *The Way to a Man's Heart Is Through His Stomach.*

The weight of the book. The glued pages. He set the book on the breakfast table. Cautiously lifted the cover. Hesitated. He lifted out the thirty-eight. Mother-of-pearl handle.

Price's boasting, "She's a great natural shot . . . it's something a person's born with, Rose is a natural shot, a natural athlete. . . ."

Bullets in the chambers. Solomon studied the gun. Nothing could happen if he stayed away from the trigger, could it? Goddammit, he hated these things, who knows, you could drop the thing, some defect, it could go off.

He'd seen it, something, this? On tv. He pulled the release, the chamber opened, a bullet slid silently out, Solomon tried to catch it, the bullet clattered on the floor.

Solomon took a deep breath, extracted the bullets, looked through the chambers, counted the bullets, felt the cold weight of the bullets in his palm.

He sighed. He sat down at the table, stared at the gun, the open cookbook, the outline of the thirty-eight gouged in the glued pages. After a long time, he closed the cover, reached up, and placed the cookbook back on top of the refrigerator.

Outside, bullets in one hand, gun in the other, he walked down the gentle slope toward the lake. At the shore, he stood looking out, the wind whipping his tie, the sun warm on his face.

He switched hands, the gun, the bullets. He threw the bullets—awkwardly—as far as he could. They scattered, splashed without sound some distance from shore. He watched a boat come about in the distance. Too far to make it out, he watched the sail fill, boat gather speed. The gun in his right hand, he felt its weight, threw; it flashed a moment in the sunlight—silver, mother-of-pearl—made a large silent splash. Solomon stared at the place where it had disappeared, watched the waves for a time, then turned.

Back up at the house, he waited in the yard for the children. By four they still hadn't come and so he walked to the car and left.

WHATEVER was wrong between Bea and Nick was worsening. They hardly spoke or looked at each other now, and Nick insisted on going to the hospital alone. The rest of the time he spent in his motel room reading mysteries and poetry or watching tv. When it was time to eat, he'd eat alone.

Several times the neurosurgeon who had become the liaison with Solomon took him aside and suggested that for the good of everyone, Solomon put Rose in a rehabilitation center and go back home to Boston. If there were any change, they would notify Solomon, do what they could.

"Especially your wife, Doctor. She's been here day and night for weeks. I admire her courage, but there's nothing more she can do now. Really."

Solomon shrugged. "I'm with you completely. I've tried to persuade her. She won't hear of it. There is no way I can get her to leave Rose. Now. Or in the future. I'm really starting to fear for her health—her clothes are just hanging on her."

And Solomon said the same thing to Bea, "Come home now, there is nothing more for you to do here, Bea—at this time."

Her voice was quiet. "As far as conventional thinking, it might appear that way. But I am here with her and she knows it. She feels it."

"Bea . . ."

"I know what I know."

Of late, any disagreements they had Bea attributed to differences in male-female thinking. Male thinking was linear. Step by step. Female thinking was associational. Leaping. There would be no real political breakthroughs, no real changes in the world, and in peace, for instance, until women were put into high political office. Not for the power. Not out of any egotistical reasoning. Many of the feminists were caught in the same ego traps as males. And they were no better off at all. Because they were emulating them. Male thought. Male ego patterns. No, there would be no real changes because change required different patterns of thought. And that came predominantly from women . . . Bea paused.

"All of this goddamned well may be, but I know a few patients who would be a damned sight worse off it it weren't for the so-called trap of my ego—my male ego."

"Dear, this is not a personal attack."

"And not one hell of a lot gets done in this world without someone's ego pushing it. . . ."

"Can you calm down? You're bright red, relax."

Bea went on and on. She gave him a problem in male-female thinking, asked him what he would do. A company located in a large office building in New York was losing millions of dollars a year because of the elevators. The entire staff would straggle in for over an hour each morning. Hours and hours would be lost each week, each month, since large parts of the company couldn't function until most of the employees were there. What would be the best way to solve the problem?

"I'd tell everybody to get the hell where they should be on time in the morning or look elsewhere for work. . . ."

"Oh, dear, look—"

"Well, is it so much to ask people to be on time? Everyone in my office knows where the hell they should be and when they should be there. I expect it and they know I expect it! And they're there!"

"Look, dear, do you want to work with this—"

"I'm telling you what I'd do."

"Well, confine yourself to solving the problem in terms of elevators. . . ."

"So what's the big problem. I'd call in half a dozen engineering firms, get their estimates, see my banker, and put in more elevators."

Bea nodded. "Exactly. Exactly. Of course. That's my point. That's male thinking."

Solomon shrugged.

Bea went on to explain that several female consultants, in looking over the situation, had noticed that as people came in to work in the mornings, they slowed up to look at their reflections in the polished marble walls on the way to the elevators. Many stopped to straighten their hair, their clothes. So the women simply suggested lining the lobby with mirrors to even out the flow to the elevators. Which is what they did. And it worked. Several million dollars, saved. Female thinking. Associational.

"So what the hell's this got to do with your staying or going or Rose or anything else?"

". . . The right hemisphere of the brain is auditory. Intuitive. The entire Third World is auditory and intuitive."

"What the hell is the Third World? And what *does* this have to do with anything?"

"Dear, why are you so angry?"

"Bea, you sit here talking about male-female thinking and the Third World, whatever that is, while—"

"What it has to do with anything is that you and I have fundamentally different ways of seeing this situation. You tend to become much more depressed, you see things in a certain light."

They went on. Bea wanted Solomon to go back to Boston, get back to work, get his mind off this. Nick could drive him back, it would be a good chance for the two of them to get to know each other again. Bea would stay here with Rose, she could be moved over to a rehabilitation center. . . .

Which is what they did do, after several tortured consultations, Solomon, Bea, and Nick walking silently behind the ambulance attendants as they wheeled Rose down the hall. The ambulance, siren off. Saint Mary's.

She'd been in the intensive-care unit fourteen weeks.

Solomon didn't want to leave without Bea, more argument, finally, Solomon agreed he would go if Bea and Nick would patch up whatever the hell was wrong between them. "You know, you might have been a little heavy-handed, too, Bea. I want you to go to Saint Mary's together before we leave. I'll talk to Nick first thing in the morning, then bring him over here and leave you two alone to talk this thing out. Then I want you to go to Saint Mary's together."

IN the morning Solomon tapped lightly at Nick's door. A long delay, voices? Solomon knocked again, louder.

"Nick? Nick . . ." Solomon listened. *"Nick!"*

"Just a second."

"What's the holdup?"

"Just a second!"

After several minutes, Nick pushed open the door a crack.

"I want to talk to you."

"Now?"

"No, tomorrow. Yes, now! That's why I'm standing here."

"Well, I'll be over in a little while. Fifteen minutes."

"No, Nick, now."

"Does it have to be now?"

"Yes, it does. It's important. What's the problem?"

"No problem."

"Well, can you let me in or are you going to keep me standing here?"

"I can't let you in right now."

"Why's that?"

"I just can't."

After a time, Solomon said, "Who's in there with you, Nick?"

Nick didn't answer.

"For Christ's sake, Nick . . . what you have on your mind at a time like this . . . do you think this is a vacation?"

Nick didn't answer.

"Christ, and this of all mornings. Look, Nick, I'm not a prude, but this morning I have something important to talk to you about. Can you get her up and out of there so I can talk to you? I'll take a walk back to my room, then I'll be back."

BEA looking up at him, "You look upset."

"No, no, I'm not upset . . . I just forgot something."

"Did he give you a hard time?"

"No, no, he just wanted to finish getting shaved and dressed, and in the meantime I remembered something I'd forgotten."

"What was that?"

"I'll find it."

Solomon pulling open one drawer, then another, pretending to go through his bags.

"What is it? Maybe I know where it is."

"No, that's okay. . . ."

"Do you want some coffee? I think I'll go over to the office while we're waiting."

"Hold on a minute, Bea!"

Bea opening the door. Standing in the doorway. Her back to him, and Solomon looking at her across the room. She stiffened, stepped back, and closed the door. Walked over to the bed, she sat down quietly.

After a moment, she said in a quiet voice, "I just don't see it."

"What, Bea?"

"I don't see it and I don't go for it. I know things are different now, but some things don't change that much, either."

Solomon looking over.

"Bea?"

"All this sleeping around they do."

"What sleeping around who does?"

"Did you find what you were looking for?"

"Yes."

"Good. They. All the sleeping around they do. . . ."

"Who, Bea?"

"Oh, I saw her leaving, the waitress who works over at the coffee shop across the street. I don't care who, really. I don't think he does, either. That's part of the problem."

Bea sighing and suddenly looking exhausted. "Really, I know they laugh at me or think I'm old-fashioned, but it does seem senseless. I really don't understand them. Either of them. All they care about is their own pleasures, their own limited concerns, the rest of the world can just go to hell. Fine, they do what they want, say it hurts no one, but when they get into trouble, who suffers . . . who pays . . . No wonder they get into trouble . . . his whole uncaring attitude, everything about the way he lives conveys this to me."

"Bea."

"That's why you're stalling around."

"Look, Bea."

"Oh, I'm disgusted, I really am. His attitude . . . I expected something from him, I really did. Something more from him."

"Look, things aren't so simple . . ."

"What's the mystery? I see how he feels. He doesn't even take any pains to hide it. He feels contempt for us, he is callous, indifferent to what happens to his sister. If anything requires any effort from him, he gives it—if at all—only grudgingly . . . he's like a few other people we know, isn't he? Out for his own pleasure."

Bea shrugged. She stood up, smoothed the front of her dress, drew herself up, and walked toward the door. "I'm going for a walk."

"Nick will be here in a few minutes. What do you want to do about this now?"

"Nothing. Nothing at all. If this is the kind of person he wants to be, let him. . . . There's so much he can do . . . I don't think we have anything to discuss, Nick and I. You boys can just go now. Just leave him the way he is now. If only he cared about his sister as much as he did about his own pleasure."

"Goddammit, I want the two of you to talk to each other before we go."

Bea stepped out, closed the door behind her.

SOLOMON sat on the bed. Looked around the motel room. Picked up a book and looked at the cover. After a few minutes, Nick pushed open the door.

"Listen, Dad . . . I'm sorry, I didn't mean to keep you waiting outside like that. . . ."

Solomon felt his vision get blurry, hands shake. Suddenly, the book in his hand, he threw it at Nick. It hit Nick and bounced off his chest and Nick, reflexively, put up his hand, winced.

"Goddamn you, Nick!"

"This what you wanted to tell me?"

Nick pulled open the door.

"Nick!"

"What, Dad?"

"Close the door."

After a long time Nick closed the door.

"Close the door. Sit down."

Nick sat down in a chair beside the door. "What?"

Solomon drew in a deep breath. Sighed.

"Let's just sit for a minute. Let's just sit here for a minute and not say anything, all right. Anything at all."

"Where's Mother?"

"She's gone out. Let's sit here and not say anything at all for a few minutes, okay?"

"Okay, Dad."

The gloom of the early-morning motel room. Disorganization. Bea's attempts at keeping things organized.

Solomon breathing quietly. Nick crossing and uncrossing his legs. The two of them sitting in silence. Solomon looking at the floor.

Nick said in a quiet voice, "I'm sorry, Dad. I really am."

"I'm sorry too, Nick. I lost my temper. I have no excuse for what I just did. I'm sorry. When I'm wrong, I'm wrong. And I was wrong." He'd wanted to ask Nick about going to Saint Mary's with Bea—the two of them, together. He opened his mouth, let out a breath, exhausted.

Nick glanced over at him, his eyes sad, distant. "Don't say anything."

"Do you want to go over and get some coffee?"

Nick shook his head. "I don't think so. I really don't think so."

Nick got up, walked out. Solomon sat in the motel room and stared at the dark tv. He was trying to imagine saying good-bye to Rose.

As Solomon walked across Rose's yard, Richard began to cry, and Doris talked to him, "Shush, that's your grandfather, don't you know your grandfather, that's not a very nice way to show him . . ."

Richard stood on the grass and cried. He cried louder as Solomon moved toward him, and so he set the toys down on the lawn table and stood where he was and Richard went on crying.

Doris said, "He keeps asking for them. . . ." She lowered her voice, "His mom. And dad."

The baby sat in the stroller blinking and squinting in the sunlight, and Doris adjusted the brim of his cap.

The screen door slammed and a skinny awkward boy came out of the house with a glass of lemonade and sprawled uncomfortably in one of the chairs, began bouncing on the chair and looking at his tennis sneakers. Solomon recognized him as the boy in the photograph. Doris's boyfriend.

Solomon drew Doris aside. He told her he was leaving, to stay in touch with Mrs. Solomon, call him about any problems with money, or anything else, that he wanted her to call him twice a week and give him a report. . . . She squinted at him through her thick glasses.

He hesitated, then said, "Could you do me a personal favor? There's a guest room in the house. I stayed in it once. It's comfortable."

She opened her mouth slightly.

"Could you sleep there? Instead of Rose's room?"

She started to say something, shrugged, said, "Okay," quickly in a high voice, turned abruptly, and walked back toward the table. Solomon turned.

Richard was staring at him.

Solomon took a step toward him, and he suddenly started to cry. Solomon hesitated, then turned and walked back toward the car.

SOLOMON watched tv as Bea finished up a few last-minute details of packing for him. He noticed a dress hanging on the closet door. The dress looked familiar; he studied it. It didn't seem to be one of Bea's, but it did look familiar.

"That's not your dress, is it?"

"No, it's Rose's."

"What's it doing here?"

Bea hesitated. "A friend wanted me to bring her something of Rose's."

"A friend?"

"Yes, a friend."

They looked at each other.

"Oh, look, dear, are you just going to get excited—I know how you feel about this—if I tell you I saw a psychic."

Solomon watched the tv screen a moment.

"Well, you don't have to say anything, I can see by your face."

"Where in the hell did you find a so-called psychic?"

"Actually, Joe, a number of people recommended this

woman, including Rose's good friend Lynn. And did you know, Rose herself had been to see this woman a number—"

"Wonderful. So why the dress?"

"She asked me to bring her some personal article of Rose's. You gave her the dress, don't you remember? She always liked it."

Solomon stood, walked across the room, and reached into his jacket pocket. "And this?" He held up the charm bracelet. "You left it on Rose's bed in the intensive-care unit."

"Dear—"

"Look, is this what's going to happen while I'm gone? Because if it is, you might as well pack a bag and we'll all go now. . . ."

"Dear, we've settled this already. And you would be amazed at what this woman told me."

"That's exactly right. I would be amazed."

They went to bed in an uneasy silence.

Solomon slept lightly, waking, turning over, falling back to sleep, the bags packed, dress hanging on the door, and finally he woke, wide awake, reached up, took the dress down, hung it in the closet, and went back to sleep.

SOLOMON carried the last suitcase out to the car, turned. Noticed a maid stripping the beds next door; she watched the tv as she shook out sheets, stared at the tv, shook out the sheets.

"We'll call tonight, Bea. Make sure you keep the door chained at night."

"Nicky, see if you can't cheer your gloomy father up. It's not as bad as he thinks. Things are going to get better. He sees gloom and doom."

"Bea, don't start that again."

"All right, all right. Take care of your father, Nick."

"We'll be fine."

"Oh, what's wrong with that? You're both my boys and I want you to take care of each other."

Bea patted Solomon's cheek gently.

"We'll be fine."

"Of course you will, I'm not saying you won't. Of course you'll be fine."

"We'll call you tonight when we stop. You're sure you're going to be all right, Bea."

"Fine. Be careful driving, Nick. You'd do well to take this time to think a few things over. You don't want to end up being the kind of person somebody else . . ."

Solomon gave Bea a quick, meaningful glance, Nick silent, staring at the dash, Bea stopping.

"This is a nice opportunity for you boys to get to know each other again—just the two of you."

"We know each other, Mom."

"Well, get to know each other better. Who knows, if you'd give each other half a chance, you might even find you have something to learn from each other."

Nick sighing. "Right, Mom."

"Wouldn't that be a pleasant surprise? My two males sitting here just bristling with their egos . . . that they could actually learn something from each other."

"Right, Mom."

"Call tonight when you stop. Before long, I'm going to have some good news for you. I can feel it."

Bea kissing Solomon good-bye and Nick letting out a loud sigh, looking at his watch. "Hey, we can't keep this up all day, let's get going . . . the idea was to get an early start, not stand around here and talk all day."

Bea looking at Solomon and patting his cheek gently.

"Things will be better, dear. I feel it. You'll see."

She kissed him again, came around to the driver's side, reached in, and hugged Nick.

Nick kept his hands on the wheel.

"Drive carefully, Nick."

"I will."

Bea kissed Nick.

Solomon peered over. "Kiss your mother, Nick!"

Nick turned and kissed her lightly on the cheek.

Bea mock-pouting, but serious. "Some kiss."

Nick started the car.

"Christ almighty, Nick, give your mother a real kiss!"

"Let's cut it out and get going. Between the two of you and this kissing good-bye—"

Bea hugged Nick again and kissed him harder, Nick pulled away.

"Drive carefully." Bea peering in the car. Bea looking at Nick, hesitating, not saying any more.

Solomon looked back and waved as they drew away from Bea. She waved. Took a step after the car. Waved harder. Solomon looked after her. "This is the first time your mother and I will have been apart any length of time since we've been married . . . Watch it, Nick!"

"I see him!"

"Well, you don't act that way."

"How did I ever manage to drive before without you—"

"From the looks of it, not too damn well."

"I can see it's going to be a long trip. Can you relax? You're making me nervous."

After a time, Nick said, "You think Mother's going to be all right back there by herself?"

"Take this exit, that's the one we're looking for. Yes, she'll be fine, I wouldn't have left her there by herself if I didn't think so."

"I don't see what she's staying there for."

"Never mind what you see."

"Yeah, that's clear."

"She's going to be fine. She's tough. You have no idea how tough your mother is, Nick. Tough and determined. This is the first time we will have been apart anytime since we've been married."

"You said so already. You just said so."

"Did I?"

Nick making a sound of disgust.

"Why everything I say annoys you, Nick . . ."

"Just let's not talk." Nick turning on the radio.

Nick glanced over, put his hand on Solomon's shoulder, squeezed. "Okay, Dad. I'm sorry, take it easy, she'll be okay. We'll be okay. We'll all be okay."

———

DRIVING on through the day, getting later and later, the sun at their backs, then slanting down, the sun setting. Nick took off his sunglasses and threw them on the dash. The air seemed the color of diluted smoke, Nick silent, occasionally fooling with the radio, his large physical presence beside Solomon, large, heavily veined hands on the steering wheel, thick forearms. Solomon remembered Nick in high school the night before a wrestling meet . . . unable to sleep, he'd hear him get up in the middle of the night, hear him moving around the house, until finally the house would be silent, and to Solomon, there would seem to be a stillness and peace at last in the house. Solomon looked at Nick's hands on the wheel.

They'd been driving for hours. Nick listened to a ball game. Solomon picked up a book of Nick's lying on the seat. Thumbed it. Read some. Read the back. Read some more.

"You read this stuff? This Gary Snyder?"

Nick glanced over, Solomon held up the book.

"I don't see it, do you?"

"Some."

"What the hell's this mean?" Solomon reading out loud. Nick listening.

"Well, what do you mean, what's it mean?"

"What's it mean?"

"Just what it says."

"What's that?"

"I can't explain it."

"I don't see why you and your mother don't get along better. You have the same way of thinking. And I don't see why it has to be a mystery and why this Snyder can't use subjects, verbs, objects, and periods like the rest of us."

"No one's asking you to read it or like it, Dad."

"What are you doing?"

"Sixty-five."

"You were doing seventy-five a minute ago."

"I can't just sit here. I'm standing still. These highways were designed for people to do eighty."

"Let other people do eighty. And get caught. You do sixty-five. I've got enough on my mind. What's the big rush. So we'll get there an hour later . . ."

149

Solomon returned his attention to the book.

Nick nodded, smiling. "Ah, Willie Stargell just hit a two-run homer."

After a couple of minutes, Solomon shook his head, dropped the book on the seat.

"Nick, can we talk for a minute without you getting excited?"

"My getting excited?"

"Yes, you."

"Not when you start like that."

"Try."

"Okay, go ahead . . . my getting excited . . ."

"Nick, what I'd like to know is, what the hell are you really going to do? You've got the start of a good education, but you're not doing anything with it. You're screwing around . . . remodeling houses, this, that, the other thing. If you want to be an architect, that's one thing. Do it right, go to school. You do a little of this, a little of that, next thing you know you're waking up one morning, you're thirty, you know a little of everything, but you can't do anything. I didn't have time to think things over when I was your age. That's what I'm asking you, what are you really going to do?"

"Don't worry, Dad."

"I worry. You're personable—when you want to be—you're nice-looking if you'd cut that mop of hair—come with me when we get home, I'm going to get a haircut—"

"Dad, do you think Gary Snyder's father takes him to get a haircut when he goes home?"

"I don't know, but from the looks of that picture, he sure could use one."

Nick laughed.

"You could change this surly attitude of yours, Nick."

Nick laughed.

"Do all right in business, law, real estate, anything. You have a nice way with people when you want."

Nick said nothing.

"Is there anything so terrible about making a buck? You're not one of those, are you? Should I hang my head in shame because I make a buck?"

Nick, quietly, "No, Dad, there's nothing so terrible about making a buck. I'm not one of those, you should not hang your head in shame about anything."

"Well?"

"Tell you what. Next rest stop we come to, you order a cheeseburger, and I'll apply to architecture school."

Solomon stared down the road in the shimmering heat. Listened to the ball game. Then, quietly, "Okay, Nick. I can't seem to tell you anything. Why you won't listen to me, I don't know. Someone else wouldn't listen to me, either." They glanced at each other. "Well, it's a fact."

"And whatever you say from now on is going to be right for me because someone didn't listen? The Someone Else who didn't listen? Or else I'm going to end up like the Someone Else who didn't listen?"

Solomon stared ahead. "All I know is I can't seem to tell anyone, anything. There's a Howard Johnson's coming up in a few miles, why don't you pull over."

THEY ate in silence, and when they had finished, Nick got up absently. "Men's room."

Solomon stood. Stiffened. Sat back down. Pushed himself up again slowly.

"You all right, Dad?"

"Oh sure, just a little stiffness in this leg . . . this is the knee I twisted last summer when I was fishing. Caught my foot in some kind of hole. It still acts up. Driving too long . . ."

Nick walked slowly beside him another couple of steps, once starting to take his arm, "Go ahead, Nicky. I'm all right, I'll pay over here, maybe just take a short walk out on that strip of grass there, get a little movement in my leg. Go ahead."

Solomon got in a short line at the register. Sighed. Watched Nick turn the corner and disappear into the men's room.

Solomon looked out the window at the strip of grass, the blue sky, a feeling of emptiness in him. He straightened his leg a couple of times, stared out the window. When he looked up, he noticed someone had stepped in front of him.

"Excuse me. I believe I was next."

The man half turned; he wore a T-shirt—Pittsburgh Steelers—and a hat with a camouflage design, the brim turned down. He was stocky and had a gut. He looked at Solomon, sucked his teeth, then turned back into line.

Solomon felt the blood rush to his temples. "I said, excuse me . . ."

The man didn't look back.

Nick was suddenly between them, the man half spun, awkwardly, a look of surprise and pain on his face. Several people close by turned to watch. Nick had the man's arm twisted behind his back, his wrist up almost between his shoulder blades, and as Nick walked him quickly out the door, the man made one sudden effort to free himself. Nick tightened his hold and the man stopped, walking quickly, awkwardly with Nick's chest pressed against his back. Solomon looked down at the check, reached into his pocket and threw the check and a ten on the counter, pushed quickly out the front door, looking both ways to see Nick marching the man around the corner of the restaurant; several people turned to stare. Solomon started to call after Nick, changed his mind, turned the corner of the building and saw Nick holding the man by the throat. He pushed him against the wall; the man struggled but Nick held him back against the wall.

"Nick!"

A family, several young children licking ice-cream cones. The children stopped and stared, their parents led them quickly away.

"Nick, let go!"

Nick held the man another moment, hesitated, let the man go, took one step backward, watching him. Took another step back, feeling carefully as he placed his foot.

Just before Solomon turned, he sensed the man's charge, he turned back, saw the punch hit Nick on the jaw.

It wasn't anything Solomon saw—a sudden movement—it was more the sound, like a rock hitting a hard melon, the man staggered back once, sank to one knee in slow motion. Nick stepped forward again.

"Nick!" He waved frantically at Nick. Felt short of breath.

The man on one knee holding his jaw among stunted ever-green shrubs.

Nick pointed his finger at the man, Solomon saw Nick say something to him, the man stayed on one knee, and Nick backed toward Solomon, his eyes blind and bright. Solomon turned, Nick backed down the walk beside him several more steps.

As they drove out of the parking lot, Nick accelerated, glanced back in the rearview mirror, and swerved onto the highway. He passed several cars, and each time, he glanced into the rearview mirror.

"Nick, for Christ's sake! *Slow down!*"

Nick kept passing cars, Solomon looking at his face, Nick's eyes in the rearview mirror, face tense.

"Yes, by God, you should be looking back over your shoulder after what you did to that guy. *Now slow down!*"

Solomon shook his head as Nick slowed down.

"Nick, I don't even know where to begin with you. Is this the way you live?"

Nick didn't answer.

"You could have killed that guy. What if he'd hit his head? Or he could have killed you. If he had a knife, a gun . . ."

Nick said nothing.

"You never know!"

Nick shook his head.

"I'm glad your mother wasn't here."

Nick still shaking his head. "Okay, next time I'll stand there and let some slob walk on you."

"Nick, there are other ways of doing things. You could have killed him."

"I should have."

Solomon shaking his head. "I just don't understand, Nick; sometimes I'm afraid for you."

"Don't be."

"But I am."

Nick shook his head and said softly, "Don't be," and turned up the ball game.

WHEN they stopped for the night, Solomon glanced around the motel room. "These places all look alike. Really, if I didn't know better, I'd swear we've been traveling in a circle all day and we're back where we started this morning."

"We're getting there, Dad."

"Oh, I know. But I feel as though I've been in a motel room for the last ten years. And when I think of your mother still back there. Well, don't mind me."

Nick squeezed Solomon's shoulder. "I don't mind you, Dad."

After dinner, exhausted, the news, part of a movie, Nick silent on the other bed, tv light flickering on his feet and legs in the periphery of Solomon's vision. Then, waking up, having fallen asleep, the tv off, Nick still reading.

"What time is it?"

"Two."

"How long have I been sleeping."

"Cary Grant just started to discover Ingrid Bergman's being poisoned."

Getting undressed. Nick still reading. Morning, Nick sleeping with his clothes on, the book fallen to the floor.

THEY reached Boston late the next night. The trees were motionless and silent beneath the silvery streetlights as they turned into the driveway.

Solomon and Nick got out, stretching, tired. Solomon looked at the house, the driveway, the linden tree in bloom on the terrace.

Nick took a deep breath. "I've always loved the smell of the linden tree."

Solomon nodded. "It's one of the things your mother always says she likes about the house . . . that linden tree."

"Who's been taking care of the house anyway?"

"The Kellys. I hope."

Nick went around to the trunk, started to open it.

"The hell with it, Nick, we can bring the things into the house in the morning."

154

They stood still a minute, breathing the summer-night air.

"The linden, the azaleas, and the lilacs in back . . . the ones under your window. And the hedge, the sense of privacy, around the house . . . that's what your mother likes."

Nick walked into the backyard, called to Solomon, "The grass is ankle-high out here."

"Not surprised."

Nick walked back. Looked into the living room from the terrace.

"It's strange standing out here looking into the living room. I almost don't want to go in there."

Solomon glanced in. The piano. "You know, after you kids left, the house was too big for us . . . we could have sold it, moved somewhere smaller with our books and the few things we wanted. But your mother couldn't bear to leave this house."

Nick stared up into the branches of the linden tree, up at the stars.

"We could have gone down to Florida six months a year." Solomon sighing. "I'm afraid the time for that has passed for good, now."

Nick's voice, weakly. "Maybe not, Dad . . ."

"I'm afraid so."

Nick walked up onto the terrace and looked into the living-room window. He stood with his back to Solomon, said quietly, "I don't want to go in."

"Well, it's a hell of a lot better than a motel room. Your mother's still in that goddamned motel room. She should have come with us." Solomon's voice was rising. "Why can I never tell anyone in this family anything, goddammit. . . ."

Nick facing into the living room. Solomon stared at his outline. The piano beyond him, a row of medical books . . .

Solomon took another deep breath, calming down. "Come on, Nick, let's go in. It's late."

Solomon opened the door. The smell of the house. "Just a second, Nick. The burglar alarm."

"Do you still have that thing?"

"Yes, why not? What do you mean, still have it? Was I going to rip it out? I'm glad I have it. A lot of the houses around here have been robbed."

Nick made a sound of disgust.

"Fine, for you that solves the world's problems. That attitude. It's not that I'm worried about being robbed, Nick. If a guy wants to steal my tv, fine, good luck. I'll probably have him in the office on Monday afternoon with a slipped disc. I just don't want to find him standing over me in the middle of the night with a gun."

Nick shook his head and laughed.

Solomon turned the alarm. "If that alarm helped your mother and me sleep a little sounder at night—gave us a little more peace of mind, is that so terrible?"

"No! Must every single thing be an issue? If you like living full of fear, if a burglar alarm gives you peace of mind, have ten of them."

"I'm not the one who makes issues of things. I simply opened the door. You—"

Nick waving his hand. "Dad, just forget it. Please. I'm sorry. I'm tired."

"So am I. Think before you say some of these things."

Nick shaking his head. "All right. *I'll* think."

Solomon noticed two coffee cups left in the sink from weeks ago. Just as they'd left them that night. He opened the dishwasher and put the two cups inside, glanced at his watch. "I'm going to make a quick call so your mother will know we're home safe."

In the front hall, they stood a moment. The house silent. Solomon stared at the stacks of mail. Nick walked to the foot of the stairs, looked up into the darkness. Looked a moment at the stairs going up into the darkness.

"I should have sold this house a long time ago. I was ready to when you went off to college. Your mother could have gotten used to the idea."

"Oh, you didn't want to sell it, either, or you would have. You always make a great show of parliamentary procedure and then do what you were going to do anyway. If the house wasn't sold, it's because you didn't want to sell it."

"That's not true, not true at all. You have no idea what

you're talking about. But, by God, maybe I'll do what I want and sell this goddamn house."

"Want a drink?"

Solomon nodded.

Nick returned with two glasses, one of brandy, one of bourbon, both glasses almost full.

"Nick!"

"Oh, take it."

"You know, I've always wanted to live on the water. A year ago, Larry Mills . . . Dr. Mills, do you know him?"

Nick shrugged.

". . . decided to pack the whole thing in, go south; he put his house up for sale—the one out in Marblehead. Right out on the point. We looked at the house three times. What a view. A beautiful large window, beautiful, just beautiful. We almost made the deal. Then at the last minute your mother just couldn't part with this house." Solomon shook his head. "So I called it off."

"You should have done what you wanted. Really. You earn the money, it seems to me you should spend it the way you want."

Solomon waved his hand. "Oh, it's done, what's the use."

"Next time do what *you* want."

"Next time, what next time?"

"Make a next time."

Solomon cleared his throat, then quietly, "Nick, in case you don't understand what's happened out there in Wisconsin, there are not going to be any more next times."

"Don't say that, Dad."

"Don't say that? Okay. I won't say that."

Solomon taking a swallow of his drink.

"I'll bet Mother had an intuition at the last minute."

"That's enough, Nick."

"You earn the money, you should have bought the house you wanted."

"It doesn't work that way, Nick. She loves this house. She has an attachment to it. Your sister did, too. . . . I can remember her sitting at the piano and saying how beautiful she thought this room . . . and never to sell the house."

157

"Neurotic!"

"Not neurotic! An attachment. And, she wouldn't have been very happy moving. If she's not happy, then what's the point? I could have done what I wanted, but she would have been unhappy. Whom would I have been kidding? If she were unhappy, I would have been unhappy, too."

"You were unhappy when you didn't take the house on the water, weren't you?"

Solomon stared at the coffee table. Started to say something, shook his head, and sighed.

"You wouldn't say so even if you were. Mother wants, Mother gets. I'd like to see you take what you want for once. . . ."

Solomon's eye caught something, he walked over to the piano, returned with a large picture. "Here, look."

"Oh, Jesus, give me that."

Solomon took the picture back. "See how nice you can look? Look."

"I was a junior in college then. No, a sophomore."

"Well, you must have had more sense back then than you have now. Was it so painful to look nice?"

Nick laughed. "Oh, Dad."

"I mean it. See how nice you look."

Solomon put the picture on the mantel. After a moment, Nick took it.

"Leave it, Nick!"

Nick returned it to the piano, face down.

He glanced up at the dark stairs again. Then he took the glass into the kitchen, returned a few minutes later as Solomon was turning off the lights. He stopped to glance at the painting of Gloucester dorymen hanging over the hall table. He looked quietly at the painting.

"I can't believe you, Dad. Three-thirty in the morning and you're still wearing a tie. You going to wear the tie to bed?"

"Two of them."

Nick laughed. Solomon checked again to see if the burglar alarm was off.

Then looking up the stairs, Solomon hesitated, and held out his hand to indicate Nick should go first. Nick walked up to the landing, stopped, looked up, looked down at Solomon, noticed the plant box on the windowsill, and said to Solomon, "Nobody watered the plants."

Nick climbed the last few stairs slowly, stopped at his room. The other room, doors ajar, dark.

Nick stood in front of his room. The trophies on his bookshelves and dresser were gleaming in the hall light.

"I don't know if I'm going to be able to sleep in here."

"You will. Why not?"

"I think I'll sleep on the fold-out couch in the den."

"That's ridiculous. I think you'd welcome a chance to sleep in your own bed."

Nick looked into the room. "It's in the same place."

"Of course it's in the same place."

"I'm not going to sleep in there."

Solomon shrugged. "Suit yourself, Nick. This is what I'm talking about when I say you make things hard for yourself."

Nick laughed. "Will you loosen that tie. Please. For me."

Solomon walked into the bedroom. Turned on the light. The bed, still unmade. The telephone by the bed. Several shirts on the dresser which Solomon had decided not to take.

Solomon sank into the easy chair.

After a minute he forced himself out of the chair, walked back into the hall. Several of Nick's trophies were on the floor by the banister. Nick was motionless in the doorway to Rose's room. Solomon walked down the hall.

"Nick?"

"What?"

"Please turn off the light in there and go to bed."

"I will."

"Now."

Nick didn't move. He stared into the room.

Solomon reached over and turned off the light.

Nick turned, his face blank, and said, "You know, I'm having trouble remembering what Rose looked like before the accident."

"You're tired, Nick."

"Are you having trouble remembering?"

Solomon hesitated. "No."

159

"I doubt if you'd say so even if you were." Nick turning on the light in the den. "I don't like coming back here."

"Nick, go sleep in your own room. And can you tell me what those trophies are doing out in the hall?"

"I put them there. I'm going to throw them out."

"Why?"

"I'm getting rid of them."

"No, you're not. I want them."

"They're junk."

"Who gave you the right to throw them out?"

"Me. They're mine. I won them. They're junk."

"You didn't think they were junk when you won them." Solomon pointed at one of them. "You got that for pinning . . . what was the name of that guy in the championship, he'd won twelve in a row and he was a wise guy, he had those cards printed up, I damned well remember, they said, *You have just been pinned by the Blue Angel,* he'd keep them in his jock and he'd hand one to the guy he had just pinned. . . . He had everyone scared as hell, and you went out there and took him apart. You are not throwing that trophy out. I want it. I want all of them."

Nick sighed. "Okay, Dad. You keep them."

Solomon straightened the bed, smoothed the cover, then got into it, settled back, after a long time, he reached over, turned off the light, remembered to set the alarm. Sounds of Nick settling down in the den.

The house silent.

After a time, Solomon heard the springs creak on the sofa bed in the den, then Nick opening a window, getting back into bed.

"Dad? You awake?"

"I'm awake. Awake is all I am nowadays."

"What do we do now?"

"I go back to work."

"What do I do?"

Solomon didn't answer.

"Dad?"

"What, Nick?"

"What do I do now?"

"I don't know, Nick, I don't know."

AFTER some time, Solomon got up, walked into the hall, the clutter of trophies gleaming on the stairs in the hall light, Solomon picked one up, felt the weight of it. The light was on in Rose's room, Solomon walked to the door, looked in.

Nick was sitting on Rose's bed in his underwear with a pile of books beside him.

"What are you doing in here, Nick?"

"I don't know. Reading. She wrote in the margins of all her books." Nick holding up *The Brothers Karamazov*.

"Go to bed."

"I will."

"Please go to bed, Nick."

"I will."

Nick turning a book sideways to read the handwriting. "She wasn't dumb."

Solomon sighed. "I know that, Nick. That was one of the awful parts."

Nick started to say something. Solomon looked at Nick sitting cross-legged surrounded by books and said, "I'm through talking."

He turned off the light and walked out.

IN the morning Solomon shaved and dressed slowly, wandering in and out of the bedroom as he buttoned his shirt, poked in his cuff links. . . . He'd go to the office first, get caught up on his mail and paperwork, go to the hospital in the afternoon, check the operating schedule. . . .

He wandered down to the end of the hall. Door ajar. Nick tangled in the sheets. Why Nick didn't sleep in his own room . . . He looked into Rose's room—a pile of books on the bed, ashtray full of cigarettes, her old albums in a stack on the bookshelf—*South Pacific, Damn Yankees, The Four Aces.* . . . The morning sunlight—in the windows, on the wallpaper—the vague smell of cigarettes, the bed rumpled . . .

In the hall, Nick's trophies . . . Solomon made several trips, carefully placing them back on Nick's dresser and shelves.

Outside, the grass long, hedges unclipped. Several papers

strayed under the hedges. Rotting. Solomon picked them up, threw them in the garbage. . . .

Just before leaving for work, Solomon left a note:

Nick, please straighten up, water the plants, do anything else that needs doing. And stay out of Rose's room, you're making a mess in there.

Bea had been right—it was good for him to go back to work. To see patients, operate. But he was aware that there was something vaguely different in the way people were looking at him. What it was, he didn't know. Something he couldn't ever remember seeing directed toward himself.

Nights, Bea would call, they would talk. She'd ask, "How are you boys getting along, is Nick helping you out . . . are you getting up to the cabin . . . are you using the Exercycle. . . ."

Solomon would stare at the tv, the tuner in his hand, sound turned off. "And what about Rose, any changes, any progress? . . ."

Bea talked about studies on the brain she'd been reading, some interesting avenues of psychic research that might pertain . . .

Solomon stared at the tv—

Bea had been exercising Rose's arms and legs. . . . Lynn had come to the center several times, they had talked, discussing ways they might communicate with Rose. . . .

One night Bea mentioned Nostradamus. . . .

"Who was Nostradamus? . . ."

"Nostradamus was a sixteenth-century French astrologer who had foretold many things."

"What things?"

"The League of Nations, Hitler . . ."

Solomon stared at the tv. Nick wandered in and out of the room, pacing, looking out the window, looking at the tv. . . .

Solomon held his palm over the mouthpiece. "Nick! Why can you *never* be still?"

Nick shrugged. "I don't know. Does it bother you?"

"Yes, goddammit, it does."

Nick walked out.

Solomon took his hand away from the mouthpiece. Bea was still talking about Nostradamus.

Solomon stared at the mute tv.

". . . I really think at this point, if we could find the right person . . ."

NICK came and went at odd hours. Some nights he seemed to be up all night, pacing; other nights, the sudden clang of weights in the basement.

Solomon would say, "Can't you keep regular hours like the rest of the world?" and Nick wouldn't answer.

Other times, Solomon would ask Nick to sleep in his own room. "You've got a perfectly good bed of your own, I'd think you'd be a lot more comfortable in it than that lumpy fold-out bed. What are your friends doing these days anyway?"

"Oh, most of them have moved away."

"Well, the ones who are here. . . . Who's here? What about Mike Walker?"

"They're just doing the usual stuff—work, school, you know. Mike Walker's married and bored."

"You're sure communicative these days. . . ."

Solomon studied *The Wall Street Journal* a moment. . . . "You know, Nick, it wouldn't hurt you any to read *The Wall Street Journal*. Your mother and I have some stock in your name and you could follow it, take an interest."

Nick nodding. "Uh huh."

"Uh huh, uh huh . . . Your mother and I aren't going to be around forever, you know; you should learn to manage these investments. Don't you take an interest?"

Nick shrugged.

Solomon read the stock-market listings in a distracted way. He said, "I can only tell you, Nick. Only tell you. After that . . ." Solomon fell silent against the closed hostile look on Nick's face. He went on reading the paper.

"You know, Nick, there's just so long a man can earn—or, let me put it this way, part of what he can earn depends not on his capabilities alone but on what the world thinks are his capabilities. Maybe what I'm talking about is confidence. How long the world has confidence in the man."

Nick looked uncertain.

"It's true in almost all of the professions. It's certainly true in medicine. To put it simply, the patients prefer the younger doctors now."

Nick looked uncomfortable.

"I'm not just making this up out of thin air. Look in the surveys in medical journals. Study the ages the patients prefer their doctors. They want younger men. Study the median incomes for doctors. They peak at a certain point—" Solomon leveling his hand in the air "—and then they start to decline as the doctor gets older. Patients want younger doctors."

They were silent a moment and then Nick said quickly, "No, Dad, they want experience. Patients want your experience."

"Nick, the younger men have the new methods, that's what they want."

"Oh, come on, who taught them those new methods?"

"Nick, there is just so much time a man has to make it and sock it away. And that's why I'm so concerned about you at this time of your life, Nicky. You should be laying the foundation for your earning power. It's not just money. You have to do something you care about. It gets harder and harder; one morning, you wake up, you're thirty. If you like remodeling houses, why fool with it?— Go to school, be an architect, do it right. There's more to life than chasing girls, getting drunk, and remodeling houses. Or why don't you let me talk to Peter Bradley at the bank . . ."

"No, thanks."

"You didn't even hear what I have to say. Talk about having a closed mind. You have these preconceptions about business and banking and Wall Street. You could at least go for an interview . . . you know, the bank can live without you. The bank will be fine without you. They don't need you. It's the bank that would be doing you a favor."

"I'm sure."

Solomon drifting for a moment. "Did I tell you that Frank Kennedy dropped dead the other day?"

"Who?"

"Frank Kennedy. He was one of the vice-presidents at the bank. Frank Kennedy liked you. Don't you remember him?"

"No, not really."

"Oh, come on, he used to come out to watch you wrestle. Remember, when you were a boy, you were sick as hell with the flu? I had just mentioned it to him in the bank while we were talking; he came out to the house later that day, he brought you a globe—a big bright-colored globe—and you loved it. You slept with it next to your bed for weeks. You asked me about all the continents and oceans . . . you learned every country on that globe."

"I don't really remember."

"You don't remember. . . . I don't know how you could not remember."

"I'm sorry. I just don't."

"It was a great thing for him to have done. He didn't have to take the time or trouble to do that for you."

"I agree. What did he die of?"

Solomon shrugged. "What did he die of?"

"Why do you always sound so angry when I ask you a question? What's so stupid about asking what he died of?"

"I'm not angry. He died of living. Just living. People wear out." Solomon shook the paper. "He was fifty-nine. He wasn't old. He got up one morning, kissed his wife good-bye, went to work; he got out of his car, walked into the bank, started taking his coat off, and dropped dead. That's it. You don't remember him?"

"No."

"Well, I'll bet I can go upstairs right now and find that globe."

Nick, quiet, looked away.

"He used to love to watch you wrestle. He was there that day you pinned that wise guy . . . with the printed card, what's his name? We were just talking about him the other night. . . ."

"The Blue Angel."

"Right, the Blue Angel. Oh, he loved that, Nick. You were so ready to throw out that trophy the other night, Nicky. Tell me the truth, now. Aren't you glad I saved it?"

Nick sighed. He got up. At the door he said quietly, "The Blue Angel wasn't all that good, Dad."

SOLOMON glanced back once more at the patient, nodded to the resident to finish sewing up, and, pushing through the operating-room doors, peeled off his rubber gloves. He dropped onto a bench. Slashes of blood on the green gown, several drops on his shoes. He let his arms fall. Closed his eyes, raised his legs onto the bench. Lockers, opening, slamming. Solomon drifted toward a light sleep. Voices, quiet, familiar.

". . . used to be so distinguished-looking. Old school. Autocrat . . . surgeon as king."

"Used to boast about what a great marriage his daughter had made. . . ."

"Seemed nothing could ever touch him all these years and suddenly this like a sword through him . . . old now . . . too old . . ."

When Solomon jerked awake, the locker was silent. He looked at the dried blood on his gown. Those voices? Had he been dreaming? He wasn't sure.

LATE September, the nights cooler, the first leaves were starting to turn. Solomon asked, "How about going to a football game, Nick."

Nick smiled at Solomon.

What the hell was there to smile about in asking someone to go to a football game? What the hell was so sad about it? Or amusing? It was either yes or no.

"How about it, Nick?"

Nick shook his head. "Thanks. No, I guess not."

"Why not? You used to love football. Don't tell me you're not interested anymore."

"It's okay."

"Well, then. Come on."

"No, thanks."

Solomon shrugged. "Suit yourself. Sit home."

166

Nick seemed unusually quiet and uneasy for several days, and finally Solomon asked him if there were anything wrong.

After a long time, Nick said, "No, but I'm going to be leaving."

Solomon silent a time.

"Where are you going?"

"Back to work. Back to Colorado."

Solomon tried a joke. "I see. It's so bad here."

"No, no, Dad. I was afraid you'd think it might be something like that. It's just that I can't stay here in this kind of limbo forever. I want to go back to work."

"But why not do what you were doing there here?"

"I've got a place there. Friends. Jobs lined up."

"You have friends here."

"It's different."

"Why?"

"Just is."

"That's some answer. Talk about vague. That's just what you get angry about with your mother: you say she's so vague."

Nick shrugged. "Some things I can't explain to you."

"Well, try. Make sense to me. How about getting a job here? Would you like to work in the bank?"

Nick shook his head. "I thought we'd been through that, Dad."

"What the hell are you going to do? This is what I'm asking. What are you going to do really?"

"I don't know, Dad. What I'm doing is what I'm really doing. What's wrong with it?"

"I run into people all the time who ask about you, ask what you're doing. I put them off. I don't know what to tell them because I don't know what you are doing."

"Well, in case you haven't noticed, I've been here with you for the last two months."

"And I appreciate that . . . but on this issue, you keep shaking your head, you don't know, you don't know, but that doesn't help me or you. You can't just sit around and not know."

"I know that."

"That's one thing you know. So? A job here wouldn't be so bad."

"I never feel right here, Dad."

"Why not?"

"I don't know. Just like I never feel right in this house anymore."

"I can't understand that."

"You should have gotten that house on the shore."

"That's all over and done. Look around you. Use your head. This town has got about ten good universities, including the one which begins with H, which I couldn't even get you to apply to. It's got theaters, it's by the water, you've always loved the water."

"Dad. Please. Stop. Just stop. I'm going."

BUT NICK put off leaving. Several times Solomon glanced up from the paper to find Nick staring at him with a thoughtful, distant look on his face. And a couple of times Nick forced a good humor, suggested they get away to the cabin, fish, walk in the woods.

In the mornings, he'd be gone before Solomon. Solomon finally caught up with Nick at the kitchen table. He was staring exhausted into a beer. His boots, crusted with mud, lay on a section of newspaper.

"I seem to keep missing you. What's up?"

"Nothing much. I've been remodeling a couple of rooms for a family over on Beacon Hill."

"Well, it's good to keep busy."

"I need the money."

"There's never been anything wrong with that as a reason for working, either." Solomon hesitated. "Nick, I think this makes my point. Why don't you work here?"

"I've got all my tools out there. I've had to borrow tools from Lou Tracy. Remember him?"

"Sure."

"And borrow his truck for hauling lumber and sheetrock. No way to work."

"This seems to prove you can find work here. Why don't you

168

send for your tools?" Solomon hesitated at the look on Nick's face, decided to drop it. "Where did you learn all of this anyway?"

Nick shrugged. "Books. Other guys. Asking questions. Just doing it." Solomon looked thoughtful. Nick picked up his expression. "You don't have to go to school for ten years—college, med school, everything, just to live."

"I'm aware of that, Nick. I'm aware of that."

Nick stared into his beer.

"May I ask you a question?"

Nick held up a dirty finger. "One. Don't waste it."

"What if these people don't like the job. If they say you did a bad job. Or say you damaged something. Sue you. What if they had a fire and said it was caused by something you did—the wiring or something."

Nick held up ten fingers. "Too many questions, Dad."

"What would you do?"

"It's never happened."

"But if it does?"

"It won't."

"Are you insured?"

"I'm like you. I don't make mistakes."

"Fine, but you're not like me in one respect." Nick raised his eyebrows without looking up. "Yes, one small detail. I'm insured. I've got all I can get."

NICK carried the second bag out to the car. Slammed the trunk.

"That's it?"

"I don't have that much stuff."

"Did you get your blue coat?"

"Which one?"

"It's in the cedar closet. I'll get it for you."

"No, wait a second. Three-quarter–length coat?"

"That's it."

"Leave it."

"But—"

"Leave. It."

Nick kissed Solomon on the cheek. Solomon reached up and hugged Nick in a clumsy way, bumping his face against his shoulder.

"Nick, don't drive all night. Drive a few hours. Get out. Rest. Stop in a motel. Don't just pull off the road and sleep. There are guys out there who think nothing about blowing your brains out for five bucks."

"Okay, Dad. Okay. I know." Nick looked around the yard. "When's Mother coming home? When do you think?"

"When she's finished doing what she has to do out there, Nick. Don't worry, I'll be fine. Here."

Solomon handed Nick a couple of twenties. Nick pushed his hand away.

"Go on."

"I don't—"

"Please just take it." Solomon pushed the money into Nick's shirt pocket.

Solomon watched Nick back out. He was in the street when Solomon waved his hand, walked quickly down the drive.

Nick pulled to the curb, rolled down the window. "What?"

Solomon reached the car and caught his breath. "I know you have a certain view of this situation."

Nick looked confused.

"The whole situation, Nick. And I knew you have a certain characteristic approach to solving problems."

Nick looked blank.

Solomon made a fist. "Get me? I don't want you to make any attempt to find Price. I don't want you to go anywhere near him."

"I hadn't thought about it."

"Thought about it or not, sometimes we're thinking about things when we don't know we're thinking about things. I've watched you. And I know you. And I know how you do things. You're moody, you're impulsive—"

"Hold on, Dad—"

"You haven't forgotten our friend out there back on the interstate."

"Who?"

"The guy who stepped in front of me."

170

"Oh, that guy. That was nothing. I'd do that again, too."

Solomon nodding. "That's just what I mean, Nick. Exactly. Stay away from Price."

Nick shrugged.

"Promise me."

Nick nodded.

"No, say it."

"I promise."

Solomon nodded. "Okay, Nick. I trust you. Whether we've agreed or disagreed on things, you've always kept your word to me. It's for your own good. For everyone's good."

Solomon patted him on the shoulder. "Have a safe trip."

"You're sure you're all right by yourself?"

"Oh, I'm fine, Nick, go ahead. Call me when you get in."

Solomon watched Nick drive off. Half a block away, Nick honked the horn. Solomon waved and turning, he walked slowly toward the house.

SOLOMON looks out the living-room window. He listens. He hears one of the children call out something in his sleep, and start to cry. He stands up, walks toward the stairs, listens, then walks quietly back toward the window; birds still silent, the sky dark, but there is the sense that soon it will begin to get light. Solomon peers out the window, his reflection dim against the glass.

SIX weeks after Nick left, Solomon flew back to Wisconsin.

Bea said, "Go see her by yourself. Be objective. Tell me what you think."

Saint Mary's. Alone. Stepping off the elevator, the sound of a person wailing. It was coming from the end of the hall. The wail reached a high pitch, quavered, broke, almost a sob, faded, quavered to a higher pitch. . . .

Solomon walked down the hall.

Doors open, overlapping ripples of television, old people, sleeping, mouths open, groaning. Nurses stood at the windows, stared out, smoked, read magazines. A wooden handrail ran the length of the corridor. An old woman stood, one hand on the rail, the other on the walker; she trembled.

The wail . . .

Solomon walked down the hall.

A man in a wheelchair tied with a restraint across the chest, head hanging almost to his knees, motionless, hair cut in rough black swatches.

The open door.

Solomon stepped into the room, approached the bed. The purple tracheotomy scar at the throat. Mouth open, lips pulled back in a grimace, the wail. Her eyes were open, the injured eye now drawn back in its socket. He stood over her. Her eyes didn't move.

The close smell of skin, urine, powder, skin lotion. He touched her hand. Hot and smooth, somehow unnatural, like something from a tropical greenhouse.

"Rose."

He leaned over her.

She went on wailing.

Her eyes showed no recognition. He looked into them.

"Rose."

There seemed to be nothing human in her eyes—nothing at all. Her eyes looked to Solomon like those of a wild animal. He got up suddenly, walking quickly, finding an exit . . . He stood outside gasping clouds of breath into the cold air. After several moments, he composed himself. In the men's room, he plugged his ears with toilet paper, returned to sit by her bed. He stared at Rose. Her rust-gold hair on the pillow. Her terrible eyes. He reached out, smoothed a curl.

Recalled Bea, circles under her eyes, cheeks hollow. "She knows, she knows everything, she is trying to communicate, that's what's so terrible for her—no one believes she *can* . . . and *that's* what's so terrible for her—she *knows* no one believes she can. . . .

"The other day I came into her room and two orderlies were joking right in front of her, calling her an animal, this, that— horrible—and doctors, who should know, say as proof of her condition, that she's incontinent. But no one *takes* her. And she can't ask, can she?"

Solomon looked again into her eyes. He stood suddenly, leaned over her. Said in a loud voice, "Rose! Do you know who I am? Do you know me? Do you know I'm your father? Can you hear me?" He held her hand. Nothing. He closed his eyes.

Suddenly, a stab of pain.

He turned. His hand in her mouth, his finger in her teeth, he yanked his hand back, glanced at his finger. The cut was deep. He could see, feel, almost to the bone, bleeding heavily. His right index finger. He flexed it tentatively. The tendon wasn't severed. He wrapped his finger in a handkerchief. . . . Started for the door. She lay on her back, wailing.

He walked back to the bed, leaned over, looked into her eyes.

No recognition.

Solomon suddenly said, "Yes, Rose, yes."

IN the emergency room, the resident had wanted to stitch the wound—insisted—but Solomon refused. The resident said that it had missed the tendon by a fraction of an inch. "Are you right-handed?"

Solomon nodded. "Never mind. I would have managed, severed or not."

He took the tetanus shot, and left.

ON this trip, Solomon finally persuaded Bea to come home. It didn't have to be for good. What was for good, in this situation anyway? But she could just come home for a respite, if nothing else. And if there were anything, anything at all to be done, they could be on a plane at a moment's notice. Gaunt, haggard, eyes distant and slightly out of focus, Bea came home.

Once home, Bea ate very little. Solomon struggled to keep from losing his temper.

"Bea, what are you trying to do? Starve yourself? If you lose any more weight, you're going to end up a prime candidate for a sanatorium."

"Oh, I had a big breakfast this morning."

"What big breakfast?"

"An egg."

"Tomorrow morning I'm getting up and I'm cooking you a nice big breakfast."

"That's sweet of you, it really is."

"And you're going to eat it."

Bea slept restlessly and never for very long. Often she woke before dawn. Solomon would wake, feel the bed empty, look around the room, find Bea in her bathrobe sitting at her desk, her elbows on it, her hands clasped in front of her; sometimes she just stared out the window. If she wasn't in the bedroom, he would get up and wander down to the kitchen to find her sitting at the table with a cup of tea, her notebook open in front of her.

"You know, Bea, some people do something very strange. Some of them even sleep at night."

"I couldn't sleep."

"Well, take a sleeping pill."

"You know how I feel about sleeping pills."

"Then have a drink. You're exhausted and I want you to get some sleep. You need it."

"Don't worry, I'll be up in a minute."

"You'll be up in a minute. How long have you been sitting here?"

"Oh, a few minutes."

"More like a couple of hours. I know what time you got up. You know, if I were going to put someone on a program to get them into a sanatorium, I'd recommend they do exactly what you're doing. Eat nothing and stay up half the night. Wonderful. What in the hell are you sitting here thinking about?"

"If you want to know, I was thinking about Richard and Tim. Richard is still so upset."

"I know that. I have walked this floor a few nights over that myself. But we can't help them right now."

"If there were some way we could take them. I don't know what Doris is doing with them. I think she slaps Richard around. Rose never even raised her voice with him. Who knows what harm she's doing? And the look on his face the last time I saw him. . . ."

"I'm watching the situation, but now is not the time and

174

we've gone over this. Price may be the biggest bastard in the world, and he's got my vote all the way, but one morning he may wake up and decide he wants his boys, and you know there isn't a goddamned court in the country that wouldn't give them to him. He *is* the competent parent, whether he's being one now or not. So we sit tight for now. Bea, come to bed."

"And I keep thinking of Rose there alone."

"Well, maybe we'll be able to move her. But, Bea, not tonight, so come to bed."

"That Sister Elizabeth is so good with her. So kind. And Lynn has been wonderful in this, too. But there is only so much time they can spend."

"Bea! I want you to come to bed! Now that's it! No argument!"

They'd go on like that.

Other times, Solomon would find Bea writing intently in her notebook. He'd make himself a cup of tea and wait impatiently until Bea looked up from her writing. She'd gaze at him, her eyes remote, and he'd say, "Bea, it's almost five o'clock, what is so important at five o'clock in the morning?"

"A dream woke me."

"What dream?"

"Not exactly a dream."

She wouldn't say any more and Solomon would ask impatiently, "Well, what then?"

Then Bea would hesitate, and finally, looking off toward the end of the table, say, "Well, I can't always put everything into words. It was more a, a feeling, a voice. Do you know what I mean?"

"No, I don't know what you mean."

Solomon looked at how loose the wedding ring had become on her finger.

"A feeling—in images—but more a voice. Like Rose was telling me something. Even though I'm here I feel her, know what she's feeling."

Solomon didn't say anything.

"I felt this way many times before the accident. Often I would know when she was going to call, I would look at the phone, and know it was going to ring, and it would be Rose."

"Uh huh."

"And when she was in trouble . . . well, you know, of course she'd refuse any help from me—get furious. But I would always know. I'm not a fool, I don't want to make this sound melodramatic but I would get, I just don't have any other words for it, this strong feeling which would interrupt everything else. Just like in the past few days I've been having strong feelings about Nick. . . ."

"What feelings?"

"That he's very unhappy. That he's in some kind of trouble, maybe with drugs or alcohol."

"He's fine, Bea, I talked to him last night."

"I don't mean that. He may not know he's unhappy, but I know he's unhappy in some way he isn't aware of . . . It's just a feeling I have."

Solomon sighed. He didn't know what the hell that meant. He looked at his watch.

"Bea, let's go to bed. I have to operate in the morning. Early."

"I know. You need to rest. You go up, I'll be along."

"This dream that woke you . . ."

"It wasn't exactly a dream, it was more a voice."

"Yes, all right, this voice, what was it saying, Bea?"

"It was Rose, and it was saying—" Bea stopped and looked at Solomon. She looked away. She looked toward the wall.

"What?"

"Oh, dear, you get this look on your face, you don't know."

"What look?"

"Belligerent. Like you want me to prove something to you. You're angry, you're skeptical. It's so hard to talk to you when you're like that."

"You see things on my face that aren't there. You interpret. Do you want to tell me what this feeling, of this so-called voice, was about or not?"

She sighed. "Dear, you look tired. Go to bed and we'll talk about it in the morning."

LYNN had some news. Bea listened, then handed the phone to Solomon. "I'll let you tell him, yourself."

Solomon took the phone. Lynn had been visiting Rose, talking to her, bringing her things that Rose had always loved and cared for—pictures of her children, a favorite necklace. She'd hold her hand, talk to her. Play cassettes of her favorite operas and musicals—then stop and talk to Rose some more. As Lynn held her hand, she asked, "Don't you miss your children?" And absentmindedly, because she had been spelling with Karen that morning, she spelled the word C.H.I.L.D.R.E.N.

Rose seemed to nod her head up and down.

Lynn looked at her eyes, squeezed her hand. "Do you know who I am?"

No response.

"You just nodded a minute ago when I asked if you missed your children. You do miss your children, don't you?"

No response.

"You know me, don't you? I'm Lynn. Remember?"

No response. Lynn tried the question several times. Then other questions. "You are a mother. You know you have children, don't you?"

No response.

Lynn tried the same questions over again. Maybe Rose had not nodded at the word children. Maybe Lynn had only seen— or thought she'd seen—the nod. Perhaps it had been a tremor. Lynn traced back. Just exactly how had she asked the question to Rose, how had she phrased the question, Don't you miss your children? And then?

Then she had spelled the word *children*.

Lynn held Rose's hand.

"L.Y.N.N. Lynn. L.Y.N.N."

Rose nodded.

"You understand when I spell?"

No response.

Lynn spelled. "Y.O.U. You."

Rose nodded.

Lynn spelled out Rose. "R.O.S.E."

Rose nodded and began to wail.

"She understands, Dr. Solomon. She understands when I spell. Why spelling, I don't know. Maybe a neurologist or speech therapist would know. But she definitely understands."

"What have you told her so far?"

"I've been careful. I told her she'd been in an accident, her children are fine, that you and Bea have been with her the entire time, almost. And will be back again. I didn't tell her that it was eight months ago. I just said an accident. And I didn't tell her anything about her condition. I just told her she was going to be okay. Was that all right?"

"Yes, wonderful, Lynn."

There was a pause.

"I didn't say anything about Price."

"That's all right. That's all right, Lynn. Say nothing about him. We'll say nothing at all about Price for now. Cross that one when we come to it."

"Doctor?"

"Yes, Lynn?"

"She's trying to speak, I think. After I told her about the children, she got very excited, very agitated."

"That's wonderful. That must mean she wants to see them."

"I'm not sure, Dr. Solomon. I think she was trying to ask where's Price. She was crying. There were tears on her face."

They talked some more. Sister Elizabeth had introduced herself by spelling out her name, the speech therapist was working with her, everyone was excited.

After Solomon hung up, Bea sat down by him and took his hand.

"Now's the time. This is what we've been waiting for. We've gotten through to her. And she to us. At last. Now she knows she isn't alone. She has understood. Understood all along. Now things will fall into place. Everything's possible. Everything. This is the beginning."

SOLOMON held her hand.

He said, "Do you know me?" And very slowly and carefully, he spelled it: "I AM YOUR FATHER. DO YOU RECOGNIZE ME?" She nodded very slowly.

Solomon smiled and squeezed her hand, and she nodded harder.

He spelled out. "I AM VERY HAPPY YOU RECOGNIZE ME. YOU ARE MY DAUGHTER."

Rose nodded.

Solomon spelled. "I HAVE BEEN WAITING A LONG TIME." He had to spell and respell the sentence several times before she nodded.

He spelled, "DO YOU KNOW I LOVE YOU?" She did not respond. He spelled it again.

She still did not respond. He squeezed her hand. He was sure she had understood. She seemed to flush, stir in the bed, there was a low cry in the back of her throat.

He squeezed her hand and spelled, "I LOVE YOU NO MATTER WHAT."

Her low cry continued.

"I WANT YOU TO KNOW I LOVE YOU."

Solomon spelled again, "DO YOU KNOW I LOVE YOU?"

After a moment, she was quiet. He knew he saw some recognition in her eyes. She nodded. She nodded a long time, yes, and Solomon felt relieved. She knew he loved her.

He held her hand and they sat in silence for a while and occasionally Solomon would squeeze her hand and she would nod, yes.

After a time, Solomon spelled, "SHOULD I SPELL YOUR NAME?"

Rose nodded.

Solomon spelled, "ROSE."

Rose nodded.

Then Solomon didn't know what last name to say. Surely not Price's. That would make her think of Price, and she would ask. Solomon? Summer?

But now Rose was agitated. She was trying to say something. Tears ran down her cheeks. She wailed and howled a sound that might be NO.

Solomon held her hand. She went on howling and Solomon was certain she was both trying to ask where's Price, and howling, no, because she already knew, perhaps had known for as long as she had known anything.

SOLOMON went back to Boston to work; Bea stayed to help the physiotherapist, the speech therapist; they fed her and she began to take Jell-O and soup. They started teaching her to eat again.

Some speech started to come back, although the speech therapist noted that she would not attempt to say *I* or *Yes*; she would leave *I* out altogether, nod for *Yes*, say *No*.

Bea said, "We are going to reverse that. She will say no, say yes, say I. She will say *I* loud and clear. And just as I have been telling you—the neurologists, the speech therapists, they all agree, she understands much more than she lets on. She is also much better than she lets on. She just doesn't want us to know."

Solomon didn't say anything.

Bea would talk about Sister Elizabeth. Her kindness. Her patience. And Lynn. How Lynn had never deserted Rose. Never.

And Solomon would say something or other into the phone.

Bea and the director agreed that soon there wouldn't be much more the center could do for Rose. Bea wanted Solomon to talk to the director himself.

Solomon flew out and met with the director. No, not much more the center could do. It would be better, if Solomon could manage it financially—to take her home. She was well enough to be moved. Start her on a program of therapy. Get her out of an institutional environment, get her children near her, if that were at all possible. The presence of her children might help bring her back to who she was. Their mother. Perhaps strengthen her will to recover. Who knew what her capabilities were? But at this point it was central, the key, that she have her children. "After all," the director looked at Solomon, "I understand her husband has deserted her. The effect of that is beyond calculation. But if she loses her children, too, she will have lost everything. What does she have to live for now but her children?"

Solomon thought it over. Maybe the children were being mistreated by this what's her name, Doris. Price sure wasn't doing anything. No one even knew where he was, what he was up to—Lynn had seen him once in a shopping mall. Well, Price sure had turned out to be a chip off the old block because there had not been a word from the Turners. And they could think what they wanted, but these were their grandchildren, too—they had sure made enough out of that when they'd been born—and it had been Rose who'd been the one who had to lie down on the goddamned table and have them. Solomon recalled them sitting in the Tavern on the Green, Price Turner, Senior's, distant smile, his silence, Mama Turner going on. With their money, why it all now fell to Solomon . . . How long had it been since he'd actually had to worry about money? But now the medical expenses alone—nurses, therapists, Saint Mary's—and running two households, one long-distance. He couldn't even begin to think of how to settle the ownership of Rose's house. Lawyers. Lawyers' fees. Custody of the children. And he'd better change his will and try to set up a trust for Rose and the children. If Solomon could get the children, he could keep an eye on them. And what if Price did want the children? Not now, but someday. And if Rose wasn't better, what then?

The money alone, just to keep up. He'd have to work as hard as he'd ever worked. Maybe harder. Sometime in the future, the children's educations . . . If something happened to Bea . . . why the hell hadn't Nick learned about money.

SOMEONE is crying. Solomon stirs. The crying goes on. . . . Solomon is wider awake. Bea next to him, Bea usually wakes to any sound, she is a light sleeper, but now she sleeps on, exhausted.

Solomon blinks in the hall light, Solomon into Tim's room, trophies shining, Nick's old room. Tim's face contorted, eyes open, but not really seeing, he screams. Solomon leans over the bed, lifts Tim in his arms, rocks him, says his name softly, Tim begins to quiet down. Tim says, "Someone's in the closet." Solomon turns, "Oh? Someone in the closet? I don't think so, shall we take a quick look—you and I—together, with the light on?" Solomon steps into the closet, turns on the light, Tim blinking, "See . . . no one here. . . ." Tim is already falling asleep. Solomon carefully puts him back in the bed, pulls the door partially closed, careful to leave a crack of light. In the den, Richard sleeping on the fold-out bed, several books on the floor. The hall light catches his blond hair.

After several sleepless nights, Solomon had canceled his appointments for the rest of the week, flown out to Wisconsin where he had collected Doris and the children, taken Rose to the airport in an ambulance, and flown them all back to Boston. There would never be a right time to get the children, never a right time to get Rose, never a right or prudent time to make a move. But now Rose would have her children near her—if nothing more. And she would be home.

Solomon looked into the room. The tv was on at the foot of her bed, the station off, the gray light shining into the room with a rush of electronic noise. Solomon took a step toward the tv. The tv was well out of reach, and the wooden floor creaked. He stopped. He looked around the room. The stainless-steel foot of the hospital bed in the tv light. On one side, the covers had been kicked off. Her foot and calf, pale, the calf atrophied, the foot without definition and pointed downward without the shoe. The shelves full of books. High school and college. Her old desk. On the desk, the stiff orthopedic shoe, the steel brace upright, straps unbuckled. A right shoe. The sole of the shoe remained smooth. Solomon looked at her foot uncovered in the pale light, put a little more weight down to take a step, the floor let out a loud creak, he stood still. She went on sleeping, the gray light on her face. The stainless-steel walker by the dresser. Vitamins. They covered half the dresser in the gray light.

Bea had started her own program of vitamin therapy, which she had designed from readings in Adelle Davis, *Prevention,* and God only knew what else. Mornings, she would stand at the dresser consulting her list, unscrewing the caps to the vitamins, counting vitamins into her palms. Massive doses of vitamin C, calcium. . . .

Throughout the day she'd give Rose pills. Tranquilizers. More vitamins. Mood stabilizers. Often she'd look at the medication in her hand, shake her head and say, "I hate giving her drugs like this. Drugs aren't a solution."

Solomon said, "Let's not go through that again. Dr. Lehman is a damned fine neurologist. You took her off the prescription that one day. Against his express advice. And against my advice, I might remind you. She was violent, unmanageable, and miserable. She was the one that suffered most. Now, please. And, Bea, you're giving her enough vitamins to choke a horse. The calcium alone, how many milligrams do you have there?"

"There can't be any harm. Calcium aids in transportation of nerve impulses."

"I know all about calcium and nerve impulses, Bea."

"Well? Don't you remember, you experimented with your patients. Pre- and post-operative. You gave them massive doses of zinc and found that it cut their healing time. I think in some cases it was as much as a third, wasn't it?"

"Did I? When?"

"During the war."

"Oh, bunk."

"Bunk? Oh, bunk? Why, 'Oh bunk'? You did. Plain and simple. As a matter of fact, that's what made me remember vitamin therapy. You forget. You were very impressed. You used to be open to a lot of things you call bunk now. I really don't know why you stopped. I thought it was a good approach."

"If I stopped, I did so because I found it didn't make a damn bit of difference."

"But it did."

"Well, if it did, not enough to matter. I'll tell you what made the difference, if you're interested in hearing."

"Of course I'm interested."

Solomon held out his hand, palm up. "This. Me. He moved his fingers. These." He touched his forehead with his other hand. "This." He wiggled his fingers again.

Bea smiled. She leaned over and kissed Solomon. "Well, of course, no one said it didn't. Sometimes I really think you misunderstand me. Of course! That goes without saying."

"Maybe it goes without saying too damned often."

"Dear, I only said they helped, not that they took the place of. You are being so sensitive. I think you'll have to agree that giving her vitamins can't do any harm."

"Fine, then give her—" Solomon opening Bea's hand. "What is each of these—a thousand milligrams of calcium lactate three times a day?"

Solomon looked at the vitamins on the dresser, and took a step toward the tv, the floor creaked louder. Solomon stopped. Rose. Still sleeping. He took another step, leaned forward. The tv still out of reach. He saw her foot pointed downward like a ballet dancer's.

He looked at Rose's head on the pillow. This was ridiculous, he'd just step into the room, turn the damned thing off.

He reached over, turned the knob, the set clicked off, a deep silence, Rose sinking in the dark, Solomon listened into the silence, sighed, started to turn, heard her suddenly stir, the word, tv, tv, louder, tv, he stood quiet holding his breath, maybe she'd stop, suddenly louder, TV! Solomon spoke quietly, "It's all right, this is Dad, the programs are off the air for the night."

"No."

"Yes, Rose. They'll be on again in the morning."

"*No!*"

"Rose, keep your voice down, everyone is sleeping."

"*No! No! Never sleep, tv! Tv!*"

"But everything's off."

"*No!*"

"Keep your voice down."

"*No!*"

"Rose, see for yourself." Solomon turned the tv back on. After a moment, the gray light, she came out of the dark, he could see her again, her head on the pillow.

"*No!*"

"No? What can I do? Put some programs on for you?"

Rose nodded.

"Yes? If I could, I would."

"*No!*"

"There's something you can do now to help me. Would you like to?"

"*Nooo!*"

"You can keep your voice down and not wake the children. We went to a lot of trouble to get them here for you, you don't want to wake them now, do you?"

She nodded.

"You do? You want to wake your own children?"

She nodded.

"I don't think you mean that. They are growing, they need sleep."

"*No!*"

"Don't you want them to grow?"

"No!"

After a long pause, she nodded.

"I thought you did. Well, then, they need sleep."

She slurred something.

He thought he understood. "Oh, they never need sleep? Why not?"

She tried to say something else.

"What?"

She said it louder.

"Keep your voice lower. No, they are not perfect. They are fine little boys just like millions of other little boys, and little boys need sleep."

"*No! No!*"

Solomon saw her head thrash on the pillows. She said the word again, slowly, "Perfect."

"Okay, Rose, they're perfect."

She pointed her finger toward him. "Perfect."

"No, I'm not perfect either. I'm just like everyone else. I need sleep."

"*No!*" She slurred something else.

"Oh, but not Mother, of course not, your mother's horrible, she's treated you terribly, hasn't she?"

Rose giggled. Nodded.

"She's been so terrible she just never left you and has done everything humanly possible for you. And is still doing so."

Rose giggled and nodded.

"It's funny? What's funny about it?"

Rose giggled.

"It's funny that she's done everything she could for you?"

"*No!*"

"Keep your voice down! Other people are sleeping. *Other people!*"

"No!"

"Yes!"

She began to cry. Solomon pushed the door closed behind him, stepped into the room.

"You want the tv on?"

185

She nodded.

Solomon looked at the test pattern, shook his head.

"Okay, Rose, it's on."

He lifted her foot, gently placed it on the mattress, covered it carefully. He stood at the head of the bed, leaned down, kissed her.

"Do you want me to take you to the bathroom while I'm here?"

She shook her head, no.

"Sure? Now's the time."

She shook her head, no.

At the door, he looked back at her in the gray light of the tv. Her eyes were open and she seemed to be staring. He started to say something, then changed his mind, lifted his hand, waved to her. She raised her hand and he stepped out of the room.

Outside, he listened for a moment. Looked into the den. Richard had rolled to the other side of the bed. He'd pulled the pillow around his ears, his arms and legs were twisted as though he were in great discomfort.

The attic stairs creaking. Solomon turned. The door pushed open and Solomon drew his robe about him.

"Doctor, I thought I heard Rose. Or one of the boys."

Doris stood blinking in the hall lights. She polished her glasses with a handful of her long flannel nightgown while she stared toward him, her gray eyes out of focus. She was fatter than ever, her cheeks white and bloodless.

"You heard something, all right. I'm amazed half the neighborhood isn't up." He waved his hand toward the floor. "Keep your voice low. I think I've settled her down."

Doris finished wiping her glasses and put them on. She looked at Solomon. Gray eyes diminished by the thick glasses. Thin pale lips. Solomon didn't like her, but he had finally decided to ask her to come, to keep as much continuity as possible while he moved the children.

"Go back to bed, Doris. I'm sorry you were disturbed. Thanks for getting up." She pulled her robe around her, turned, started back up the stairs.

They needed her, but no longer was there any privacy in the

house. Doris thought nothing of walking into their bedroom or going through their books. Solomon wondered if she went through their dressers and closets. One day he had come in and she was sitting barefoot, cross-legged on their bed, watching tv.

"Hi, Doctor."

He nodded. Sat in his easy chair. He raised the paper, ignored the tv.

After a moment, Bea's voice, formal as she came into the room. "Doris, the doctor and I have something to discuss. There's a tv downstairs."

After she'd left, Bea said, "You didn't have to put up with that."

"Well, I'm trying to humor her a little."

"I don't know what she's trying to pull. And sitting on our bed like that with those dirty feet." Bea kissed him. "There *is* a tv downstairs; it's not as though this *is* the only tv in the house. On our bed. Did you see the look on her face as she walked out of here? She wanted to kill me."

"Things are going to be different in this house and maybe at times not to our liking. We're going to have to humor some of these people, bend a little . . ."

"Not in our bedroom."

". . . bend a little more than we like at times. Because you know something, Bea? Much as we may not like it, we need these people. Like Doris. We're going to have to live with them."

Two nurses came to sit with Rose. Violet, from eight to three, and Teresa from three to eleven. Violet was good with the children, but not so good with Rose. She read magazines and watched tv. She paid little attention to Rose. Once she went out of the room and left Rose with a burning cigarette and when Bea happened in, Rose was quietly watching the corner of her skirt blacken and smoke. Rose had a way of making inopportune remarks—once she said, "Violet smells funny." She said it clearly enough so that Violet stood up. "Oh, you think black peoples smell funny, we good enough to sit

187

here and take care of you, you beginning to stand on my nerve, Rose, you really are. . . ."

It had been all Bea could do to quiet Violet down while Rose looked confused and giggled.

Teresa came in from three to eleven. She was good with Rose, patient, tried to talk to her, work with her speech; she couldn't stand Violet and in the brief moments when they passed each other, it would take all Bea could do to get them past each other without an exchange. Once they had faced off in the front hall, and Solomon had to step in and separate them. . . . Eventually Bea had to resort to having them use different doors. Violet would miss the bus and then not call or come in. Or Teresa would call and need a ride because she and her husband had just had a fight and he had told her to go to hell and taken the car. Well, if she couldn't get a ride, she couldn't come in, could she? Unless Mrs. Solomon wanted to pay for the taxi—and give her a ride home later. . . . Teresa reported Doris had slapped Richard when Mrs. Solomon was out. Doris denied it. Richard wouldn't say anything. He just whimpered. Doris would help with the laundry, picking up clothes in slow motion and saying out loud, "I'm supposed to be here to take care of the children, not be a maid. . . ."

Violet and Doris had both worked as nurses aides in hospitals. Sometimes they'd sit around the kitchen table, smoke cigarettes, and Solomon would hear them talking.

". . . even washin' 'em didn't bother me that much, dead is dead, but when it came to stuffin' the asshole with cotton . . ."

". . . yeah, I never liked it, didn't like washin' 'em, either."

Solomon putting down his coffee cup. "All right, that is enough of that!" They would stay awhile—the Violets and the Teresas—several weeks, several months—and then there would be new referrals, new interviews, Bea's "I know this one will work out, she seems to have a real feeling for Rose." Then, new problems—liquor disappearing, a watch gone from Bea's top drawer, someone slapping Rose in frustration, denials. . . .

Bea would have Rose quieted down, Richard would wander in and ask, "Where's Dad?" Rose would suddenly thrash in

188

her wheelchair, become wild-eyed, cry, "Where's Dad, where's Dad!"

Mrs. Pasternak, the speech therapist, came mornings, but Rose wanted to lie in bed with the tv on.

Bea and the speech therapist would be patient. They would get her up. Rose would wail.

Rose would refuse to say the word *I.*

Bea said, "Don't you want to say *I,* Rose. *We* like *you.* Don't *you* like *you?*"

Rose would shake her head, no.

"Won't you change your mind and say *yes* for us?"

Rose would shake her head, no, and slur, tv, tv, or cigarette.

"You want a cigarette. Work with Mrs. Pasternak, then you'll have a cigarette."

Mrs. Pasternak would add in a forced, bright voice, "Come on, Rose!" and clap her hands together.

In the afternoon, Rose and Doris stared at the soap operas or afternoon movies and smoked cigarettes. Occasionally, when he was home, Solomon would hear their conversations.

Rose might ask, "What time is it?"

Doris would tell her.

A few moments later, she would ask again. "What time?"

Doris would say, "Two minutes later. I just told you! You're driving me crazy!"

Rose would giggle.

Doris might say, "Well, what do *you* need to know the time for anyway. Where ya goin'? Got a date?"

Rose would giggle and nod, yes.

"Oh, really? Who do ya got a date with? Got a boyfriend?"

Rose would slur, "Price."

Solomon wanted to intervene, but he hadn't wanted to show his anger in front of Rose, waiting for a moment when he'd be able to get Doris alone.

Doris, with a slight smile on her thin lips, "Got a date, huh? Where is he? I don't see him."

Rose would say, "Downstairs."

"He's downstairs, huh? Well, looks like ya gotta get up outta that wheelchair if you're gonna keep your date."

Rose would start to thrash in the wheelchair.

"Ya sure ya got a date?"

Then Rose would scream, her legs would kick and tangle and Doris would get up, her voice would soften, she would put her hand on Rose's shoulder. "Hey, I was only kidding, Rose, calm down. . . . You asked me what time it was. Remember? So I'm tellin' ya, it's two twenty-five. Rose. It's two twenty-five. Plenty of time still! Come on, work on your hand exercises."

Rose would calm a little.

"Hey, want a cigarette?"

Rose would nod.

Doris would light a cigarette, hold it for her, and Rose would inhale as hard as she could, then let out a series of coughs, they would stare at the soap operas or game shows.

After a time, Rose would say, "Doris?"

"What?"

"What year?"

"Are you playing a game with me?"

"No."

"You're not? 'Cause if you are, I'm gonna punch you in the nose."

Rose would reach up and try to touch her nose. She would bend her neck forward, her feet would kick and tremble, her right arm tremble.

"Yes, your nose!"

Rose shook her head, no.

"Okay, it's 1970."

"It is?" she slurred in a hoarse voice.

"Would I kidja? Aren't I your friend?"

Rose nodding, yes.

"Am I your best friend?"

Rose nodding, yes.

"It's 1970."

"Why?"

"Why what?"

"Why 1970?"

"People don't ask questions like that 'cause there's no answer. It just is."

"Why?"

"You're driving me crazy!"

Rose staring at the tv.

Doris sighing. "Whatja lookin' so sad about now?"

"Not sad."

"You look sad."

"No."

"You're never pleased, are you?"

Rose shook her head, no.

"Don't look sad like that, you're making me nervous. It's 1970."

Once Doris came in with a picture of Rose in her early twenties and said, "Is this you, Rose?"

Rose nodded.

"You were so pretty. Just so pretty. Weren't you, Rose?"

Rose didn't say anything. After a long time, she nodded, yes.

Doris said, "We'll set the picture right here on the dresser so we can see it." Rose sat quietly a long time, and finally Doris looked at her, looked at the picture, got up, and took it out.

Rose would ask Solomon, "Kitty. Where's Kitty?"

"Kitty's married and has children."

"Why?"

"Why? Why? People grow up, get married, have kids. Don't you remember sending her a wedding present?"

"No."

"Well, you did."

"No."

"All right, then, you didn't."

Rose giggled.

One afternoon, Solomon came in and heard Bea singing a series of sentences to Rose.

When she came out of Rose's room, Solomon asked, "What was that all about?"

Bea explained she had read an article on aphasia where speech was recovered more quickly if the sentences were sung to the aphasiacs. "And she did once love to sing."

"Uh huh."

"Yes, the explanation seems to be that the right hemisphere of the brain is able to handle words better if the material is coded in rhythm. If I could just get her on a regular schedule,

191

get her up in the morning . . . she's impossible to get up. She thinks she has nothing to get up for and that's a problem in itself. She wants to lie there, watch tv, have cigarettes . . . she could be much better. . . . I don't think it can be very good for her to be in her old room. She's very sensitive to the things around her. Moods. Places. For her to be lying in the same bedroom she grew up in, it's regressive . . . she is really sensitive. . . ."

"I am tired of hearing how sensitive she is. We're all sensitive. What do you want me to do with her? I've run out of places to put her. It's either here or in a nursing home."

"Dear, no one is criticizing you. Keep your voice down. The children."

"Now, goddammit, that's it!"

"Your voice."

"I don't give a goddamn about my voice! That's it! Now I'm going to read my paper and I don't want to hear another word about her or her room or anything else from you or anyone else!"

Bea patted his arm. "All right." A very quiet voice, "Read your paper. I'll bring you up a drink."

She pulled the bedroom door closed quietly as she walked out.

AT first, people came to the house, old friends, family friends, friends Rose hadn't seen in years, since before she had been married. Some were high-school friends who were now married and had kids, or were divorced. Rose sat in a wheelchair in the sunroom with an afghan over her lap and the friends would come in and as they stepped into the room and saw her something imperceptibly passed in their faces, but they would say, "Hello," in bright, forced voices, as though they were talking to a child. "How are you, Rose?" Sometimes she would slur in a hoarse voice, "No good, no good, no good."

Bea might say, "Oh, she doesn't mean that, do you, Rose? You remember Peter, don't you? You used to be such good friends. Remember. He took you to the senior prom. He's married and has two lovely little girls."

"No!"

"Remember Sally Clark?"

"No. . . ."

"Sure you do. . . . She was in your class . . . well, Peter married her. . . ."

Rose would go on slurring, "No, don't remember," or "Don't like you." They would sit down and talk to Rose and Rose would speak her words in a hoarse voice and they would smile uncomfortably, try to think of things to say, and ask, "What? I'm sorry, Rose, could you just repeat that, I got the first part all right, but . . ." Rose would take a deep breath, her feet tangling spastically with the effort, and try to repeat what she had said, exhaust herself with the effort, notice the uncomfortable looks, and start wailing, "No, no, *no*," or screaming, and Bea would have to walk the people back into the other room, talk to them, go back, talk to Rose, talk to the people who were in the other room, either saying they understood, it was all right, or standing with blank, pale faces. Bea invited them into the kitchen, where they would talk, or else Bea would say, "Well, come back another day, she seems tired and upset." She would walk them back to their cars.

Dom still came to the house to deliver groceries. His father had died several years before and the business was his. Long gone was the chopped, channeled, and flamed Ford. He now drove a van with a cross on the dash.

And Dom himself—bald, heavy, with a white belt, white shoes.

The first time Bea led him in, he stood uncomfortably in the doorway. "Rose, look, you remember Dom."

Rose looked up.

"Hi ya, Rose. How are ya?" Dom took a step toward her. "How are ya, Rosie?" he said softly.

Finally she said in a hoarse voice, "No good, Dom."

"Ah no, Rosie, you'll be okay, I know you, Rosie, you're tough."

No one said anything more. Dom looked at his watch. "Well, I gotta make my deliveries." He turned, then hesitated. "Rose . . ." He looked at her. "Remember that book ya gave me once, the lady who had ya talking funny that summer?"

Rose stared out the window.

"I still got the book. The other day I was reading it to my daughter. Camille. I'm gonna bring Camille by and show her to you one day. She's ten now. Anyway, Camille loves that book, Rose. Ya remember, what was her name?"

Rose looked out the window. Dom hesitated.

"No? Well, I'll bring Camille by one day, you'll like her. I'll see ya next week, Rose."

He turned and Bea followed him. As they reached the door, Rose said in a hoarse voice, "Ger—trude. Ger—trude—"

Dom turned and smiled. "Gertrude Stein."

Bea repeated it softly: "Gertrude Stein."

Rose stared out the window and wouldn't look at them.

Each week, Dom would deliver the groceries, often bringing something for Rose, a dozen carnations, a melon—and leave quickly and uneasily.

Solomon noticed there were those who came back, seemed determined, took Rose's hand, talked to her, brought her something, anything—a flower, candy, a picture of their kids— and those who never came back, and that group included many of the people Solomon had known and worked with for years. He tried not to blame them.

Once, after Rose's screams had driven away some visitors, she sat quietly in her wheelchair looking out into the yard. Solomon noticed the bowing of her body to the right side, the rigid hold of the paralysis—the rounded shoulders, the vulnerability of the bowed neck, pale, white, the soft ridges of the neck vertabrae.

He wanted to say something to her, but just didn't know what. He walked over and placed his hand on her shoulder, felt the brittleness of her delicate shoulders through her shirt, her body grown brittle and inflexible through lack of movement, like someone old and immobile. He took her clenched right hand, opened the fingers, held her hand a moment. She turned her head awkwardly and looked up at him. He looked at her a moment, squeezed her hand. "Rose. Can I get you something? Some tea?"

She shook her head, no. He looked down at her. She went on shaking her head slowly and silently, no, for a long time.

In the kitchen, Bea said in a quiet voice, "Sometimes when she does this—screams like that—I swear she knows exactly what she's doing. Don't you see what she's doing? She does that purposely to see if she can frighten people away—she's saying, 'I *know* perfectly well what's happened to me.' I think she wants to see if they will come back and accept her—you notice she rarely does it a second time. She is just so proud. She knows exactly where she is, what's happened. She knows everything. She screams to drive people away."

Bea looked out the window. She said, "Come to think of it, in a way, isn't that what she's always done?"

MORE and more Solomon felt relief just to get in the car in the morning, get out of the house, away from Doris and Violet, who sat over cups of coffee at the breakfast table, just away from the house. He exhausted himself in heavy, complex surgery. Bea would often greet Solomon saying, "She seems so much better today, have a look at her, tell me what you think." He didn't like to lie to Bea, to discourage her, but it was hard to know how to say he didn't see any change in her.

Several times Solomon said, "Look, Bea, I want you to get away. . . . Call a friend, take two weeks, go to Puerto Rico, read a few novels, relax, swim, you really have not taken any time off on this thing . . . go on, the break will do you good."

But, oh no, she could not hear of it, who would run the house, keep the help straight, who would get his meals? He came home and she felt it was important for her to be there for him, get his drink, make time for him to relax. And now, particularly now, was not a good time, Bea had been to see an astrologer and the astrologer had said now was not a good time to travel but to stay at home and look after things. . . . There will be some unexpected changes on the domestic scene. . . .

"Bea, because some astrologer—"

"No, I just feel now isn't a good time, felt that before I went to the astrologer. Rose particularly needs me now, she is struggling with something in herself and she is going to make a big breakthrough. . . ."

"So she'll make her breakthrough when you come home."

Solomon said, "Did you ever think you might do yourself, and her, more good if you let it rest awhile."

But Bea had reasons for everything.

ONE afternoon, Rose would not cooperate with the physiotherapist. Rose was still excited when Solomon came home, and Bea was trying to talk to her in a quiet voice. "Don't you want to get better? Do the things you used to do? Swim? Sing?"

"No."

"The piano's out there in the other room—you always loved the piano. Come on, sweetie, let's go play the piano. Right now. Come on."

"*No! No! No!*"

"You want your children, don't you?"

"No . . ."

"Yes, you do. You know you do. Don't let your children hear you say that. You don't want to hurt their feelings, do you?"

"Don't care."

"Yes, you do. You have to get better to take care of them. They need you. They want *you* to take care of them. They're yours."

"*No.*"

"You want to get better for your children, don't you?"

"No. No. *No. No.*" Rose suddenly bit the back of her hand. "No, no."

Bea grabbed her hand. "Calm down, now stop—"

Rose bit at Bea's hand. "Kill me, kill me."

"Calm down, Rose. Who would take care of your children?"

"You. Don't care. Kill me."

"No, not us. We're not going to take care of your children. That time in our life has passed for us."

"No."

"Yes. You want to get out of here, don't you?" Bea tried to joke. "And remember, I'm such a terrible mother. You've always told me so."

"You are!"

"I know that. You wouldn't want such a terrible person taking care of your children when you could do it so much better. Wouldn't you like to get away from me? I'm so awful."

"Hate you!"

"I know you do. Because I want you to be better, isn't that so?"

"Hate you!"

"Well, get better so you can get up and walk away from me." Rose struggled in the wheelchair, quivered. "Hate you!" Lurched forward, fell to the floor, and hit her head.

Silence. She lay quiet and motionless on her side.

Solomon and Bea kneeled down beside her.

"Rose, sweetheart."

Rose lay on her side, her eyes moving, the rest of her motionless. Solomon put his arms under her, lifted her up, dabbed at Rose's temple with his handkerchief. "It's all right, Rose. All right. Nothing at all."

Solomon kneeled, wiped the blood off the linoleum with his handkerchief.

Rose stared at the spot on the floor.

Bea took Rose's hand. "Rose. Sweetheart. Would you like a cigarette?"

Rose reached up, hand shaking, felt her head. Looked at her finger several times. Solomon wiped her fingers, wiped her fingertips. "It's nothing, Rose. You're all right, I'm just going to put something on that. It's a little cut."

Solomon put a dressing on her temple.

Rose stared from the floor to her fingertips. Solomon lit a cigarette and held it for her. "Here, Rose."

She stared at the tip of the cigarette.

"Go on, Rose. Take a puff. You've always liked cigarettes. Come on."

After a time, Rose took a puff, then reached up to touch her head again.

"Rose, you are all right."

She stared at the floor. She was still sitting quietly staring at the floor when Solomon walked in the other room and took off his coat. Bea followed him. Put her arms around Solomon. "You're pale." She reached up and touched his cheek.

"I'm all right, Bea. I'm all right. I really am."

Bea pressed her face to his shoulder and hugged him hard. She placed her hand gently behind his neck, pulled him to her, kissed him. "Dear, dear. I would give anything never again to see your face as it is now. Anything."

"I'm all right, Bea. All right."

She kissed him, hugged him hard, blinking, her eyes bright and shiny.

SOLOMON was quiet most of the night and finally Bea said, "I can see you're so depressed. Dear. Aren't you?"

"Just tired, Bea."

"I think we have to try to see this as a temporary stage. It's difficult."

Solomon had been looking through a magazine. He put down the magazine and said in a quiet voice, "Bea, can I say something? Can you remain calm while I do so?"

"Of course." Bea's hands in her lap.

"I appreciate what you're trying to do."

"We're both trying."

"Yes, but I appreciate the special way you've been trying."

She didn't say anything. Solomon fished out one of Rose's cigarettes and lit it. Bea didn't say anything, but she watched him closely.

"Bea, there's a point at which you might be making things a lot worse for her. By conveying to her the expectation that she will recover."

"That's exactly what I want to convey to her."

"She is becoming more and more frustrated. She simply does not have the capability. I think at some point you would be helping her a lot more if you would start trying to help her accept the way she is. She might find a way to live with it."

"She does have the capability."

Solomon measured his words. "She might, if given the right expectations, make a reasonable adjustment. Not be happy. No. But maybe enjoy a few small pleasures. A cigarette. A tv program. Her children. And not be miserable, either. She has to do what we all have to do. Adjust to the way things are, not the way we want them to be. Make some compromises. Perhaps if she had learned to adjust sometime earlier in her life, she wouldn't have—" Solomon waved his hand at the air.

Bea was silent. She studied her hands. Her fingers. Finally she spoke in a measured, controlled voice.

"You see, dear, that's what she wants. She wants us to believe she can't be better. To give up on her. Because she doesn't think she's worth saving. She feels she's nobody or nothing . . . that's the reason she won't say *I*. She's never felt she's been worth anything. And if she can get us to stop trying, then she can stop trying. The fact that she is so frustrated demonstrates to me she has the will to do it."

"I'm not talking about quitting. I'm talking about trying for something different. Something a little more realistic."

"I know what you're talking about."

"I'm not sure you do."

They remained silent a long time. He put out the cigarette. After a moment, he reached for another.

"Dear . . ."

He looked at her.

She said nothing more. He lit the cigarette.

"I want to say a couple of other things. Can you remain calm while I do so?"

"I'm calm, aren't I?"

Solomon didn't answer. "I think at some point, you might have to get used to an idea you are not going to like."

"Yes," she said in a quiet voice.

He paused a long time. He looked at the cigarette.

"You might have to get used to the idea that she'll have to be in an institution."

They were both quiet.

"Go ahead, dear, say what you want to say."

"I said it. In the long run, they might be better equipped to deal with her. She might even be happier. You yourself said it can't be very good for her to be in the room she grew up in."

Bea said nothing.

"We don't have to make a decision tonight."

"No, we don't."

"But it's something to give serious thought to. One other thing, Bea."

"Yes."

"It might not be such a bad idea to consider a little outside help for yourself."

"What kind of outside help?"

"Therapy. We don't have to decide anything tonight, but you can give it some thought."

Bea didn't say anything more.

BEA had been writing to Nick, and Nick replied with neutral letters about his job, a house he was working on; Bea would hold Nick's last letter in her hand, gaze out the window. "He shares nothing of his feelings with us. He might as well not write at all, for what he tells us."

Bea would write him back. "What is it you are doing there that is so important? You could give your family some time and consideration. You can't go through life thinking of only your pleasures and happiness. That isn't life. You know, Price didn't like the way things were. Do you think he'll be any happier? And remodeling houses—with your education—is that living up to your potential?"

And Nick would write back neutral letters.

Bea talked to Solomon: "Why don't you write him, dear, maybe you can get through to him. I certainly can't."

Solomon said he would write Nick, but he put it off. He didn't like to write letters. He felt Nick should come home, too, but really, he didn't know what to say, or how to say it. Bea went on giving Rose massive doses of vitamins, getting her up mornings, singing to her; seeing to an endless succession of neurologists, observers who might bring fresh perceptions, speech therapists, physiotherapists. She spent a lot of time on what she called concentrating on Rose being well.

EACH morning, Bea and Doris, or Bea and Violet, would swing Rose's legs over the side of the bed. They would rest her feet on the floor, Rose slumping. Sometimes she would fall to one side or the other as if in slow motion; if left alone momentarily, they might find Rose fallen on her side, her arms pressed under her, legs hanging at an awkward angle. Back upright, her feet on the carpet, her atrophied calves seemed childishly straight, the skin so white it seemed you could see through the skin, see the bones.

They would help her dress.

Bea would say, "Come on, dear, let's get up and get dressed."

Rose would say, "Why?"

"Because, Rose. We get up and dress and do things in the morning, that's why. We have lots of things to do."

"No."

"We've been through this. We have plenty to do. What do we have to do?"

"Nothing."

"I know, it's a big game, isn't it?"

Rose giggled and nodded. They would get her dressed.

Some mornings Rose sat on the edge of the bed, Doris bracing her shoulders, Bea placing her legs into pants, Rose staring out the window.

Bea asked, "You're depressed this morning, aren't you, sweetie?"

Rose nodded.

"Try not to be. That's negative energy. Think of the good. You're better than you were at this time last year, aren't you?"

Rose would say, "No."

"Yes, sure you are."

"Where's Price?"

"Now we've been through that a thousand times."

"No."

"Yes."

"No."

"What did I tell you?"

"Forget."

"Can you say *I* forget?"

Rose shook her head, no.

"You haven't forgotten. Not really."

Rose nodded, started to tremble.

"Now . . . Rose . . . none of that. Calm down. Sometimes we have to accept things."

"No!"

"You know where Price is."

"Forget. Where's Price?"

"You know. That's why you're smiling, isn't it? You're playing a little game. Pretending not to know things you do know. You know everything."

Bea caressing Rose's head, touching her shoulder. "Right inside you, is a person who is perfectly healthy, perfectly capable of doing everything for herself. I see that person every day. Do you?"

"No."

"Yes, you do. I send you an image of that person. Concentrate and you will see her, too."

"No."

"Come on, now, sweetie, let's get up and exercise. Everything we do is bringing you closer to that person."

"Where's Price?"

"You don't need Price. You'll get better, you'll walk. You will walk toward that healthy person inside you. You'll find someone else and get out of here and have your own house again and forget all about Price."

"No, never forget."

"Come on, now, we're going to get dressed and do some work. Would you like a cigarette?"

Rose nodded yes.

"Then get up, let's get something done, come on. Then we'll have one. After."

Bea would fit her foot into the orthopedic shoes and strap on the brace below the knee.

"Don't like it."

"I don't like it, either. And I don't like to see you wear it. But we'll do it. Just for now. This is a passing stage."

"Hurts."

"I know, dear. I know. This morning we'll stand again."

"No."

"Yes. And we'll stand every morning until we are used to it again."

"No."

"Yes, and then one morning we'll take a step with the walker."

"No."

"And then another."

"No."

"Yes. And then eventually we'll walk."

"No."

"Would you rather just lie there in bed?"

Rose nodded.

"While other people are out being busy and having fun?"

Rose nodded, but she had a faint smile.

Bea said, "You're smiling. I didn't think that's what you want, to be here. Come on. Up. There's nothing wrong with trying and not being perfect."

Bea put cosmetics on Rose. Bright lipstick. Nail polish. Perfume. Necklaces.

"Come on, now. We're as pretty as we feel."

"Not pretty."

Rose reached up, her hand quivering, to touch her nose.

"Sure you are. Come on. Up."

"Never pretty."

"See. Here's Dad. He's been watching all this time from the doorway. Did you see him?"

Rose shook her head, no.

"Show him what you can do. Wouldn't you like to walk for him?"

"No."

"It would make him happy. You'd like to make him happy, wouldn't you?"

After a long time, Rose slurred in a soft voice, "No . . . es."

Solomon spoke. "Walk. That would make me very happy."

"Walk for you, Dad," Rose slurred. "Not for her!" Rose pointed at Bea. Her voice rose. "Not for her!"

"No need to shout, I'm right here. No, of course not for me. Do it for your father. Do it for yourself."

With Doris behind, and Bea in front, they pulled and pushed Rose into an upright position beside the bed and guided her hands to the walker. Bea pried open the clenched fingers in her right hand.

"These nails are awfully long, Rose. They're splitting. Won't you let me trim them a little?"

"No!"

203

They would guide her hands to the walker; she stood beside the bed, shaking, trembling, Doris holding her shoulders from behind, Bea in front. Solomon watched her. Behind, the flow of morning light in the window illuminating her hair, the white wallpaper with the white velour urns of antiquity glowing softly, the flash of sunlight on the aluminum walker. The rows of her books from high school and college bright in the bookshelves opposite the bed. The photos of Gertrude Stein and Robert Wagner still Scotch-taped to the dresser mirror.

Bea nodded, and Doris slowly released her hands from Rose's shoulder, held them poised above Rose's shoulders a moment more, letting them hover, and took them away. Bea took her hands away. Rose stood holding on to the flashing bar; she swayed, looking down at the tan orthopedic shoes whose soles always remained smooth; she looked down at her feet as though they were far away; she looked down at her hands clawed by paralysis. Turned her head and looked out through the veil of sunlight made by the screen.

Bea stepped back. "Good, Rose! Good!"

Rose turned her head suddenly, swaying, starting to lose her balance. Doris grabbed her shoulder—"Whoa, Rose!"—and steadied her, then slowly drew her hand away.

After a few more moments, Rose trembled with fatigue, and Bea nodded, and, together, Doris and Bea lowered her to the bed, Doris massaged her shoulders, Rose sat, panting, the air coming in hoarse gasps, and when she could catch her breath, she said in a hoarse voice, "Cigarette."

"Yes, Rose, I promised you a cigarette. Wouldn't you rather have something else? An apple? Some fruit?"

"Cigarette!"

Solomon said, "For Christ's sake, give her a cigarette."

"Dear . . ."

Solomon lit her a cigarette, turned, and walked out.

Afterward, Bea looked at him expectantly.

"Well, what do you think? Isn't she better?"

"You want the truth?"

"Yes."

"I don't see it. How?"

"She stood longer, she seemed steadier. She didn't seem as tired afterward."

"Maybe."

"But you heard that business of hers, that I'll walk for you, Dad, but not for me . . ."

"Bea, don't let that bother you."

"It doesn't bother me in the least. Not at all. That's not my point. I fully understand she still has old animosities toward me. I understand. Don't you see? That's why I just know, I have a definite feeling that Nick is the one who could work with her. She's always loved and admired Nick. Inside, I've known it all along. Nick could help her if he cared."

"Bea, I don't think that's such a smart idea to propagate for a lot of reasons."

"All right, let's not get into that again. But at least he could help out around here."

Bea looked out the window.

"Nick had it once. Feeling for others. He can relearn something he once knew. In the bargain, he can do something for his sister. And himself."

Solomon looked at his watch. "I've got to get down to the hospital." He kissed Bea, lightly, squeezed her shoulder.

AT Bea's urging, Rose had tried several times to take a step, but each time, simply in trying to lift her foot from the floor, she had trembled violently and fallen.

Often, Solomon glanced up to see Rose reaching toward the straps on the brace and trembling.

Bea asked, "What is it?"

"Hurts."

Then Bea might hesitate and look at Solomon and he would look at his book. Bea would say, "All right, let's loosen the straps for a few minutes . . . Dear?"

"So loosen them five minutes."

Rose digging toward the brace. "Throw away."

"I'd like to, Rose."

"Now!"

"We'll throw it away sometime soon. Work hard and we'll throw it away sooner."

"*Now!*"

"Now we'll loosen the straps for a few minutes."

After a few minutes, she would run her hand through Rose's hair, and then tighten the straps.

In the evenings when Bea would remove the brace, there would be red marks from the strap, the brace, and the shoe.

Bea would shake her head, and say in a soft voice, "I'm sorry, sweetie."

"Throw away."

"We will. Soon."

"Now."

Bea would massage Rose's leg with oil and Rose would slur, "Don't like you."

Bea would nod. "I know. Does that feel better?"

Rose would nod. After a moment say, "Don't like you."

Bea would nod. "I know, I'm awful."

"You are."

Bea would go on massaging. After a time, Bea said to Solomon, "You know, she complains so much when we put her shoe on in the morning."

"I don't blame her. It's not much fun."

"She says it hurts."

"Maybe it does a little."

"But I've noticed it is getting harder to fit her foot into the shoe."

"Go on. A lot of people wear a brace, it's not so terrible."

OVER and over, Richard asked, "What's wrong with Mom? Where's Dad?"

Each time he would ask where's Dad, Rose would slur, "Where's Dad?"

There was no way Bea or Solomon could get Richard to stop asking that question, and each time he would ask, Rose would slur in a loud hoarse voice, "Where's Dad," turn red, and tremble.

Rose would try talking to Richard, but he would have trouble understanding her speech.

He would come and stand next to her uncertainly and she would reach out with a shaking hand, bracelets jangling, touch his head, and slur his name, Richard, and, after a moment, he would move out of reach.

Bea asked, "Don't you like to be touched by your mother?"

Richard wouldn't answer.

Bea said in a soft voice, "Rose, maybe if we cut your nails . . ."

"No."

Rose would look at Richard sadly, longingly, as he stood beyond her reach.

Bea repeated, "It's all right, Richard, you can tell me, why don't you like to be touched by your mother?"

"I do." He moved a little closer. "But she looks—" he stopped.

"Yes, go ahead, Richard, it's all right . . . say what you feel."

"Funny."

Rose giggled. "Do. Look funny. He's right. He's smart. Always smart. Can't fool him." She giggled. "Richard, where's Dad?"

"I don't know."

"Don't know, either."

"All right, Rose, that's enough of that."

"No, not enough."

"Rose, we've discussed this. You're not helping him."

"Don't care."

"All right, Rose."

"No."

"Yes, Richard, you are right, your mother is different. She looks a little different for a time."

"No. For always."

"People sometimes can't help the way they look. But she's still your mother. And she still loves you. And she likes to touch you. The way she always did." Bea's voice quiet, "Go ahead, now. Go back to her. She's your mother. She likes to touch you."

"No, no, don't like to. No more."

"Go ahead, Richard. Your mother doesn't always say what she means."

Rose's arm trembling, the bracelets on her wrist jangling, she reached out her hand to touch his head. She touched his hair gently. "Richard," she slurred softly.

BEA said, "The other day I came in and she was reading a magazine Doris had left on the table. You know how she will just turn the pages. But she was actually sitting and reading it. She was perfectly calm. I watched her for a minute and then asked her if she liked what she was reading.

"She just went into a rage, started screaming, 'No, no, no . . . good . . .' tore the page, threw the magazine on the floor. . . ."

"Well. What is your point?"

Bea looked at Solomon with exasperation. "Sometimes, dear . . ."

"Don't 'sometimes' me . . . What *is* your point?"

"Don't you think it's obvious? She can do so many things if she would try. She doesn't want us to *know* what she can do."

ROSE continued to complain about the brace and shoe, and Bea speculated on what might be causing so much pain. Solomon remained vague.

In fact, he had begun to ask Rose questions. Could she bring her toes up?

No.

Could she turn her foot outward?

No.

There was no ankle reflex, no knee reflex, and of course no response to touch or pinprick. There was atrophy of the calf, no active power in the extensor of the foot or ankle, no strength in the peroneals.

But she could turn the foot in. She could pull the foot down. There was a good pulse in the foot. Solomon noted all of this, but thought no more. But, finally, as Bea went on speculating, Solomon said, "Look, Bea, there is nothing to guess about here. This is the onset of an equinovarus deformity."

She looked at him blankly, almost as though for a moment she were going to say, No, it isn't. She seemed at a loss for words, then said, "Are you sure?"

Solomon just turned and stared at her.

"What a look! Do you have to look at me that way?"

"Well, Bea, for Christ's sake, am I sure! I may not know much in this goddamned situation—but after almost forty years of practicing orthopedic surgery, I do know an equino-varus deformity when I see it."

"All right, dear, all right. I'm only asking."

"Am I sure?! Really, Bea!"

"What will happen if nothing is done about it?"

Solomon looked out the window.

He put his palm flat on the table. "This is the bottom of her foot." Put his forearm at a ninety-degree angle. "This is her calf." He raised his palm from the table and put his fingertips on the table. "That's what could happen. Not *will* happen. But could. Her foot would no longer lie flat on the floor—it would make it impossible for her to walk. Even if she could."

Bea looked at her hands. They were crossed in her lap. "Oh," her voice soft, "Oh."

Solomon sat down next to Bea and took her hand.

Bea said in a soft, tired voice, "What can be done about it?"

"A few things. Why speculate? Let's not get into this now. Please."

Bea looked at her hands in her lap. She didn't say anything. Solomon looked at her. Her eyes were closed and there were deep lines on both sides of her mouth. "Would physiotherapy help?"

"Would it matter to you if I said it would or wouldn't help?"

"Dear . . ."

"Would it?"

"You have become so defensive . . . I'm only asking."

They sat side by side on the edge of the bed. Finally Solomon said, "Physio can't do any harm." He took her hand. "It couldn't do any harm, if you can get her to do it."

SOLOMON was struggling to get Rose up the stairs.

Solomon caught his breath. Rose giggled. "Yes, Rose, it's very funny."

"It is," she said.

"What's funny about it?"

209

"You."

"Why me?"

"You are."

Bea came to the top of the stairs. "Where's Doris?"

"I think she went to the store."

"Why didn't you wait for her to help you?"

"It's all right."

Rose slurred, "It's not," and giggled.

Bea came down the stairs, they struggled with her, got her upstairs and into bed, and as they were walking out of the room, Bea said suddenly, "Damn him! Just damn him! This is ridiculous! He could at least save you from having to do that!"

Bea went on writing to Nick and Nick finally sent back a postcard with one word written on it, ALRIGHT!

Within three days, he sold his car, truck; sold or gave away everything else he had—stereo, tv, tools—and flew home.

. THE moment Nick walked in the door, Bea gave him a big hug. Nick glanced at Solomon. Solomon nodded. Nick pushed Bea away, took a deep breath.

Bea led Nick into the sunroom. "Look, Rose, I have a wonderful surprise for you. Here's your brother!"

Rose sat in the wheelchair, her shoulders rounded, her back to the door. She was looking out the window. She turned her head, and her foot kicked awkwardly with the effort.

Solomon watched Nick. Rose pushed her foot against the floor, the wheelchair swung, a flash of sunlight on the stainless steel, Nick's face empty, surprised.

Bea took Nick's hand, led him over. "Look, Rose, your brother, he's come a long way to be with you again, aren't you glad to see him?"

"No. *No!*"

"That means 'yes' with her, Nick, don't—"

Rose began to scream, and Nick's face went pale.

"All right, now, all right. Rose. This is your brother."

She went on screaming.

Solomon waved to Nick, and Nick walked slowly out of the room, and Solomon waved him toward the kitchen. In the kitchen, Doris smoked a cigarette and was leafing through a magazine.

Solomon gestured toward the sunroom and the noise.

"Doris, I think Mrs. Solomon could use a hand."

Doris stood up, looked sullenly at him through her glasses, eyeshadow streaked, smiled at Nick, and waddled past.

Solomon closed the door to the kitchen and the screaming became muffled.

He shrugged and held out his hands. "That's the way it is."

Nick still hadn't managed to say anything. Finally he just shook his head.

Solomon nodded. "Yes."

"I really thought from Mother's letter that she was recovering. Maybe a little more speech therapy and some physio or something."

"Yes. Or something. All she has to do is give one of those little performances if and when the court sends psychiatrists to look at her and that will be the end of everything I've been trying to do. . . . God knows what will happen to those kids. . . ." Solomon trailed off.

"I didn't do anything, did I? I didn't even open my mouth. I just walked in and stood there."

The sound of screams muffled through the kitchen door.

"You don't have to open your mouth or do anything else, Nick. You can just forget everything you think you understand about human behavior here."

"I just had a different idea from Mother's letters."

"Your mother has a way of seeing what she wants to see here, thinking what she wants to think, and simplifying. She has from the beginning. As you might recall. And it's getting worse." Solomon held up his hands. "It's just so goddamned complicated and if it's not one thing, it's another, or another, and it's one thing after another, and all of it costs, I really don't know what the hell I'm going to do about money, I haven't worried about money in years, I just really don't know how the hell I'm going to pay for all of this . . . we've got problems with nurses, problems . . . Never mind, Nick." Solomon stopped, collected himself. "I'm glad you're here."

After a moment, Nick said, "But what is *really* wrong with her?"

"Plenty. Head injuries, Nick. Violent behavior and head injuries. Trauma. Paralysis. Plenty. It would take an hour to tell you."

"But Mother sees a change?"

"Oh yes, big changes."

"How?"

"All I know is I'm the guy who pays the bills around here. I feed this outfit, your mother sees miracles, I don't do miracles, I fix broken arms and legs, slipped discs." After a moment, Solomon said, "There are a lot of things your mother and I don't agree on, but we try not to clash." As an afterthought, Solomon said, "You have to learn to give a little, compromise."

Nick looked at Solomon and laughed. "Is that you talking? Did you say compromise?"

"Yes, and I mean it."

"That's the first time I've ever heard you say anything like that in your life."

"If you're smart, you'll learn now. You particularly could learn. You might even become happier for it."

Nick shook his head and smiled at Solomon. He looked embarrassed. Then he stared at the floor.

Solomon said, "What's the matter? You look disappointed."

Nick didn't answer.

"So what are the choices? It's compromise or what else?"

"I don't know, I don't know."

"Tell me."

"I don't know."

"Then I'll tell you since you don't know. It's compromise. And if you're smart, you'll listen to me for once."

"The way she's got Rose dressed. That bright-red nail polish. The lipstick. All of those necklaces and junk rings."

"Your mother thinks it will help her morale to dress her up a bit."

"But—"

The door opened and Solomon put his finger to his lips. Bea came in.

"All right, Nick. She's calmed down. Now don't let that screaming bother you. Rose does that with almost everyone she cares about. She's testing their reactions. She was just testing you, Nick."

212

Nick and Solomon looked at each other.

"Why don't you go back out there and sit with her for a while. Show her that you think nothing of that screaming, that it doesn't faze you a bit, that you love her and accept her. Go ahead, Nicky. It will be good for both of you. Don't let her drive you away."

"Well, what will I do if she does scream?"

"Just talk to her. Don't let it upset you."

Again Nick looked at Solomon and Solomon made a slight nod.

Nick turned. He was pale. He walked out of the kitchen.

After a moment, the sound of Rose screaming. Then the screaming stopped and Bea turned to Solomon in the silence, looked at him once, and nodded with certainty.

WHERE to put everyone? Tim was already in Nick's room, Richard in the den, Rose in her old room. Doris moved into the same room with Rose, Nick took the attic room.

For the next few weeks, Nick helped carry Rose up and down stairs, tried getting her to practice her speech, exercise her hand.

He seemed always to be in motion, from early morning until late at night—pacing, sitting down, crossing and uncrossing his legs, slumping, adjusting a lamp, sitting up straight, pulling the lamp still closer, getting up again, scratching his head, suddenly doing push-ups in the middle of the floor, lifting weights in the basement. At night, Solomon would hear him overhead in the attic, still pacing, suddenly coming down the attic stairs, just as suddenly up again, pacing In and out of rooms pacing, leaving behind crushed and twisted cushions on the sofa.

ONE morning, Solomon found Nick lying face down on the living-room floor, a book beside him, the radio softly giving out the news, weather, and early-morning traffic report, the lights on. A glass beside him on the rug. Solomon picked it up. Sniffed. Scotch. Solomon touched Nick lightly with the toe of his shoe. Nick stirred. Blinked.

"What?"

"People sleep in beds."

"This is my bed."

"This is the living room."

"I'm living."

"Go up to bed if you want to sleep. We have two small children around here. I don't want either one of them finding his uncle passed out on the living-room floor with a glass of Scotch next to him."

"Go away."

"Get up."

Nick got up slowly, rubbed his neck, winced with pain.

"Well, that's what you get for sleeping on the floor."

"IT's getting so I hate to ask him to do anything. The other day the dryer wasn't working. I asked him to help me hang up some clothes. He gave me such a look. Everything he does around here he does so grudgingly. He doesn't sleep, he's up at all hours of the day and night, pacing. He doesn't know what to do with himself. You might talk to him about getting a job here."

But Nick didn't want to get a job. "I don't know how long I'm going to stay here, what's the point."

"We've talked about this before."

"Yeah, you're right, we have, so let's not talk about it again now."

"It would be good for you to have a job."

"I had a job where I was."

"Nick, get a real job, get out. You want to remodel houses—fine, be an architect, apply to school here, do it right."

Nick shrugged. "What am I supposed to be doing here? What *can* I do here?"

"You're supposed to be helping us. Is it so much? So hard to understand?"

"She just kept writing me and writing me. So now I'm here. I'm the right person, that's what she wrote me."

"And we're happy you're here."

"Now I'll spend the rest of my life taking Rose up and down

the stairs and walking her to the bathroom."

"That's the last thing I want to see you do."

"My ass it is."

"Nick, help your mother. Do what she says. Take an interest in the children. You know Richard could use someone to take him out, play with him. He's been through plenty, this hasn't been easy for him. He remembers a certain . . ." Solomon lowering his voice, ". . . man whom we don't mention around here, and he wonders what's wrong with himself that this man disappeared. He thinks he did something—to make it happen. That he's responsible for his disappearance, you get me?"

"Sort of."

"What don't you get?"

"I get you!"

"All right, well, either you do or you don't, not sort of, there's nothing to get excited about, you could spend time with him."

"I do."

"Well? Is it so awful? Keep on. That's something you can do. And it would be good for you. Nick, do me a favor. Watch your language and don't drink in front of him."

"Anything else?" Nick held out his hand. "Fingernails okay?"

"No, I have a reason. I don't want any lawyer or court psychiatrist getting this kid up there saying his uncle's passed out on the living-room floor and that he likes to drink some pale-brown substance that smells like turpentine. You know we have no idea what Price is going to do about these kids."

"Oh, Dad."

"Don't oh-Dad me! Listen to me for once. What do you think I was worried about with you lying there in the middle of the living-room floor at eight in the morning?"

"He wasn't even up!"

"That's not my point! What if he were?"

"And I hadn't drunk too much."

"The hell you hadn't."

"I'd just fallen asleep."

"Nick, I can't fight with you over every little point. I have enough problems without you, too. Either you're here to help and you'll do what we want or—"

"We? Who's we? I'm talking to you."

"We? I . . . your mother and I."

"Just say I. One of you at a time is enough."

Solomon shrugged. Nick stared out the window.

Solomon looked at his watch. "I've got to get to the office. I'm already late. Listen to me for once. And you might consider what I've told you about getting a job here. As a matter of fact, I'm supposed to see Peter Bradley from the bank later on this afternoon. He'll be in the office."

"What's the matter with him?"

"Oh, I'm not sure. Sounds like it might be a pinched nerve in his neck."

"Oh, tough shit."

"You've got some attitude. He likes you. Do you want me to talk to him about it?"

Nick stared out the window. "This is what you want, isn't it? Me to get a job at the bank, sleep in the attic. . . ."

"You can help out. And working in a bank, what are you doing that's any better?"

"What's wrong with what I do?"

Solomon staring at Nick. Nick, square-jawed, staring out into the yard.

"What's wrong with banking?"

"I'm not interested in banking."

"There's nothing to hang your head over in banking. How else do you think businesses are created? I'll tell you, Nick, if I hadn't some of that awful stuff called money put away, where do you think I'd be now with your sister?"

"Where are you now?"

"I'll tell you where I am now with your sister. Right here. In my own house. At least she isn't a ward of the state. Yes, don't look at me. A ward of the state. You ought to see how *those* people are treated. No, you don't have to . . . it still hasn't dawned on you, you still didn't see how they treated her in Saint Mary's. That was good. Wonderful. And I was lucky to have the bucks to pay for that, too. And Doris. Violet. And Teresa. And Mrs. Pasternak. And a few other things around here. You don't know a few things, buster. As a matter of fact, maybe you've got the right idea, maybe you'd better sit on your butt in this chair a little while longer and do a little thinking, you're such a wise guy. Sit and think."

"You're right here in your own home, with your money, right?"

"You're damn right."

"You remember telling me you wished you'd sold this house?"

"No."

"Come off it. Coming back from out there. You sat right over there on that sofa and told me."

"Well, vaguely."

"Yeah, vaguely, vaguely my ass. You remember, you wished you'd sold this house and gotten a house on the water in Marblehead. But Mother couldn't bear to part with the house. This wonderful house."

Solomon looking out the window.

"Yeah, look out the window."

"Well, what of it?"

Nick held out his arms to take in the house. He stared at Solomon.

"Okay, so stare at me. What of it?"

"You *know* what of it."

"No, what of it? As it turns out, I'm damn glad I didn't sell it. If I had, I'd be sunk now. Where do you think I'd be putting everybody. In the park?"

"You wouldn't have to put anyone anywhere."

"Why not?"

"Because if you'd sold the house, you wouldn't be stuck in this madhouse."

Solomon looking at Nick. "If I'd sold the house?"

"If you'd *done what you wanted*, and sold the house."

"Yes."

"It just couldn't have happened."

"I don't get you. What's *it*?"

"Just it. Everything. None of this could have happened."

"Why not?"

"It just couldn't have."

Solomon looked out the window. He looked at Nick. Circles under his eyes. Light striking his face. Whiskers. Unshaven.

217

Solomon looked at his watch. "I'm late. I don't have time for this now." Solomon lowered his voice: "Think about what I said. About the job. And it might help you to sleep at night when the rest of the world sleeps and get up when the rest of the world gets up."

"I don't need help and the rest of the world can go to hell."

"That's what I mean, Nick. I'll talk to you later."

Nick didn't answer. He stared out the window.

SOLOMON noticed Nick did make more of an effort with Rose and the children. He played with Richard and Tim, walked them to the park, took them on the swings, built models with Richard, made things out of clay—dinosaurs—which lined the floor of the basement, burned-out spark plugs and pencils stuck in their backs and heads. Nick carried Rose up and down the stairs, spent time trying to talk to her, get her to speak, help her with exercises, tried to encourage her to use the clenched fingers of her right hand.

Bea would say to him, "What you're doing is so vital, if she can relearn the use of her right hand, it will wake up old pathways in her brain, old memories."

Nick would say, "Is *that* right?"

"Yes, it is."

"How?"

Bea would look confused a moment, then say, "Well, there are certain pathways to the brain which carry messages. . . ."

"Certain pathways. Which ones?"

"Oh, I'm not going to talk to you when you're like this. You are so impatient and short with people. You do exactly what you accuse your father of doing. You're just like him."

"Thanks. That's nice to know. But why don't you just tell me, which ones?"

Bea starting for the door. Nick turning to Solomon.

"Which ones? that's all I'm asking. Which nerves, which pathways, Mom?"

Bea walked out of the room.

"Why do you do that, Richard?"

"I'm Nick, remember, Dad?"

"Sorry. Nick. But why do you do that?"

"Do what?"

"Bait her like that? Take that tone with her?"

"Why do I have to listen to her nonsensical wishful thinking about brain pathways and messages? She doesn't know anything at all about it."

"She's been doing some reading."

"She doesn't have the slightest concept of anatomy. So where does she get off telling me about brain pathways."

"Does it hurt you to let her talk?"

"I don't want to hear it! Why do you apologize for her when you *know*—and you've always known—she's in dreamland on this? Why?"

"I'm not apologizing for anyone. I'm asking you to be a little more tolerant. This is making it a little easier for her. Why be so angry?"

"I'm not angry. I just *don't want to hear it.*"

"Nick, remember our little discussion the other day?"

"We're always having little discussions."

"The one just after you got home. About compromise?"

"Yeah, I remember."

"Compromise a little, Nick."

After a few moments, Nick said, "My being here is my compromise."

"So. It's not so bad, is it? Compromise a little more."

"I don't want to hear any more about brains and nerves and messages!"

NICK was teaching Richard to wrestle. Solomon watched Nick's gentle patience with Richard. Nick taught him several holds and then started teaching him how to put them together in different combinations. Richard, in his delight, played rougher and rougher. One of his knees hit Nick hard in the eye. Nick suddenly shook him, Richard's face went bright red, Nick caught himself, seemed to wake up, tried to joke, hugged Richard, Richard pushed away, burst into tears, ran from the room. Nick remained on his knees a minute looking at his hands. Solomon sitting in the chair shook his head. Nick got up slowly, walked toward the door. He stopped, glanced back quickly at Solomon; they exchanged glances. He walked out.

A few minutes later, Nick appeared in the yard. He walked in tight circles, stopped, put one hand down in the grass, then the other, stood on his hands. Balanced a moment. Walked on his hands. Fell. He lay still a minute. Got up, paced around the yard, distracted, stopped. Seemed to be thinking of something. He patted his pockets for cigarettes. He pulled out a bent cigarette, straightened it, examined it minutely, lit it, and took a puff. He walked in tight circles smoking the cigarette; suddenly, he threw the cigarette down, ground it out, and threw the pack into the hedge. He did a handstand, stood motionless several moments, came to his feet, returned to the hedge, felt into the hedge, pulled out the pack, inspected it. He dug out another cigarette.

Later, Nick still hadn't settled down. He turned the tv on, switched the channels for several minutes, turned the tv off, then turned it back on without the sound, and began to read, glancing up at the tv from time to time. Solomon came in and Nick was reading standing up, walking back and forth with a book in his hand.

"What are you doing?"

"Reading."

"Why don't you sit down? Are you watching that tv or aren't you?"

He turned off the tv, closed the book, looked at Solomon. "Is she ever going to get out of that goddamn bed again or do we all just stay here forever?" He walked out of the room.

Solomon heard Nick close the door and slowly climb the stairs to the attic.

SOME time later, Solomon heard a commotion in Rose's room, Bea went to investigate, and after a few minutes, Solomon went into the bedroom to find Rose excited, slurring "Shut him up."

"What's the trouble here?"

"Oh, Rose is upset, she says Nick is disturbing her."

"How?"

Bea pointed at the ceiling. "Well, the attic room is right over-head and she says she can hear him moving around."

Rose slurred, "Can! Nick keeps moving. Make him stop!"

Bea walked closer to the head of the bed. "No, Rose, I won't make him stop, nobody is making anyone do anything around here. Nick has a right, too."

"No, no."

Doris sat up in her bed. She lit a cigarette and pulled the ashtray closer to her on the bed table. The gray tv light flickering on them. "See, Rose, what'd I tell ya, he wasn't really making so much noise. I told her, Mrs. Solomon."

"Yes, Doris. Thank you. And Rose, I don't think you can really hear him, can you?"

"Can!"

All four stopped for a moment and listened.

"I don't hear anything."

"Make him stop."

"I can't make him stop. He has a right."

"No, no, no!"

"No? He doesn't?"

Rose half smiled. *"No!"*

"I see you smiling. You know he has a right, don't you?"

Rose suddenly screamed, *"No!"*

Solomon felt Nick behind him. He waved Nick back with his hand, stepped farther into the room.

"You hear Nick overhead disturbing you now?"

Rose nodded.

Solomon nodded to Nick and Nick stepped into the room.

Rose looked from Nick to the ceiling and back to Nick. "Hate you!"

Nick stared at Rose.

She slurred again, "Hate you!"

Bea said, "Rose, we'll have none of that, what kind of example is that for your children?"

"Hate you!"

Nick flinched. He looked at Rose another moment, turned, hesitated, "Go to sleep, Rose." He left.

Rose suddenly half rose up in her bed and slurred, "No no no, never sleep, never sleep, never sleepneversleepneversleep . . ."

221

Bea gestured toward the door. Downstairs, Solomon found Nick sitting in the kitchen. They sat at opposite ends of the table, but didn't say anything.

Bea came in. "Do you want a cup of tea? Joe? Nick?"

They shook their heads, no.

Bea made a cup of tea and sat down. Nick glanced up at the ceiling. Took a deep breath and sighed. Bea said in a hushed voice, "Don't you see, she is very sensitive. She has very sensitive ears. She hears and feels everything that happens in this house. You have to be a little more careful."

Solomon and Nick exchanged glances.

"I know how hard some of this is. Her saying 'hate you,' I know that's not easy. But she can't help it."

"Why not? She says hate you, she means it. Why are you always apologizing for her? Hate you means I hate you. Not I love you, not I like you . . ."

"No, it's not that simple. Though you find it convenient to think so."

"I do, do I?"

"Yes, you do. It makes it easier for you to despise her. That way you don't have to lift a finger and can go on your merry way. Though you're finding that not so easy to do, are you?"

"And you've appointed yourself my conscience, is that it?" Nick asked.

"If I have to, I have to. Too bad, at your age. I thought I'd raised you better. The thing you don't see is that Rose loves, too. Sometimes that hate-you business is her way. I don't let it bother me. Some people have a harder time loving than other people."

Bea glanced at Nick, tried to meet his eyes, but he stared at the table.

"She's not so different from someone else I know around here, is she?"

Bea reached over to touch Nick's hands, but he pulled them away.

Bea went on speaking in a hushed voice: "Nick, you of all people could do so much good for her—and for yourself—if you could get over these negative feelings you have. Don't think she doesn't know how you feel about her. You might not say in so many words, but, well, for instance, just now, in her

222

room, your tone of voice when you said, 'Oh, go to sleep,' she is *very* acute, she knew you were saying 'Oh, just go to hell.' She picks these things up, that's what you both do not seem to understand at times. But she does understand. Everything."

Nick took another deep breath. His eyes momentarily went to the ceiling. "She knows everything and she hears everything, right, Mom? Just how do I feel about her?"

"Well, it's clear. You resent her. Isn't that right? Now that you've brought this up, you've resented her from the beginning. You're selfish, and she interferes with any pleasures or whims you might choose to indulge at any given moment. So what's the big secret? Tell me if we're wrong."

Nick didn't answer. He stared at his hands.

"Nick?"

Nick stood up. He crossed the kitchen floor, turned, took another deep breath.

"Nick?"

"What?"

"You didn't answer us."

He nodded. "Us. We. Why do you always say *we*?"

"When did I say *we*?"

"Just now. *Tell me if we're wrong*. And, *you didn't answer us*."

"Did I say *we*?"

"Yes."

"Well, what of it, you're nit-picking, what's that have to do with anything?"

"I'm not nit-picking. You're saying Dad feels the same way you do."

"Yes, if I said *we*, I assume I speak for your father and myself. What's wrong with that?"

"Why?"

"Well, look, Nick, you haven't answered my question."

Nick pacing. Thinking. "And you do it, too, Dad. You said *we* the other day—for Mother and you."

"Why quibble over something like that? I, we, what's the difference, it's a minor point. The real matter at hand here is your mother's question—which you seem to be avoiding as hard as you can. Why don't you answer your mother's question?"

223

"I don't think it's a minor point. Not when Mother says I'm selfish and I resent Rose, and then says she's speaking for both of you. Is that what you think, too?"

"Goddammit, why don't you just answer her question?"

"Is that what you think, too? Is she speaking for you, too? I just want to know who *we* is around here."

"You're avoiding her question."

"And you, mine."

"And so, since you avoid answering, we assume you have something to hide and we will assume your answer is yes, you resent your sister. Which comes as no surprise to us."

Nick pacing. "We. Us. Because when you talk to me—both of you—you both say *we,* but when I talk to you separately, you don't agree with each other half the time."

"We do on basics, Nick."

"You just did it again. We. Dad and you agree. You hide behind each other."

"Oh, no one's hiding anything here except maybe you—and all this Women's Lib business about sex roles . . ."

"What's that got to do with anything, sex roles?"

"I'm just telling you, if you'll give me a chance; your father and I might say 'we' because we don't go for that sex-role stuff around here. I help him, he helps me, if there's something that needs doing, one or the other of us just does it. We've always been that way. Our friends, too.

"And, Nick, why don't you answer my questions instead of dodging around with this word game?"

"You didn't answer my question. You don't even take it seriously. Oh, forget it." After a moment, Nick said, "That sleep business, I just said, 'Go to sleep,' and she went crazy."

"What's the point of talking to you, Nick?" Solomon making a sound of disgust.

"I'll tell you why she got so upset, Nick. First, it was your tone. And the look on your face. But beyond that, don't you understand what she was saying?"

"No."

"She was as good as dead for months. Unconscious. And then, for months after, she lay in bed in a strange place, helpless, unable to move, feed herself. And the people around her in Saint Mary's, not all of them but some, unfortunate, uneducated people, made jokes right in front of her, said she was nothing. And she could hear and understand it all. Did you know that?"

"No."

"Well, see, dear, this is what I'm talking about, if you had taken an interest, you'd know."

"But no one tells me."

"We don't tell you because you show no interest. We feel we can't depend on you so we don't tell you."

"Depend on me for what?"

"For anything."

"Okay, you can't depend on me for anything. Are you going to tell me what it means, this 'never sleep.'"

"'I never sleep.' She's saying, 'I'm not dead.' Isn't it clear to you?"

Nick sighed. Started pacing again. Solomon watched him. Nick carefully placed his feet in all of the black tiles as he walked toward the table, the white tiles going away. "And goddammit, Nick! Can you stop this goddamned pacing! This is just what started all this commotion in the first place. You are never still. Rose is right. It's damn irritating! Why can you never be still? What is wrong with you? Just stand still, goddammit!"

Nick stopped. He stared at Solomon.

"Dear, keep your voice down."

Solomon glared at Nick.

Bea reached over and said in a quiet voice, "Calm down, dear."

Nick turned and started for the door.

Solomon half stood. He was trembling. Bea held his hand. "And after all of this, you still didn't ever answer your mother's question, just how you feel about Rose, did you? Nick! Did you?"

Solomon heard the door slam, felt Bea's hand on his. He sank back in the chair.

SOLOMON held Rose's foot gently in his hand. He felt the calf, the rigidity of the paralysis in the bowed foot. He held her

225

foot a moment longer, kneeling on the floor in front of her wheelchair.

"Hurts!"

Solomon looked up at her. "I know," he said softly, "I know."

"Fix it!"

Solomon was quiet. He slid her sock on, fit her foot back into the stiff shoe, and tightened the straps to the back.

"Throw away! Hurts!"

He remained kneeling in front of the wheelchair another moment, then pushed himself up, grunted.

"Fix it! You can! Cigarette!"

Solomon lit a cigarette and held it out to her, Rose puffed the cigarette hard, gasped, puffed again.

"Easy, Rose."

She smoked the cigarette down to the filter, Solomon put it out.

She was still. She looked out the window. Look at her long red nails. Several rings on her fingers. Her wedding ring. She touched it with the pad of her thumb. Her fingers trembled suddenly. Solomon looked at the skin on the backs of her hands, her wrists. Pale-red discolorations remained from the lacerations, poor circulation, a bluish cast. Her eyes sad.

"What's the matter, Rose?"

"You look so old," she slurred. "Tired."

"Yes, well, people get older, Rose."

"Work too hard," she slurred. She coughed. Tapped herself. "My fault. You need rest."

"I'm fine, Rose."

"No, not fine, work too hard."

"I like to work, what else would I do?"

"Rest. Fish. Have fun. Done enough work."

"Rose . . ."

"You are right. Always. Perfect." Her hand trembled toward herself. "Wrong. Always."

Solomon sat down next to her. "Rose . . ."

"Don't want you old, Dad. Please."

"Sweetie, people get older. That's the way it is. But I'm a long way from being old."

Her hand trembled toward herself.

226

"Made you old."

She trembled. Her hand trembled toward her hair, she convulsively grabbed a handful of hair and made a noise which was somewhere between a sob and a whine, "Made you old, God! God!" She tossed her head from side to side.

"Calm down, sweetie. I'm not old and no one's made me old or made me anything else in my life I haven't wanted to be. Want another cigarette?"

She nodded. Solomon held another cigarette, again she puffed the cigarette, puffed, puffed, smoked, was quiet.

"Want to walk again. For you, Dad."

Rose made a convulsive move in the wheelchair.

"Easy, Rose."

"Walk for you, Dad. Won't have to work."

"Calm down, Rose," Solomon hesitated. "You will walk. In time, Rose. In time."

"Will?"

"I hope so."

"Now! Want to walk now!"

"Relax, Rose. Everything in good time. You're getting better. I'm happy working. I'm thankful I can work and I'm happy working."

"No, no, you are not. Can see. You are tired."

"I'm all right, Rose, and everything's all right. We have the boys here, they're good boys, we're glad to have them, glad to take care of them, everything's fine."

"Where's Price?"

Solomon didn't answer. Rose stared out the window a long time in silence. She tapped herself with her hand. "Can walk, then you can rest. Be young again," she slurred.

"No, Rose, I could not become young again."

"You could. You will!"

"Calm down. I'm happy to be exactly what I am."

Rose tapped herself. "Walk and you will become young again!"

"No, but that's why we have the children. They are young."

"You!"

"All right, Rose."

Rose caught her breath. She stared at the floor a long time.

227

She slurred, "Sorry, Dad, sorry."

Solomon took her hand. "I know you are, Rose. But it's not your fault."

She nodded.

"No, Rose, some things just happen. And we don't know why."

She shook her head, no, tapped her chest. "My fault. Sorry, Dad."

"I'm sorry, too. We are all sorry."

"Made you old," she slurred. "Wrong, always wrong."

"Rose."

"Sorry, Dad." Rose trembled. Her face flushed red, she began to cry. Solomon got up, put his arm around her. He could feel her frail rigid back and shoulders beneath her shirt, feel her shoulders shake.

He wiped her cheeks. He tried to say something to her, but couldn't think of anything. He said her name once, "Rose," but could think of nothing more to say.

"NICK, of all the places in the house, do you have to sprawl right there, in that particular place, on the living-room sofa?"

"I'm not sprawled."

"I do try to keep one room neat and looking nice."

"I'm wrecking it."

"Those jeans don't look exactly clean. . . . Look, Nick, this does not have to be half as bad as you're making it. You could have your friends in here, you could . . ."

Nick looked at Bea. He looked at Solomon. He made a face.

"Well, why not?"

"Are you kidding. In here?"

"Why not?"

"With what goes on in here?"

"I think you'd find your friends a lot more tolerant—and sympathetic—than you've given them credit for. Are you ashamed? Your father's a grown man and he's not ashamed. You might learn a few things from him, you know."

Nick shook his head.

"Nick, why can't we talk to each other?"

"Talk."

"How can I talk when you take that tone?"

"You'll find a way."

"Sometimes I think you see us—your father and me—as we used to be—why don't you see the way we are now, today? We change. You change. People change. We've changed and you've changed. We both have to give a little."

Nick didn't say anything.

"I feel you're reacting to us the way you see us at some point in the past."

Nick didn't say anything.

"You still see us as though you were fifteen and we were your parents. But so many things have changed. Maybe we should all take a good hard look at ourselves."

Nick made a face.

"So wrinkle your nose. But do you ever offer anything constructive? No. You wear this look on your face. What's it say? Oh, we get it. The message is clear. Yes, we're all a big bunch of bastards, aren't we?"

Nick still didn't say anything.

Bea looked over at Solomon—at last—and Solomon waved for her to stop. Either it didn't register or she ignored him.

"I don't know why you must think that we're so terrible. It makes something about all of this easier for you, doesn't it? Exactly what, I don't know. Would it be easier for you to turn your back and walk out on us, then? Nick?"

He shook his head. "I am not going to get drawn into anything with you." He said each word precisely as though he could allow just each word, no more, no less. Anything more might be dangerous.

Solomon shook his head at Bea to let it drop right here. She hesitated. He turned. Paused. She said in a quieter voice, "What do you mean, 'get drawn into'? I'm trying to have an exchange of ideas with you. So what is there to 'get drawn into'? People talk. People understand."

Nick gave Bea a strange smile.

Bea said, "I'm interested in what you have to say."

Nick turned to Solomon, nodded several times, and smiled. It was a peculiar smile and it made Solomon uneasy.

229

"I repeat, Nick, what are you so afraid of?"

Nick said in a mocking voice, "Oh, you, I'm afraid of you."

"Why can't we talk?"

Nick sat up. He looked at her. His voice changed. "I don't want to talk to you."

"Why? Am I so bad? Do you have something to hide?" She paused. "I don't."

"I have nothing to hide. And if I did have something to hide, why would it be from you?"

"I don't know. Why would it?"

"I don't and it wouldn't be."

"Well, then?"

"Talking to you is a waste of time."

"I see. Very nice. Do you want to tell me why?"

"It's a can't-win proposition."

"And what does that mean?"

"I don't know, but I know when I can't make myself understood."

"Do you understand yourself?"

"Does anyone? Do you?"

"Yes, I do."

"You do, do you? You're the only person I know who could sit so smugly with their hands—"

"Her hands, Nick."

Nick turned and looked over at Solomon. "What?"

"His hands. Only *person*, you know, *his* hands."

"Just be quiet."

"That certainly is a nice way to talk to your father. Full of respect."

Nick took a deep breath. Paused. Closed his eyes. Opened them. Started again: "Only person I know who could sit there and smugly say you know yourself."

"I don't think so at all. I think your father could say the same thing. Couldn't you, dear?"

Solomon didn't answer.

"Dear?"

"Look, please . . ."

Bea said, "I think we understand ourselves."

"He doesn't answer and you say *we*. I can't talk to you."

230

"You're talking to me."

"But you is always *we*."

"Well, we'll just talk, you and I. Your father wants to sit and read the paper, he can read the paper. So? So let's talk."

After a long pause, Nick said, "What would you do if I were married and had a wife and kids of my own now?"

"You're not, so what's the point?"

"But if I were?"

"Well, what of it?"

"Would you still expect me to sit here and take care of her kids and her and do whatever else it is you expect?"

"I'd expect you to be a person and have feeling for another under any circumstance, Nick."

"Yeah, but that's not what we're talking about now, is it? Having feeling for someone is different from being on twenty-four-hour call."

"No one's got you on twenty-four-hour call."

"Would I be here if Price had stuck around?"

"If, if, if. What's the point of *if*? This is reality, here, the way things are. Let's get out of the past. Move on. Be constructive. We've asked you to help us out at this difficult time. It's not going to last forever."

"The hell it's not. She's turned the clock back on us, and we're going to be here forever."

"You know, you are so afraid to give one single bit of yourself. You're selfish. In plain English."

"I'm selfish? You don't care about me or my life and *I'm* selfish?"

"Well, what were you doing that was so important that you couldn't give up something of yourself to help us? If you were going to school, that might be one thing. Oh, look, it's your whole attitude—"

"You don't see or care about my life."

"Nick, if you feel that way, then you're twisted."

"I'm twisted."

"When you talk like this, you are."

"You'd use me up, and Dad up, and everything and everyone else up."

After a long time, Bea looked up from the floor and said in

231

a quieter voice, "You think I made your father take this on, don't you?"

"You're damn right I do. I know it."

"He wouldn't have wanted it any other way, go ahead, ask him, he's sitting right here."

"I know what he'll say. *We. We. We. Your-mother-and-I.* But he doesn't know himself anymore."

"But you know. We're all bastards, aren't we, Nick? This makes it easier for you. Somehow. But go ahead, ask him. What are you so afraid of? He's sitting right over there. Dear?"

Solomon shook his head. "Look, you two."

"Why don't you ask him, Nick?"

"Why don't you both stop?"

Nick said, "You'd use me up. You'd use him up. He's sixty-three and working like a horse."

"I don't mind, Nick."

"You like it, don't you, Dad?"

"If I have to, I have to."

"He likes it, Mom. *If he has to, he has to.*"

"He's not afraid, you are."

"Talk about compromise, maybe if you'd stop yammering at him, and made it more acceptable, he could have found some way to have at least a little rest. But no, you wanted all of it— her, the kids, miracles, everything! Now let him work himself to death."

"This is the first time I've seen you show any concern about your father."

"You're going to kill him."

There was a long silence. Then Bea said in a quiet voice, "I pity you, Nick. You must be very unhappy."

"I don't want pity or anything else from you."

"You have no compassion. If you had any real compassion for your father, you wouldn't talk this way. And her children, do you really think your father doesn't want to do this for her children? They're helpless in this situation. But all you can do is hate them. No compassion. None. Not even for yourself. If nothing else comes of this, let's hope that you can develop some feeling for other people."

"People who don't feel the way you do have no feeling! She—" Nick nodded up toward the ceiling "—made a mess of everything in her life. Even suicide. Here we are living in the afterlife of a failed suicide."

Bea stood up. She walked deliberately over to Nick and slapped him hard. Nick stood holding his cheek. He looked down at Bea. Solomon quickly stepped between them.

"That's all. That's it."

Bea was trembling.

Nick seemed oddly calm and quiet. He held his cheek.

His voice was very soft, "She's been waiting to do that from the beginning."

His voice was distant, and he seemed almost calm for the first time since he'd come home. He took his hand from his cheek and Solomon saw red finger marks and a bruise from Bea's ring. Bea turned and walked from the room. Solomon looked at Nick. Started to say something.

Nick said, "Don't. You talk too much when I need you to be quiet and don't talk at all when I need you. Don't talk anymore now, please."

He turned and walked out the front door.

Nick was gone several days, he wasn't at any of his friends, or at least, if he was, they weren't saying. One evening, he just walked in. Solomon had been dozing in front of the tv with Tim on his lap. He woke suddenly and Nick was standing in the dark.

"Your mother's been worried sick."

Nick didn't answer. Solomon shifted Tim in his lap.

"You might have called—at least called me, Richard."

"I'm Nick."

"Nick, I'm sorry. I'm tired. Nick. I understand you're angry at your mother, but you might have called me. If you were trying to upset her—upset her even more—you succeeded. What were you trying to do?"

"I needed to get out."

The color from the screen flickering on Nick. A bruise and swelling on Nick's face?

"For Christ's sake, what happened to your face?"

"Nothing."

"Nothing? I can see from here, nothing. You've got a black eye, you're all banged up. Turn on the light. Come here and let me look at you."

"I'm fine."

"You're not fine!"

"If there's one thing I don't need, it's a doctor!"

Solomon shrugged. "Suit yourself. I can only offer."

"Don't."

"What happened to you?"

"What do you care?"

"You're my son. I care. I know you find that hard to believe or accept right now, but I care."

Neither spoke. Solomon watched an ad for Krazy Glue.

Nick said, "Buy some."

Solomon said, "I will."

Solomon said, "Are you going to tell me, Nick?"

Nick shrugged. "What's there to tell? I was in a bar. The news was on and then there was something about Nixon. Some slob at the end of the bar bought a round for everyone and said, 'Here's a toast to Nixon, our greatest president.' "

"So?"

"So everyone threw down the toast. I just left mine sitting on the bar. After a minute, the guy noticed and called down to me, 'What's the matter with you?' I didn't say anything. He got up and said, 'What's the matter with you, don't you like Nixon?' I still didn't say anything.

"This guy comes over and says, 'I'm talking to you. Don't you like Nixon? Pick up your drink and drink it.' "

"Well, from the looks of your face, you didn't, did you?"

"Drink it? No, but you haven't seen his face, either."

"I'm not interested in his face. I'm interested in your face. All right, what happened?"

"I said 'No, I don't like Nixon.' Since he was asking me."

"And you hit him."

"No, see, you've got me wrong. I was trying to let it go. It was getting a little tougher, since the guy gave me a direct order to drink. Then he pushed the drink toward me. 'Drink

234

it,' he said. I pushed it back. He slid it over again. 'Pick it up.' I picked it up. I finally figured if this guy liked Nixon so much, he could drink the drink himself. So I threw it in his face."

Solomon was silent.

"You should have known I'd do that, Dad. You've always told me I didn't know how to serve a drink properly."

"Why couldn't you just have thanked the guy, sipped the drink, and let it go?"

"I did. I left it alone on the bar. He wouldn't leave me alone."

"You know what I mean."

"Is that what you would have done?"

"I don't drink in bars, so I wouldn't have had this problem to begin with. But yes, that's what I would have done."

"I doubt it."

"I would have."

"Well, too bad for you. I didn't feel like it."

"You like being banged up any better?"

"No, but I drink what I want when I want. I don't drink to Nixon. And it wasn't even that guy who hit me. I had a bead on him the whole time, I knew what he was getting ready to do."

"Then why are you all banged up?"

"Some other guy hit me from the side."

"Wonderful."

"I got him. Then I got the other one."

"Wonderful."

"Not wonderful, but those were the cards."

Solomon was silent. "You didn't have to pick them up."

"Okay, I didn't. Whatever you say, Dad."

"So you're a bar fighter."

"I didn't start it."

"And you're all banged up. I know a little about this. Some of my patients come in, I have a look, ask a few questions, how'd you get this scar across your cheek. Oh, a little cut? I see. Four inches long. Shaving? I know where they get their scars. And you wanna know something? I know all about their scars—the ones who are still walking around and can answer. The blacks make long ones with razors and the Puerto Ricans

235

have nice neat holes. The ones still walking around. You know why the Puerto Ricans have nice neat holes? Because they stab each other. They don't like razors, they like to make a nice neat hole. You know, you've got something in common with each of these guys—they all thought they had to pick up the cards and play them, too. And you know, this goes on every night of the week and on Friday night starting at eight o'clock, they do a special feature. Want to come down to the emergency room with me and watch the parade? Every night of the week, but Friday night they really get warmed up. But you know something? That's nothing, either. Because Saturday night is the big one. Then they really do it up big. It goes like this. There's usually an intern, a resident, a trail of blood from the parking lot, and two women sobbing and tearing their hair in the waiting room. But by then it's too late. Now for variations—"

"Why don't you stop it?"

"You don't like what I'm saying? You're all banged up. But it's not so bad because two slobs you don't give a shit about— to put it in a way you'd understand—got worse. So what's the point? You've accomplished something?"

"You asked me, I told you."

"Yes, I guess you've accomplished something. The first guy who hit you didn't have a razor. Or a knife. And you lived." Solomon was silent. "You know, I already have one in there." Solomon gestured toward Rose's bedroom. "You know what I mean, Nick?"

"You asked me, I told you."

"And I'm telling you. Has your mother seen you yet?"

"No."

"Well, when she asks, tell her— Let me see that, turn toward me."

Nick turned toward Solomon.

"Tell her you banged it on the car door or something."

"Yeah, I'll tell her I banged it on the car door."

Nick turned and started out.

Solomon stared at the tv a moment more. Felt Tim's warmth against his lap.

"Nick?"

236

"What?"

"Why are you like this?"

"Who started the fight, Dad?"

"It takes two. You have to learn to walk away." Solomon reached down to shift Tim's weight as he spoke. "What's happening to you, Nick?"

"HAS he spoken to you?"

"Yes."

"He'll barely even look at me, much less speak to me. And what did he do to himself?"

"Oh, it's nothing. He's got a little black eye."

"No, it's not a little black eye."

"He's fine, he banged it on the car door."

"He'll barely even look at me." Bea sighed. "Sometimes, I don't know why, I feel I'm fighting both of you. And her, too. Am I the only one who wants her better?"

Bea sat down and held her hands in her lap. She looked exhausted. She stared beyond her feet at some point on the floor. She said quietly, "Well, if I am, then I am."

SOLOMON couldn't remember when he knew for sure. In a sense he'd known from the beginning. But to put Rose through all of that . . . and then, what was the best way to tell Bea? And when?

Without getting into anything too clinical, Solomon sat Bea down and began explaining about the foot. He groped for an analogy. A spring. A series of springs. Since the muscles which brought her foot up—one set of springs—were paralyzed, there was an unopposed and unbalanced force—a second set of springs, if you will—which brought her heel up and turned it in. That's why she was having so much pain. Follow? Yes, of course.

All right, an operation might—"and I am only saying might"—improve this. The Achilles tendon could be lengthened so that the foot could come up to a right angle. Then, by transplanting the tendon which turns the foot in from the inside to the outside of the foot, the relocation of the tendon could keep her foot in a neutral position. It might even allow her to bring her foot up some. Now, in addition, to help her foot remain stable, the astragalus, the os calcis—"Let's call them the ankle bones."

"Dear, I do remember some of my anatomy. . . ."

"Still, let's call them the ankle bones for now. All right, the ankle bones are fused to help hold the correction. Then she'd be in a plaster cast for three months. And after all this, and the physiotherapy, the heat, the massage, she would have to be retrained to use the tendon.

"Remember, the tendon has been moved to its opposite side. So you have to retrain the patient to pull the tendon over—the patient thinks, Pull the tendon over—when she wants the foot to straighten—the opposite. After a while it does become second nature."

Solomon glanced at Bea's face. It was enough to absorb for now.

"It's painful, Bea. Make no underestimation about that. And the time in the cast afterward, that's depressing. There's always the possibility of infection. And I couldn't guarantee anything."

She glanced up at him sharply.

"What is it?"

"What you just said."

"Well, there are no guarantees. And the pain, Bea. After all she's been through . . ."

"You said; I, Joe. 'I couldn't guarantee anything.'"

"Yes, I. Not that anything would happen, but I wouldn't want to blame anyone else if it did. I, yes, I."

"Dear, you've already been through so much yourself. . . ."

"And the younger doctors don't do as much of this operation since the Salk vaccine. I think I'm best for this."

"Why don't we talk to her. Quietly. You and I. See what it is she wants." Bea's eyes remained distant.

"What?"

"Nothing, dear."

"I can see it's something."

"Rose."

238

"What about her?"

"Walking. Rose walking."

Solomon suddenly saying: "I have not said a word about her walking! This is not a question of her walking, but of trying to make her more comfortable—maybe—in the long run!" She looked at him quietly. "No, Bea, don't look at me like that!"

She remained quiet. After a moment she held her hand out. "Shall we talk to Rose? Quietly. You and I."

Solomon took Bea's hand, but he saw she didn't really believe him. She believed Rose would walk.

THEY sat with Rose and she looked from one to the other, suddenly looked frightened and slurred, "Cigarette!"

Solomon gave her a cigarette.

Bea looked at Solomon, and then said, "Dear, I want to talk to you for a minute about the pain in your foot. . . ."

"Hurts!"

"I know."

Then Bea softly explained about the operation and said, "Dear, it's not a dangerous operation, at this point it's just a question of whom you would be most comfortable with. You could have another doctor, you could have your father—"

"Dad!"

"Another surgeon—"

"Dad!"

"Think about it a bit, dear."

"Dad!"

"Are you sure you understand what we're talking about? Everything involved?"

Rose nodded. "Foot. Hurts!"

"And Dad will operate on it. That's what you want?"

Rose nodded.

Solomon said, "Now don't get the idea there will be any miracles."

"Will be."

"No, because there won't be." Solomon explained and demonstrated the operation. "But there will be no miracles. This is not the movies."

Rose giggled. "It is, you will."

Bea suddenly said, "Rose, are you sure you wouldn't rather have someone else do it?"

"Dad is best."

They were quiet a moment. Rose stared at Solomon; her eyes were sad.

Bea said, "Why wouldn't you rather have someone else do it?"

"No! Dad. He must."

"Dad must?"

Rose nodded.

"Why?"

Rose tapped herself. "Made Dad old."

"What?"

"Oh, she went through this with me the other day. She thinks she made me old." Solomon smiled. "I'm an old man, all right, Rose. That's me. Old and washed up."

Rose slurred, "Made you old."

"No, sweetheart, Dad's not old."

"Old!"

Bea looked at Solomon, shrugged. "Maybe another doctor would be better, Rose. You think about it a little more. We don't have to decide this morning anyway."

"No!" Rose tapped herself. "Made Dad old!"

"All right, dear, but what's this have to do with anything?"

"Make him young again."

Solomon looked at Bea.

Rose nodded, giggled, puffed her cigarette with loud gasps, went on nodding, her one blind eye staring off. "Make him young again."

Solomon stood up.

Rose suddenly said in a hoarse voice, "Dad!"

"Yes, Rose."

"Come here!"

"I am here."

"Closer!"

Solomon came closer, stood beside her. "Dad," she slurred in a hoarse voice, "promise—"

"What?"

"Promise you won't put—" she tapped herself "to—" She seemed to search into the corners of the room, search the air, the sunlight coming in the window, then in a hoarse voice, whispered something.

Solomon bent his ear closer. "I'm sorry, Rose, I can't hear you. Whisper it again."

Rose whispered again, nodded.

"Won't put you to *sleep?*"

Rose looked around the room.

"*Sleep,* Rose?"

"No, nononever sleep . . ."

Solomon looked at Bea.

"You mean anesthesia, dear?"

Rose nodded.

Solomon said, "Of course, we'll have to use anesthesia, Rose, but it won't be for long."

"Nonono . . ."

Solomon looked at Bea. Then said, "No, Rose, you won't go to . . ." Solomon lowered his voice and whispered ". . . *sleep.*"

Rose slurred, "Neversleep, neversleep."

Solomon took her hand. "You won't go to sleep, Rose. And I'll be with you the whole time. Every second."

Rose nodded, a faint smile on her face.

"Neversleep," she slurred softly.

"No," Solomon said, "never sleep."

EACH morning, Solomon would come down to work and find Nick in the chair by the window, his back to the living room, the radio playing. Afternoons, he would still be there. One afternoon, Solomon dropped his briefcase on the hall table, walked over, and stood in front of Nick.

"Look, Nick, I went ahead and talked about you with Peter Bradley at the bank. He was in the office again the other day. I mentioned the possibility, and he seemed genuinely delighted. So there it is. Go down to the Co-op, get yourself a suit, shave, cut your hair, clean yourself up, and that's it. You'll have something."

Nick stared out the window.

"Nick?"

Nick looked up.

"Did you hear me?"

"Yeah, Dad, I did. Thanks."

"Go ahead, give him a call, he's expecting it."

Nick said quietly, "I don't think so. Thanks anyway."

Solomon could hardly hear him.

"Richard . . . I'm sorry, Nick." Solomon put his hand on Nick's shoulder. "Are you aware that you've been sitting in that chair for, I don't know, days, weeks?"

Nick looked down at the chair. "This chair?"

"Yes! That chair."

"No, I really wasn't." Nick's voice quiet, toneless.

"Well, you have."

"Oh." After a moment, Nick said, "Well, so what?"

"People don't sit in chairs for days, Nick."

"Before you bitched because I wouldn't stay still."

Nick reached into his pocket and pulled out a cigarette. Lit it.

"Got another, Nick?"

"Last one. Here."

"That's all right."

"Take it."

Solomon hesitated, took the lit cigarette.

Nick stared out the window, then said, "She thinks she'll walk, doesn't she?"

"She thinks? . . . Look, I haven't told her any such thing. As a matter of fact, I've told her the opposite."

"But she doesn't really believe you. She thinks you can do anything. You haven't told her she won't walk."

"I've told her what I think is adequate for now. Look, none of us likes this, Nick. I've been watching this situation develop with her foot for some time, I just didn't wake up one morning—"

"Why does it have to be you, Dad?"

"I sewed you up plenty of times and it didn't seem to do you too much harm. And you seemed to be glad when you dislocated your shoulder and were lying out there on the mat and

I went out there and got it back in place for you. Or am I wrong?"

"You got more applause for that than I did for wrestling."

"Sorry, Nick. I'm awful. I'm a terrible guy. I should have left you lying there with a dislocated shoulder." Solomon lowered his voice, "Look, Nick, I realize there are an enormous number of things in this situation which deeply trouble you. Trouble all of us. Maybe we've made some mistakes. Here, in this situation, I feel I can do something. I feel I'm the best person—just being objective—the most capable, for this type of operation."

"No one else could do it?"

"I didn't say that."

"Remember the speech you gave me. About compromise?"

"Yes, sure, it wasn't a speech, it was—"

"It's for others, isn't it? Not for you."

"I've compromised plenty. And don't you forget it! I feel I'm the best person to do this. The best qualified. And it's what Rose wants. If something happened, I wouldn't want to blame someone else."

"Only you are good enough to blame."

"I don't know what you mean by that."

"A member of your family—"

"It's not unprecedented. Gutman did a spine fusion on his daughter. Harry Albright delivered both of his daughters."

Nick shook his head and stared out the window. "She never got away from you and she'll never get away from you."

"I don't know what the hell you are talking about."

"Doctors at the hospital think you've no business operating on your own daughter."

"What the hell do you know? Doctors at the hospital! You know nothing about doctors or hospitals. You're the one who says the whole world can go to hell. Now suddenly you're very sensitive and worried about what people will say. Just what do you know?"

"What do I know? Remember Tad Wilson? I used to wrestle with him—he's a resident now. And he's the one who told me. And where's he getting it, Dad? From *your* peers! Doctors!"

"I should start listening to a bunch of interns and resi-

243

dents? The trouble is you care about what everyone has to say except your father."

Nick looked disturbed.

Solomon shrugged. "I've been criticized before. Many times." Solomon's voice quiet, resigned, sad, "When you do things, you get criticized. It's part of living. There's always someone standing on the sidelines who knows how to do it better."

"Dad—"

"But it did not keep me from doing what I thought I had to do. Listen too much and you'll end up doing nothing but worrying about what other people think."

"Oh, Dad, come on. Please. I didn't mean it like that, don't take that tone of voice."

"Come on, what, please? I see how you feel about me."

Nick suddenly lurched forward and put his head in his hands. "No, you don't. Dad. Please. Stop. Forget it."

"I fished with Jack Murphy for thirty-five years. That's some time, isn't it, Nick? Remember? He was terrific. A good fisherman, a good sport, a great guy. We had great times together. One day, he came into the office with a pain in his foot. It turned out to be cancer. I knew that most of his foot would have to be amputated. I told him so. And you know something, Nick? I didn't like it. You know what I mean, Nick?"

Nick held his head.

"No answer? That's funny, you usually have answers for everything. I'll tell you more. I didn't like telling Jack that he had cancer. Or that his foot had to be amputated. And you know something else, Nick? I didn't like seeing him cry, either. That's right, he cried. He didn't cry much. He cried a little."

"Okay, I get your point, please—"

"No, you don't get my point at all, and now you are going to listen! I told Jack and he cried."

"You never understand."

"Then he pulled himself together and asked me if I would do the operation and oh, you know how much I enjoy these things, I love them. My ego. My enormous ego! This is just what I want and need to satisfy my enormous ego." Solomon gazed out the window, fell silent.

After a moment, he said quietly, "Jack asked me if I would do it, Nick. And I said, yes. I would rather not have. Because I was close to Jack. I hate to amputate. I have always hated it. I hate it each and every time. Amputation, whatever else might necessitate it, is a purely destructive operation. It is a defeat for the surgeon. I do not like to be defeated." Solomon paused. "But Jack asked me. So I did it for him. He was glad I was there. If it helped him that little bit, then I'm glad.

"Afterward, he was great, too. You know, I see a lot of people. I have a pretty good idea when they're faking. Jack really did take it like a man. He didn't complain. He didn't feel sorry for himself. He used the crutches, made the best of things. Even joked about it. He was great."

Solomon silent again. Nick stared at the floor. Solomon took a deep breath and said, "So the boys at the hospital think I'm what? wrong to do the best I can for my family. Well, let them."

Solomon gazed out the window. Repeated, "Let them. You know something, Nick? You live in this world, you get to know a few people. If you're a doctor, you have to take care of them. A lot of them want it that way. That's all. It's not a perfect world. I'm glad I was able to do what I could for Jack Murphy.

"And you know something else? Now I'm glad I'm still well enough and have these two hands and my health and wits and can take care of your sister. Why shouldn't I be able to do everything I can for my daughter?"

Solomon stared at Nick. Nick stared at the floor.

"You, you can sit there and ruminate on all of the gruesome aspects of this and on what a horrible, egotistical son of a bitch I am; and by all means, listen to your know-it-all friends, the interns and residents who are telling you what a sick old man your father is, how horrible that he should do what he can for his daughter. Listen to everyone but your father."

Nick stared out the window.

"Sit here by the window, feel sorry for yourself."

"Dad—"

"Don't call Peter Bradley about the job at the bank because I'll tell him myself you're not interested. Maybe your mother's been right about a lot more than I've realized."

Solomon turned to go. Suddenly turned back. "And about sitting around discussing me with your friends. Think what you want. How horrible I am. Whatever."

"I never said that."

"But don't you dare say another word to anyone about what goes on in this house. Ever! Too bad I have to tell you. You don't have the brains to keep your mouth shut."

SEVERAL nights before the operation had been scheduled, Solomon awoke. Sleeping lightly, on and off in a fever, something had been calling him out of sleep from somewhere in the house. He closed his eyes. Bea's breathing beside him. He drifted back toward sleep, again felt something calling.

He swung his legs over the side of the bed. Reached for his robe.

Blinking in the hall light. Nick's room, gleam of light, the trophies half in shadow. Solomon looked in. Tim sleeping, animals about him on the pillow and floor.

Solomon looked into Richard's room. Richard. Sleeping.

He slowly pushed the door to Rose's room. The wooden floor creaked under his weight. The hall light followed him in.

Doris in one bed. She suddenly let out a snore. Her glasses on the table. Solomon looked around. The vitamins on the dresser. Medicinal smell. Rubbing alcohol. Dermassage. Brace on the chair. A twisted sheet on the floor. Solomon looked at Rose's bed. Empty.

Solomon stepped into the room, stood by the bed, actually felt the sheets. He turned suddenly. Looked behind him. Walked quickly to the bathroom. Turned on the light. No one.

He stopped, stood still, took a deep breath. Listened.

As he started downstairs, he felt a draft, walked to the bottom of the stairs. There was a chill, a breeze.

The front door was wide open.

Solomon stared at the open door. His heart pounding. He looked at the open door, the silence beyond the darkness, the lawn somewhere out there. He'd never, in all the years he lived in the house, come down to see the front door standing silently open like this, in the middle of the night.

It was another moment before he could move. He stepped into the living room, picked up a poker from the fireplace, stood a moment, his eyes moving back and forth in the dark. Again he heard a low sound. He listened, then took several steps, stopped, listened again, suddenly looked behind him. Raised the poker. He reached the heavy front door, but did not close it. He looked back toward the burglar-alarm light. He held his breath, again heard the sound, long, low. He wasn't sure he was imagining it now, he was listening, his heart was pounding hard, loud, in his ears, but he thought the sound had come from the outside.

He stepped into the vestibule, looked behind him. Stepped outside. The night was cool, dark. He looked around, stepped out on the front steps, felt the immense darkness held by the linden towering overhead. Beyond, in the darkness between the house and the elms, a band of bright stars. He listened. He heard the sound louder, but still low. On the lawn, something pale, glowing. He walked through the grass, the poker in his hand.

"Dad."

"Rose?"

"Knew you'd come."

He kneeled. "Rose, how long have you been lying here?"

"Long time." She giggled.

"But how did you get here?"

"Walked." She coughed.

He reached down in the dark, found her hand. Cold. He took off his robe and spread it across her.

"Just a minute, Rose. I'll get your brother to carry you in."

"Knew you'd come."

He remained kneeling beside her. "Rose, where were you going? Where was there to go?"

"A date."

"Now? At four in the morning? Couldn't let it ride until tomorrow?"

"No."

Solomon felt the cool grass at his knees and ankles. The trees stirred. He looked up. Above, darkness, the stars.

He sighed. "A date. I see. Where was the date?" He could

see her, pale, glowing in the grass beside him.

"Florida."

She let out a hoarse laugh in the grass beside him. The laugh, low in her throat. "Florida." Solomon heard himself repeating the word, "Florida," felt something give way in his chest, heard himself suddenly laughing. Florida. The stars bright. Florida. He held her hand, leaning on the poker. "Florida," she slurred, laughing.

It was quiet and Solomon felt cold. He started to his feet.

"I'll be right back, Rose. I'm going to get your brother. He'll carry you inside."

"No. Not inside."

Solomon walked back toward the house, turned once, saw her body glowing in the grass. She was talking, her voice hoarse. She laughed; he walked quickly back toward the house to wake Nick.

BEA stood at the counter fixing a tray. Violet and Doris smoked at one end of the kitchen table, Doris reading *Valley of the Dolls*. Occasionally her lips would move. Solomon nodded to everyone, said good morning to Nick. Nick didn't say anything. Once there was a loud clatter as Nick's hand brushed a cup and saucer. Solomon noticed Nick's hand tremble. Nick didn't raise his eyes from the paper.

Solomon picked up his briefcase. Bea took Solomon's hand, led him out to the living room.

"How long's he going to keep this up?"

"Until he's tired of it, I suppose."

AFTER several more days, Bea said, "Look, Nick, we get the point, we're all monsters and directly responsible for whatever's wrong in your life. You could still make an effort to be civil, don't you think? It would make it easier for everyone—yourself included."

Nick looked up.

After a moment, he said, "There is a shrink in town—Dr. Kramer."

"Yes. We know who he is. We've heard of him."

"I've been to see him once, myself. I want us to go see him."

Bea looked toward Solomon.

Nick added, "Now."

Solomon said, "I thought you were the guy who didn't like doctors. And why must *we* go? You need a shrink, you go. It might not be such a bad idea for you either."

"*We* go."

"Why we? What's wrong with us, your mother and me? We don't feel any need for it."

"I'm not going to talk to you anymore without someone else there."

Bea nodded. "Yes, we're so unreasonable. Look, Nick, let me make it clear how I feel. I think there's altogether too much of this people running to the psychiatrist. Sometimes life isn't a bed of roses. All right. That doesn't mean we have to go running to the psychiatrist."

Nick looked away.

"So look away. Your father's not been happy about a few things. Need I explain? Yet he doesn't go running to a psychiatrist. You don't need a psychiatrist—or a shrink, as you put it—any more than I do. What's your problem? Plain and simple. You don't like the way things are now and you're trying to find any excuse you can to run out. So run. We can't stop you. You can. Run. You'll never have a moment's peace. I know you, Nick. You're sensitive. Is a psychiatrist going to change the way things are, Nick? No, I don't believe in it, I—"

Nick stood up. His face went white. "I don't care what you believe in. I don't want to hear another word about what you believe in. My whole life I've heard nothing else but what you believe in. And for the last four years, positive this, negative that, pathways to the brain, and all the rest. Now you don't have to believe in shrinks just to go with me."

Bea looked at Solomon. "This is exactly what I've been talking about." She turned and walked out.

Nick turned toward Solomon. Solomon said, "I'll consider it."

"Don't do me any big favors."

"As a matter of fact, that's exactly what it will be. A big favor to you. It's sure not for me."

SOLOMON nodded toward the doctor, whom he was sure he
had once met briefly, maybe at a party. He nodded for a glance
of recognition, but Kramer either didn't remember him or
didn't choose to recognize him. Solomon glanced around the
room, some children's blocks on the floor near the window;
the psychiatrist, jacket folded over a chair, in a blue shirt, tie.
A digital clock pulsed softly on the table beside Solomon.

Nick sat near the window and seemed uninterested now
that they were here. He looked out the window. Solomon felt
Bea next to him, the smell of her perfume. Dr. Kramer had
finished his settling-down motions. Still, now Solomon felt the
concentration of his gaze. Solomon looked back. The doctor
had a heavy dark beard, thick black glasses; the gray glare
from the window shined on his glasses. Solomon felt him looking, now at Bea, now at himself, now at Nick. As he turned
his head, there was a flash of light from his glasses. Behind
the glare, his eyes appeared, disappeared. Solomon felt his
eyes on him, again gave a slight nod. The glasses flashed.

The silence seemed to lengthen. Solomon looked to Nick.
Nick slumped by the window. Solomon felt the clock pulse
beside him. He said, "Well, since no one else has much to say
at this point, I'll set the record straight by saying we're here
because Nick requested us to come. Not because we ourselves
feel any particular need."

They were quiet. Solomon looked over at Nick. Solomon
thought he saw Nick nod slightly toward the psychiatrist, but
wasn't sure.

Again the silence grew. What had Nick nodded about?
Again the silence grew. Had he nodded?

"Oh, was it the *we*, Nick? I said *we*, didn't I? Our son seems
lately to have taken violent exception to the use of the word
we by his mother and myself." Solomon smiled slightly at the
doctor. "Terrible, isn't it?"

Dr. Kramer still didn't say anything.

Solomon looked at Nick. "That is it, isn't it, Nick?"

Nick didn't say anything.

Solomon smiled slightly. "In my son's eyes, I just cut and

saw people." Solomon shrugged. "A glorified carpenter. I don't know anything, and have managed to learn very little about human feelings. So I'm a very slow, ignorant guy, I'm insensitive, so I don't understand why *we* is such an awful word from my wife or myself." Solomon sat up slightly. "Except it's rather significant to me that my son, who can't stand the use of this terrible word, *we,* my son insisted that my wife and I— *we*—come to see you." Solomon said, "We're so terrible, we don't want him to be happy, but you see we've come here today."

The psychiatrist, a vague nod?

"So let me ask something of Nick now that we're here. Nick?"

Solomon turned toward Nick. "Nick, suppose you explain to us—all of us—Dr. Kramer, your mother, and myself, just what is it which is so terrible about the word *we?*"

Nick half turned toward Solomon, but did not look at him. He lifted his eyes slightly toward Dr. Kramer, made a slight nod, a faint smile. The doctor seemed to show some recognition in his glance. Nick still didn't look at Solomon or answer.

"Nick, go ahead, why don't you answer or say something? Dr. Kramer and I are both doctors, we're both objective, your mother's not insensitive. This is what you wanted, isn't it?"

"Yes, Nick," Bea's voice behind him. "You've asked us to come, which is a lot more than many other people in our position would have done, we've come, we're here now, so talk. Explain yourself."

Nick looked up. He had that faint smile which Solomon had noticed in the last few months. He nodded several times. "You see." He nodded toward them. He nodded toward the doctor. "You see. This is the way it is."

Solomon said, "What is the way it is? What is so significant here? He's asked us to come, we've come. *What* is the way it is? Nick?"

"Doctor, I'll give it to you in a nutshell. I'm sure Nick's given you an idea of the situation we're in with his sister. We've asked him to help out. It's not easy. Not easy for any of us. He resents the situation, he resents us, he's looking for any way he can to get out, and if he can make us out to be terrible and

251

tell himself what a bastard his sister was—that's the way he'd put it—then he could leave and not feel so bad. Isn't that it, Nick?" Bea said.

Nick stared out the window.

"It's just that he's not finding it so easy to walk away. And we aren't fools. I know who I am and what I am and so does his father. We don't let ourselves get pushed around and we don't swallow a lot of nonsense."

Bea's voice softened. "The thing is, Dr. Kramer, he's really sensitive to other people's needs. I know. Perhaps that's why he's having such a hard time. He doesn't need a psychiatrist. He needs to make up his mind, come to terms with this. It's hard. So what in life isn't hard? Tell me? Some things are hard and we do them anyway. Was it so easy to go through medical school and be a doctor?"

Dr. Kramer turned his head, looked at Bea. Solomon thought he might have wrinkled his forehead. He didn't say anything.

They were silent.

Bea suddenly said, "Now that we're here, he doesn't say anything. He sits there and nods or smiles. This is to signal he feels superior to his mother and father. Yet he wanted us to come, we've come."

Solomon looked over at Nick. Nick stared out the window. Solomon said, "Why don't you answer your mother, Nick?"

Nick's hands were clasped loosely over his lap.

After a moment, Solomon looked at the psychiatrist, shrugged, and said, "He doesn't really seem to be here, does he?"

Dr. Kramer said, "Why don't you say that directly to Nick?"

Solomon said, "I imagine he's heard me."

Kramer glanced at the clock. There were a few minutes left.

Solomon said, "We don't want to take up any more of your time."

But no one moved. They sat in silence.

After a few minutes, Bea said, "I find all of this very unnecessary and very sad."

Kramer said quietly, "The time is up now."

They stood without looking at each other. Dr. Kramer held

the door open. Outside, there was a man reading a magazine. "I'll be just a few minutes." The man nodded without looking up from his magazine.

IN the parking lot, Nick walked toward the street. Solomon called him. "Don't you need a ride home?"

Nick shook his head, no.

Bea said, "Just one minute."

Nick stopped.

"Where are you going in such a big rush that you can't talk to me for one minute? Show some courtesy and come over here."

Nick hesitated. He walked slowly toward her.

"You were the one who wanted to see a psychiatrist. So we went. All you did was sit and stare out the window. You acted totally uninterested. That was the message, wasn't it?"

Nick didn't answer.

"Fine, don't answer. You didn't say more than five words. And yes, you smiled your special smile, which is to convey to us some secret about how awful we are."

Nick stared at the ground.

Bea said, "It isn't cheap, you know."

Nick looked up. He searched her face. "You've spent a fortune on her, her kids, doctors, hospitals, now you tell me a few sessions with a shrink aren't cheap?"

Bea smiled slowly. She shook her head. "So. That's it. That's what's been bothering you. The money we've spent on your sister." She laughed once. "I wouldn't have believed it of you, Nick. Thinking of that money's made you green with envy, hasn't it?"

Nick turned and walked through the parking lot toward the street.

Solomon waved Bea toward the car. Bea called after Nick, "If that's the source of your misery, then go and be in your misery."

AT the next session, Nick would not look at Bea. Once Bea said, "Well, if he doesn't talk, I don't see much point in this, we might as well go." But no one left. They sat in silence for some time, Dr. Kramer watching them.

Toward the end of the session, Dr. Kramer said softly, "I think it might be a good idea if I saw Nick separately for several sessions, then saw the two of you, together, you and your wife, Dr. Solomon."

Nick saw Dr. Kramer for several sessions, but still would not look at or talk to Bea, and once, at home, Bea said, "If this is what Dr. Kramer is doing for you, it can't be very much."

SOLOMON and Bea had been talking to Dr. Kramer for some time about the accident and Solomon had lapsed into silence. Dr. Kramer asked Bea about the way Nick had behaved at the time of the accident and Bea said, "I thought he was callous and indifferent. He just didn't care."

"Why did you feel that way?"

"His whole look, his appearance, his hair, his clothes, they were all part of the life he'd been living.

"And what about the life he'd been living?"

"He was secretive. He'd share nothing with us. He had some job, remodeling houses, but he wasn't really doing anything with himself. All I saw was a kind of hedonistic self-centered preoccupation. He really had no time for anyone else. He showed his concern for his sister by sleeping with waitresses."

"What would you have liked him to do?"

"Not that."

"We've already discussed her husband's behavior at that time."

Bea was silent a long time. "I see what you're trying to do."

"What is that?"

"Suggest I took things out on Nick for the way Price behaved. I can assure you I've never had any problem keeping Nick separate from Price."

Dr. Kramer didn't say anything.

"Isn't that it?"

"I heard no suggestion from me that you took things out on Nick."

Bea looked out the window. After a long time, Bea said, "Whatever is said and done, the truth remains. I know in my heart that we can't depend on him. For anything. We can sit here and add and subtract from now until Doomsday, but that simple fact remains, I know it, and he knows it. Nothing we say or do makes that simple fact more palatable."

Dr. Kramer said, "Some individuals, and Nick may be one of them, simply do not cope well with the kinds of injuries his sister has."

"I think he might make an effort to learn how."

NOTHING changed. They stopped seeing the psychiatrist, Nick drifted around the house without saying or doing anything. He looked at nobody.

Solomon went to see Dr. Kramer once more, alone.

He sat facing Dr. Kramer. He looked at the empty chair by the window, where Nick had sat, the other chair, where Bea had sat, also empty.

They had been talking about Bea and Nick, and Solomon said, "I really don't understand his feelings toward his mother. They can't stand each other, yet Nick used to be closer to his mother than anyone else."

"Until what age?"

"Oh, right up until he went away to college. They actually liked each other's company. They'd sit and talk to each other for hours. About anything. Nick was open. Trusting."

Dr. Kramer didn't say anything. He looked a little surprised.

"Why do you ask?"

"Oh, it's somewhat later than is usual, that kind of mother-son closeness. It usually ends before."

"Well, I'm just telling you. And I don't see anything wrong with it. People being close. From what I see around me, we could use a hell of a lot more of it."

Solomon felt the psychiatrist studying him. He felt uncomfortable and added, "That's what makes his behavior—their behavior—so odd to me now. I'd have expected them to be closer in this situation. They have a similar approach to things. I certainly don't understand why he won't talk to us. He was the one who asked us to come see you. We came. And you saw yourself, all he did was sit in that chair and look away from us, look at the floor, look out the window."

Kramer nodded. "I was watching what went on there."

"Could you make anything of it? I couldn't."

"You and your wife are both very forceful people, you're extremely articulate, highly verbal. . . ."

The psychiatrist thought for several moments. He gestured toward the empty chair. "Nick sat and he looked away or looked out the window—or from time to time looked over to me for help or understanding. At the same time, you said of us, 'We are both doctors, your mother is not insensitive, explain yourself to us . . .' that was what you said?"

"That's right. I think those are almost the exact words. I'm impressed by your memory. What's wrong with that?"

"I didn't say there was. Or wasn't. Did you notice the look on his face?"

"Sullen."

"I don't know if I'd characterize it that way, myself." Dr. Kramer gestured toward a pile of blocks near the window. "I work with children. I've seen that look on the faces of some of the children who come in here."

"Yes, I am glad you see it, too. I'm not alone in this, I'm not seeing things, and I think Nick's been goddamned childish."

The psychiatrist looked at Solomon. He said quietly, "I didn't say that. I said I've seen that look on the faces of children— children who have given up trying to reach anyone because they feel it won't do any good. They feel they can't make themselves understood or get any real response."

Kramer hesitated. "I suspect that this isn't something which started with the accident but is an old pattern of behavior that has reached a crisis situation."

Solomon suddenly thought of Rose. He took a deep breath. "You make it sound like he has something he wants to tell me—or needs to tell me."

"Perhaps."

Solomon turned up his palms. "But what is it they want to tell me?"

"*They?*"

Solomon took a deep breath. "*He*. Nick. What is it he wants to tell me. I've always listened to him. What would he tell me?"

After a time, Kramer said, "I don't know. I don't know if Nick knows himself."

Solomon said, "I've always listened to him."

"Nick might not know himself. He might not even know he wants or needs to tell you something."

Solomon sat quietly. He shrugged. He made a gesture at the air. "Something he wants to tell me. Needs to tell me. Something he doesn't know. Something I don't know. Out here. In the air. Between us. Why such a mystery?"

"I didn't say that."

"Is it such a mystery? Does it have to be such a mystery?"

They were both silent.

"I don't believe in mysteries, Dr. Kramer. Questions, yes. Answers, yes." Solomon drifted. He stared out the window.

"The question came to me as I watched you and your wife, and it struck me, Why are they all so highly verbal? Because they're intelligent, yes. Educated. Yes. But so insistent with words. All the verbalizing. Verbal, but with no trust. Or, verbal, in place of trust. Why no trust? I don't know. And I would have to work with you—all of you—much longer, before we could even begin to approach an understanding in that area. But," the psychiatrist hesitated, "it is all very much in line with several observations I've made of Nick. After talking to him alone, I asked if I might mention whatever I felt could be important in any subsequent sessions with either of you. He pretended to be indifferent, but he actually said I could do what I wanted. I definitely had the feeling he wanted me to transmit his feelings. One thing which came out is that Nick feels there's nothing he can do in this situation."

"Oh, now, that's not quite true, he knows of a number of things . . ." Solomon trailed off under Kramer's gaze.

Kramer repeated, "He feels that there's nothing he can do in this situation. He feels powerless. He feels that whatever he does, it's not right. Or enough. No matter what he does, it is not enough. Or can never be enough."

The psychiatrist thought for a moment. "How long has it

been since he's spoken to either of you?"

"Well, he's said a couple of things to me, but I don't think he's spoken to his mother for weeks."

Kramer nodded. "Nick, in his last session with me, used the words *tricked* and *crazy* several times. Nick said, 'she tricked me,' referring to his mother; he said, 'she has tried—and is still trying—to make me think I'm crazy.' And he said several times, 'she almost did it.' At the end Nick said, 'I'm not crazy.'"

"Why should he think he's crazy? Even ask?" Solomon said, "Do you think he's crazy?"

Kramer said, "What matters right now is the fact that he is very worried about it. And also, that he feels betrayed."

"But who has betrayed him? This I don't understand. His mother has done nothing wrong that I can see. Who has betrayed him? How?"

"What he said is, 'I'm not crazy, they tricked me, but I'm not crazy.' He'll say, 'Everything I'm saying must sound like craziness because I can't tell you how they did it.' He says, 'I haven't figured it out yet. But they did it.'"

"I don't understand."

"Neither does he. I think that is one reason he is not talking anymore."

SEVERAL days later, in the evening, Nick told Solomon that he was leaving.

"Mike Walker is driving to San Diego and I'm going with him. I'm meeting him on the Common at seven tomorrow morning."

Solomon put down the paper. "Just like that. Tomorrow morning. No warning, no nothing. What's the rush?"

Nick didn't say anything.

"And I thought Mike Walker was married."

"He's left his wife."

Solomon studied Nick. "But what are you going to do there? How are you going to live?"

Nick walked out of the room.

Bea said simply, "If that's the way he feels, let him go. I'm sick to death of fighting him."

In the morning, Nick stood in the dark kitchen drinking a cup of coffee, a duffel by the door.

Bea turned on the light.

Nick took another sip of his coffee and looked at the clock on the stove. At Solomon, unshaven in his bathrobe.

Bea said, "All right, Nick, if this is what you want to do."

Nick rinsed the coffee cup in the sink.

Solomon asked, "Have you said good-bye to your sister?"

Nick nodded, yes.

"I don't think so. I looked in. She's still sleeping."

Nick said, "Last night."

Bea said, "I'm sorry for you, Nick. I really am. You're miserable now and you're only going to be more miserable."

Solomon said, "How are you getting down to the Common?"

"Bus."

"No, just a minute, I'll take you."

Upstairs, Solomon pulled on a pair of slacks, a jacket, over his pajamas.

As Solomon stepped into the kitchen, Nick picked up his bag. Bea looked at Nick, looked away.

"Just a minute, Nick, have you said good-bye to your mother?"

"Never mind, dear, just let him go now."

Nick opened the back door.

"Nick, kiss your mother good-bye."

Nick stepped outside.

"Nick, I want you to come in here and kiss your mother good-bye."

Nick stepped into the driveway.

Solomon followed him out.

"Nick!"

Solomon walked to the car. He opened the door. "Just get the hell in."

Nick got in the car. Solomon stared at Nick hard. Nick put his hand on the door handle. Solomon started the car. They drove in silence, Nick staring straight ahead.

When they stopped at a light, Solomon said, "I know you don't want to hear any more out of me, but I have a couple of

259

more things to say and I think you'll be able to stand them." Solomon paused. "You know, Nick . . . someday, I'm not going to be around. Are you listening? All right, I know you're not answering. You don't have to answer. Someday, I am not going to be around anymore."

Solomon glanced over at Nick, thought he saw something pass over his face.

"I'm not being morbid. And it's nothing to get upset about. It's just a fact. I plan on being here a while more. I've just had a checkup and I'm healthy. Pump's fine, blood pressure, the works; maybe I'm more healthy than I've got any right to expect, considering recent developments. But I'm fine, for now. But someday, Nick, I won't be here. And someday, your mother won't be here, either. Before that time comes, I hope you'll be able to change your attitude about a few things."

Solomon glanced over at Nick.

"I'm not asking you to give up your life. Far from it. I'd like you to find something you like to do. Have kids. Don't be like me. I got a late start. I was thirty when I married your mother. That was the situation for residents in those days. I'd like you to have your own family, Nick. No matter what people say, no matter how much fun it is to fool around, at some point none of it matters. . . ." Solomon paused.

Nick was still staring ahead.

"When we're gone, if you don't have strong ties with your sister's kids, if you don't at least take an interest and look after her, then who will? No matter what else you might think, these kids are victims. I want them to have a chance. They deserve a chance. I've tried to talk to Mama Turner about setting up a trust fund for them—so they'll be educated—but she won't even talk. We're all dead to her. Okay. I'll still manage, they'll grow up, be educated, be loved, have a life. I wanted you to start developing a relationship with them, but I see you can't right now."

Solomon watched a street cleaner come toward him. The light changed. Solomon saw the Common. "I hope someday you will be able to. Where did Mike say he'd meet you, Nick?"

Nick pointed at a Ford parked across the street. Solomon swung around, pulled up behind the car.

Nick reached into the backseat, picked up his bag. His face blank. "Thanks for the ride."

"Will you write me when you get wherever you're going?"

Nick didn't answer. He got out, walked up to Mike's car, tapped on the window. Mike leaned across and unlocked the door.

THAT evening, both Solomon and Bea were quiet a long time. After a while, Solomon looked over at Bea and said, "What are you thinking so hard about?"

"About Nick."

"What about Nick?"

"What a pity. For him."

"What else are you thinking?"

"It will only irritate you."

"At this point, I think there is not much that will irritate me."

She paused. "I was thinking about some theories of motion and regeneration I've been reading about. Whether it's dance therapy or Eastern thought, so many of these disciplines seem to be saying the same thing in different ways."

Solomon said nothing.

Bea fell silent. After a moment, she said in a quiet voice, "I know this may sound odd—egocentric perhaps, but I don't mean it that way." She stopped. "Well, it's just that I feel certain I am on the verge of making some important basic discovery about the brain—about thought process, consciousness. I don't know exactly how to put it into words. I've had dreams and—"

She looked up at Solomon. She stopped abruptly.

She smiled, sadly, gently, "You asked me, I told you. I also said it would only irritate you. It's all right, dear. I do understand how you feel." She stood, came over, kissed him.

SOLOMON stands. Stiff. The living room is light. He walks to the end table, turns off the lamp. Outside, the lawn gray, the sky pale, without color. He steps over to the bookcases, the ship's clock and barometer, side by side. Solomon opens the glass, feels for the key behind, winds the clock. Sets the needle on the barometer and taps it.

Bea in her bathrobe, Tim in his pajamas holding her hand.

"You're up early, dear."

He doesn't answer. Nods slightly.

Solomon hoists Tim. Smelling of sleep.

Solomon holds him. "You're my early bird?"

Tim nods.

"Did you have a good sleep last night?"

"Yes."

"That's the boy, what did you dream?"

"I can't remember. Can I watch you shave again?"

He puts his hand on Solomon's chin and scrapes the whiskers. "Not this morning, Timmy. You go have breakfast now. Go on."

Tim walks into the kitchen. Bea puts her arms around Solomon, kisses him lightly.

"Are you hungry?"

"A little."

She turns and goes into the kitchen.

Upstairs, Doris stands in the hall rubbing her eyes. Whispers in a voice hoarse with sleep, " 'Morning, Dr. Solomon."

In the bathroom, Solomon drapes his robe over the towel rack, steps into the shower.

Then, opening the door to let out the steam, he shaves carefully, trims his mustache, combs his hair, and momentarily leans into the light, exploring his face for something.

The kitchen, the *Globe* on the table. He pushes it away, glances at Bea, her back to him, and picks up the paper, makes a show of reading it.

Bea brings him his coffee. "Anything new?"

Solomon shakes his head. "Same stuff. Inflation. Still Watergate."

Solomon watches Tim play with his eggs, smiles a moment. "Tim! Don't play with your food. It's for eating. Now eat those eggs."

Tim looks back at him. Stops, then goes on poking the eggs.

"Did you hear me? Go on, get busy."

Solomon looks at Bea, smiles faintly.

Bea, softly, "Eat your eggs, sweetheart."

Solomon has another cup of coffee. A piece of toast. "Well, I guess I'll go along."

Bea looks over. "Is that all you're going to have, dear?"

Solomon nods. "It's plenty."

Solomon picks up his coat. Leans down and kisses Tim. "Stop playing with those eggs." Solomon kisses him again.

"What're you doing this morning, Bea?"

"Oh, I have plenty to do. I want to go through the cedar closet in the attic. I remembered the other day there were several boxes of Nick's old clothes from back when. I have a hunch a lot of those things will fit Richard. Or if not now, in six months." Bea hugs Solomon hard. "All right, dear. Relax. Be calm."

"I'm perfectly calm. I'm fine. There happen to be one or two people out there walking around who . . ." Solomon trails off. "I didn't exactly start doing this yesterday. I'm fine, Bea."

"I know you are. Call me when you're finished."

She squeezes his arm and kisses him again.

IN the locker room, Solomon strips slowly—jacket, tie, shirt—strips naked and changes into pajama pants and shirt. At the sink, scrubs for a full ten minutes, hands to elbows, cleaning carefully under his nails with a rosewood stick.

In the operating room, the instrument nurse greeting him with a soft good morning, holding out the gown, he places his arms in the sleeves—she ties the gown behind him—then works each hand into an outheld glove. Again, a quick glance at the instrument table, the inflatable tourniquet. He scans the X rays placed on the viewing box, the milky glow of the bones. Studies them a moment more.

When he turns, he sees she has been silently wheeled in. He bends down. "Rose."

Her eyes thick and closing with sedatives. "Dad," she slurs. Her lips move, but he can't make out what she is saying. He leans over and places his ear close to her lips. ". . .Sleep."

He looks at her face. She is asleep.

In another moment, low murmur of voices, the resident, orderly, the anesthetist stops and stands beside him.

"Tom . . ." Solomon's voice trails off. They look down at
Rose sleeping.

"Okay, Joe. Okay."

The placement of the electrocardiograph over her heart, the
sound of the bleeper, and the pattern of waves on the monitor.

The pentathol. Needle being withdrawn from her arm, the
insertion of the rubber airway into her mouth, a moment later
the mask. Baldwin is taking her blood pressure as Solomon
directs the orderly to hold the leg at the knee. The resident
scrubs from the knee to the foot, scrubs the foot and toes carefully for ten minutes. Then the orderly elevates her leg overhead for ten minutes, and Baldwin places the tourniquet above
the knee, turns to Solomon, Solomon nods, and Baldwin in-
flates the tourniquet.

They drape the leg and the orderly and resident turn her to
a semiprone position. Baldwin takes her blood pressure once
more. Pulls back her eyelid, studies her pupil. Glances back at
Solomon, softly, voice distant behind the mask. "Okay, Joe.
She's ready."

Solomon looks at the square of draped flesh. Luminous. The
familiar press of the resident and instrument nurse at his
sides. Steady beep of the heart monitor. Solomon hears his
voice. The knife in his hand, the familiar balance, the belly of
the blade, the flesh glowing. In a gentle motion, he draws the
knife across the skin, the skin parting, the sudden rise of blood
to the light.

Epilogue

SOLOMON passes the nurse at her station, nods. The long hallway of the nursing home, doors ajar. Tv sets flickering. In one of the rooms, Solomon can see an old woman, white hair on the pillow, mouth open to the ceiling. Her body makes almost no rise in the blanket. In a chair beside her, a fat black nurse, cigarette in her mouth, watches tv and knits. Solomon hears sudden snores and groans as he walks down the long hall.

Ahead, through the partially opened door, he can see the back of Rose's head. She turns to look at him as he comes in.

Bea on the bed, Richard in his Cub Scout uniform watching tv. Tim lies coloring on the floor.

Solomon draws up a chair.

Rose watches Tim color, then turns her wheelchair slightly toward Solomon.

"Dad, cigarette."

"She just had one."

"In a minute, Rose. How are you tonight?"

"No good, Dad."

"The children look good, don't they?"

Rose nods.

Solomon says, "Richard, why don't you tell your mom how you're doing in Cub Scouts?"

Richard shrugs. "Nothing much, Mom."

"Oh, that's not quite true, Richard. Tell your mother."

"Tell me," she says.

"Rose, your speech is so much better. Really."

"Tell me."

Richard looks at the tv and says nothing.

"Tell her what your new merit badge is for."

265

"Stars, Mom. Planets and stars."

"Richard," she says, "love you."

He stares at the tv. He says, "I love you, too, Mom."

Rose says, "Richard's pants too short, Dad." Rose giggles.

Solomon nods. "I know. It's all I can do to keep these boys in pants. Those vitamins your mother gives him."

Tim looks up from his coloring.

"Cigarette."

Solomon fishes out a cigarette from Rose's night table. The Kodak print of the children. He steadies it while he closes the drawer. A streak of gray at her temple as she leans into the light. Solomon lights two cigarettes. Sits down. Stares at the tv. No one says anything.

Bea stands. "Come on, you two. I better get you home to bed."

"No," Rose says.

"Oh, it's way past this one's bedtime." Bea gestures toward Tim. "Come on, you. Kiss your mother good night, let's go."

"No," Rose says.

"We'll be back tomorrow, sweetheart." Richard stares at the tv. "Come on, Richard. Kiss your mother, Tim."

Tim walks over to Rose, hugs her, kisses her.

"Love you," she says. She kisses him.

Richard moves quietly toward the door.

"Richard, kiss your mother good night."

He glances at the tv a moment, then walks to her side, hesitates, and kisses her cheek quickly. She reaches out and touches his hair. He seems to freeze, says softly, " 'Night, Mom."

"Love you, Richard."

He steps into the corridor.

Bea touches Solomon's hand. "See you at home, dear."

Solomon watches them walk down the long darkened hallway. Tim walking, then running, then walking again, Richard suddenly swinging against the handrails. Rose watches them through the doorway, then turns in her wheelchair. Solomon picks up a crayon from the floor, puts it on the night table.

"Dad, where were you?"

"Just now?"

Rose nods.

"Well, just as I sat down to dinner, the phone rang."

Rose says, "Remember. Phone always for you at dinner."

"That's just about right."

"It is right."

"So same stuff. Someone fell down and broke his wrist."

"Phone always for you, Dad."

"That's where I was. The emergency room. I wanted to get it taken care of quickly."

"You're tired."

"It was no big deal."

"Walk for you, Dad."

Solomon glances at the tv a moment.

"Soon."

Solomon nods.

"Dad!"

"What is it?"

"Answer something?"

"I'll try."

Rose whispers, "What year is it?"

"I told you."

"Tell me again."

"It's 1976, Rose."

She touches her forehead. "1976. Forgot. Sorry, Dad."

"It's all right, I forget a few things, too."

"No, no you don't."

He lights another cigarette. Looks at his watch.

"Not yet, Dad. A few more minutes."

Solomon smokes his cigarette.

"Dad, the children, do they know"—she tapped herself—"love them, can't be with them?"

"Yes, of course, Rose. Of course they know you love them."

She doesn't say anything. She stares at the floor. Solomon can't look at her eyes; he gazes toward the window.

"Dad . . . where's Nicky?"

"Nick's working in California. I told you that last night."

"Will he come back?"

"I don't know, Rose. I don't know. I doubt it."

"Does he write?"

"Not much."

Solomon stands, "Well, Rose, I've got to go along now."

"No."

"I've got a full schedule tomorrow. Surgery at seven-thirty."

"Walk for you, Dad."

"Yes, Rose."

"Soon."

He leans over and kisses her. "Good night. Want the tv on?"

She nods.

"I'll see you tomorrow. Get some sleep."

"No, no, never sleep, never sleep."

"I know, I'm sorry, Rose."

He kisses her again. He walks to the door, looks back at her. She looks at him, glances toward the tv. The Kodachrome of her children on the night table. He hesitates.

"Good night, Rose."

She looks up at him. Her lips are still moving. She looks back at the tv. He turns and starts down the darkened corridor, her voice fading behind him.

". . . never sleep, never sleep . . ."